THROUGH HER EYES

Through
Her
Eyes

Jennifer Archer

HARPER TEEN
An Imprint of HarperCollinsPublishers

HarperTeen is an imprint of HarperCollins Publishers.

Through Her Eyes
Copyright © 2011 by Jennifer Archer

Library of Congress Cataloging-in-Publication Data
Archer, Jennifer.
   Through her eyes / Jennifer Archer. — 1st ed.
      p.   cm.
   Summary: Sixteen-year-old Tansy is used to moving every time her
mother starts writing a new book, but in the small Texas town where
her grandfather grew up, she is lured into the world of a troubled
young man whose death more than seventy years ago is shrouded in
mystery.
   ISBN 978-0-06-183458-5 (trade bdg.)
   [1. Supernatural—Fiction. 2. High schools—Fiction. 3. Schools—
Fiction. 4. Photography—Fiction. 5. Grandfathers—Fiction. 6. Moving, Household—Fiction. 7. Family life—Texas—Fiction. 8. Texas—
Fiction. 9. Mystery and detective stories.] I. Title.
PZ7.A67462Thr 2011   2010018440
[Fic]—dc22   CIP
                                                             AC

Typography by Torborg Davern
11 12 13 14 15   LP/RRDB   10 9 8 7 6 5 4 3 2 1
❖
First Edition

For Jeff,
who makes this possible.
Thanks for your love and support
throughout the years.

Henry

I died on a bitter, cold night. Beneath a black sky and a bruised winter moon, I tried to fly, hoping my arms might act as wings. When the howling wind refused to lift me, I closed my eyes and willed death to take me away.

The end came quickly and without pain, but no angel of mercy appeared to help me escape this place; I'm as trapped here as I was in life, forced to roam Father's remote house, the barren fields, this dusty wind-battered town full of small-minded bores. And it's all the worse because the girl I love is gone.

At least in the afterlife I fly with ease. I have learned to hover like mist and to soar like a bird. Today I mix with particles of debris and ride the wind as it circles the turret. I rattle the roof beams and roar at the sun, swoop down and around to the front porch, swirl up the steps and shove the old swing, causing the rusty hinges to screech.

I push out into the yard, where a gust of wind carries me

around to the side of the house and lifts me to the top of the mulberry tree. Green leaves tremble, and gnarled branches shudder beneath my breath. A small space between a dirty glass window pane and its frayed wooden frame allows me enough room to squeeze through into one of the house's second-story bedrooms.

Once inside I rush down the hallway past more vacant rooms, my silent screams bouncing off walls. Father's precious house has sat empty too long, devoid of life except for insects and rodents, and they can't help me ease my pain; they can't accomplish what needs to be done.

At the uppermost landing of the staircase, I slip beneath the door to the turret, my refuge in both life and death. I circle the room twice, once fast, the second time more slowly. Soothed by the plaster and wood that still contain strains of my violin music, I float on lost notes that echo from a time when I played for *her*, when I hoped my melodies might drift across the field and reach her ears.

The wind calms outside, and the sound of a sneeze startles me out of my reverie. Curious, I sweep to the window that overlooks the land behind the house. The root cellar door stands open. Someone—*a person*—is climbing inside! A hand reaches up from the cellar and grabs a bag and two books from the ground beside the opening. The title on the spine of the top volume scatters particles of hope through me. *Finally . . . finally. A lover of Yeats and Shelley, of Shakespeare and Dante. The sort of mind that I might reach . . . or possess.*

The cellar door closes. Drifting through the window and down, I sift through the minute cracks in the splintered wooden door, eager to meet my guest, hoping that *this* one will be my salvation. At last.

1

One Month Later

Most people run from nightmares; my mother seeks them out. Her name is Millicent Moon, and she's a horror novelist—the female version of Stephen King, minus the megabucks and movie deals. Whenever Mom starts working on a new book, she scouts out the perfect setting. Then she, my grandfather Papa Dan, and I move there. We've lived in a lot of cool places: the Queen Anne neighborhood in Seattle; a loft overlooking the Cumberland River in Nashville; a neighborhood in southwest Boston where writers like Ralph Waldo Emerson and Henry David Thoreau used to hang out. But we've never lived anywhere like the place we're moving now, and I'd be a whole lot happier if we never did.

"We're almost there, Tansy," Mom says, tucking a lock of straight black hair behind one ear and staring ahead at the dusty, rutted road as if it's paved with diamonds.

In the backseat, Papa Dan whistles. Loudly. I recognize the tune. The lyrics have something to do with mares eating oats and little lambs eating ivy.

The novel Mom's currently writing, *The Screaming Meemies*, takes place in the town where my grandfather spent his childhood: Cedar Canyon, Texas, population 2,250. Which, after driving through the town for the first time a minute ago, is a nightmare in itself, if you ask me. This will be my first small town experience, which is one reason why this move is the hardest one I've made so far.

After he finished school, Papa Dan left Cedar Canyon and never returned, so I haven't been here before and neither has Mom. She keeps saying it'll be easy to make friends in a little town, but I know that the size of the place won't change anything. There's no convincing her of that, though. Mom's chasing miracles by moving here. She hopes that Cedar Canyon will (1) make her forget and (2) make Papa Dan remember.

"I wish you would look at the photo." Mom slides her cat-eye sunglasses to the tip of her nose and glances across at me. "The place is incredible. Eloise said there's an old wagon bridge at the edge of the property near the canyon."

I turn to stare out the window at a dark cloud in the distance and try to tune out my grandfather's whistling. Over the past two days, I haven't spoken more than five words to Mom. But then, since she told me we were moving again, I've hardly spoken much more than that, anyway. Maybe she's getting used to my near-silence. Usually, it worries her and she asks me a million questions. *Are you feeling okay? You want to talk about anything? Is something bothering you?* But on this trip, she hasn't seemed fazed. Not that she's gone mute. Far from it. I guess that's a good thing; somebody has to speak for this family.

She could give it a rest, though. For hours on end, she's rattled on nonstop about the old house she rented after finding a crumpled picture of it in a shoe box in Papa Dan's room. She's never seen the place except in that photograph, and Eloise—the leasing agent—said it's been empty for years. Before Mom found that picture, we were going to live in a house in town, instead of out in the boonies. But she called and asked about the place, and just my luck, Eloise confirmed that the house is in Cedar Canyon and that it was available.

"It even has a turret!" Mom gushes. "Can you imagine a turret in the middle of the Texas Panhandle?"

I shoot her another glance. I haven't seen my mother so excited since the day we first pulled up in front of our tiny bungalow in California, the place we just left. The day after my fifteenth birthday, we parked the U-Haul in San Francisco and stayed almost fourteen months, the longest I've lived in one place. I met Hailey there. Hailey Fremont. The best friend I've ever had—the only close friend, really. We shared more than rides to the movies and homework answers; we shared our secrets and dreams. I should have known not to get close to anyone. I let down my guard and forgot that making friends is a waste of time. It's easier to move when you aren't leaving behind something that matters.

I'm supposed to call Hailey tonight. I would've tried sooner, but since we left San Francisco, I haven't had a second alone to talk without Mom listening. I want to ask Hailey about Colin—a guy in our class who she's been working with all summer at a music store. Hailey warned me that he was bad news, but I didn't care. I think she just didn't want me having a boyfriend unless she did, too. The first time Colin and I hung out, Mom ruined everything after I got home by telling me we were moving here. Colin called later, but we only saw each other once more. He probably thought going out with me was a lost cause, since I was leaving.

"Say something, Tansy, would you?" Mom sounds exasperated, which makes me happy, though I'm not sure why.

Without looking at her, I mumble, "I'm suffocating."

Aiming the air-conditioner vent at my face, she says, "Papa Dan, are you hot, too?"

Mom doesn't get it. I've never seen a more wide-open space; there's hardly a tree or a tall building in sight or any sign of life whatsoever unless you count cows and prairie dogs. Just miles of flat, parched fields and endless sky. Yet, ever since we crossed the border into the Texas Panhandle, I've felt more trapped than ever . . . like I can't breathe.

Five minutes pass. Ten. While I've been watching the bland scenery pass by, my cheek numb from the stale, frigid air blowing at me through the vent, Mom has become abnormally quiet. I have a feeling she's freaking out, worrying about my state of mind. But before I can even brace myself for an interrogation, the questions start.

"What are you thinking, sweetie?"

"About what?"

"The turret, the bridge, the house, I don't care. Anything. This silent-treatment bit you've got going on is getting really old."

So she did notice. My mother only listens to me when I'm not talking. "You've told me about the tower or turret or whatever it is at least ten times now. If I had something to say about it, I would've already said it. Why don't you ask Papa Dan what *he* thinks?"

Mom's fingers grip and release the steering wheel, again and again. "Sarcasm isn't very flattering on you, Tansy," she says.

Shame tightens my throat. Papa Dan can't help that his mind has flickered from bright to dim. He's my dad's father and the last person on earth I would ever want to hurt. My grandfather has lived with us all of my life, ever since Dad and my grandmother died in a car accident a few months before I was born. The doctors think Papa Dan has some kind of dementia. But they're stumped about why he clammed up and quit talking so suddenly a few months ago. I don't know why, either, but I guess he has his reasons. If Papa Dan wants to be quiet, that's fine with me. What's hard, though, is the fact that the dementia has slowly changed him from the person I always leaned on most into a person who needs to lean on me. All my life, Papa Dan has been there for me. He's going through a crappy time; I owe it to him to be strong for him.

Mom reaches across the seat and touches my shoulder, as if she knows I feel like the world's lowest living creature at the moment. "So what did you think of your first glimpse of Cedar Canyon?" she asks. "Isn't it quaint?"

"Yeah, quaint. A couple of gas stations and convenience stores. Oh, and let's not forget that rodeo arena we passed. Every kid here probably wears a cowboy hat."

She blows her bangs off her forehead and sighs. "Didn't you see all the antique stores and that cute old-fashioned diner on Main Street?"

"Dairy Queen?"

"No, not the Dairy Queen, the Longhorn Café."

"How could I miss that statue of a bull out front? Something tells me they don't have a vegetarian menu." I nibble my cuticle. "Did *you* notice they only have one theater and the movie that's playing is over a month old?"

"You could always stay busy by taking pictures again. I can't remember the last time you picked up your camera."

My first camera was a gift from Papa Dan on my tenth birthday. We had just moved to Seattle, and the two of us walked around the city that summer taking pictures. Mom taped the photos all over her office walls. She says I have an eye for light and shading and atmosphere, for capturing beauty in unexpected things and places.

"Maybe I will take some shots," I tell her.

"Great." Cautious relief trickles through her voice. "I really miss having your photos for my research. Taking pictures will be good for you."

Translation: It will force me to quit feeling sorry for myself, keep me from going "peanutty as a Payday candy bar" in this boring town. That's Papa Dan's expression, one he used to describe our San Francisco neighbors the Cranes, "artistes" who painted faces on the rocks in their yard.

We turn onto a dirt road and hit a pothole. The van rattles. Papa Dan whistles louder. From the corner of my eye, I glimpse Mom's smile. "Look!" She steps on the brake, slinging me toward the dash before my seat belt jerks me back. "There it is!" Mom sticks her sunglasses onto the top of her head. "It's *perfect*," she says.

I glance through the windshield at three stories of pure creepiness as Papa Dan ends the oat-and-ivy tune and starts whistling *The Twilight Zone*'s theme music. He couldn't have chosen a more perfect song. Mom's beloved turret tops the right side of the roof where it points like a finger at the gray cloud above. A little more centered and I would think it was flipping us off. The paint on the house, which might have once been a pretty shade of blue, is faded. A shutter dangles across a second-floor window, as if it's unsure which would be worse—hanging on to the monster or the long drop to the ground. Weeds cover the yard, and the branches on the only tree in sight, a twisted giant on the house's right side, start low on the trunk and reach wide.

"Oh, look at that wonderful old mulberry!" Mom exclaims. She pulls the van into the rocky driveway and we climb out. As I'm helping Papa Dan from the backseat, Mom says, "Someone's supposed to come by to talk about painting and repairs and cleaning up the yard. Eloise said the house is

10

nice on the inside, though. She already sent over a cleaning service, and the owners left some furniture behind."

"That's good. We'd never come close to filling up a house this big with our stuff."

A warm gust of rain-scented air flutters my hair. Without traffic noise, it's spooky quiet outside. The only sounds I hear are a low rumble of thunder, the hiss of the wind, the twitter of a bird or two, and the constant chirp of insects—crickets or maybe cicadas.

Beads of sweat break out on my forehead. Papa Dan grasps my hand tighter, as if he senses my tension . . . or shares it. A quiet, strangled noise escapes his throat. I follow his gaze to the house's dark windows. A covered porch wraps around the front of the house. On its left side, a wooden bench swing hangs crooked from rusted chains that are attached to the ceiling. "It doesn't look like anyone has lived here in a long time," I say, squeezing my grandfather's fingers like he does mine. "At least nobody with flesh on their bones."

As if on cue, another blast of wind blows the porch swing back and forth and the rusty hinges creak. "Come on," I say to Papa Dan, tugging his arm gently. He tugs back, and I feel a shudder pass through his body. Behind his round glasses, his eyes are pale green, confused . . . and scared. "You sure Papa Dan didn't live here?" I ask Mom.

"He lived somewhere in town."

"Why would he have a picture of *this* house?"

"Maybe he knew someone who lived here. Or maybe he just liked the architecture. It's fairly unusual for this part of the country."

I finally coax Papa Dan to follow Mom and me up the steps. "This is our new home," I say to him, though I doubt he can hear me, since he's not wearing his hearing aids. He always misplaces them, along with just about everything else. We step onto the porch, and I notice it's made of warped gray boards. A few of them look as if they might cave in beneath our weight. "I hope you got a good deal on the rent," I mumble to Mom.

She slips the key into the lock and turns it. "We're practically living here free."

I feel impatient as she jiggles the doorknob. I'd never admit it, but part of me can't wait to explore this weird place. Something about the house, that creaking porch swing, even Mom's precious turret, intrigues me. My grandfather's sigh gives me the impression he doesn't share my curiosity, though. He starts whistling so quietly, I can't make out the tune. "Papa Dan doesn't seem very happy to be here," I say.

"Oh, I think he is." Mom swings open the door and steps across the threshold. "Before he got sick, he told me he wanted to come back to Cedar Canyon for a visit."

"Maybe he changed his mind."

A flock of birds takes flight inside my chest as I peek inside the house. Suddenly I'm not so eager to explore it anymore. I don't know why I feel so conflicted—I mean, the house is definitely interesting. But I've just lived in too many rentals, and I sort of dread facing more rooms full of memories that aren't mine. I wish Papa Dan would have a clear moment and say, *Don't worry, Tansy girl, it's just another house in another town. No big deal. I'll show you around my old stomping grounds.* Instead he squints at the swing and keeps whistling.

I pat his hand. "Go with Mom," I say to him. "I'll be there in a minute."

Mom glances at me. "Aren't you coming in?"

"I want to look around outside first."

Nodding, she says, "Okay. But don't wander off too far. The movers should be here soon, and I'll need your help getting organized." She shields her eyes with one hand and tilts her face up toward the sky. "You may get wet. Looks like it's about to rain."

When I reach the bottom step, she calls my name, and I turn around.

A groove dents the space between her brows. "Give Cedar Canyon a chance," she says. "If you like it, I promise we'll stay here until you graduate from high school."

"And if I don't?"

"Then I'll write fast." Her face softens. "And I'll set the next book back in San Francisco."

"And stay *there* until I graduate?"

Her smile fans tiny wrinkles at the corners of her eyes. "You drive a hard bargain, but you've got yourself a deal."

And I'm holding her to it. I can't wait to call Hailey and tell her I'll be home soon. I'm going to hate Cedar Canyon. I've already made up my mind.

2

Rain sprinkles down. I run around to the side of the house and duck beneath the mulberry tree. Becoming a human lightning rod doesn't interest me, but I can't resist the canopied branches. The knot in my chest loosens as I wipe dampness from my cheeks and listen to the soothing patter of raindrops on the leaves above. I stare at the house and wish that I was back in my tiny San Francisco bedroom, curled up on my bed, surrounded by every stuffed animal I've saved through the years. I know every scratch and dent on those four bedroom walls, every floor creak, the slant of the morning sun through the window, each dust mote dancing in that hazy beam.

Light suddenly spills from the first-floor windows of our new house. Minutes later, the second story glows, too. Mom appears at a window—a city slicker in an old Victorian house on the West Texas prairie. Leave it to her to set such a scene. I don't think she sees me, but I'm sure she's thinking about me. She's wondering if she should call me in out of the weather. She's worrying that I'm too upset by this move. And she's feeling guilty, which explains the deal she just made.

Staying here for two years so that I can graduate would be a huge step for Mom to take. She seeks out nightmares, but she runs from memories. She's been running my whole life, ever since Dad died. That's really why we move all the time. Mom has convinced herself that it's because she needs to be in her story's location in order to write a good book, but I know better; Papa Dan helped me figure it out. He said that sometimes facing what might have been is harder than living what *is*. Mom's trying to escape reminders of the past, of what might have been. She's looking for a place where the memories won't find her. Crazy, right? But Papa Dan also told me that hearts are seldom rational.

The wind dies and the August rain shower stops as quickly as it started. I push away from the tree trunk and step out from under the dripping leaves. I walk around to the back of the house, where I find a faded red barn so rickety that I wouldn't be surprised if it fell to the ground if I touch it. Only one other house is visible in any direction, and I'm guessing it would take a good ten minutes to reach it on foot. With no hills, trees, or anything else to block the view, I can see a lot of details about the place. The farmhouse is neat, normal, and white. The roof is red. I'm sure it fits right in with the rest of conservative Cedar Canyon, while our radical house with its turret, dingy peeling primer, and dull-eyed windows seems as out-of-place here as my family does.

An old-fashioned windmill sits off in the distance beyond the barn. It towers over the dead grass like a giant, fat-stemmed metal flower. The dark gray petals rotate slowly in the wind, moaning with each turn, complaining like Papa Dan does when his joints ache.

Halfway to the barn, my heel hits something solid, and I'm thrown off balance. Steadying myself, I look down and see a wooden door in the ground. *The entrance to hell,* I think. Fitting, since our house could easily serve as the reception area. I kneel, grasp the damp, rusty handle, and pull. The door rasps and lifts an inch. I tug harder and it swings wide, revealing stairs that drop into a pitch-black hole. The second step has a gap in it, leaving only a shoe-width piece of board on which to step. I've never been inside a cellar and don't have a clue what I might find. Possibly some great material for Mom's research.

Leaving the door open, I run to the van, dig through the boxes packed in back, and find my camera and a flashlight. Then I hurry back to the cellar, switch on the flashlight, and point the beam into the darkness below. Taking cautious steps, I start down the stairs.

The cellar is about half the size of my bedroom in San Francisco. It could hold a twin-size bed and maybe a chair, but not much else. When I reach the bottom step, I set my camera bag on the dirt floor and sweep the flashlight beam across the cement walls, down at the floor, then up at the ceiling. Cobwebs stretch from corner to corner. Something makes a scratching noise beneath the steps and I jump, the transfer of my weight causing the board beneath my flip-flops to shift. I take a breath, step down, and crouch to lift the loose plank, surprised to find a container the size of a jewelry box beneath it.

Sitting on the stairs, I balance the flashlight on the step beside me and pull the box onto my lap. I aim the beam so that I can see every nick and scratch on the rose-tinted wood. Beneath the lid, I find a worn leather book, a gold pocket watch, and a tear-shaped crystal pendant. A tiny wire loop connects to the top of the crystal. I search the box for a necklace chain but don't find one. The crystal pendant feels cool and smooth as I hold it up and twist it left to right. The cut glass catches the light, throws it at the opposite wall, scattering colored dots across the cement.

Thunder rumbles quietly outside the cellar as I remove the pocket watch from the box. Etched into the gold on back are the words *To Henry on your 17th birthday. From Mother and Father. 1939.* One push of a tiny button opens the cover, revealing the timepiece inside. The hands have stopped at 12:22. Placing the watch on the step beside the crystal, I lift the book from the box, open it, touch pages yellowed at the edges. I position the flashlight so that I can read the poem scribbled in black ink on the first page, the tiny cursive letters sharp and tight—a guy's handwriting.

Down in the cellar, under a stair
Covered with cobwebs
Nobody cares

Withered and pale, forgotten it seems
That's where I hide them,
Yesterday's dreams.

Shake out the memories, blow off the dust
Smooth out the wrinkles
Rub off the rust
Remember the times they sparkled so bright
Then put them away
Far out of sight

Down in the cellar, under a stair
Covered with cobwebs
Nobody cares
Withered and pale, forgotten it seems
That's where I hide them,
Yesterday's dreams.

"Tansy!"

Startled by Mom's shout, I drop the journal and push to my feet. "I'm here!" I hurry up the stairs, careful of the rotting boards, and poke my head through the cellar's entrance.

She stands at the door of a screened-in porch at the back of the house. "Some neighbors just dropped by. Come say hello."

"I'll be right there!"

Avoiding the narrow second stair and the open space

where I removed the bottom plank, I ease back down into the cellar and place the journal and other treasures inside my camera bag. I return the box to its nook and lay the board atop it. Climbing out, I lower the door.

The poem plays through my mind like a familiar song, and I forget to be nervous about entering the house for the first time as I hurry across the yard toward the back porch. I wish I didn't have to meet the neighbors so soon, though. I didn't see them walking from their house when I went to the van to get the flashlight; they must've driven over while I was in the cellar. They sure didn't waste any time coming over to check us out.

"Eloise told us you write books, Miz Piper."

"That's right," Mom answers the man. "Horror novels. I write under the pseudonym Millicent Moon. And please, call me Millie. Everyone does."

I enter the living room in time to see the old man's gap-tooth grin disappear. "You mean like those chain-saw movies?" His upper lip curls over that rancid possibility. He glances at the short, round woman beside him, but she just keeps staring at Mom and chewing her gum, her face a wrinkled blank page.

Mom laughs. "I don't think I've used a chain saw in any of my books yet. I like to dream up my own unique methods of dismemberment." When she motions me over, I walk around a couch with a flowery sheet draped over it and stop beside her. "I'd like you to meet my daughter,

19

Tansy," Mom says to the couple. "Tansy, this is Mr. and Mrs. Quattlebaum. They live in the farmhouse across the way."

"Howdy-do, young lady." The old man tugs the brim of his John Deere hat.

"Hi," I murmur.

"We was driving back from town and thought we'd stop by. Already said 'hello' to your grandpa. I remember him from when we was kids. He was five or so years ahead of me in school, though." Mr. Quattlebaum shifts back to Mom. "Guess y'all don't mind the rumors about the house, seeing as how you write scary books and all."

"Rumors?" Mom asks.

"The house is haunted." The farmer's voice drops. "So they say. Didn't Mr. Piper tell you?"

"No." Mom leans forward, a slow smile spreading across her face. *"Really?"*

"Eloise don't usually tell newcomers about the ghost." Mr. Quattlebaum pauses to scratch the beard stubble on his chin. "News has a way of gettin' around, though. Been six years since she's found somebody to rent the place. Before that, nobody ever stayed long."

"Why?" I ask. "Did something happen?"

"Imagination got the best of 'em, I'd guess," he says. "Back in the twenties, a rich rancher name of William Peterson built the house. When his son was a teenager, he killed hisself. Jumped off the old wagon bridge into the canyon that borders this property. His folks left town

20

afterward. Couldn't sell the house, though." He pauses, then adds, "Rumor has it the boy's ghost still hangs around here."

A fluttery feeling fills my chest. Touching the camera case hanging from the strap over my shoulder, I feel the sharp edge of the journal inside and think of the poem scribbled onto an old yellowed page.

"Oh, I hope the ghost shows up," Mom says, scanning the room. "I've written about restless spirits, but I've never actually met one. Except Tansy, that is." She laughs at her own joke, and I roll my eyes. She's the restless one, not me.

Somewhere upstairs, Papa Dan begins whistling shrill and fast. Mr. and Mrs. Quattlebaum look up at the ceiling. His brows tug together. She chews faster.

"Mr. Piper might recall the tragedy," Mr. Quattlebaum says. "He would have been close to the Peterson boy's age."

"What was the boy's name?" I ask.

"I think it was Herman," says Mr. Quattlebaum. "Isn't that right, Myra?"

The old woman stops chewing, her puckered lips twitching as she meets my gaze. "His name was *Henry*," she says in a raspy voice. "Henry Peterson."

3

Soon after the Quattlebaums leave in their big, noisy truck, the moving van arrives.

"Which is my bedroom?" I ask Mom. She'll be preoccupied with the movers for a while, and I'll have time to find a hiding place for my camera bag. I can't wait to take another look at Henry Peterson's things.

"Papa Dan's is the last one on the second floor," she says. "Take one of the others."

I choose the smallest room. It's painted a pale blue and doesn't have any furniture, which is good; I'd rather use my own dresser and sleep in my own bed. A window overlooks the backyard, and another window shows the huge mulberry tree in the side yard and the Quattlebaums' farmhouse off in the distance.

I'm heading for the closet when I hear a loud thump at the window and turn to look. Nothing is there, but I get the weirdest feeling that I'm being watched. *Get a grip*, I tell myself. A gust of wind probably made a limb on the tree scrape against the pane. I study the rain-glossed green leaves on the branches a moment, think how pretty they are, and unzip my camera bag. Reaching inside, I pull out my camera. I left color film in it the last time I used it, and for the first time in a long while, I have the urge to capture a scene.

I look through the viewfinder, my breath catching when I see a little gray bird perched on the window ledge. I'm sure it wasn't there before, but now it faces the window, as if it's staring straight at me. "Hey, there," I murmur. "Where did you come from?" Stooping and leaning closer, I adjust the lens for a clearer view, but something isn't right. The windowsill should be blue, but it looks as gray as the bird. Standing, I turn around, and still peering through the viewfinder, scan the room; everything within the frame looks gray and dreary. The walls. The hardwood floor. The light. The lens must be dirty. When I glance to the window again, the bird is gone.

Disappointed, I return the camera to the bag, then pull out Henry's pocket watch. I pop the latch, reset the time, and wind it, listening to it tick. I wish I could sit down right this minute and flip through the journal. I'm dying to learn more about Henry, but I don't want Mom to find me reading his poems. I'm not going to tell her about his things. He must've hid everything for a reason, and I feel a responsibility to respect his privacy.

After putting the watch in the bag again, I place the bag on the highest shelf in the closet, then head down to the kitchen. The room could use a major remodel. The linoleum floor is yellowed and scuffed, with faded black diamonds in the design. The off-white painted cabinets are chipped and dull. At least it's clean, I think, noting that the movers have already stacked boxes against the walls and on top of an old gray Formica table.

Through the window over the sink, I see two men unloading a mattress from the moving truck parked behind our van in the driveway. They carry it across the yard toward the front porch as I start opening boxes. I unwrap plates and bowls and glasses, my thoughts on Henry. Did he like living in Cedar Canyon? Did he have a best friend? A girlfriend? What were the dreams he mentioned in his poem? Why did he end his life?

Mom pushes through the door. "Wow, Tansy. You're already hard at it." She sets the box she's carrying on a chair. "Take a break. It's been a long two days in the car. After the movers finish up, let's go get something to eat. We can start fresh in the morning."

"I'd rather keep working and get it over with." I climb up a stepladder I found in the pantry and place a jar on the top shelf.

"You feeling okay?"

"I wish you'd stop asking me that."

Silence stretches. She sighs. "I know moving is hard on you, Tansy, but it's how I work. I have to support the three of us, and that means writing the best books I can."

"I'm sick of moving," I blurt out, ignoring her attempts

to smooth things over. I hear my grandfather mumbling and glance over my shoulder to see him wander into the kitchen, scanning the floor as if looking for something. "He's sick of moving, too. Look at him, he's upset. Aren't you tired of moving all the time, Papa Dan?"

"Tansy . . ." Mom lowers her voice. "You can't speak for your grandfather."

Papa Dan turns and retraces his steps, leaving Mom and me alone in the kitchen again. I shake my head, hating the tears that burn the backs of my eyes. "And you *can* speak for him? I don't think so. While you're all caught up in writing your stories, he and I are together. I know him a hundred times better than you do."

Sounding exasperated, she says, "We raised you together. I think I know the man."

"Okay, then tell me what he misses most about Dad."

Mom stares at me like she's shocked to discover that a demon has possessed her silent, okay-whatever-you-say-I'm-a-doormat daughter. "I don't know, Tansy." Her voice is as soft and ragged as the map in our van's glove box. "What does he miss most about your father?"

"Everything." I bite my lip to keep the tears from falling. I miss everything about my dad, too, as crazy as that sounds. Ever since Papa Dan got sick, I think about Dad all the time. How could I miss someone I never knew? I don't even want to imagine how it feels to lose someone I *do* know.

I face the cabinets again so I don't have to look at Mom's

sad expression, and movement outside the window over the sink snags my attention. Papa Dan passes by with his head down. Mom must see him, too, because she says, "I'd better go round up your grandfather before he walks all the way into town."

Remembering the cellar, I tell her about it. "The door's pretty heavy," I mutter, "but he might be able to open it if he tries hard enough."

"We'd better buy a padlock. We can't risk him venturing down there and getting trapped. Or worse, falling in." Her cell phone trills in the living room—the *Twilight Zone* music that Papa Dan always whistles, her signature ring. "Would you grab that?" Mom calls as she starts for the door to get Papa Dan. "It's probably Jayne. She said she'd call."

I head for the living room, hoping it's Hailey instead of Mom's editor. My cell phone's dead, and Hailey knows Mom's number.

The phone is on the fireplace mantel. I press Talk and say hello without looking at the display, disappointed when Jayne's voice says, "Tansy? Are you guys in Texas yet?" I talk to her for a minute then, when Mom enters the room, pass over the phone. As she raves to her editor about how "fabulous" the house is, I return to the boxes in the kitchen.

After the movers are gone, we drive into Cedar Canyon to eat at the Longhorn Café. Our van jostles over the redbrick streets, past Cedar Canyon Hardware, the public library, and the two-story courthouse with its tall clock tower. We turn on Main, a street lined with shiny black lampposts and storefronts flanked by wooden barrels of mums. Mom parks in front of the newspaper office—the *Cedar Canyon Gazette*—which is directly across the street from the Longhorn Café.

Walking past the bull statue, we open the door and step into a sea of denim jeans, sneakers, and work boots. Nothing sets a single person apart from anyone else; at least that's what I think until a door beneath the Restroom sign at the back of the café opens and the one exception walks out—a girl about my age. She wears white shorts, sparkly black flip-flops, and an orange cheerleader jacket. Her cheerleader status must be a big deal to her; it's short-sleeve weather, but I guess she thinks the jacket is worth the sweat.

The girl stares at us as she parts the denim sea. She looks a lot like Hailey. She has the same big eyes and pale blond hair that she wears in a ponytail. The girl is tall and thin like Hailey, too. I watch her cross to a table where two people sit who I didn't notice before—a girl with long, wavy auburn hair and a freckled guy with messy curls. Seeing them all together, I feel a stab of loneliness. Just before the cheerleader slides in across from her friends, she turns to speak to a woman at the table behind her, and I see the name *Alison* written across the back of her jacket.

A waitress leads us to a booth on the far side of the room. Everyone in the café seems to know everyone else.

They call out to one another as we weave around them. *Hey, Bud, hey, Sarah. Billy, how's work? We missed you in church on Sunday. How are the kiddos?* A lot of talk. A lot of laughter. I'm pretty sure we'll soon be the topic of conversation, since most of them look at us as if we just flew in from outer space. I could be imagining this, but I doubt it. We don't exactly fit in. Papa Dan wears his beret slanted to one side and the lenses of his round, tortoiseshell glasses are so thick that his eyes look like bulging green grapes. Mom wears a pink satin blouse with a mandarin collar, baggy black pants, and pink ballet slippers. Then there's me; I like hats, my grandfather's mostly. He has a collection—berets, fedoras, old-fashioned newsboy caps. Today I'm wearing a gray felt fedora with a black satin band. The brim hides my eyes. A bonus.

I was right when I guessed the Longhorn Café wouldn't have a vegetarian menu. At first I think that means no dinner for me, since I don't eat meat. But the waitress points out a salad bar, so I walk over to check it out. The containers are filled with more pasta, canned peas, and mayo-coated salads than fresh vegetables, but it's better than nothing. I pick up an empty plate and put some carrot and celery sticks on it.

"The potato salad's good," a guy's voice says beside me. "But I'd stay away from the cottage cheese gelatin mold."

I look up into the bluest eyes I've ever seen. The guy grins, and I remind myself to breathe. We stand almost elbow to elbow, and everything about him hits me at once.

Tall, but not too tall. Wide shoulders. Hair the color of honey. I lower my gaze to his black T-shirt, which reads *Bobcat Football #10*. Just my luck—a jock. Translation: huge ego. I smile anyway; I can't help myself. "Thanks for the tip," I say.

"No problem." He hands me the spoon for the potato salad as I look back at the containers of food. "You passing through town?" he asks.

"You could say that." I scoop the salad onto my plate and move down the bar.

"We get a lot of travelers off the highway."

After placing wilted spinach leaves on my plate, I lower the tongs. He reaches for them and our fingers brush. I glance up quickly, embarrassed because I'm so flustered. "Your family owns this place?"

"My uncle does."

I move to the next container and spoon more food onto my plate.

Following me and filling his plate, too, he asks, "Where are you from?"

"California."

"I like your hat."

I frown and look up again, thinking he's making fun of me. But he isn't laughing. He looks sincere. "Thanks. It's my grandfather's," I say, and he glances across the café at Papa Dan, then back at me. We smile at each other again. I've reached the end of the salad bar, and I feel like a total idiot standing here grinning at him, but I can't seem to stop. "Well, I'd better go. Thanks for warning me off the cottage cheese."

"Anytime. Have a good trip."

As I make my way toward the booth where Mom and Papa Dan sit drinking iced tea, I feel better than I have since we left California. But just after I pass Alison's table, I hear a girl say, "Oh, *please*. Look at that corny, lame hat."

I glance back. The girl with auburn hair is staring at me and laughing, one hand covering her mouth. I look quickly at the guy beside her, and one corner of his mouth curves up. "Corny and lame, but *awesome*," he says. I can't tell if he's being sarcastic or if he means it. *Sarcastic*, I decide when the cheerleader named Alison hisses, "Shanna! Jon! Shut up!" She swivels around to face me, her eyes wide and apologetic.

I start for the booth again, walking as fast as I can, scanning the room until I spot the guy from the salad bar. He sits at a far-off table with a man. They don't act as if they heard anything, but I still want to crawl underneath the booth as I slide in beside Papa Dan.

"Do you have a fever?" Mom says, one eyebrow raised.

Scowling at her, I say, "That's random. What are you talking about?"

Mom gestures at my plate, and I glance down at a mound of ham salad next to a few spinach leaves covered with bacon bits and the scoop of potato salad. I look up quickly, and Mom nods at the football jock across the café. "Good-looking hunks have the same effect on me." Grinning, she adds, "See? Not everyone in Cedar Canyon is a cowboy, after all."

"*Mom.* Be quiet," I whisper, ducking my head. "You know I don't like jocks. And he isn't a *hunk*. Which is a stupid word, anyway."

She laughs. "When do you want an appointment to have your vision checked?"

Glaring at her, I mouth *shut up,* but Mom only chuckles. I turn my attention to Papa Dan, wanting to change the subject. "What did you order?" I ask, not expecting an answer.

Later, after we eat, we head to the register to pay the bill. Mom has her cell phone pressed to her ear. Her editor called again halfway through the meal and they're brainstorming the best way to "off" one of Mom's characters. From what I can hear, they've narrowed down the weapon choice to either a blowtorch or a Weed Eater. I step closer to the door and pull the brim of my hat a little lower.

Neither of us notices until it's too late that Papa Dan has wandered to a stranger's table and sat down. Mom ends her phone call quickly, and we dart over. While she apologizes to the lady, I hurry my grandfather toward the door. The laughter seems louder as we work our way around tables and chairs. I hear the girl named Shanna mumble in a disgusted tone, "Ohmygod. Did you *see* him?"

I look over my shoulder, hoping the guy from the salad bar isn't watching. The man with him is leaning across the table, talking and glancing our way. The hot guy cuts his gaze in my direction, his expression odd and strained. Unsure of what to make of their exchange, I turn away, and for only a second, my eyes lock with Alison's. The sympathy on her face stiffens my spine. I don't need her or anyone else to feel sorry for me—besides, it's probably fake compassion. I should be the one pitying *her*. I only have to live in Podunk, USA, for a few months, but I have a feeling that she grew up in this rinky-dink Dairy Queen town.

We stop at the Food Fair grocery store on our way home. It has six aisles and two checkout lines, with only one checker working tonight. Country music cranks out from the sound system. We have to hurry because the place closes at 7:00 p.m. The whole town probably shuts down then, every light goes out, and the sidewalks fold up. I wouldn't be surprised.

The store has no deli, which makes me glad I'm a vegetarian, since all they have is nasty-looking prepackaged sandwich meat. Based on the amount of bologna in stock, I guess it's Cedar Canyon's top seller, with pickle loaf coming in at a close second. *Disgusting.*

The checker talks on her cell phone as we unload our cart. She's short, pudgy, and cute. She doesn't look much older than me, but she wears a wedding ring. "That's the day of the Watermelon Run and the Pruitts' fund-raiser," she says into the phone, watching us while she talks. "We're working the bake sale, remember?"

Mom and I only grab a few essentials, including a

combination lock for the cellar door—the kind used on school lockers. I push the empty cart to the corner up front where the others are shoved together as Mom places the last item on the counter. It's a blue notebook full of blank pages she's buying for me. She keeps bugging me about starting a diary, saying that writing down my feelings about the move will make me feel better.

"Hey, Sis, I've gotta go," the checker says. "Call me tomorrow." I turn around and return to the checkout line as she's putting the phone in her purse on the floor behind her.

"Hi," Mom says to the girl.

"Hi, Miz Moon."

Mom tilts her head to one side, her eyes surprised. "I'm sorry. Have we met?"

"No, Aunt Eloise told me you guys made it in."

"Eloise Moyer who leased us the house?" The girl nods, and Mom squints and says, "You do look a little bit like her. You have her pretty red hair."

Mom chose the right profession when she decided to write fiction. She lies with ease. Unless Mother Nature took psychedelic drugs the day Eloise Moyer was conceived, this girl didn't inherit her red hair from her aunt. It came from a box in aisle two.

The checker starts scanning our purchases. "My cousin Jeri works over at the Longhorn," she says. "Jeri reads all your books. She called a sec ago and told me y'all were eatin' over there. She heard you say you were headin' this way."

34

Mom laughs. "Cedar Canyon has quite a grapevine."

"You don't know the half of it. When I was goin' to school? If I got in trouble last period, my mom knew about it before the bell rang. It's pretty much that way with everything around here."

Translation: The people in Cedar Canyon are a bunch of gossips. I cross my arms, wondering if the whole nosy town's going to read about Papa Dan sitting down at that lady's table in the paper tomorrow. That probably qualifies as big news around here.

"So you grew up in Cedar Canyon?" Mom asks.

"Yes, ma'am. I was salutatorian of my senior class year before last."

"Good for you!" Mom exclaims. I know her well enough to read her mind, though. She's wondering why the girl didn't go on to college with credentials like that.

The checker runs the last item across the scanner, then tells Mom the total. While Mom swipes her bank card through the machine, the girl bags our groceries and keeps on talking. As if she read my mother's mind, too, she says, "Soon as my husband, Tyler, and I save up the money, I'm going to quit working and start taking classes at the junior college in Amarillo." Laughing, she holds out her left hand and wiggles it so that the tiny solitaire diamond on her ring finger sparkles in the light. "Tyler and I started kindergarten together. We tied the knot last year. He works at the beef processing plant."

He and the rest of the town. Mom told me that Texas

Beef Processors is Cedar Canyon's main employer. I guess if you're from here, your options for the future are either cutting up cow corpses, farming, being a store clerk or waitress, or getting out of Podunk as fast as you can after graduation. I'd choose the "get out" option. I wouldn't have to think twice about it.

"I'm Reagan Blake," the checker says as she finishes bagging our groceries.

"Call me Millie," Mom says, gesturing toward a wire rack a few feet away where Papa Dan stands. "That's my father-in-law, Dan, rearranging the books. Sorry about that."

"Oh, no problem. Every kid who comes in here moves those around." Wincing, Reagan adds, "I'm sorry. I didn't mean that he's—"

"It's okay," Mom hurries to assure her, but I'm less forgiving. I hate it when people act as if my grandfather is five years old.

Reagan waves at Papa Dan. "Hello, sir!" Then she grins at me and says, "Tansy Moon . . . what a cute name."

"It's Piper," I tell her.

She frowns. "Piper Moon? I thought it was Tansy."

"It is."

Reagan's face goes blank. "Oh," she murmurs. Behind her on the floor, her cell phone trills in her purse and she stoops to look at the display.

I take the opportunity to glance at Mom and cross my eyes.

Mom sends me a quick scowl before Reagan stands up again.

I grab two sacks and head for the door. The girl is about as bright as a dusty lightbulb. If she was the second smartest kid in her graduating class, what does that say about the Cedar Canyon school system? I decide to ask Mom that question and to point out the risk to my young, impressionable mind she's taking by having me educated here.

At home, I help unload groceries then hurry upstairs, maneuvering my way through the minefield of boxes and furniture in the middle of the living room floor. When we pulled out of the grocery store parking lot, Mom got all over me for being rude to Reagan. I defended myself by saying I didn't speak more than two words to the girl, and she snapped, "Exactly."

Maybe I *was* rude—I don't know. Reagan just rubbed me the wrong way, as Papa Dan used to say. So far, *everyone* here has left me feeling raw. Except the guy at the salad bar. He didn't say anything stupid. He was totally friendly, even if he *is* a jock.

Mom lectured me the whole way home, accusing me of being difficult. She said I'm judging the people around here without getting to know them. I didn't waste my breath arguing with her. Lately, she rubs me wrong, too.

I put sheets on my bed and plop onto it, too numb to move. I want to read the journal, but knowing Mom she'll barge in without knocking and ask me what I'm doing; better to wait until she's asleep. I haven't hung any posters in my room yet, and everything about the small space, from the pale blue walls to the scratched wooden floors, seems unwelcoming and cold. As reluctant to accept *me* as I am *it*. Only the tree outside the window feels friendly, the scratch of leaves against the side of the house a familiar sound. I had a tree outside my bedroom window in San Francisco, too. The wind didn't blow as much there, but when it did, I'd hear the same noise.

Sighing, I get up and dig through all the junk on the floor that I dumped there earlier until I find the book I was reading in the car. Propping up on pillows, I open the novel to the chapter where I left off.

It's almost eleven o'clock when Mom pokes her head in to say good night. "You forgot this." She puts the blue notebook on my dresser, then says, "I hope you'll use it."

I shrug. "I don't see why a diary is such a big deal to you."

She stares at me a few seconds, then says, "Get some sleep." Before she closes my door she adds, "My bed is piled high with stuff, and I'm too tired to make it up anyway, so I'll be on the couch downstairs if you need me."

"Okay." I close my novel and set it aside. "G'night, Mom." I smile, hoping she's over being ticked at me. I sort of regret not talking to her the entire trip. And I feel bad about being a jerk at the grocery store. She does her best. The cities and houses I live in change, as do the schools I attend and the kids I hang out with. But Mom and Papa Dan are permanent; I can always count on them to be there for me.

Mom smiles back. "I love you, Tansy."

Relieved, I say, "Love you, too."

She closes the door, then I take my camera case from the closet and spread Henry's things across the bed. I promised Hailey I'd call tonight at nine o'clock California time. She said she'd stay home and wait. I have five minutes. Plenty of time to read Henry's next poem, but for some reason, I can't bring myself to open the journal. I don't want to rush when I read it. I want to savor each word. I'll wait until after Hailey and I talk.

Earlier, I reset Henry's watch and wound it. I pop open the cover, and when the minute hand points straight up, I punch Hailey's number into my cell phone. After the tenth ring, I end the call and dial her landline. Mrs. Fremont picks up right away.

"Hi, this is Tansy," I say. It's great to hear her voice. I like Mrs. Fremont. She's an old-fashioned stay-at-home mom who makes the best brownies ever. We talk about the trip and Cedar Canyon for a little while, then I ask if Hailey can come to the phone.

"I'm sorry, Tansy," Mrs. Fremont says. "Hailey went to a concert."

"A concert?" I sit up.

"Yes, with that boy from work. Corey—no, that's not right, it's—"

"Colin?" My stomach drops.

"Yes, that's his name. They went to see a local group . . . Kinky Red?"

"Blue," I murmur. "Kinky Blue." Colin's favorite band.

"Hailey won't be home for a while. I know she'll be sorry she missed you. I'll tell her to call you tomorrow."

My throat hardens, and I can barely choke out a goodbye. All Hailey's warnings about Colin being bad news echo through my mind, followed by her promises. *Call me your first night there. I promise I'll be home. . . . I don't care how far apart we live, you're my best friend. Nothing will change that.* Yeah, right. I've only been gone a few days and she not only couldn't care less if she talks to me, she's going out with the guy I like. I can't believe Hailey would do this to me. I trusted her. How could I have been so stupid?

My hands shake as I open Henry's journal to the second poem and read . . .

Don't believe the words they speak
When they look into your eyes,
When they swear to stand by you
Till the sun falls from the sky.
Don't believe the hollow vow
Said with ease to humor you,
Woven stories sewn to please
But the golden threads aren't true . . .

Henry. I would swear he is speaking directly to me, reaching out from the page, through the years. How can someone who lived and died here so many decades ago know exactly how I feel?

I jerk awake from a dreamless sleep and blink until my eyes adjust to the darkness. The curtains hang limp in the stale, stuffy air. Earlier, before I turned out the light, I opened the window just enough to let in a little of the cool, blustery air. But the wind has finally stopped blowing and the room is sweltering hot. Mom said she'll have air-conditioner units installed soon, so we can survive the Texas heat.

Somewhere in the distance a train wails, the sound reminding me of some of the lonely harmonica tunes Papa Dan used to play. I kick off the sheet, and a breeze sweeps across me, pebbling my skin with goose bumps. *Weird.* Where did such a cool draft come from on such a hot, still night? My door is ajar, but I remember Mom closing it long before I turned out the light. Could the wind have blown through the window earlier and forced the door open? Even though the latch is as old and worn out as the rest of the house, that doesn't seem possible. Besides, the door opens *into* the room, not out of it. Mom might've looked in on me again before she went to bed. That explains the door but not the breeze.

Too tired to worry about it, I glance at the clock on my nightstand. 12:22. I burrow deeper into the pillow. Outside, a bird whistles then breaks into song, the warble low and strangely sad. For a moment, I recall the bird that I saw on the windowsill through my camera's viewfinder. Then my thoughts drift to Hailey and Colin and I squeeze my eyes shut, fighting tears. Right now, Henry Peterson feels like my only friend. Some social life I'm going to have here—me and a dead guy hanging out on Saturday nights.

I read his second poem several times after I talked to Hailey's mom. I don't really believe his words were meant for me—advice from the grave. *Yeah, right.* But shaking off that uneasy feeling is hard to do, anyway. I think of him living in this big, gloomy house, walking the narrow hallways, maybe even sleeping in this room. Did he leave the window open in the summer? Did he lie awake and listen to a night bird's song, the train's sad wail, the monotonous hum of cicadas? I wonder if he found comfort in the dark isolation, in the creaks and whispers, the quiet sounds of a country night. Or did he feel as lonely as I do?

The bird's shaky lullaby relaxes me. But just as I'm in that twilight place between reality and dreams, the singing stops and I'm snapped awake again by the sound of a man's voice. It drifts to me from the direction of Papa Dan's room. Could it be him? Eight months have passed since my grandfather has spoken more than a mumbled word or two at a time. But now I hear full sentences delivered in a steady stream. I can't make out what he's saying, just his quiet angry tone, rising . . . rising, then falling to a low, rolling mumble. I don't remember Papa Dan ever sounding so tense or hateful. His tone of voice scares me.

Sitting up, I strain to hear more clearly. I tell myself he must be talking to Mom, but my stomach tilts anyway.

Why don't I hear *her*? The muscles in my legs twitch as I push from my bed and tiptoe to the door. Standing at the threshold, I count to three, draw a breath, and hold it. Then I poke my head into the dark hallway and look toward Papa Dan's room. No light shines beneath his door.

"*I won't,*" he says in a quiet, threatening voice that doesn't sound like him at all. He must be talking in his sleep, having a nightmare. . . . I should wake him. The hallway between my room and Papa Dan's seems a mile long as I make my way to his door. Pausing, I reach for the knob.

"*Listen to me. . . .*"

Now that I'm closer, Papa Dan sounds more like himself. But then I hear two voices at once . . . overlapping. A sharp "*Leave!*" A pleading "*Watch out!*"

Panicked, I step back. What I heard . . . what I *think* I heard . . . is crazy. Impossible. Still, the echo of those two separate voices speaking at the same time reverberates inside my head. Someone *is* in the room with my grandfather. I know I should go downstairs and get Mom, but I can't leave him alone and defenseless, even for a minute.

Poised to pounce on a burglar if necessary, I grab the doorknob and turn it, pushing open the door. Cool air rushes past me then disappears, leaving me standing in the same fog of heat that hangs heavy in my own room. A yellow moon spills enough light through the gauzy white curtains to highlight my grandfather's silhouette. He's sitting alone at the edge of the bed, facing me, his back to the window, quiet now. Still.

"Papa Dan?" I whisper. "You okay? I'm going to turn on the light." I flip the switch, squinting against the sudden glare.

My grandfather blinks and glances at me. His eyes flash confusion at first, then recognition and relief.

I scan every corner, look under the bed and in the closet, relaxing little by little when no one jumps out at me. I tell myself I only imagined two different voices speaking at once. But I'm still trembling when I sit beside Papa Dan. I hug him and notice he's trembling, too. "You're afraid, aren't you?" I squeeze his shoulders, hoping he'll answer me, but he's not talking now. "It's okay. This place freaks me out, too."

His arms come around me. Against my chest, his heart thumps hard and fast.

"It's okay . . . it's okay. Everything's fine." I try to reassure him, as he always used to reassure me whenever I was afraid. But it's all a lie. Everything *isn't* fine. Something is wrong with this house. Papa Dan knew it the minute we arrived. "You don't want to live here, do you?" More than once, Mom has mentioned that before he got sick, he told her he wanted to take a trip to Cedar Canyon. Now I wonder why he would want to come back after so many years away. Did he want to dig up a memory—or bury one?

My gaze settles on a photograph on the nightstand: Papa Dan and my grandmother with my dad between them. I study their faces, remembering an album I found in Papa

Dan's closet when I was about six years old. Inside were black-and-white snapshots with yellowed edges, images of people from another time, faces I didn't recognize. Surrounded by his shoes, I sat on the floor and flipped through the pages. When Papa Dan found me there, he took the album away. That was one of the few times he ever scolded me.

He has other photo albums that he leaves out for anyone to see, and on a night months ago when his mind was still clear, we looked through them together. Papa Dan talked about places he had lived and visited. He didn't mention Cedar Canyon, though. Not once. Most of the pictures were of him and my grandmother, a few of my dad. Some were of his parents and Papa Dan as a boy. He didn't show me the photograph of this house that Mom found, and there were no shots of his childhood friends. No school group pictures.

In the photograph on the nightstand, my grandparents' shoulders press together; my dad clings to Papa Dan's leg. Sitting back, I take my grandfather's hand in mine, startled by how weak his grasp has become over the last few months.

I can't remember my dad's touch. Even so, I've mourned losing it. How much worse will it be to know a touch and have it taken away?

5

The next morning, I'm up before seven, wide awake in spite of my restless night. I pass Mom's bedroom on my way to the stairs. Small cartons and suitcases cover the bed. Boxes fill every corner. A grating noise overhead that sounds like a piece of furniture being moved tells me she's on the third floor, already arranging her office, even though the rest of the house is so cluttered that I have to watch my step to avoid tripping over something.

My growling stomach leads me downstairs to the kitchen, where Papa Dan sits looking out the side window at the mulberry tree, a pile of shredded paper napkin on the table in front of him. He glances my way and a smile flickers at the corners of his mouth. His eyes are bloodshot, his face ashen, his thick silver hair a tangled mess.

Dread sinks like a stone to the bottom of my stomach as I lift a box and move it into the corner. Papa Dan never joins us in the morning until he's dressed and shaved, hair combed, teeth brushed, shoes on his feet. Ready for whatever surprises the day might bring. That's what he always used to say. This morning, he wears wrinkled pajamas, and his feet are bare. I kiss his head on my way to the refrigerator. "Morning."

Top o' the morning to you, Tansy girl. The words echo from mornings long past, an Irish greeting spoken with the slight Texas drawl he never quite shed.

I grab a pitcher of orange juice from the refrigerator along with a bowl of grapes we bought last night. Placing the bowl at the center of the table, I pour two glasses of juice. "Having trouble getting started today?" I ask Papa Dan.

His hand shakes when he takes the glass I hold out to him, and everything inside of me shifts downward. Papa Dan doesn't normally tremble. Despite the problems with his mind, his body has stayed healthy and strong. His hands have always been steady enough that he was able to keep carving and sanding some of his woodworking projects in San Francisco, even though we had to take away his electric tools. When he started forgetting and losing things, Mom wanted to take away *all* of his tools, but he loves working with his hands so much that I convinced her not to. She agreed that he could continue to carve, sand, and polish any unfinished pieces as long as someone stayed with him.

He doesn't make anything you can recognize or use anymore. But Papa Dan used to carve awesome birds and fish. He made tables, chests, and the most beautiful jewelry boxes. My breath catches. *Beautiful boxes.* Like the one I found in the cellar out back.

I sit down across the table from my grandfather and lift my glass, then set it down again without drinking. Leaning toward him, I say, "Why did you have a picture of this house? Did you used to come here when you were a kid?"

He only blinks at me, and I'm not sure he understands my question.

Reaching across the small table, I take his hand and whisper, "You talked last night . . . I heard you. Why won't you talk to me now?"

Papa Dan's blank expression shifts to one of worried confusion. He touches my cheek, and I realize then that he only understands one thing—that I'm upset.

I smile at him, tears blurring my vision. "I'm okay," I say, my voice too high. Sitting back, I reach for the fruit bowl and pluck a grape from the stem.

Mom walks in and opens the refrigerator. "Good morning, early bird," she says.

"The *early bird* was outside my window last night. It woke me up after midnight and kept singing off and on until morning." I sit back and look at her, hoping she doesn't notice I'm emotional. "Didn't you hear it?"

"No. Are you sure it was a bird?" She takes out the juice pitcher, then faces me. "That's odd for one to sing during the night."

"I didn't see it, but I know what a bird sounds like. I'm surprised all the birds around here haven't been blown to Oklahoma, there's so much wind."

Mom frowns. "Is something wrong?"

Thinking of my conversation with Hailey's mother, of the voices coming from Papa Dan's room, I shake my head. Mom studies me a moment longer before pouring juice into a tumbler. She's already dressed, her hair pulled up into a knot on top of her head. "When did you get up?" I ask.

"Over an hour ago. I put that padlock on the cellar." She sips the juice, then opens a loaf of bread, takes out four slices, and drops them into the toaster. "I've been trying to get my office in order so I can start working."

Glancing at Papa Dan, I stand and walk over to Mom. "He doesn't like it here," I whisper.

"What are you talking about?" She leans against the counter, her back to the sink.

"Papa Dan. He seriously hates it here."

"Not this again." She sighs. "How do you know?"

I widen my eyes, hiss, *"Look* at him. He didn't get dressed before he came down."

Papa Dan's chair scrapes the floor as he pushes away from the table and stands. "Don't you want some toast, Dan?" Mom asks him, but he turns toward the door that leads to the living room and leaves without acknowledging either one of us.

"We shouldn't talk about him like he's not even in the room," I say.

"I know." She touches my arm. "The move has thrown him off, that's all. The doctor warned us that things like this would likely happen, even without the move."

"I heard him talking in his sleep."

Her eyes widen. "Talking?"

I nod. "Full sentences. He sounded upset."

"What did he say?"

"I couldn't hear all of it." I don't mention that he spoke in two different voices or that they seemed to overlap. She would either think I was dreaming or worry that I'm going peanutty because of the move. This morning, I'm not so sure I don't agree with her.

The toast pops up. Mom places the slices on a plate and takes them to the table. "He may be a little stressed out from the trip."

"Maybe." I cross my arms. "Or maybe this place gives him the creeps."

"I thought coming here might do him some good." Turning, she takes jam and butter out of the refrigerator, then returns to the table and we sit across from each other.

"You said that Papa Dan told you once that he wanted to come back here. . . ."

She nods. "A while ago. Before he stopped talking."

"Did he say why?"

"Just that he had some old business to set straight. Something to do with a childhood friend who had died. He said she was like his sister when they were growing up. I can't remember her name, but she was living on the East Coast when she passed away a year or so ago. Her attorney sent Papa Dan a letter she wrote to him before her death."

"What did it say?"

50

"He didn't tell me, and I didn't ask, because he didn't seem to want to talk about it. He was really upset over the woman's death, so I urged him to arrange for a trip out here. I thought it might help him find some closure, if that's what he needed. Then his health went downhill, and he didn't have a chance to follow through. I never found the letter."

"Maybe he threw it away."

She studies me for several quiet moments. "I knew moving would be hard for both of you, but I thought it would pass and you'd get a kick out of exploring this old place. There are a lot of great photo opportunities here. I hoped—"

"I might take some pictures after I shower," I say quickly. I don't want our conversation to head the direction she's trying to take it. It will just lead to Hailey and Colin, and I don't think I can talk about them without crying. "Can I set up Papa Dan's workshop in the old barn?" I ask. "It would be the perfect place for him to put his stuff."

Mom averts her eyes. "I don't know, Tansy. The barn is too far from the house."

"It's not that far."

"I'm not sure it's a good idea for him to be way out there alone tinkering while you're in school and I'm working."

"Why not? I know we have to keep his tools put away, but why can't he just hang out there by himself if he wants to? He likes to be around the things he's made. And you locked the cellar door, so we won't have to worry about that."

"I'm afraid he'll wander off. I didn't tell you, but last week in San Francisco, I found him out in the yard in the middle of the night a couple of different times. When the handyman comes, I'm going to have him put a lock on the outside of Papa Dan's bedroom door so he can't get out at night." She glances briefly at the ceiling, frowning. "What about that big room on the third floor for his shop? The one across from my office, beneath the turret. I'll help you lug everything up there later. I could have a lock put on that door, too."

"You're going to start locking him up like a prisoner?" I don't even try to control the infuriation in my voice.

"Honey . . . he could get lost or hurt."

"So we're going to treat him like a baby now, is that it?"

Her hand covers mine on the tabletop. "This is hard for me, too. But we have to think about Papa Dan's safety. We have to do what's best for him."

I squeeze my eyes shut. "I hate what's happening to him. I *hate* it."

"I know, Tansy. I hate it, too."

"It's like he isn't even here sometimes. Just his body. And even it—" The words catch in my throat. I open my eyes and look at her. "It's so weird. He looks the same on the outside, but he's getting all shaky. And when he holds my hand, he doesn't feel as strong."

"He's always taken care of us. Now it's our turn to take care of him," Mom says softly.

Fighting tears, I say, "I miss him, Mom. I miss him so much."

After breakfast, I take another look at the third-story room. Mom's right; it's perfect for Papa Dan's shop. Just the right size, and the lighting is good.

Mom wants to get in another hour of organizing her office before we start hauling his stuff upstairs, so I make sure Papa Dan wears a cap and plenty of sunblock, then I grab my camera and zoom lens, put his Havana straw hat on my head, and we take off. I'm anxious to see the canyon and the bridge, but Mom said it's too far for Papa Dan to walk there, so I decide to save that trip for another time.

The wind has given way to a gentle breeze, and the sunshine and bright blue sky make the overlapping voices I heard last night seem like a dream. I force my thoughts to other things, but when I picture Hailey with Colin at the Kinky Blue concert, I feel worse than ever. *I won't cry,* I tell myself. *Not over them.*

We head for the field behind the house. Just ahead, the old windmill's blades spin slowly, like a twirler's baton in a marching band. I wonder if Cedar Canyon High School has twirlers—the old-fashioned kind with white ankle boots, short flirty skirts, and fringed jackets. Perky little cowboy hats perched at an angle on their heads. The image pulls a laugh from me, and it feels as good as the sun on my face. Papa Dan lags behind. I turn to check on him, and movement over at the Quattlebaum farmhouse catches my eye. Lifting the camera, I zoom in for a better view, using the lens like binoculars. A man—Mr. Quattlebaum,

I guess—shovels the yard at the side of the house, tossing each scoop into a pile beside him. He's wearing a dark coat and hat, even though it's warm outside. Weird. Everything framed in the viewfinder looks colorless. I adjust the focus, but it doesn't help. I must need to clean the lens.

Pausing to wait for Papa Dan to catch up, I watch the rhythmic plunge and lift of Mr. Quattlebaum's shovel. Somewhere close to his house, a bell clangs. A second later, a big black dog prances up to the farmer. Mr. Quattlebaum leans on his shovel, takes something from the dog's mouth, and throws it. The object sails through the air and disappears behind the barn. The dog bolts after it and out of sight. Mr. Quattlebaum pulls off a glove and holds his hand to his mouth, as if he's warming his fingers with his breath.

Now, that's *pretty freaky,* I think. The man must be really cold-natured; the temperature outside is at least sixty-five degrees.

Before I can wonder any more about it, Papa Dan's whistling draws my attention and I lower the camera to look at him. Wiping the lens with the hem of my shirt, I say, "Hey, slowpoke. What took you so long?" I glance at my watch: 8:15. "At the speed you're moving, we'll reach the windmill in time for lunch," I tease. I take his hand, and we start walking again.

A cloud moves over the sun, casting a shadow across us. When I look toward the Quattlebaums' farmhouse, the farmer and the dog are gone, and something about the scene seems off—different somehow. Releasing Papa Dan's hand, I pause and use the zoom lens to zero in on the farmhouse again. Cleaning the lens worked; the image is bright and colorful. The yard is smooth, untouched.

The hair on the back of my neck prickles, and goose bumps scatter up my arms. What was Mr. Quattlebaum shoveling? Something that he tossed into a pile at his side—a pile that's no longer there. How strange is that? Beyond strange. Maybe Mom wasn't teasing when she said I need glasses. Shaking off my unsettled feelings, I lower the camera and hurry to catch Papa Dan at the windmill. He holds his cap and shades his eyes with one hand as he looks up at the twirling blades.

In that instant a shaft of sunlight illuminates my grandfather. My breath catches and I stop. *Luminosity*. In photography the term refers to the brilliance created by a light source or radiated back from the face of something. Right now, it seems as if the sunbeam doesn't shine down on my grandfather, but rather that *he* emits the ray that stretches between him and the sky. Amazed by the beautiful sight, I lift the camera and take the shot.

After I shoot several more pictures, we make our way back to the barn where I take photographs of the ramshackle building at different angles. The camera feels good in my hands. I've missed it. Life always seems so clear when I'm seeing it through a lens.

I hear Mom talking in the front yard as we make our way in that direction by way of the side of the house. Papa Dan pauses beside the mulberry tree and his whistling stops. A breeze flaps the fabric of his baggy pants. Birds chirp, filling the air with music. I follow my grandfather's gaze to a nest tucked in the crook of a bent-knuckled branch.

"You want me to take your picture?" I ask him, but the tree holds his attention. He doesn't seem to be looking at the nest anymore but at the limb beneath it. "Papa Dan!" I call, laughing, feeling better after spending this time with him outside. "Look at me! Smile!" Though he doesn't turn, I lift the camera, peer through the viewfinder . . . and freeze.

The image in the frame is completely still. Black, white, and gray. Like a photograph already shot. Snow dusts the scene like powdered sugar. A guy about my age occupies the space where Papa Dan stood only a moment ago. He wears a coat and a woolen scarf, an old-fashioned winter hat with earflaps, heavy boots on his feet. A sparrow hovers above him, paused in midflight. The mulberry tree seems smaller and the limbs are bare. On one of them, I see a faint, blurred silhouette—a second guy dressed in bulky clothing. The boy on the ground stares up at the guy in the tree, and the guy in the tree stares back, his eyes the only distinguishable feature in the white smudge of his face.

The wind has died. The birds no longer sing. I don't hear Mom's voice around the corner. Only silence. Adrenaline shoots through me, and my stomach flips over. I jerk the camera away from my face.

At once, birds chirp and chatter, and Mom's laughter drifts to me again, carried by a whispering breeze. No phantom sits in the tree, and only blue sky fills the spaces between the limbs. Papa Dan gazes up into the flickering green leaves, his focus on the branch beneath the nest where the sparrow lands with a flutter of wings. At my feet, patchy grass covers the ground instead of snow.

"Papa Dan," I whisper. But he won't turn to me. He won't glance away from the tree. A chill ripples through me as I lift the camera again and look through the viewfinder.

Silence. Everything black and white and gray, everything frozen in time, snow on the ground. The boy standing in Papa Dan's place stares up at the tree where the blurred guy sits with his legs draped over a limb. But the pale, hazy phantom no longer stares at the boy on the ground.

He stares straight at me.

6

Somehow I manage to press the shutter release and take the picture before I drop the camera; only the strap around my neck saves it from hitting the ground. Grabbing Papa Dan's hand, I practically drag him behind me as I hurry around the corner of the house. Mom stands in the driveway talking to a small blond man with a deep Texas drawl. He wears a brown uniform and tan cowboy boots. Relief sweeps through me when I see letters plastered across the door of his white SUV that tell me this man is the county sheriff. My first instinct is to tell him what I saw. But what *did* I see?

"There you are," Mom says. "Come meet Sheriff Ray Don Dilworth. Sheriff, this is my father-in-law, Daniel Piper, and my daughter, Tansy."

"Mornin', young lady . . . sir," he says, smiling.

I pause beside them and open my mouth to reply, but I'm too shaken up to speak.

Mom pulls off her sunglasses. "What's wrong?"

More than anything, I want to tell them, to hear the sheriff laugh and say: *Oh, that? Nothing but a hologram the prior renters left behind. I turned it on to show your mother. Conditions have to be just right.* An unlikely explanation, but at least it doesn't question my sanity, which is exactly what I'm starting to do. First the voices last night, now this. Maybe Papa Dan's condition is hereditary.

The dread in Mom's expression changes my mind about speaking up. She's already worried enough about me. Sometimes she acts like she thinks I'll unravel if everything isn't *just right*. I don't want to make her even more anxious. "Nothing's wrong," I tell her, dropping Papa Dan's hand and crossing my arms.

Mom searches my face, as if she isn't sure she believes me. "The sheriff drove all the way out here to welcome us to town. Isn't that nice?"

I nod, then pull the brim of my hat down a bit farther so Mom can't see my eyes.

The sheriff chuckles. "Word around town is your mama was over at the Longhorn last night devising a scheme to murder some poor sucker with a Weed Eater, so I decided I'd better come have a little talk with her."

Mom tips her head to one side, a teasing glint in her eyes. "I'm afraid you're too late, Sheriff. But I used a blowtorch instead of a Weed Eater; it was much more efficient."

While they snicker over her joke, I glance behind me, half expecting to see those two guys from the tree standing there. When I turn back, the sheriff stops laughing, peers at the sky, and says, "Beautiful morning, isn't it? We could sure use more rain, though. A real downpour, this time. It's supposed to get hotter 'n all get out this afternoon."

"Yes, a shower would be nice," Mom murmurs, her voice trailing, her attention fixed on the sheriff in a flirty way that would probably disgust me if I didn't have more important things to worry about. Was what I saw at the mulberry tree real, or was I hallucinating?

The sheriff twirls his cowboy hat between his hands. He looks as antsy as I feel. I'm pretty sure Mom's scrutiny has him flustered. Either that or his collar is too tight. "I bet y'all are going to feel right at home here before you know it," he says. "Texans are a friendly bunch, and the folks in Cedar Canyon are even more so than most."

"We've already found that to be true," Mom says.

While I squirm and look back toward the tree again, the sheriff puts on his hat. "Are y'all going to the Watermelon Run on Sunday evening?"

"The Watermelon Run?" Mom shakes her head. "I haven't heard of it."

"It's held every August to kick off the school year and the new football season. Everyone goes. The tradition dates back to when my grandparents were in school."

"In that case, we'll definitely be there," Mom says, sounding overjoyed.

"It's at the stadium . . . over by the school complex. Have you had a chance to visit the schools yet?"

"No, we haven't gone by," Mom tells him. Placing

her sunglasses on top of her head, she asks, "How does watermelon figure into all this?"

"The Food Fair brings in the melons—enough for each football player to choose one," the sheriff explains. "The team meets at the store to pick 'em up, then it's a footrace to the stadium where everyone's waiting. When they show up, the players are introduced and the pep rally starts." Grinning, he adds, "It's quite a deal. It'll be a great chance for you to get acquainted with folks."

"It sounds like fun," Mom says.

More like pure torture, I think, but nobody asks my opinion. And, anyway, I'm not sure it could be any worse than what I'm going through now. My heart's thumping so hard, I'm surprised they can't hear it. Was there someone in that tree? Or am I losing my mind?

"This year the booster club's sponsoring a fund-raiser for the Pruitts at the same time as the run," the sheriff continues. "Their house burned down a couple of weeks ago. Folks are donating baked goods and crafts, and businesses around town are providing merchandise for a raffle."

"I should donate some of my books," Mom says. "I'll call my publisher today and ask them to overnight a box or two."

The sheriff's face lights up. "If you'll give me your phone number, I'll tell Della Shroeder to get in touch with you. She's headin' up the thing. She'll be tickled pink."

Mom tells him her number and he pulls a small notebook from his shirt pocket and jots it down.

"Well, I best be letting you get back to your business." Returning the notebook to his pocket, Sheriff Dilworth says, "Y'all be careful out here all alone."

"Careful?" Mom frowns.

"Not to worry you, but previous tenants reported some strange things going on around the property. Recently the Quattlebaums have, too."

I was wrong to think that my heart couldn't beat any faster. If others have seen the same sort of thing I did, then maybe Mom won't think I'm going crazy . . . and neither will I. "What kind of reports?" I ask.

"Noises," he answers. "A break-in or two. Hank Quattlebaum thought he saw someone prowling around here at night a week or so back."

"Oh, you mean the ghost." Mom laughs. "Hank told us about him. Actually, I'm hoping we meet."

"Seriously, Ms. Piper." Sheriff Dilworth scratches his chin and squints. "Is it Moon or Piper?"

Mom looks flirty again as she answers, "It's Millie."

He smiles. "I don't particularly believe in ghosts, Millie, but you might want to keep your eyes and ears open."

"We'll call if we hear one rattling around the place." Mom pulls a serious face and adds, "Especially if he's carrying a blowtorch or a Weed Eater." She slides her sunglasses onto her nose again, and the tiny rhinestones at the corners sparkle in the sunlight.

Chuckling and blushing, Sheriff Dilworth reaches to open the door of his vehicle.

"I think I just saw someone," I blurt out, afraid for him to leave us alone.

"What?" Mom says.

The Sheriff pauses with his hand on the door. "You saw a prowler?"

"I was taking Papa Dan's picture, and I thought I saw someone in the tree behind him. But when I lowered the camera the guy was gone."

Mom touches my shoulder. "It was a man?"

"I'm not sure. Maybe. Or he could've been closer to my age."

Closing the car door, Sheriff Dilworth says, "Let's go take a look."

Holding my grandfather's hand, I lead them to the tree. We don't see anything strange, so we walk around back to the barn but don't find so much as a footprint other than mine and Papa Dan's. After returning to the driveway, the sheriff warns us again to be careful and reminds us to call if we need anything. He studies me a second, concern wrinkling his forehead. Then he climbs into his SUV and backs out. Mom, Papa Dan, and I stand in the yard, watching dust billow on the road behind his vehicle as he drives away.

"Honey, are you sure about what you saw?" Mom asks, turning to me.

I shrug. "I don't know. It was probably just a smudge on the camera lens."

"We're so isolated out here that it can mess with your

mind, if you let it," she says.

Her concern makes me wish I'd kept quiet. I laugh, hoping to disguise my anxiety. "I guess this house has me spooked. And Mr. Quattlebaum's story about the ghost."

"This *is* a pretty spooky house. And this is such desolate country. Did I tell you what I dreamed last night?" she asks, starting for the porch, her voice lighter.

Papa Dan and I follow her. "No, what?"

"I dreamed someone was screaming out in the canyon. Out in the direction where the bridge is supposed to be. It was that bird screeching, I bet. The one that kept you up all night. My subconscious must've turned the noise into a scream."

Apprehension strokes up my spine like an icy finger as we climb the porch steps. I don't mention to my mother that the bird didn't exactly screech.

She glances back at us and says to Papa Dan, "Ready to set up your workshop, Dan?" The screen door squeaks when she pulls it open. "The sooner we put the house in order, the sooner it'll start to feel like home."

"Can we wait just a little while?" I ask. I don't want to spend too much time around her when I'm feeling so edgy. "I'm really tired. I think I'll go lie down and read for a while." I want to draw the curtains, pull the covers around me, curl up, and shut everything out. Forget the mysterious frozen world; push the image of it out of my mind.

Mom faces me and frowns. "You just got up. Are you sick?"

"No, I'm okay. I think the trip just wiped me out. But you're right; I probably shouldn't be lazy or I won't sleep tonight."

Holing up in my room wouldn't have worked, anyway. Even with the shade drawn, I'd sense the mulberry tree on the other side of the window. It doesn't seem all that friendly anymore. I'm not sure which scares me worse— that I might have imagined what I saw or that I didn't. But I need to figure it out, and the sooner the better.

"I still don't feel like starting on the shop, though," I tell Mom. "I'd rather take my film into town to have it developed. You want to go?"

"I think I'll stay here. I don't want to miss the handyman if he drops by. Papa Dan might enjoy the ride, though."

"Where do you think I should take the film?"

"Probably City Drug on Main. Did you see it last night?"

"No, but I'll find it."

She must sense that I'm nervous about leaving her out here alone, because she touches my arm and adds, "I'll be fine. You two go ahead. And pick up some ibuprofen for me. My back is killing me already from tugging furniture around."

I hurry inside to get my keys and some money from Mom's purse, wishing I had already set up a darkroom. A few years ago, Papa Dan bought me the equipment and supplies, but everything is in boxes.

I should've known Cedar Canyon wouldn't have a place to process film. Which is one more reason I should ask for a digital camera for Christmas. Putting away my 35 millimeter would be hard, though. It's been a friend for so many years. A better one than Hailey, that's for sure.

While Papa Dan scans the magazine rack, I talk to the pregnant woman behind the counter at City Drug—Mary Jane, according to the name tag on her blouse. "Saturday, I'm driving into Amarillo. I'd be happy to drop off your film at the one-hour photo," she says.

"Thanks, but you don't have to do that."

"If it was any trouble, I wouldn't offer," she assures me. "I'll run my errands and pick it up when I'm heading home."

I hesitate a moment before handing Mary Jane the film. I don't even know this woman. But I'm not sure how long it will take to get my darkroom up and running, and I doubt Mom and I will be going to Amarillo anytime soon.

Mary Jane drops the film into her purse. I have a sudden urge to grab it, to not let it out of my sight. That roll contains the proof that I'm either losing my mind or I'm not.

"Write down your name and number and how you want the pictures," Mary Jane says, handing me a pad of paper and a pen.

"How I want them?"

"The size and finish." Reaching behind her, she presses a hand against the small of her back, winces, and mutters, "Roger better not expect me to cook dinner tonight. In fact, I think I'm swearing off cooking until after this baby comes."

As I'm writing down the information, a tall, balding,

middle-aged man wearing a white pharmacist's smock walks up to Mary Jane behind the counter. He winks at me, points at her stomach, and whispers, "Being pregnant makes her cranky."

One row behind us, Papa Dan flips the pages of a magazine and whistles a jazzy tune. Satisfied that he's occupied, I hand the paper to Mary Jane.

"I don't think we've met," the pharmacist says. "I'm Jim Bob Cooper, chief pill pusher, bottle washer, and owner of this bustling enterprise. Call me J. B."

Jim Bob, Mary Jane, Sheriff Ray Don Dilworth. Does everyone in this town over the age of thirty have two first names? I introduce myself and we shake hands.

"Oh, you're the writer's daughter."

"Yes," I murmur.

"I heard you folks made it into town. Nice to have you here." J. B. gestures toward the cashier. "The ray of sunshine behind the register is Mary Jane McAllister."

"Nice to meet you," Mary Jane says. "You'll have to come back for a chocolate soda or a root-beer float some afternoon. The fountain's a popular after-school place." She nods toward the far side of the shop, where a row of chrome stools with round red tops lines an old-fashioned soda fountain counter. Glasses in all shapes and sizes are stacked on shelves behind the bar, and the wall is covered with a chalkboard menu and old signs advertising Coca-Cola and Hires Root Beer.

Before I can respond, the door opens, and two girls

and a guy walk in. I flinch when I realize it's Alison and her A-hole groupies. The freckle-faced guy struts in like a puffed-up rooster. His gaze cuts in my direction, and his mouth curves up at one corner. He nudges Alison with his elbow, and she looks at me and says, "Oh, hi."

"Hi," I say quietly, grateful the brim of my hat hides my eyes when the other girl smirks and glances away. Lowering my head, I take off to look for Mom's ibuprofen.

"Hey, hoodlums," J. B. calls out to the threesome, and they tease back and forth with him while I scan the aisles.

"My kids have missed you, Alison," Mary Jane says, sounding cheerful now. "You sure you can't squeeze in a little time to babysit for me every once in a while?"

"Sorry," Alison replies. "I wish I could, but between school, cheerleading, and volunteer work in Amarillo, my weekends are going to be totally packed this year."

Mary Jane sighs. "Your mom told me you were crazy busy. She said you're shooting for the honor roll this year. Good for you."

"Yeah, Alison's become completely boring," the rude girl says. "She has this sudden bizarre obsession with the letter A."

"That's 'cause she never learned the rest of the alphabet, Shanna," Rooster Boy calls from the direction of the soda fountain.

Alison laughs. "*Shut up*, Jenks."

"I'm just sayin' . . . ," he mutters.

I find Mom's ibuprofen, then slowly start up front again.

From the corner of my eye, I see Rooster Boy spinning in a circle on one of the soda fountain stools. As I place my purchase on the counter, he gets up and starts toward me. "Hey, I don't think you've had the pleasure of meeting me," he says. "I'm Jon Jenks."

"Idiot," Alison murmurs, her mouth pulling into a tight smile that isn't really a smile at all. She and Shanna wander over to a candy rack and disappear behind it.

"I'm Tansy," I tell Jon.

"So I heard. Welcome to the big city." He nods toward the girls. "Don't worry about the wildlife; they aren't as fierce as they seem."

"I'm not worried."

"Now I, on the other hand, bite." Wiggling his brows, he starts off toward the magazine racks.

J. B. shakes his head and sighs. "Always the clown." Shifting his attention from Rooster Boy to Papa Dan, he asks, "Is that gentleman looking at magazines your grandfather? I heard he used to live here way back before I was born."

"Yes," I say. "His name's Daniel Piper." When the pharmacist calls out a greeting to Papa Dan, I lower my voice and say, "He doesn't talk."

As soon as the words are out of my mouth, Papa Dan yells, *"Woo-wee!"*

Giggles drift from behind the candy rack.

"He doesn't talk *much*," I add, my face heating up when I notice that my grandfather is looking at a *Cosmo* magazine while Rooster Boy snoops over his shoulder.

"Well, I'm pleased to meet both of you. I look forward to meeting your mother, too. It's not every day I get to talk to a famous author." J. B.'s smile is kind, but I don't feel any less mortified. "What else can I help you with today?" he asks.

"You don't sell film, do you? I need five rolls of black-and-white."

"Yes, we have film." He stoops to search beneath the counter.

I scan the store but don't see the girls. Rooster Boy has moved to the opposite end of the magazine rack from Papa Dan. I feel Mary Jane watching me and glance at her. She settles one hand on her bulging belly and says, "When we heard a published author was moving to town, my husband bought one of your mom's books at the grocery store. Something about a zombie girl."

Rooster Boy sputters a laugh, and I wish for the hundredth time my mom was a secretary or a nurse or a lawyer.

"Roger stayed up till two this morning reading it," Mary Jane continues. "Said he had to leave the lights on, it scared him so bad."

I shrug. "I'm pretty sure that's the goal." Faking interest in the merchandise on a nearby shelf, I pick up a box, then realize I'm reading the directions for applying hemorrhoid medication and set it back down. I search the shelves for something else to help me escape the woman's scrutiny.

Enemas. Home pregnancy tests. Condoms. Tampons. No place is safe.

"The Peterson house ought to give your mom plenty of material for her books," Mary Jane goes on.

Hoping she'll forget about me if I ignore her, I move to the analgesic creams. I hear a girl's giggle in the next aisle, hear my name whispered, followed by a *shhhh.* Ducking my head, I read the label on a tube. *Apply small amount to cut, abrasion, or wound to reduce sensitivity.*

"Here you go, Tansy," J. B. calls, and I walk over to the counter as he hands Mary Jane the film. "Sorry that took so long. We don't get many requests for black-and-white."

Mary Jane rings up the sale. "Have you heard that the Peterson kid who lived in your house back in the thirties committed suicide?"

Startled, I nod and say, "Mr. Quattlebaum told me."

"My grandma says he was nuttier than a fruitcake. He was a class ahead of her in school, but she and pretty much everyone else steered clear of him. I grew up hearing her stories about the strange things he'd do. Grandma said he used to walk the railing on the old wagon bridge that crosses the creek in the canyon. Have you been out there?"

"Not yet."

She shakes her head. "A person would have to be crazy to do that. It's a long drop to the creek bed. Sometimes people would see him sitting alone in the canyon, playing his violin. Grandma said he was an artist, too. He painted pictures."

And wrote poems . . .

"He was a loner. A real oddball."

"Aw, now . . . maybe he was just eccentric, Mary Jane," J. B. says. "Or he might've been depressed. Back then, nobody thought kids suffered from depression."

"If he walked the railing, why do they think he jumped?" I ask. "Maybe he fell."

"It makes for a better story," J. B. says, winking at me.

"I don't recall all the details," she says, ignoring him, "but I've always heard he committed suicide."

I pass Mary Jane some money and ask, "Is your grandmother still alive?"

"Yeah, she's in Willow Grove nursing home in Amarillo. I hate it, but what can you do? She's close to ninety and can't take care of herself anymore." Mary Jane closes the register and eases down onto a stool, sighing long and loud before returning to the subject of Henry. "The turret in your house was the Peterson kid's bedroom."

"Don't start in on that." J. B. frowns at her. "It's nonsense, if you ask me."

"I didn't ask you," Mary Jane says, then turns to me and adds, "Sometimes he'd hole up in there for days at a time to play his violin when his parents were on one of their trips, and it was just him and the housekeeper. Wouldn't even come out to go to school. Myra and Hank Quattlebaum swear they still hear him playing up there sometimes."

"Come on, Mary Jane." J. B. glances at me, flinching like

he's embarrassed by her claims. "You're going to scare her. Surely you don't believe that bunk."

She scowls at him. "Tansy's mom writes *horror* novels; she can handle it." Turning back to me, she says, "Myra Quattlebaum insists she's seen a light burning up in the turret when the house was vacant."

J. B. cups a hand around his mouth and whispers loudly, "Mary Jane is a sucker for a ghost story."

I rub my hands up and down my arms to chase away a sudden chill. Could Henry's ghost be one of the figures I saw through the camera lens?

Ignoring J. B., Mary Jane says, "Hank was even considering buying a dog so he and Myra would feel safer out there all alone. He put it off when he heard you and your family had rented the place."

"No, they have a dog," I say. "A big black one."

J. B. shakes his head. "They don't have a dog. They were here this morning and Myra was on Hank's case about getting one."

"They were here?" I take the sack off the counter, press it against my stomach.

"They were waiting outside the door when I opened up," Mary Jane says.

"What time do you open?"

"Eight o'clock on the dot," she answers.

"But I saw Mr. Quattlebaum in his yard this morning a little after eight. He was throwing a ball to a dog." J. B. and Mary Jane stare at me, silent. Flustered, I say, "Maybe

73

they have company staying with them, or it could've been a workman, I guess."

Excusing myself, I walk over to the magazine rack to get Papa Dan, ready to make my escape. Rooster Boy is flipping through a car magazine as I pass behind him. "Let's go," I say to my grandfather. I put back his magazine and lead him down the aisle.

"See ya Monday at school, Zombie Girl," Rooster Boy mutters as we pass by.

Heat scorches my neck. I don't look at him, just keep my focus on the door.

"Glad you came in, Tansy. You, too, Mr. Piper," J. B. calls as I hurry Papa Dan outside without looking back.

As I'm driving through town, every person we pass waves at us as if we're old friends. I feel weird waving back, but I don't want to seem unfriendly and earn another lecture from Mom. I brush aside thoughts of Alison and her friends, how self-conscious I felt around them, how Shanna completely ignored me. Instead, I think of Henry Peterson and Mary Jane's grandmother. I wonder if Mom would let me drive the forty miles into Amarillo. I could tell her I want to go shopping. She hates malls, so maybe she'd let me go alone. I want to go to Willow Grove and ask the old woman about Henry.

We cross the city limits, and the landscape empties. In my mind, I picture Henry sitting in the turret with only his violin to keep him company, shut off from the world. Mary Jane called him an oddball for it, but I don't consider his behavior to be all that strange. Maybe Henry and I are two of a kind.

As I make the turn onto the road that leads to the house, I glance at Papa Dan and the hairs on my arms stand on end. He stares out the windshield, a far-off, haunted look in his eyes. I wonder if he sees what I see: the dirt road ahead, the man mowing the tall weeds in the parched yard alongside our driveway, the Cedar Canyon Handyman Service truck parked there. Does he see the house? The hollow-eyed windows? Henry's turret sticking up from the roof like a vulgar insult?

A shiver snakes through me. I have a feeling he's looking at a very different scene. One I might see, too, if the light shifted.

Or if I looked through my camera's viewfinder.

On Saturday night, Papa Dan's voice wakes me sometime after midnight. Again, I find him sitting up in bed, staring into the darkness, and shivering. I settle him down, tuck him in, and hold his hand until he snores softly, wondering why moving here has him so upset. When he lived in Cedar Canyon as a kid, he must've known Henry Peterson; nobody is a stranger in a town this size. Does Papa Dan remember that this was Henry's house? Did he think Henry was some sort of freak? Did he keep away from him, along with Mary Jane's grandmother and the rest of the kids? Could it be that, back then, Papa Dan wasn't allowed to come out here—maybe he didn't *want* to—but now he has no choice and he's afraid?

Returning to my own bed, I slip under the sheet and listen to the sorrowful cry of a train passing by on distant tracks. I ran some errands in town for Mom late this afternoon and stopped by City Drug to see if Mary Jane was back from Amarillo. She wasn't there, so J. B. called her house. Mary Jane's husband said she hadn't returned yet. I carried around my cell phone all evening, hoping she'd call, but she never did.

My cell is still close by, on my nightstand, and when it trills quietly, I sit up, grab it, and look at the display. *Hailey*. I turn off the phone and slam it down a little too hard on the nightstand beside my camera. She's tried to call me several times since I talked to her mom, but I haven't answered. I have other things more important than her and Colin to worry about now. I couldn't care less what she has to say.

Just as my head hits the pillow, I hear a rattling sound outside. I sit up. The noise stops. Recalling Mom's dream, I listen for a scream but only hear the bathroom faucet dripping and the sudden singing of a bird in the mulberry tree. For no reason at all, I think of the crystal and close my eyes. I imagine the cool, smooth feel of it against my palm, picture it shimmering like an icicle in the sunlight. The urge to get up and take it out of the camera case is strong, but my dread is stronger. I'm *afraid* to get out of bed; I don't know why, but I am. Opening my eyes, I stare at the ceiling and listen to the bird sing for more than an hour before falling asleep again.

The house is quiet when I awake the next morning. I blink up at the ceiling and notice the dingy paint. The curtain flutters at my open window, and birds chatter outside. Somewhere in the distance, a bell clangs, prickling the hairs at the nape of my neck.

Grabbing my camera from the nightstand, I get up, walk to the window, and push the curtains aside. I use the zoom lens to look across at the Quattlebaum farm. The man and dog I saw the other morning stand in the side yard. The man is dressed in the same dark hat, gloves, and coat, with a shovel at his side. He takes something from the dog's mouth and throws it behind the barn. The dog bolts after it, out of sight. The man pulls off a glove, holds his hand to his mouth as if to breathe on his fingers. Same as before.

Goose bumps skate across my skin. Lowering the camera, I turn my back to the window and lean against it. The clock on my nightstand reads 8:15.

"Tansy? Are you awake?" My bedroom door opens, and Mom looks in.

I glance across at her, but I can't speak.

"What's wrong?" she asks, stepping into the room. "You're shaking."

"I don't feel good." I set my camera on the windowsill and cross my arms.

Mom quickly closes the distance between us, her brows puckering. She presses a cool palm against my cheek as I face the window again and squint across at the Quattlebaums' yard. The man and dog are gone.

"You don't have a fever," she says. "What's the matter?"

Turning, I look into her eyes. I want to tell her about the man and the dog, but if I do, she'll worry about me . . . and I'll feel crazy. What I've seen twice now over at the Quattlebaum farm is too strange to be real, which means

I'm imagining it, and that I probably imagined those two hazy guys at the tree, too. It would freak Mom out to know that her father-in-law and daughter are losing touch with reality at the very same time. It freaks *me* out. "Maybe I just need to eat," I tell her. "I'm sort of dizzy."

"I'll scramble some eggs."

"You?"

Laughing, she says, "Surely I can't ruin eggs." She crosses to the bed and sits, her gaze never leaving my face. "Are you nervous about school?"

I shrug and turn away. "It's no big deal."

"I faxed over your transcripts before we left California. All you have to do now is take a few papers by the office before homeroom and you're all set. The lady I spoke with on the phone was very nice."

"Okay," I murmur. She's already told me all this at least ten times.

"When I was your age, I always got a little antsy the day before school started." Mom pauses, as if waiting for me to say something, and when I don't, she says, "I won't work today. We'll do whatever you want until it's time to leave for the Watermelon Run this evening. We should go out to the canyon, see that old bridge."

"The Watermelon Run . . ." I groan. "Do we *have* to go?" I carry my camera to the dresser and set it down next to a pile of books and other items I still need to organize.

"Don't you want to? I think it sounds like a lot of fun. But if you're sick—"

"I'm not sick. I told you—I just need to eat. But a bunch of guys running onto the field with watermelons while the whole town cheers?" I roll my eyes.

"Oh, come on, sweetie. That's what's great about small towns—people carry on the same traditions their grandparents did."

I sit next to her, cross my arms. "Maybe stupid traditions shouldn't be carried on."

Mom tucks a strand of hair behind my ear. "If you're feeling better by then, I hope you'll go. The booster-club ladies are setting up a booth for me to sell my books."

I sigh, remembering the boxes from her publisher that I picked up at the post office yesterday. "Okay, but I'd rather work on my darkroom today than go to the canyon."

Yesterday, I hauled out the junk in the turret that the owners left there. The turret has a bathroom, which is perfect, since I need a sink and water to use for processing. And maybe I'll feel closer to Henry there, if Mary Jane at the pharmacy knows what she's talking about. My feelings about our resident ghost are all mixed up. The thought of Henry's spirit hanging out here scares me a little, but I read another of his poems last night and I don't care if he was a freak or not; he feels like the one person who understands me.

"Fine," says Mom, "I'll help you. What do we need to do?"

"Vacuum and paint the walls," I tell her. "It's so windy all the time that dust is all over the place up there. A speck of dirt can ruin the processing."

"I saw some white paint in the garage. But we don't have to do it. The handyman is coming back tomorrow to get started. I'll tell him to add painting the turret to his list."

"I don't want to wait. I'd rather do it myself so it'll be right."

Mom smiles wryly. "Okay then, Miss Perfectionist. We'll get to it after breakfast." She kisses my forehead, then stands and starts toward the door. "I'm glad you're taking pictures again. You should bring your camera along to the stadium tonight."

At six o'clock, we drive into town to join the rest of Podunk at the football stadium. As our van moves down the redbrick streets, people on the sidewalks wave. "I don't get it," I say from the backseat. "They don't even know us."

"It's called being neighborly," explains Mom, her voice delighted. Grinning, she honks, then lifts her hand from the steering wheel to wave back at a couple I'm pretty sure she's never met in her life. Papa Dan sits up front with Mom, waving, too.

"*Mom* . . . did you have to honk?" I slouch down in the seat behind my grandfather.

Mom turns a corner onto Sixth Street. "I think that's your school up ahead."

Cedar Canyon High is a two-story brown brick building that sits directly across the street from a trim row of old houses with postage-stamp yards and the biggest trees

I've seen in this town. Wide cement steps on the school building lead up to two marble columns set between three arches. Each arch adorns a massive double door. *Only the gargoyles are missing,* I think. It's that sort of place. Ancient and brooding beneath its rusty red-tiled roof. The building isn't large, but it dominates the neighborhood, silently watching and listening, as it has for maybe a hundred years or more.

Papa mutters beneath his breath, and I say, "*That's it?* It looks about the size of two hallways at my old school."

Slowing the van to a crawl, Mom laughs. "It probably only *has* two hallways. Eloise told me they graduate around fifty seniors each year."

"Fifty," I whisper. "*Pathetic.* I wonder if Papa Dan went to school here?"

"I'm sure he did," she says.

So I'll walk the same halls that my grandfather did at my age, sit in the same classrooms, stare out the same windows. Which is sort of cool but also sort of freaky.

Mom speeds up. We pass the middle school a block down on the opposite side of the street, and directly across from it, the elementary school and the cafeteria that serves all twelve grades. At the end of the street, we circle back behind Cedar Canyon High, where three tennis courts are surrounded by a chain-link fence. Metal bleachers about eight seats tall are on one side of the courts, and the school parking lot is on the other.

The brick street ends, replaced by black pavement. Giant,

bright orange paw prints appear on the lane. Sighing, I ask, "What are those?" I brace myself for the answer, since I'm pretty sure it'll have something to do with some stupid small-town tradition.

"They're bobcat paws!" Mom exclaims. "The school mascot. They must lead to the stadium. Isn't that cute?"

I puff out my cheeks and refrain from answering that question as she follows the paws around another turn. A white water tower looms at the end of the road, with *Bobcats* painted across the top in giant black letters, and beyond it, tall stadium lights appear. We pass the tower and pull into a large parking lot scattered with cars and people.

"Here we are," Mom declares, throwing the van into Park. When I climb out, the scent of freshly cut grass surrounds me along with echoing drumbeats and the blare of a marching band tune. After unloading Mom's books from the back of the van, we start off toward the football field, following the trail of orange paw prints across the parking lot. I have my camera slung over my shoulder by the strap and it bangs against my side as we walk, comforting me in some weird way as we merge with the flow of bodies headed for the stadium entrance. People call "Hello" to us and "How are you?" Mom makes idle chitchat, but I only murmur "Hi," and walk a little faster.

The football field opens up in front of us, a long stretch of green divided into grids by straight white lines. A curving red track with seven lanes surrounds the field, and it's cluttered with makeshift booths—card tables filled with crafts, baked goods, glasses of lemonade, and other items for sale. At least fifty band members, dressed in their regular clothes, stand in rows, center field, warming up.

"The woman I spoke with on the phone said to look for her on the track directly beneath the press box," Mom calls back to me. She leads Papa Dan in that direction, and I follow behind, watching the opposite sideline, where six female cheerleaders in short orange skirts practice backflips and cartwheels. Alison's bouncing blond ponytail is hard to miss. I keep my gaze on her, wondering what it would've been like to grow up in a town like this. Do the kids here know there's more to life than football? I seriously doubt it.

The band breaks into a familiar fight song, and like programmed robots, the cheerleaders' pom-poms snap into position as they begin a dance routine. "Go, Cats! Fight, Cats! Win, Cats!" they yell, pumping their pom-poms into the air. Alison bumps her hip against the girl on her left, and I realize it's Shanna beside her. No surprise. Fans whistle and clap, chanting along with the cheerleaders. The school mascot wears a cat suit, complete with a tail and claws. He runs up and down the sidelines, then pulls off the bobcat head to yell at someone in the bleachers. *Rooster Boy*. I groan out loud.

People of all ages laugh and talk on the bleachers, wander around the sidelines, and visit with one another at the booths. All so at ease, so familiar with one another. My stomach wobbles. How will I ever feel like I belong in this little town where everyone else seems to have known one another all of their lives? In the cities I've lived in before, the schools were full of unknowns—outcasts, or other transplants like me, just passing through.

"Millicent!" a shrill voice calls, and I turn to see a tall, skinny woman in jeans, a Bobcat T-shirt, and tennis shoes waving frantically at us from beside a card table. The table is decorated with black crepe paper that flutters in the breeze. "Millicent Moon!"

"Della?" Mom calls back.

She nods. "Della Shroeder. We spoke on the phone?"

"Oh, look what you've done!" Mom exclaims, guiding Papa Dan toward the grinning woman. I follow, mortified by what I see. A little boy and girl dressed in torn black clothing stand next to Della Shroeder. Their eyes are smudged black with makeup, and red lipstick is smeared on their faces to simulate blood. Mom sets her box on the table and says, "Well, hello, little zombies!" Della and Mom shake hands. "You've gone to so much trouble," my mother says. "This is so creative. I love it!"

"No trouble at all," says Della. Indicating the zombies, she says, "These are my twins, Lacy and Luke."

Mom introduces Papa Dan and me, then settles my grandfather in one of two folding chairs on the opposite side of the card table. I open a box and begin setting books next to a bouquet of black and gray carnations as fast as I can, ready to go off on my own before anyone my age wanders by and sees the whole lame setup. After we finish arranging the display, I stack the empty boxes under the table, then catch Mom's eye from where she stands talking to a group of ladies. I lift my camera, and she nods.

In the past few months, I've noticed that Papa Dan seems uncomfortable around large groups of people. But his foot taps to the band music now, and he appears content sitting with Mom and watching the activity on the field, so I climb the bleachers toward the press box. I pass Mr. Quattlebaum sitting with three other elderly men, eating orange sugar cookies and drinking lemonade from clear plastic cups. He tips his stained John Deere hat when I pass by, says, "Howdy-doody, young lady." I say hi back and smile, and the other old men grin at me and call out greetings. One of them says my great-grandmother Piper used to babysit him, and he remembered "looking up" to Papa Dan, who was a teenager.

The upper third of the stands is empty. I make it to the press box and sit on the low cement wall alongside it, above the top bleacher bench. I can see everything—the band on the field, the cheerleaders and Rooster Boy on the opposite sideline, the townspeople milling about. When I look straight down and use my zoom, I see Mom and Papa Dan from behind. The gaudy black booth has attracted a small crowd. I recognize some of the group—stone-faced Mrs. Quattlebaum, Reagan from the grocery store, Della Shroeder and her zombie twins, J. B. the pharmacist and Mary Jane—who didn't even contact me today about my pictures. I felt funny calling her on a Sunday, so I didn't. The truth is, I was a little afraid of seeing the photos, anyway, so I put it off. I'm still afraid. Or more like freaked out, I guess. I'll go by City Drug after school tomorrow, first thing, and pick them up. Might as well find out the truth about what I saw—or didn't see—in that mulberry tree, one way or the other.

Aiming the camera randomly from the field to the sidelines to the bleachers across the way, I shoot pictures quickly—band members marching, Rooster Boy strutting, cheerleaders bumping and grinding. A father chasing a toddler away from the field; families cheering in the stands. I shift again to Mom's booth. Sheriff Ray Don Dilworth is there now, too.

It's only then that I tune in to an argument going on a few feet behind me, on the other side of the press box. Two male voices—one older, the other young. "We've already talked this to death," the older man says. "Get your butt over to that grocery store and join your team. You're suited up and ready to go. Now get out of here."

"Dad, I—"

"Don't argue with me, Tate. I thought we decided—"

"*You* decided. I just gave in, like always. I'm not you. I don't want to play football this year. I want to—"

"Waste your time on a bunch of nonsense? Give up the sure bet of a football scholarship for the slim chance you might win a stupid contest?"

"It's not a contest, Dad, it's—"

"Do you want to go to college or don't you?"

"If I win, it'll help pay tuition."

"*If* you win," the father says with a dismissive huff.

"If Mom were here—"

"Well, she isn't. *I* am. As long as you're living under my roof, you listen to *me*."

"Forget it," the guy says in a clipped, defeated voice. After a long pause, he says, "It's too late for me to catch the team, anyway. Here they come."

A roaring cheer rises up from below me, and I glance down to see football players in uniform rushing onto the field, each one carrying a watermelon. "Ohmygosh," I murmur. Some of the players haul the melon cupped in one arm as they run; others cradle it with both arms. A few show-offs shoulder the fruit, holding it in place with one hand.

The man behind the press box yells something at his son, but I can't make out the words over the voice on the loudspeaker. *"Ladies and gentleman . . . ,"* it booms, *"the Cedar Canyon High School fighting Bobcats have arrived!"* The band begins a rousing chorus of the school song. People in the stands and on the sidelines lift their hands above their heads along with the cheerleaders, moving their arms left to right with the music and singing. The players deposit their watermelons into a pile on the grass at the edge of the field.

I take shot after shot, moving quickly, but my mind is on the quarrel I overheard between the guy named Tate and his selfish father. *Good for you, Tate,* I think. *Good for you for not giving in this time. For standing up for yourself.*

The band plays a second song as the football players

88

form a single line. The crowd claps to the beat of the music. The cheerleaders prance. Rooster Boy in his cat uniform pulls a small, round melon from the pile, then tries to drop-kick it toward the goal. The melon makes a short, sharp arc into the air before falling a few feet away from him and splattering onto the field, shooting red mush everywhere. Laughter erupts as he falls to the ground, grabbing his toe, and I catch myself laughing, too.

Seconds later, the band stops playing and moves to the end of the field. In the press box, the announcer begins introducing the varsity team members, and one by one they leave their line and run to the center of the stadium. *"Number seventy-three, Blaine Carter, offensive guard. Number twenty-one, Dustin Blades, fullback. Number thirteen, Cody Riddlesborough, wide receiver. Number ten, Tate Hudson, quarterback."*

Tate Hudson. I pause, zoom in closer on the quarterback. The man I heard arguing behind the press box called his son "Tate." The quarterback's helmet is off, and I recognize the golden hair, the sharp-angled face—though the last time I saw him, he didn't look so unhappy. Tate is the guy I met at the Longhorn Café our first night here. The one who was so nice to me at the salad bar. I snap his photograph, feeling bad for him and disappointed that he didn't stand his ground, after all. But I understand. Lately, I feel powerless over what happens in my own life, too.

We're pulling out of the stadium parking lot when Mom says, "Look in my purse, Tansy. The lady who works at the pharmacy gave me your pictures."

"Mary Jane?" I take her purse when she hands it back between the seats.

"She apologized for not calling you earlier so that you could get them. Apparently she got in late yesterday, and she's been busy today. It slipped her mind."

I turn on the overhead light, find the photo envelope, and shuffle through pictures of our house, the land around it, Papa Dan at the windmill, until I find the one I want. The photo is in full color as it should be, since my camera was loaded with color film. Papa Dan peers up into the mulberry tree—not some boy dressed like he's out of the past. And no phantom sits on the tree bough, either.

Switching off the light, I sit back in my seat. The fact that everything about the picture appears normal makes me queasy instead of relieved; weak in the knees, scattered, and unsteady. I tuck the photos into the envelope, confused and unsure what to think.

When we get home, I go straight to my room. Tossing the envelope onto my bed, I head for my closet, slide hangers across the metal bar, trying to push thoughts of the photograph out of my mind so I can decide what to wear to school in the morning. I don't want to call too much attention to myself, though I'm pretty sure there's no escaping it, no matter what I choose. I decide on my newest pair of jeans, a dark purple T-shirt, and my plaid Converse sneakers with the yellow laces. From an overhead shelf, I grab one of Papa Dan's berets. Probably a big mistake, I know, but I can't help myself. I didn't wear a hat tonight, and I felt a little lost without it. I have to be me, and wearing my grandfather's hat will be the next best thing to having him with me.

Satisfied, I hang the clothes on my closet door and put the beret on the dresser, wondering if Tate will like it as much as he did the fedora. Asking myself why I even care, I gather Henry's treasures and the envelope of photographs and take them up to the turret. Flipping on the overhead light, I stand in the middle of the room. The scent of fresh paint hangs heavy in the air. Mom and I made good progress up here today.

The turret has three windows: One overlooks the front yard; a second one, the back of the house, the storm cellar, and the field beyond; the third overlooks the mulberry tree and the Quattlebaum farm. I wonder if the old couple sees the glow from the window up here, if they're freaked out over at their farmhouse, thinking Henry's ghost is in the turret playing his violin.

I walk to the second window, sit on the sill, and place Henry's treasures and the photo envelope beside me. Lifting the crystal, I turn it left then right, hoping the cut glass might catch the overhead light and scatter colored dots across the walls like it did in the cellar. When it doesn't, I set it down and open the pocket watch. The hands are stopped at 12:22, the same time they showed when I first found the watch. Strange. I remember setting the timepiece to the correct time and winding it. I lay the watch on the sill alongside the crystal and the photographs.

My thoughts drift to school, to the Watermelon Run, to Tate and his father. I feel tugged one way and then another. I hate being alone, but why try to make friends when I'll be leaving soon? Besides, the idea of trying to fit in with the kids here makes me sick to my stomach. They all seem so tightly bound to one another, I doubt there'd be room for me, even if I wanted into their space. And, thanks to Hailey and Colin, I don't trust friendships anymore. How can I be sure who's real and who isn't?

I touch Henry's watch and wonder about Cedar Canyon High. What's it like beneath that red tile roof? Behind those old brick walls with their curlicue trim? Beyond the arched marble columns and the heavy double doors? I guess it doesn't matter. I've had a lot of experience being the new girl at school. I know the routine. *Pretend not to care what they think. Smile, but only if someone smiles at you first. Blend in the best you can.* I hope Tate is in some of my classes. At least he'll be a friendly face. A sexy one, too.

Only a sliver of moon shines tonight—a toenail moon, Papa Dan used to call it. Henry's journal lies in my lap. I run a finger along the leather binding and peer into the night. My breath catches when I see someone standing beside the storm cellar, looking up at the turret window. At me. Pushing to my feet, I press my hands against the window and look closer, but the person moves quickly out of sight. I step to the side of the window, too, take a deep breath and hold it, risk another peek. Shadows have swallowed the person I saw or *think* I saw.

Trembling, I turn away from the window, sit on the floor, open Henry's journal to the page I've marked with a ribbon, and read. . . .

Clock is ticking,
Ticking, tricking
Night to day and day to night
Sun is rising,
I'm despising
Pain ahead, the same old fight
Footsteps clicking,
Children kicking
Stones along the rotting walk
Laughter pealing,
I am feeling
Eyes that follow, words that stalk

Leaves are falling,
Someone's calling
Someone's name: could it be mine?
Lies are spreading,
I am dreading
Empty smiles, the same old lines

I am fading,
Dissipating,
They can't see me, they don't know

I am ending
Breaking, blending,
Soon, so soon now, I will go

Clock is ticking,
Ticking, tricking
Night to day and day to night
Moon is rising,
No disguising,
Darkness brings a whole new light

Darkness. I turn to look out the window again. Henry once sat here, too; I sense it. Watching the night and searching for something . . . or someone . . . in the shadows.

Outside the window, the insomniac bird begins its nightly serenade, his lonely song more faint than usual since the windows up here are closed. I take out the color snapshots again. On top is the picture of Papa Dan beside the mulberry tree, squinting up through the thick lenses of his glasses at the leafy green branches. Was Henry the phantom image I *know* I saw in the mulberry tree, even though it doesn't show up in the photo? Or is he the boy I saw peering up at the branches? Was it Henry I saw a moment ago in the shadows outside, staring up at me?

After studying the snapshot a long time, I lay it aside and pick up Henry's pocket watch, close it, trace the engraving on the back with my thumb. I wrap my fingers tightly around it and lift the crystal with my other hand for a closer look. The cut glass catches the overhead light, releasing a shimmering prism of radiance that reflects off the shiny surface of the picture with the same luminous intensity as the sunbeam that touched Papa Dan by the windmill.

The image in the photograph shimmers, shifts, fades to black-and-white. My hand trembles, and I drop the crystal as the scene in the snapshot broadens and surrounds me . . .

. . . *I stand in snow across from the still figure of the guy looking into the tree. His squinting eyes are exactly like my grandfather's, his face like photographs I've seen of Papa Dan as a boy. A sparrow hangs motionless above his head.*

Henry's pocket watch presses against my palm. I spread my fingers, and the cover pops open. The hands have moved to 8:15.

Thump, thump. Thump, thump. Thump, thump.

My heartbeat is the only sound I hear. No wind blows, but the air is so cold that goose bumps scatter up my arms. I exhale, and a white puff of breath suspends in front of my face like a tiny, low-hanging cloud. I step closer to the tree where the phantom guy sits as still as a doll upon a gnarled, barren branch, his black button eyes staring down at me. His face is no longer blurred. Startled by his resemblance to Tate Hudson, I back up, whirl around, come face-to-face with the teenaged version of Papa Dan. Hysteria spirals up inside of me, twisting like a tornado, swelling. I reach my hand toward my boyish grandfather but stop short of touching his face.

Thump, thump. Thump, thump. Thump, thump.

The house looms in front of me, the paint no longer chipped and peeling. I tilt my head back to look up at the turret, feel dizzy, and close my eyes—

"Tansy!" Mom calls from somewhere far off, and I feel myself sucked back into the turret. "Hailey's on my cell phone. She said you haven't been answering yours."

Opening my eyes, I jump to my feet, but my knees feel like putty, so I immediately sink to the floor and prop my elbows on my knees. Shivering uncontrollably, I cover my face with my hands and surrender to a bone-deep chill. "Ohmygod, ohmygod," I whisper, rocking back and forth. *What just happened?* The air in the room is still, but a cold wind swirls inside me, murmuring an answer that I can't hear.

"Tansy?" Mom yells louder. "Hailey—"

"Tell her I'm in the shower," I call back, my voice unsteady and raw. Realizing that I'm clutching Henry's watch so tight that my nails are digging into my palm, I splay my fingers to find the cover open, though I know I closed it only moments ago.

The hands on the face read 8:15.

8

At seven thirty on Monday morning, I walk beneath the center archway at the entrance to Cedar Canyon High School, down the noisy first floor hallway, and into the office.

Clock is ticking . . . ticking . . . tricking . . .

The secretary welcomes me and gives me a locker assignment, a lock, and my class schedule. We go over it together and she tells me where to find my homeroom.

I walk in and see the teacher's name, Mrs. Tilby, scrawled in red marker across the front eraser board. There are four rows of five desks, a few of them filled. Five lab tables form an L down one side and across the back of the room. I head for the empty table closest to the door, then sit and watch the Cedar Canyon Bobcats file in.

Footsteps clicking . . . clicking . . . clicking . . .

On top of having the new-girl jitters, I can't quit thinking about what happened in the turret last night and wondering if I'm going insane. Is this how Papa Dan feels?

Scared and confused and out of control? As if his mind is teasing him cruelly?

Trying to calm my nerves, I look around the room, avoiding eye contact with everyone. On the opposite wall, someone has used black paint to scrawl the words *Science*, *Matter*, *Energy*, *Atoms*, and *Observe* in big cursive letters. Colorful construction paper orbs hang from the ceiling. From prior science classes, I know they're called icosahedrons and that each one has twenty sides. The spheres hover above me, as motionless as the sparrow in the frozen world I stepped into last night. That's how it seemed—as if the crystal's radiance transported me into the photograph. Crazy.

As the bell rings, Mrs. Tilby walks over, carrying a box of lab equipment. She sets it on my table and says quietly, "I need this space. Would you mind moving to the back?" She motions to a lab table where a tall, thin girl sits writing in a spiral notebook with her head down. Her long, dark hair gleams beneath the fluorescent lights and falls forward to hide her face. All the desks are full now, so I make my way to her table.

Textbooks are stacked on the tabletop opposite the girl so I lay my backpack on the floor next to the stool beside her. The moment I sit, she says, "Hi." I smile and turn to her, my heart dipping when I realize it's Shanna, and that she isn't talking to me but to Tate, who is approaching us. I smile again—at him this time—but he doesn't smile back. I avert my gaze quickly, wondering what's changed since the other night at the Longhorn Café. Was he just pretending to be friendly to the weird new girl on a dare or something? Mad at myself for being such a dope, I grab my backpack, and take out a notebook and a pen.

Tate sits across from us, pushing a stack of books on the table aside to make room for his backpack. "What's up, Shanna?" he asks, but I feel his gaze on me. I glance up to find his blue eyes narrowed and brooding, just like the phantom guy's black eyes last night. I must have fallen asleep in the turret; I must have been dreaming. Why else would Tate and the ghost look alike? I had Tate on my mind after hearing him argue with his father at the Watermelon Run; that's the only explanation that makes sense.

"You haven't been hanging out with anybody much lately," Shanna says, her smile seeping into her voice. "How come?"

Tate shrugs. "No reason."

Shanna wears dark eyeliner and too much mascara. She doesn't spare me a glance; she's too busy staring at Tate with a dopey grin on her face. I can't blame her. Even though I pretended otherwise to Mom, Tate might possibly be the hottest guy I've ever seen. Not perfect or pretty. Not even handsome, really. He's . . . startling. Imposing, my mother would say; an oak tree in a mesquite-dotted field. He is definitely the most interesting guy I've spotted so far at Cedar Canyon High School. Which isn't saying much, since in a school this size, there aren't many guys to choose from, hot or otherwise.

As the principal welcomes us to a new school year over the intercom, then begins reading announcements, Rooster Boy walks in wearing diarrhea green high-top sneakers and a T-shirt with some old dead rock star on front. Damp curly hair falls into his eyes. "Sorry," he says, nodding at the teacher. "Couldn't find any clean undies this morning." Everyone laughs except Mrs. Tilby.

"Take a seat, Mr. Jenks," she says.

He heads for the empty stool next to Tate, and I add one more reason why this morning sucks to an already long list. "Hey! Zombie Girl," he whispers, shooting a blast of heat up my neck. Ignoring him, I start writing in my notebook, making an inventory of supplies I need for my darkroom. Anything to make me look busy. Since I'm not cooperating with Rooster Boy's antics, he makes kissing noises at Shanna. She looks up from the note she's writing to give him a stop-it-or-die glare.

The principal talks on and on while Mrs. Tilby unloads lab slides and beakers onto the table up front. Quiet laughter drifts on the air like a breeze. I pretend to concentrate on my list while sneaking peeks at Shanna's note to someone named "Beeyotch." Ironic, since I've been thinking that name would suit Shanna perfectly.

Where were you before school? Shanna's note asks. *Emily and I looked for you in the parking lot. We were so nervous about walking into the building that we had to sneak an early-morning beer in Em's car to calm our nerves.*

That surprises me. Not the beer so much but the

nervous part. Shanna doesn't seem the type. I wonder if "Beeyotch" is Straight-A Alison. Would she risk her goody-two-shoes reputation by drinking beer in the morning? Or any other time? She looks too sweet to be real, but I think she has a lot of people fooled. Especially the adults in this town, if Mary Jane and J. B. are any indication. I might've fallen for her pious act, too, if I hadn't caught her, Shanna, and Rooster Boy making fun of me at the Longhorn Café, if I hadn't heard Shanna's disgusted comments about Papa Dan. And they all laughed at him when we were at City Drug. As bad as Shanna and Rooster Boy are, though, at least they don't pretend to be something they aren't. Alison is like Hailey—a fake. Must be exhausting to put on an act all the time, to try to look perfect.

On the intercom, the principal asks us to stand and say the Pledge of Allegiance, and after we do, we have a minute of silence. Must be one of those small-town traditions Mom was talking about. Except in elementary school, I've never been required to recite the Pledge in any of the other places I've lived. And the silent thing is definitely a first.

Mrs. Tilby calls roll, and when she says my name, I answer, "Here."

She looks up from her attendance book. Finally some attention. Lucky me. "You're the young lady from California?"

"Yes," I say, and every gaze in the room darts in my direction.

She taps her pencil against the earpiece of her glasses. "Welcome to Texas," she says. Her smile is like plastic wrap, thin and transparent. Pointing the pencil at my head, she adds, "We don't allow hats in the classroom."

The heat in my cheeks spreads up to my forehead. Serenaded by snorts, snickers, and whispers, I pull off the beret.

Laughter pealing, I am feeling eyes that follow, words that stalk.

I cram the hat inside my backpack, and throughout the rest of roll call, stare over Mrs. Tilby's head at a narrow strip of poster paper attached on the wall above the eraser board that reads: *The Important Thing Is to Not Stop Questioning.— Einstein.*

Questions. All at once, they flood my mind. Was what happened last night a dream, even though it didn't seem like one? Or is Henry haunting our house . . . haunting Papa Dan and me? Is he the phantom in the mulberry tree? I think of the young image of Papa Dan staring up at him through the branches. Were he and Henry friends when they were young? Enemies? What does my grandfather remember that has him so upset?

Another bell rings. Stools scrape the floor, voices rise, and a minor stampede ensues as everyone heads for first period. I push away from the table and stand, aware that two sets of eyes are watching me. "Zom-bie Girl-y," Rooster Boy says in a singsong voice. He extends both arms out in front of him and walks stiff-legged into the hallway.

I dart a glance at Tate. Something in his stare bothers me more than Rooster Boy's teasing. Is distrust what I see in his eyes? Or is he pissed off at me? Either option is totally bizarre, since we don't even know each other. My stomach clenches as I start for the door. I've dealt with plenty of Rooster Boys in plenty of towns. But I don't know how to deal with what I see in Tate Hudson's moody blue eyes.

Clock is ticking . . . ticking . . . tricking . . .

In the school's hallways it's easy to disappear. I'm just another body hurrying along, which should relieve me, but it doesn't.

They travel in groups.

I travel alone.

They call out to one another, laugh together.

I move quietly, unknown, unnoticed.

They exist.

I am fading, dissipating; they can't see me; they don't know. . . .

I'm not sure what I want anymore. I hate being watched, laughed at, and whispered about. But maybe it's worse not to be seen at all, passed by as if I'm invisible. Is that what happened when I held Henry's crystal over the photograph? Did I fade from this world, scatter to dust, then reappear in the picture?

My beret flattened my short hair. I want to try to make it look halfway decent before my first-period class starts, so I head for the restroom. I open the door in time to hear someone say, "—and her disgusting hats are so unbelievably lame."

Stepping inside, I see two girls standing at the sinks with their backs to me. Straight-A Alison and Beer-for-Breakfast Shanna. Shanna is distracted by her own image as she applies even more mascara to her already clotted lashes, but Alison sees me in the mirror. Before she can jab her friend with an elbow to shut her up, Shanna continues, "I heard she's one of those West Coast whack jobs who only eat green stuff."

The elbow works. Shanna's gaze shoots up to mine in the mirror as Alison swivels around to face me, wearing a guilty smile. A whisper weaves through my mind. . . . *Lies are spreading, I am dreading empty smiles, the same old lines.*

Alison looks so pretty, so Betty Crocker cake mix wholesome and fresh, like she got a full eight hours of sleep last night instead of tossing and turning like I did. She wears a crisp white sleeveless blouse, sky blue denim capris, silver sandals. Her pale hair falls in soft, gentle waves to her shoulders.

A toilet flushes. Moving past Alison and Shanna to escape into a stall, I run into someone. Or, to be exact, she runs into me. My backpack falls from my hands and lands upside down on the floor, scattering the contents.

"Ohmygosh," a voice screeches. "Oh, geez. Darn and double darn."

I'm only five feet four inches tall, but the girl in front of me barely reaches my shoulders in height. Her clothes are too big for her stumpy frame, and she's stepping on the hem of her pants in back. One look at her thin, straight, mouse-brown hair, pulled back at the sides with little-girl barrettes, and I'm sure she cuts her bangs like Mom says my grandmother used to cut hers—with Scotch tape and sewing scissors. They're straight across and blunt, with a jagged spot in the center. The girl drops to her knees on the scuffed bathroom floor and crawls on all fours, chasing a rolling tube of my lip balm.

Behind me, Alison and Shanna giggle. "Stinky!" Shanna exclaims. "Did you just use a curse word? Shame on you. What would your mother say?"

Kneeling, I begin scooping my stuff into my backpack. The strange little girl is in a stall now, still in pursuit of the fleeing tube of lip balm. Considering where it's been, I'm not so sure I want it anymore. "O villain, villain, smiling, damned villain!" she shrieks.

Shanna rolls her eyes and mutters, "What a whack job."

"You okay?" Alison asks me quietly, but I detect a smothered laugh in her voice.

"I'm fine." Keeping my head lowered, I push to my feet. Alison hands me my comb, and I stuff it into my backpack.

"Let's go," Shanna says with a groan. "We're going to be late."

"'Bye," Alison murmurs over the noise that floods in from the hallway as she and Shanna push through the door and leave.

"Gotcha!" Stinky calls from the stall. She crawls out, sits back on her heels, and lifts the tube up in front of her for me to see. Her grin spreads wide, exposing a mouth full of red, white, and blue braces. I take the tube from her and, holding it with the tips of two fingers, give it a quick rinse in the sink before returning it to my backpack.

The girl stands, swiping at the knees of her baggy pants. "Sorry for the run-in," she says. "I was in a hurry. Don't want to be late to classes on the very first day." When the bell rings, she makes a face, then grabs a huge pink book bag from beneath one of the sinks. "Well . . . I go, and it is done; the bell invites me. Hear it not, Tansy Piper, for it is a knell that summons thee to heaven or to hell."

I'm not about to encourage more conversation by asking how she knows my name. Managing a quick look into the mirror, I start for the door. My hair is even worse than I thought—smashed so flat it looks like a dark, frayed cap—but there's no time for repairs. I run my fingers through the short locks quickly and leave it at that.

The girl follows me out, her short legs hurrying to match my long strides. "That's Shakespeare, in case you didn't know. William. From *Macbeth*." When I don't respond, she adds, "I'm Bethyl Ann Pugh. Better known as Stinky Pugh to the natives."

"And that doesn't bother you? Being made fun of by a bunch of jerks?"

"I hold the world but as the world, Tansy Piper, a stage where every man must play a part. And mine a sad one." She sighs dramatically and shrugs. "Shakespeare again. *The Merchant of Venice*."

106

"Which means?"

"It means Stinky Pugh is my part right now. But one day the roles will change." She grins. "Not to boast, but I have a genius IQ."

"That's random," I say, glancing at her.

"Well, I said it to point out that there'll probably come a time when some of those jerks will call me *Miss* Stinky Pugh as I'm signing their paychecks."

Not slowing down, I say, "No wonder you have such a great attitude. Miss Stinky Pugh is a huge improvement."

Bethyl Ann drags her book bag behind her on the floor as she hurries along. "I'm a sophomore this year." She holds up one hand, as if to stop me from interrupting. "I know what you're thinking. I don't look old enough. I bypassed second grade, then sixth."

"Which makes you what? Fourteen?"

"Thirteen, actually. Until my birthday next month." She falls behind me, skips once, twice, then she's at my side again. "Enough about me. You are—"

"Tansy." I scan the numbers over each door along the hallway.

"Piper, I know. Daughter of author Millicent Moon. *Tears of Blood* deserved a Bram Stoker Award, in my opinion. To this day, the scent of roses makes me shudder."

I speed up, afraid she's going to start quoting Edgar Allan Poe.

Bethyl Ann jogs to catch me. "My mom is the local librarian, and I archive the town newspaper for her every summer. Sometimes I read back issues. The really old ones can be quite informative, if you dig through all the garbage about potluck suppers and who came to visit the natives on the Fourth of July. I know a lot of things no one else does." She stumbles on the hem of her pants, then rights herself. "You'd be surprised."

I'm relieved to see 121 above the next door. Finally I can be free of Bethyl Ann and her random information. She's the friendliest person I've met but annoying, too. If there's anything I don't need, it's the eccentric thirteen-year-old brain everyone calls "Stinky" trying to be my best friend.

At the door, I manage a small smile for Bethyl Ann. Yeah, I wish she would go back to middle school, but I sort of feel sorry for her, too. "Here's my English class," I say.

Bethyl Ann pulls her schedule out of the pink book bag and looks at it. "Oh, super! Mine, too." She flashes her red, white, and blues. "Lucky us. Want to sit together?"

"I thought you were a sophomore? What are you doing in a junior English class?"

"Blowing the curve," Bethyl Ann says with a sniff.

I enter the classroom to find the teacher hugging Alison and gushing, "I was just so proud of you when I heard you spent the summer volunteering at the hospital in Amarillo."

Beside me, Stinky coughs and the teacher glances up. Silence falls over the room, like someone unplugged a blaring television. At least twenty pairs of eyes aim our way.

Bethyl Ann leans close to me and whispers, "Asses are

made to bear, Tansy Piper. Shakespeare again. *The Taming of the Shrew.*"

I stifle a laugh. Bethyl Ann is weirdly funny. But then I see Tate Hudson sitting at a desk by the window, and my sense of humor evaporates. His eyes pierce me, and not in a good way. I flash back to his frozen twin in the mulberry tree and shudder.

Two empty desks sit side by side in the front row. The teacher nods us toward them. I draw a deep breath. *Yeah, Bethyl Ann. You and me? We're the luckiest girls alive.*

Clock is ticking . . . ticking . . . tricking . . .

I was too jittery to eat breakfast before school, and by lunchtime my stomach is so empty that it hurts. Most of the kids my age are heading out the front doors, but I don't have anywhere to go and wouldn't eat alone in a restaurant, anyway. So I dump my backpack at my locker and follow the stay-behinds out a side exit and across the street to the cafeteria, wishing I could forget Henry's words for a while. It's eerie hearing a dead guy in your mind and freaky how his poem from last night seems to be talking about my morning today.

I enter the foyer and walk toward the open double doors leading into the lunchroom. Voices and laughter pour out of those doors, making me freeze beneath the entrance. My mind spins back to other cafeterias on other first days at new schools. I'm not ready to do this. Nothing's more totally embarrassing than eating alone.

A tray hits the floor. Startled, I back out into the hallway. Forget this. I'll spend the lunch hour in the library. It's not like I'm all that hungry, anyway. Not anymore.

When I smell the yeasty aroma of warm bread, my growling stomach forces me to admit that I'm lying to myself. Not hungry? Yeah, right; I'm starved. I've got to face everyone sometime. It's not like I haven't survived this sort of scene before. I return to the open doorway, ready to walk inside and fill my tray. But then my gaze settles on Bethyl Ann. She's sitting alone at the end of a table, reading a book and nibbling on a sandwich, a paper sack folded in front of her. I turn around fast and walk out. She's an odd girl, but she was nice to me, too. I should sit with her. I know I should, but I can't do it.

As I walk out of the building and across the street, I try to look as if I'm in a rush, as if I have somewhere important to be. I enter the high school and hurry down the hall to my locker to get my backpack. Seconds later, I glance over my shoulder before ducking inside the library, then cut across to the farthest cubicle from the door, the one in the very back corner. I shouldn't miss Hailey after what she did, but I do. Or maybe it's just having a friend that I miss. I almost wish I had taken her phone call last night. I ache to tell someone about Henry and all the strange things that have happened since we moved here, about my suspicions that he's reaching out to me through his poems. Someone other than Mom who won't worry themselves sick about me. But there isn't anyone. My days of talking to Hailey are over, and Papa Dan is lost to me now.

I take my spiral notebook from my backpack and stare down at the instructions for the assignment that my English teacher, Miss Petra, already dumped on us. *Write a story from the viewpoint of one character. Three pages double spaced.* The words swim through a blur of tears. Did Henry eat alone in the cafeteria? Or did he sneak away at lunch to hide? Did his classmates humiliate him? Ignore him when they passed him in the hallway?

Terrified I'll start sobbing if I sit here a minute longer, I gather my things and leave the library as quickly as I entered it. I hurry down the deserted hall to my locker again, use the combination to open the lock, then trade my backpack for my camera. I brought it today to take photos after school, since Mom isn't picking me up until four. Exiting the building, I walk toward the corner.

The elementary school sits up ahead across the street. Children stroll in a line down the sidewalk, making their way toward the playground. One little girl calls out to another, making me think of Hailey again. The girls' laughter floats to me on a breeze that rustles the tree branches overhead.

Leaves are falling, someone's calling someone's name: could it be mine?

Snoopy, pregnant Mary Jane from City Drug waddles at the head of the line of children; she must volunteer in one of her kids' classrooms. Today she wears a red-and-yellow-striped smock that makes her look like a hot-air balloon. She tilts her head back, wiggles her hips, and, waving her hands out in front of her, starts to sing. . . .

> *Peanut, peanut butter*
> *And Jelly*
> *Peanut, peanut butter*
> *And Jelly*

Pausing, I lift my camera and focus on Mary Jane and the children. After snapping several pictures, I continue to the corner, turn, and circle around to the back of the school to the tennis courts, surprised when I spot Bethyl Ann sitting at the bottom of the metal bleachers. She must've left the cafeteria while I was in the library. She feeds a skinny cocker spaniel from a sack in her lap. The dog's tail sweeps the ground like a broom.

A fist clenches inside my chest. How can she look so happy? Bethyl Ann Pugh has a horrible name, bad clothes, and even worse hair. She's a lot younger than everyone else in her class but twice as smart. As far as I can tell, she doesn't have a single friend.

I aim the camera to take her photograph, and through the viewfinder, I watch her stroke the spaniel's head and offer it another bite of food. The dog licks her fingers then barks. Bethyl Ann giggles.

At once, I realize I'm wrong about this girl. Bethyl Ann isn't only book smart, she's wise in other ways, too. A lot wiser than me, that's for sure.

She chose a friend who will never hurt her.

9

I leave campus at noon the next day with my camera. Cedar Canyon is so small that the walk to Main Street and back only takes twenty minutes, and that's walking against the wind and sticking to side streets to avoid mixing with other kids headed for the handful of restaurants in town. Along the way, I snap photos of buildings. Houses. A plant nursery with dead flowers and bushes out front. An out-of-business gas station with boarded-up windows and *gone fishing permanently* scrawled in red paint across the planks.

On Wednesday during lunch break, I take pictures of people. A painter on a ladder in front of a worn-out house, trying to convince a skeptical woman that chartreuse would be a good color. Sheriff Ray Don leading an escaped cow down a residential street. A young mother and her giggling toddler shampooing a dog in a plastic swimming pool.

I arrive home after school each day to the smell of fresh paint. The handyman, whose name is Bill, replaced the warped boards on the porch first thing, then moved inside.

While Mom works on her book, rearranges the furniture for the millionth time, unpacks another box, or drives Bill crazy with instructions, I organize my bedroom and continue setting up a darkroom in the turret, working only while daylight streams in through the windows. After the freaky incident with the crystal, I'm afraid to be alone up there when it's dark. I guess I could have Papa Dan sit with me while I work, but who knows what might happen? I don't want to take the chance of something upsetting him.

When Mom and I were putting together Papa Dan's shop, we found a purple velvet chair and a round claw-footed side table in the barn. I move them into the turret and place them next to one window. Henry's treasures fit nicely inside the table's curved center drawer. Mom might find Henry's things if I leave them in my bedroom, but I doubt she'll come into my darkroom often, if at all. I still don't want her to know about the artifacts. More than ever before, they've become a secret Henry and I share.

By dinnertime on Wednesday night, the interior of the house looks fresh and bright, thanks to Bill's hard work, and my darkroom is almost ready, thanks to *my* hard work. I need to cover the windows with black plastic trash bags to block out any light, and then I'll be set. I make a mental note to buy some when I'm in town. Then all I need to do is get up my nerve to be alone in the turret in the dark.

The next day, I walk to City Drug during my lunch break to buy the trash bags and some school supplies. Turning onto Main, I hesitate. People cluster on the sidewalks, and cars fill every parking place. Taking a deep breath, I jaywalk across the street, headed for the pharmacy, garnering a few glances, a few hellos, and more waves than I can count.

A huge pot of dark orange mums sits at one side of the entrance. I push through the door. Inside, every stool and booth in the soda-fountain section on the left of the store is full. The place pulsates with conversation. A woman about Mom's age waits tables, scurrying back and forth across the black-and-white checkerboard floor. A young guy fills orders behind the bar. It looks like a fun place lifted straight out of a decade when girls wore bobby socks and guys raced hot rods. And it only makes me feel more out of place.

On the other side of the store, separated from the soda fountain by aisles of merchandise, J. B. stands behind a tall counter filling prescriptions for an elderly couple.

"Hi, Tansy," Mary Jane calls out from behind the front register. "You here to eat?"

"No, I need to pick up some trash bags and permanent markers."

"School supplies are on aisle two," she says. "The bags are at the end of aisle three, directly across from the pharmacy."

It doesn't take long to find the markers. Grabbing a box, I make my way to the back of the store. When I reach the end of aisle three, J. B. calls out a greeting. The old couple he's waiting on turn around, and I realize they're my neighbors, the Quattlebaums.

"Howdy-do, young lady," the old man says, and his wife

nods, her face as grim as ever.

"Hi, Mr. Quattlebaum . . . Mrs. Quattlebaum."

I turn and search the aisle endcap for the plastic bags as J. B. comes around the prescription counter and hands Mr. Quattlebaum a sack. "So what did you think of the Watermelon Run?" he asks me, putting an arm around Mr. Quattlebaum's shoulder.

"It was different," I say. Locating the bags, I grab a box.

J. B. laughs as we all start up front together. "Not something you see in San Francisco, I bet. Your mom was quite the celebrity."

We pause at the register, and Mr. Quattlebaum hands some money to Mary Jane. Shifting his attention to me, he says, "Myra bought a copy of that zombie book. I finished reading the thing last night." He shakes his head. "Good lord, where does your mama come up with that stuff?"

Mary Jane gives him his change, then rings up my purchases while they discuss the strange workings of my mother's mind.

"Now, here comes someone who would probably love to meet your mom, Tansy," J. B. says. He nods toward the soda fountain and smiles.

I turn, and my heart does a swan dive when I see Tate Hudson approaching. I've been completely ignoring him at school. I have enough to worry about, without obsessing over what I might've done to make him so angry.

But I can't disregard him now. Not with J. B. standing next to me and calling him over to join us. Besides, Tate looks too good in well-worn jeans and a white button-down shirt with tiny blue stripes. His stride is long and unhurried, and he seems so sure of himself. I wish I didn't love the way his hair falls over his forehead so much. Or the way he jams his hands into his pockets as he pauses beside the pharmacist. His sleeves are rolled up to his elbows, exposing tan forearms sprinkled with tiny gold hairs. And I'm pathetic to notice such things. I should only pay attention to the complete disinterest in his eyes when he looks at me. Because of that, none of the rest of it matters.

"Have you two met?" J. B. asks, glancing between us.

"Sort of," Tate murmurs, capturing my gaze, and for once not looking away.

Quietly, I add, "We have a couple of classes together."

J. B. gives Tate a friendly slap on the back. "Did he happen to mention he's one heck of a writer?" Tate cringes and looks down at the floor. "Well, you are," J. B. says, chuckling. "Tate was chosen to go with a group from the Panhandle to a national poetry event last year in Washington, DC. What was that called?"

"Brave New Voices," Tate mutters.

"The International Youth Poetry Slam Festival?" I ask.

Tate's surprised eyes flick to mine again. "Yeah."

I'm impressed. Being chosen to participate in the festival is a very big deal. "A few kids from my old school went," I say.

"Tate made it to the finals," Mary Jane chimes in from behind the register.

"That's really great," I say, but Tate only shrugs.

"Tansy's mother is a published writer," Mary Jane says to him.

He nods. "I heard."

"Maybe she could give you a few pointers," she adds.

"She'll have you writin' *killer* poetry in no time flat," Mr. Quattlebaum interjects, chuckling at his joke. Beside him, Mrs. Quattlebaum surprises me by snickering.

When Tate doesn't comment, J. B. says, "Tansy has a creative streak, too. She's a photographer. Pretty accomplished, too, according to her mom. Cedar Canyon is becoming quite the artistic community all of a sudden."

I see a change in Tate's expression, a faint glimmer of interest. "I just play around with it," I say. "I haven't won an award or anything like that."

"I've seen you around town taking pictures." He stares at me a moment longer, then looks down to the camera hanging at my side.

Encouraged that he's finally speaking to me, I continue, "I want to take some shots of the canyon and that bridge I keep hearing about, but I haven't had time to go out there yet." Hoping he might offer to take me, I add, "I'm not sure where the bridge is, anyway."

"You can walk out there. It's not that far from your house."

So much for subtle hints, I think.

"Just make sure you stay on the bridge and off the railing," Mr. Quattlebaum warns, shaking his head. "Crazy damn kids climb all over that thing . . . dangling off the sides and whatnot so's they can scribble graffiti on any bare space they find."

Tate glances up at the wall clock behind Mary Jane and says, "I need to talk to Coach before class starts. See ya later."

The Quattlebaums say good-bye, too, and follow him out the door.

"What do you suppose is bothering that boy?" J. B. asks Mary Jane.

"What do *you* think? Just 'cause a kid's in high school doesn't mean he doesn't need his mom." Mary Jane glances at me, adding, "She moved away over the summer."

J. B. shakes his head. "The kids are always the hardest hit when a marriage splits up." He sends me an apologetic smile and sighs. "Tate's usually such a friendly kid. I'm sure the way he acted toward you wasn't anything personal."

I cross my arms. "It's okay. It's not your fault."

I pay Mary Jane, tell them good-bye, and step outside, pausing on the sidewalk to search the street for Tate. I don't see him, so I cross at the intersection, then turn onto a side street and head toward school. Something nags at me, and it takes me a minute to realize what it is. Not only does Tate look like the phantom in the tree—the boy I think is Henry, at least in my dreams—they both write poetry.

A block from campus, I pass an alley lined with tumbleweeds trapped by the fence. An old blue Mustang sits alongside a Dumpster, and a couple leans against the car kissing as the wind scatters leaves and litter past their feet. The guy wears coveralls—the sort mechanics pull over their clothes. He looks nineteen, maybe twenty, and his hair is pulled into a short ponytail. The girl's back is to me. Long blond hair covers the name on her Cedar Canyon High School cheerleader jacket, but I recognize her, and in an instant, the coincidence with Tate and Henry flees my mind. I can hardly believe my eyes.

I duck behind a bush, my dislike for Alison swarming inside me like bees. What is it about her that bothers me? Yes, she reminds me of Hailey. Yes, she's a phony. Yes, her friends are epic jerks. But I don't know Alison well enough to let her get to me so much.

When she and the guy stop kissing, Alison backs up a step and glances toward the street, but she doesn't spot me. I can tell by her expression that she's afraid of getting caught with this guy, of everyone discovering she's not as squeaky-clean as they think.

Then she laughs, and the sound takes me back to the times she and her friends made fun of my hat, of Papa Dan—even Bethyl Ann Pugh—and anger coils in the pit of my stomach. The guy lights a cigarette, and when he offers it to her I see a tattoo on the back of his hand. Alison shakes her head, but he prods her to take it, and she finally caves.

She lifts the cigarette to her lips.

I lift my camera.

Alison isn't Hailey. I shouldn't hate her because she

reminds me of another girl who hurt and humiliated me, who stole my almost-boyfriend and betrayed me. Even though she hasn't told her friends to back off, Alison hasn't ever said anything mean to me—I'm not even sure she laughed at me or Papa Dan; she just didn't try to stop the others.

I know it's wrong to spy on perfect Alison and her less-than-perfect boyfriend. I know it's wrong to sneak their photograph. I should just walk away.

Alison tilts her head back, blows out a stream of smoke.

I hesitate half a second, then—*click*—snap the picture. Immediately, I take two more, unaware of the gray mutt running up beside me until it barks. Alison and the guy jerk their heads toward me. I duck farther behind the bush, unsure if I escaped being seen.

Friday at noon, I find Bethyl Ann on the bleachers at the tennis courts. The truth is, I'm tired of eating by myself. And Bethyl Ann isn't threatening like the other kids.

The spaniel's tail wags when it spots me, but I doubt Bethyl Ann will be as friendly as the dog. Tate isn't the only one I've ignored all week. I wouldn't blame her if she snubbed me. On the second day of English class, I even moved to a different chair to avoid her constant chattering. I'm not proud of it, but I never claimed to be a saint, either.

Patting the dog's head, she looks up when I pause in front of her. "Oh. Hi."

I lift my lunch sack. "Mind if I eat with you?"

Her eyes widen and her scraggly brows shoot up. She scoots over and I sit beside her. Opening the sack, I remove my peanut-butter-and-jelly sandwich and offer her half.

Bethyl Ann takes the triangle and bites off a corner. "I waited for you the first day in the cafeteria. I don't usually eat there, but I thought you might need someone to sit with." She nods toward the school building. "The natives can be brutal to newcomers."

Shame rains down on me. "That was nice. I couldn't get the nerve to go in there, you know?"

"Do I ever." She pinches off a piece of the sandwich and feeds it to the dog. "It's better out here, anyway. Unlike the natives, Hamlet is civilized."

"Hamlet?"

She points at the spaniel, and I smile. We stare out at the tennis courts for a minute, chewing in silence. The breeze is gentle today, but it smells like dust with a faint whiff of cattle feed yard mixed in. "What do you do for lunch when it's cold outside?" I ask.

"Wear a coat. But it's never as cold out here as it is in the building. Not that the natives get to me anymore; I'm used to them. Sometimes I just need a break."

I pull a bag of chips from the sack and pass one to her. "Bethyl Ann—"

"Call me Stinky. Everyone does."

"I'm not going to call you that. It's a horrible name."

"You think Bethyl Ann is any better?"

She has a point. "Okay. Beth, then."

Popping a chip into her mouth, she squints at me, as if trying the name on for size. "That which they call Stinky by any other name will smell as foul," she says.

"Please." I roll my eyes. "I don't speak Shakespeare."

We continue eating in silence. The breeze rustles the sack, but the weight of the candy bar inside keeps it from blowing away. "You must miss going to school with kids your own age," I say.

"Are you kidding? Middle school was worse than this. I spent more time stuffed in my locker than I did in the classroom."

"That's terrible."

"Most of the time the kids here pretty much leave me alone. And they're a lot more interesting than the naive middle-school pubescents. Some of them are even having S-E-X." She wiggles her brows, then taps her temple with a fingertip and adds, "You'd be surprised what I've stored up here since I transferred to high school. Since I'm basically ignored, it's easy to accumulate blackmail material without rousing suspicion."

"I could help. With the blackmail, I mean. You should see some of the pictures I've taken this week."

"Aha!" Leaning closer, she whispers, "Anyone I know?"

"You know everyone, don't you?"

"Better than they think I do."

"What do you know about Alison?"

"Alison Summers? Hmmm." I sense a sudden reluctance in Bethyl Ann as she reaches to take another chip from my bag. "Some are born great, some achieve greatness, and some have greatness thrust upon 'em," she mutters slowly.

"*Beth.*"

"Okay," she says. "Alison expects a lot from herself. She has an image to uphold."

"I've noticed." I lick jelly from the corner of my mouth. "I could blow that image."

She looks down at her lap. "I wouldn't do that to her. She's nice to me."

"Alison is your friend?"

"We don't have sleepovers or go shopping together or anything like that, but she's friendly—you know, when we're face-to-face. She usually says hi and stuff."

"Only when her friends aren't around, right?" Bethyl Ann shrugs, and I add, "If Alison is so friendly, why are you out here with Hamlet instead of inside with her?"

"As I said, Alison has an image to uphold. Nobody wants to be seen with me. Some kids even hide behind doors to avoid it."

I want to crawl beneath the bleachers and hang out with the gum wads where I belong. "Sorry about that," I mutter.

"I understand." There's a lightness to her voice, but she won't meet my eyes, and I can tell her feelings are hurt. "You're the new girl. I have an image. Alison has an image. You're trying to find yours. I'm not exactly the friend you had in mind." She sighs. "I have a perfect quote from *All's Well That Ends Well*, but for your sake, I'll refrain."

"Thanks." I shrink inside to think I have anything in

common with Alison. Ever since I caught her in the alley yesterday, I'd swear she's been looking the other way when we pass in the hallways, careful not to glance in my direction in class. Of course, I could be imagining this, due to the fact that I'm afraid she might have seen me taking her picture. Even though I don't like her, I feel a little guilty about that.

"By the way, I never said I wanted to blow Alison's image," I tell Bethyl Ann, "I just said I could." When she doesn't respond, I ask, "How about Tate Hudson? What's he like? Could you blow *his* image?"

"*Tate Hudson!*" Bethyl Ann's voice booms like a sports announcer. "Football god! Worshipped by the masses!" She scratches Hamlet's head then, in a scoffing tone, says, "He used to be really full of himself. Him and his Tate-a-licious blue eyes."

Smiling at her description of Tate's eyes, I say, "*Used* to be? What changed? His mom leaving?"

"I'm not supposed to gossip, but if you already know—"

"I heard the pharmacist and Mary Jane talking about it."

Words rush out of Bethyl Ann as fast as air from a punctured balloon. "It was right before school let out last year," she says eagerly. "That's when Tate got all quiet and moody. His older brother, Evan, was away at college and he didn't come home for the summer, so Tate was left alone with his dad."

"Why'd his mother move out of town?"

"Who knows? Mom says Mrs. Hudson has city blood."

"I can relate," I murmur.

"Tate's dad is a farmer. I can't see him living in a city."

I toss Hamlet a crust of bread. "I don't think Tate likes me."

"Yond Tate has a lean and hungry look. He thinks too much; such men are dangerous, Tansy Piper."

I groan, and one corner of her mouth curves up.

"Sorry," she says, "I can't help myself. Don't worry about Tate, though. These days, he doesn't seem to have much use for *anybody*. But I can put out my radar for you. If I hear that he has something against you, I'll let you know. That's not really gossiping, just helping out a friend, right?"

"Whatever you say." I take out the candy bar, break it apart in the center, and pass half to Bethyl Ann, wondering what she knows about Alison that she's not willing to share.

Bethyl Ann eyes the candy bar, then shakes her head and points at her braces. "Can't have peanuts," she says.

Chattering and laughter draw my attention toward the side street where Mary Jane is leading her kid's class down the sidewalk. I look at my watch. Five minutes until the bell.

"Is it spooky living in the Peterson house?" Bethyl Ann asks.

"Sometimes. In a way I like it, though."

She leans closer, a secretive smile on her face. "I went there a few times," she says quietly. "Mrs. Quattlebaum had gallbladder surgery a few weeks before you moved here. Mom and I would take casseroles to her and Mr. Quattlebaum, and while they visited, I walked over to your house. It was empty then."

"You went inside?"

Her smile falls and she shakes her head quickly, like she's afraid I'll get her into trouble. "No, just outside, but that was enough." She folds the paper sack into a square, avoiding my gaze. "No wonder everyone says it's haunted."

"Why do you say that?" I ask too quickly, leaning toward Bethyl Ann. "Did you see or hear something?" Henry's rosewood box comes to mind, and before she can answer me, I ask, "Did you *find* something?"

Eyeing me suspiciously, she asks, "Did *you*? Is that why you're so overwrought?"

I lean back, embarrassed. "I'm not overwrought. And that sounds like a word my mother would use."

She lifts her chin. "You didn't answer my question."

I shrug. "I've heard a few strange noises at night. It's an old creaky house, and the wind blows constantly."

Bethyl Ann keeps staring at me with that skeptical look on her face. I can't tell if she knows I'm keeping something from her, or if she's the one who's keeping something from me. She never answered *my* question, either.

She sits back and flattens the paper sack between her knees. "I wish I'd been around when Henry Peterson was alive," she says. "He's probably the most intriguing person who ever lived in this two-horse town."

"Intriguing?" I squint at her. "How?"

"Sometimes he hurt himself on purpose."

"What do you mean?"

She lifts a shoulder. "People say he'd get mad at his parents or somebody else and hurt himself out of spite. I've read articles about him in the library archives."

Disturbed by the rumor, I ask, "Will you show the articles to me?"

"Sure. We could walk to the library after school. I usually go see Mama, anyway."

"My mom's picking me up today. Can you meet me there in the morning?"

"Okay." She hands me the paper sack. "Is ten o'clock okay? I like to sleep in on Saturdays."

"Okay." I stand.

The bell rings. Bethyl Ann sends Hamlet off with a pat to the rump. "Come, Tansy Piper." She hooks a thumb toward the building. "Let's away to prison."

Mom makes chicken noodle soup out of a can for dinner. One of her specialties. While we eat, she talks nonstop about how much she loves small town life. She mentions that Mrs. Pugh called her today about presenting a program at the library sometime. I tell her a tiny white lie—that Mrs. Pugh's daughter and I are getting together to do research for a school project in the morning. Mom's face lights up. I'm not sure what pleases her more—the fact that I've made a friend or that I'm doing homework on a Saturday.

Maybe if she thinks Bethyl Ann and I are becoming best buds, she won't ask me about Hailey anymore. More than once, she's brought up the fact that I'm not answering

Hailey's calls, and I can hear the worry in her voice.

As I'm clearing the table, I notice that Papa Dan's soup bowl is almost full. Pausing with the bowl in my hand, I watch him follow Mom from the kitchen, startled by how thin he looks. He's lost weight in the short time we've lived here. He looks older, too. Though I ate plenty, my stomach feels hollow as I pour his meal down the disposal. The television comes on in the next room and a few moments later, Mom returns and joins me at the sink. When I mention the changes in Papa Dan, she assures me the new medication he's taking is probably the cause, adding, "Loss of appetite is one of the possible side effects."

But I'm not convinced that pills are the reason for his weight loss or anything else that's going on with him. A nagging voice in the back of my mind tells me this house has something to do with my grandfather's problems. Now, if I could only figure out why.

After dinner, I sit in the turret on the purple velvet chair. The trash bags I bought at City Drug cover the windowpanes to keep out daylight during the day, so as not to disturb the developing process. No chance of that now, anyway, since it's dark outside. I haven't been up here at night since I dreamed the crystal's beam carried me into the photograph, and I'm so antsy I can't sit still. I need to prove to myself that what I experienced *was* only a dream. I refuse to accept I'm a loony tune, and that's the only other option.

I tap my foot against the floor as I study the room. It's quiet up here. The television Papa Dan watches in the living room downstairs and the click of Mom's fingers on her laptop don't reach me. I only hear the old house's creaking joints. A soft glow cast off by the lamp brightens the tarnished gold of Henry's pocket watch, open on the round table, stopped again at 12:22. I look at the black-and-white photos I developed earlier, spread out on the floor at my feet, and rub my thumb across the crystal teardrop.

The pictures I took at the Watermelon Run are of cheerleaders jumping, Rooster Boy strutting on the sidelines in his bobcat suit, family members clapping and cheering in the stands as the football jocks rush onto the field. I look at the photo of Tate, the tense set of his jaw, his beautiful, unhappy eyes. Setting that shot aside, I look at the one of Bethyl Ann feeding Hamlet. She looks so happy, like life could not be better. I scan the image of the painter in town arguing with his client from the top of a ladder, the woman and toddler washing the dog in their yard, the line of little kids dancing behind Mary Jane, who is as big as the cow Sheriff Ray Don leads down Main Street in another photo. I pause on the next picture, the one I shot of Alison exhaling cigarette smoke, then glance at a second shot of her coughing as her boyfriend laughs.

I puff out my cheeks. How does the camera see things that I miss? All these people seem different in the pictures than they are in person. Not ominous at all. So why can't I give them a chance? Why am I so afraid?

Shifting again to the picture of Tate Hudson, I wonder for the millionth time why he's so pissy around me. Could

I remind him of someone he wants to forget, like Alison reminds me of Hailey? Deciding I'm wasting my time trying to figure out Tate, I pull the photographs I had developed in town from the table drawer. When birdsong twitters outside, I jump and glance at the rattling window, amazed any bird would be out of its nest on this blustery night. The bird has been silent lately. The last time I heard it sing was the night I had that freaky experience with the crystal. Or dreamed it.

Do it, I think. *Or you'll never know.*

My hand shakes as I pull the photograph from the envelope and lay it in my lap. I reach for Henry's pocket watch and close my fingers tightly around it. Just as before, I tilt the crystal until it catches the lamplight. Just as before, a shimmering beam extends toward the fading image on the picture . . . expands . . . surrounds me.

Suddenly I'm back in the frozen, black-and-white world of the photograph, standing beside my young grandfather, who is as still as a mannequin. The guy who resembles Tate stares down at us from where he sits above in the mulberry tree's barren branches.

Thump, thump. Thump, thump. Thump, thump.

A bell clangs, shattering my nerves and the silence. I tell myself to turn toward the Quattlebaum farmhouse, but I'm afraid. I know the man is out there, bundled up in warm clothes, a shovel in his hands. Snow. That's what he shovels; I know that now, too. There's a black dog . . . a ball . . . white smoke drifting from the man's mouth when he removes his gloves and blows on his fingers. No, not smoke . . . the cloud his breath makes when it hits the air. Because

131

it's winter and freezing outside. Everything is clear to me now—

"Tansy?"

Air moves around me in ripples . . . lake water touched by a breeze.

"Do you want to watch a movie with us?"

The air settles as I'm pulled back to the velvet chair by my mother's voice. The room is warm. I shiver. I'm afraid to answer Mom, afraid to open my eyes. Terrified of what I might see.

She knocks at the door. "Hey! Are you okay in there?"

"Just a second," I call, my throat as scratchy as if I'd swallowed sand.

I blink and look down at the photograph in my lap. Papa Dan—old, feeble, and in vivid Kodak color—squints up at tree branches heavy with leaves, like he did as a frozen boy in the surreal world I just left. The branches, though, were bare in that world, and the tree was smaller. In the dead grass at his feet, something glimmers, an object I am sure was not in the picture before. I look closer, and feel a shifting take place inside me.

The item is round and gold, the size of a gingersnap cookie.

I lower my gaze to my lap and open my hand.

Henry's pocket watch is gone.

10

"You're up early." Mom slides her sunglasses to the tip of her nose as I walk down the porch stairs the next morning. Clutching a thorny weed in her gloved hand, she crouches next to the barren flower bed that borders the front of the house. A few feet away, Papa Dan sits in a lawn chair, looking lost.

"I'm meeting Beth at the library at ten."

"Beth?"

"Bethyl Ann Pugh. The librarian's daughter. For our project, remember?"

"Oh, that's right." Sitting back on her heels, Mom wrinkles her nose. "Her name is *Bethyl Ann*? That poor girl."

"Yeah, her parents pretty much doomed her to geekhood." I tug my camera strap up to my shoulder and dart a glance toward the side of the house. After what happened last night, it wouldn't surprise me if those mannequin boys came alive and walked around the corner. I almost wish they would, so Mom would see them, too.

Mom glances at her watch. "It's a long time until ten."

"I thought I'd go into town a little early and take some photos."

"Good idea." She puts on the sunglasses again and tugs down on her straw hat when the breeze picks up. I don't have to see her eyes to know they scrutinize me from behind those dopey pointed frames. "The library on a Saturday . . . that's something new. I could get used to it."

"Don't," I say. Raising the camera, I adjust the focus. Mom strikes a pose and I snap her picture. "Can I take the van?"

"Do you think you'll be gone long?"

"I should be home by lunch."

"Okay." A strand of hair escapes her hat and blows across her eyes. "Haven't seen you wear that cap in a while. It's one of my favorites."

Papa Dan's leather newsboy cap is a favorite of mine, too. I considered giving up his hats after what happened with Mrs. Tilby but decided against it. I'm wearing them outside of school, whether people make fun of me or not. My grandfather's hats are a part of me, and now that I might be losing my mind, holding on to every other piece of myself that I can is a priority. I wonder: Did Papa Dan feel the same way? Does he still?

"Why don't you and Beth have lunch on me?" Mom asks. "My purse is in the kitchen. There's a twenty in my wallet."

Lunch in town with Bethyl Ann—just what my reputation doesn't need. But it'll be worth it if I find out more about Henry. And maybe something about Papa Dan's past, too.

Clasping my hands behind my back, I walk over to Papa Dan. "Morning," I say.

He fidgets, his fingers gripping his knees, off in his own world today. Papa Dan's expression has never been so blank, and his sudden frailness strikes me again like a slap in the face. How did my stout grandfather become so thin in such a short time?

Feeling helpless, I return my attention to Mom. "Why are you pulling weeds?"

Clods of dirt fall off her gardening gloves as she brushes her hands together. "Don't you think they need to be pulled?"

"Yes, but weeds have never fazed you before."

A horn honks, and I shift to see the Cedar Canyon Handyman Service truck turn onto our road. It's become a familiar sight, but something's different this time; I think I recognize Sheriff Ray Don in the passenger seat.

Mom waves and grins. "They're going to start painting the outside of the house."

"The sheriff paints, too?"

"He helps out sometimes. Ray is Bill's brother."

"The handyman's name is Bill *Dilworth*?" She nods, and I mutter, "That's almost as bad as Bethyl Ann."

The truck swings into the driveway and pulls to a stop beside our van. As Mom hurries over to greet the Dilworth brothers, I wander to the side of the house and inspect the grass beneath the mulberry tree. Last night after Mom and Papa Dan went to bed, I returned to the turret and searched everywhere for Henry's pocket watch. I couldn't find it. It's not out here, either; how could it be? I was holding it when I stepped through that prism of light and into the picture. That sounds absurd, I know; how could I possibly do such a thing? I couldn't, which brings me back to the insanity theory, an explanation that twists my stomach into knots. But if I'm crazy, how did the watch wind up in the picture? Was it there all along? Did I only imagine finding it in the cellar? Holding it in my hand?

A rustling in the hedge beside the house draws me over. Bracing my hands on my knees, I lean forward to peer into the bush and spot a little bird ruffling pale brown feathers. I expect it to startle at the sight of me and fly away, but instead it climbs out and hops to the top of the hedge. The bird's straight legs move restlessly. Its chestnut tail twitches. I wonder if it is the same bird I saw on my windowsill my first day here.

"Did you lose something?" Mom asks from behind me.

"Come here," I whisper, turning to motion her over. "I think I found the loudmouth that's been keeping me up at night." She pauses at my side, but when I face the hedge again, the bird is gone.

"What is it?" Mom moves closer, leans down.

"There was a bird here. We must have scared it off."

"You'd think we would've seen it fly away."

I frown. "Yeah, I know."

136

Mom steps back. "Aren't you going to say hello to the Dilworths?"

"I guess." Hoping to startle the bird from its hiding place, I shake the bush gently. No luck. I have the weirdest sense that a puzzle piece is within my reach. *Pieces*, actually, not just one. The bird. The man and dog I've seen at the Quattlebaums' farm. The scene I stepped into last night. The artifacts from the cellar. The lost watch and how it's always set to 12:22. Henry's resemblance to Tate. All clues . . . but to what?

I follow Mom up front again, where the men are unloading supplies from the bed of the truck. Lifting a hand, I yell, "Hello!" and the Dilworth brothers call back a greeting.

While Mom talks to the two of them, I go inside the house, find her purse in the kitchen, and take the money from her wallet. When I return to the yard, she's on her knees in front of the flower bed, tugging at the weeds again. "You leaving?" she asks.

"Yes." I start toward the driveway, then hesitate. "Mom?"

She drops a dandelion into the small pile of weeds at her side and glances up at me.

Words pummel my throat, the truth wanting out. Taking a breath, I push the words back. For some reason, I feel ashamed. What will Mom think if I tell her about what I've seen through the lens of my camera? About stepping into the photograph and hearing the voice in Papa Dan's room? What would she do? Would she be worried enough that she'd take me to a doctor? Maybe. I'm no expert on mental illness, but I'm pretty sure what I'm experiencing is symptomatic of schizophrenia or something worse. *Delusional.* Isn't that the label shrinks slap on whacked-out people who see and hear things that can't exist?

"Tansy, what is it?" Mom asks.

"Nothing," I say. "Never mind."

Mom tugs off a glove. "I know how upset you are about moving. I wish you'd talk to me about it."

"I'm okay."

"I was hoping for better than okay."

I walk over to her, kiss the top of her head, and step back. "I am. Better than okay, that is." I manage a smile. "Don't worry about me so much."

"Are you using that new notebook I bought for you?"

"*Mom.*" I make a face at her. As if a diary would solve anything.

Mom hesitates, then says, "Do you like it here?"

"You mean Cedar Canyon?" She nods, and I shrug. "Do *you* like it?"

Mom darts a look toward the driveway, where Sheriff Ray Don is bent over the bed of the truck. "The people are nice enough."

"What about the house? Are you happy with it?"

"Yes. Aren't you?"

"Yeah, but I just meant, you know . . . is it right for your story?"

"It's perfect, as a matter of fact. Being so isolated out

here really helps me set the atmosphere." She shakes loose dirt out of her glove, then puts it on again. "Oh! I forgot to tell you that Papa Dan and I drove to the canyon and saw the bridge yesterday. It's fantastic! If only it could tell me all its secrets. Now, *that* would be a best seller for sure."

Leave it to my mother to talk about an inanimate object as if it's a living, breathing thing. "Did Papa Dan act like he recognized it?"

"Funny that you ask that—he wouldn't get out of the van."

I search her face for clues that she might've noticed something strange out there or something even more odd about my grandfather's behavior. Maybe, like me, she's just afraid to admit it. But the sunglasses hide her eyes, and I only hear wistfulness in her tone, so I say, "Maybe I'll go out there later today."

"Tansy . . . If something's wrong at school, you'll tell me, won't you?"

I start to assure her again that everything's fine, but then the toll of a bell vibrates the morning air, making me jump. "Did you hear that?"

"What?" Mom pushes to her feet.

"A bell. Over at the Quattlebaums'."

"A bell?"

She follows me to the side of the house, where I squint across the field at our neighbors' property.

"Looks pretty quiet over there," Mom murmurs in a baffled voice.

She's right; there isn't a person in sight at the Quattlebaums' farm.

"What a pretty place," she says. "So peaceful. You should take a picture."

Murmuring, "I will," I look through the viewfinder and see the man with the shovel and the black dog running toward the barn. I know without looking at my watch that the time is 8:15. A ringing starts in my ears, and scattered pinpoints of light fill my narrowing vision. The camera feels too heavy to hold. I quickly turn away from the scene.

"Tansy?" Mom lays her hand on my arm. "You're shaking."

The truth knocks at my throat again, and for a moment I'm ready to tell Mom everything and risk having her think I'm hallucinating—maybe because I'm thinking it, too. But then Papa Dan wanders around the corner to join us, and I can't do that to my mother. How could she handle knowing that Papa Dan and I are losing our marbles at the very same time? I have to work this out on my own.

"I just had a chill," I say, pulling away to head for the van and my escape.

Papa Dan leans against the repair truck, watching the Dilworth brothers stir paint. I'm startled by how young he looks with his elbow propped on the hood of the truck, his ankles crossed, and his hat at a crooked angle atop his head. I pause, tightening my grip on the camera, dread coiling in the pit of my stomach. I can't resist; I have to look.

The scene the lens reveals is black-and-white. Our van,

on the far side of the drive, has disappeared, and an old-fashioned car replaces Bill Dilworth's truck. The black car—a convertible—has fenders around the tires that look like doughnuts cut in half, and the headlights remind me of tiny, round spectacles. Papa Dan *is* young, a teenager with suspicious eyes that peer from beneath the brim of his cap—the same newsboy cap I'm wearing now. He stares at something or someone offscreen.

In books about photography, I've read the term *parallax*, but I didn't understand the meaning until now. Parallax refers to a difference in what the photographer sees through the viewfinder and what shows up on the film once the picture is shot. I capture the scene in front of me, certain nothing I'm seeing now will appear in the actual picture.

"Ohmygosh! Listen to this!" Bethyl Ann touches the microfiche screen.

Expecting her to recount the boring details of yet another of Mr. and Mrs. Peterson's trips "abroad," I continue looking through a book about birds I found on the library's nonfiction aisle. I scan the pages for a picture of the bird I saw in the hedge. My two hours with Bethyl Ann at the tiny old house that serves as Cedar Canyon's library have been a total waste. I can't help wondering if her claims of finding articles about Henry were a scheme to get me to hang out with her. We haven't run across a single one.

"Maybe we should go to the newspaper office," I say absently, flipping through the pages of colorful bird photos.

141

"I bet they have archives of old papers, too."

"*Look*." Beth nudges me with an elbow.

"Just tell me what it says."

"It's about a Christmas party at the Peterson place. I didn't find this one before."

I turn another page in the bird book, pause, and announce, "This is it!" Smiling, I press my finger against a photo of a small bird with pale brown wings and a brownish red tail. "My insomniac bird is a nightingale." I clear my throat and read, "The sun-shy nightingale is one of only a few bird species that sing primarily at night. Known for its melancholy serenades sung in low, haunting whistles and refrains, the nightingale has been a frequent subject of mythologists, poets, and songwriters throughout time."

"Sorry, Charlie. Impossible." Bethyl Ann gives the page a dismissive glance. "Nightingales don't exist in North America, only England. Unless your bird swam the Atlantic, it's something else."

I read further into the text and sigh. "You're right. But I swear this is the bird I saw." Or did I? Maybe that was a figment of my imagination, too.

Bethyl Ann blinks at me and sniffs. "As I was saying . . ." She returns her attention to the microfiche. "The Petersons were having a Christmas party and the ten-foot blue spruce tree in their parlor went up in flames."

"When?" I close the book and lay it in my lap.

"Henry was seventeen. A reporter interviewed one of the guests, and he said everyone was in the parlor for the tree lighting while Henry played his violin for them." Squinting at the screen, she twirls a strand of hair around her index finger and continues, "When Mr. Peterson plugged the tree in, it exploded. Everyone except Henry screamed and got the hell out of Dodge. He kept playing 'Silent Night' as if nothing had happened."

I laugh. "The paper says they got the hell out of Dodge?"

"No, *I* said that, smarty-pants. The paper said they ran." She smirks at me. "Henry did it, of course."

"Did what? Blew up the tree?"

"Big *duh*."

"But why would Henry blow up his parents' tree?"

"Though this be madness, yet there is method in it." Bethyl Ann shrugs. "Maybe he wanted to get their attention. Maybe he didn't like them."

"He was a spoiled rich kid. They probably gave him whatever he wanted."

"Rich gifts wax poor when givers prove unkind," she says.

I decide it's a waste of time to try to silence her Shakespearean tongue. The quotes are so much a part of Bethyl Ann, I doubt she could speak without them.

"Here's another one." She leans closer to the screen and reads, "William and Lenore Peterson were summoned home early from a business trip to Chicago when their teenaged son, Henry, suffered a gunshot wound to the foot while cleaning a hunting rifle in the turret of their mansion east of town. Though recorded as an accident, Miss Adeline Ivy, the Petersons' housekeeper, suggested the wound was self-inflicted. Miss Ivy resigned from her job and left

Cedar Canyon soon after our interview." Bethyl Ann lifts her wide-eyed gaze to mine. "Wow. See? I told you he hurt himself on purpose."

Uneasiness flutters in my chest. If the rumors are true, why was Henry so disturbed? I've been pretty unhappy at times. Depressed, even. But I can't imagine shooting myself in the foot or anywhere else.

I recall the pale face of the guy in the tree, his black marble gaze staring down at me. He's Henry. I don't know why I'm so sure of it, but I am. I wish I was as certain of everything else—that I had answers to all the questions crowding my mind. Does he want something from me? Why is he upsetting Papa Dan? And what's up with his resemblance to Tate? Does Tate have something to do with all of this?

I watch Bethyl Ann study the screen, the corners of her mouth curled up in that sly Mona Lisa smile of hers. For a second, I wonder if she's hiding something from me, if she knows more than she's willing to tell. Sighing, I sit back. That's silly; what reason would she have to keep information about Henry from me? What I *should* be wondering is: *What's wrong with me?* How can I even consider that any of this might be real? The guy in the tree—the entire episode, in fact—was nothing more than a daydream or an illusion, a latent image created by exposure to a bright reflection. A distorted photograph.

I've been thinking about Tate nonstop, watching him in school, wondering why he hates me and wishing he didn't. Every time our eyes meet, he looks away. Or his face flushes bright red, like he's angry with me. In the hallways, I've seen him go out of his way to avoid passing me. Just yesterday, he turned midstride to walk the opposite way. I conjured him into that photograph, superimposed his likeness over that of the tree. I turned Tate into our resident ghost. A hot, brooding monochrome figment of my imagination.

I take off my cap and fan my face with it, assuring myself the reason I'm so warm has nothing at all to do with Tate Hudson. The library doesn't have central air.

"Oh, geez . . . are you okay?" Bethyl Ann presses her palm to my forehead just as her mother appears at our table. "You're burning up. Isn't she red as a beet, Mama?"

If I didn't know better, I would think Mrs. Pugh is Bethyl Ann's grandmother instead of her mom. She wears her gray hair pulled into a ponytail, and her face is a roadmap of wrinkles. "You do look a bit flushed, Tansy," she says. "Are you feverish?"

"No, but I'm a little dizzy."

"Looking at microfiche makes some folks a bit seasick, believe it or not." Mrs. Pugh blinks rapidly, her eyes concerned behind her giant wire-framed glasses.

"It might just be because I didn't eat breakfast," I say. Or sleep last night.

"We have leftovers at home, Bethyl Ann," she says. "Cold meat loaf and pasta salad with extra mayo, just like you like it. Why don't you girls go make yourself a plate?"

"Oh, good! I love meat loaf." Bethyl Ann flashes her red, white, and blues.

"My mom gave me money for lunch. Enough for both of us to eat out," I say.

Bethyl Ann looks disappointed. "Mom makes really good meat loaf," she says.

I start to say that I don't eat anything that once had eyes, a nose, and a mouth, but her hopeful expression stops me, and I feel a pinch of guilt for ever thinking that someone as young and innocent as Bethyl Ann might be scheming me. "Okay. We'll go to your house." Lifting the bird book from my lap, I add, "I want to check this out first, okay?"

"Of course." Mrs. Pugh takes the book from me. "I'll make you a library card."

Bethyl Ann and I follow her mother to a desk up front. The truth is, I'm really not all that hungry, and even if I was, I would never eat meat loaf. The thought of mayonnaise-covered pasta makes me nauseous, too. But I'll force down the noodles. Bethyl Ann has been helpful, and I should be nice to her. She's the most normal thing in my life right now.

Beside me, she yawns noisily, and Mrs. Pugh looks over her shoulder, frowns, and says, "Don't forget you're in a library, young lady."

"Sorry, Mama. Couldn't help it." She yawns again, quieter this time, then leans close to me and whispers, "Life is as tedious as a twice-told tale. Shakespeare, in case you're wondering. *King John*. Act three, scene four."

I bite the inside of my cheek. Bethyl Ann, normal? If I'm starting to believe that, I really *do* need an appointment to have my head examined.

11

As I'm driving home after lunch at Bethyl Ann's house, I can't quit thinking about Henry hurting himself on purpose. I wonder if that's true or just another rumor. One of my classmates in San Francisco was a cutter. Even during the hottest days of summer, she always wore long sleeves, but once I caught a glimpse of her wrist peeking out from the black cuff of her shirt, and I saw the horizontal red scars on it. Why would someone do that? Just thinking about it scares me. I felt so sad for that girl.

I arrive at the house and park alongside Bill Dilworth's truck. Sheriff Ray Don stands at the top of a ladder that's propped against the front of the house, painting a small section of the siding a pretty shade of sea foam green. I kill the engine and climb out.

The sheriff turns to look down at me, the paintbrush poised in his hand. "Hi, there."

"Hey." I shut the van door.

"So, what do you think of the color? We'll paint the shutters cream."

I lift my gaze to the painted patch. "It's all wrong." The certainty comes to me from out of nowhere. "The siding should be white, the shutters black."

"Oh." He frowns. "This is just a test sample." Squinting at the paint again, he mutters, "White, huh?" When his brother comes around the corner of the house carrying another ladder, the sheriff says, "Bill, did Eloise put white on the list of approved colors?"

I don't wait to hear Bill Dilworth's answer. Muttering another hello, I walk past him and up the steps to the front door.

"Tansy?" Mom calls down from her office when I enter the house. "That you?"

"Yeah, it's me." I start upstairs, and she meets me on the second-floor landing.

"Hailey called."

I flinch. "What did she want?" The moment the words are out, I regret my harsh tone. It isn't Mom's fault that Hailey betrayed me.

"She wants to talk to you. Why haven't you called her back?"

"I don't want to," I say, moving past Mom. Hailey's the least of my problems now.

Following at my heels, she says, "Do you want to talk about it?"

"About what?"

"This thing between you and Hailey that has you so miffed."

I stop in front of my bedroom door, but I can't bring myself to look at her or answer her question.

Mom places a hand on my shoulder. "What's wrong?"

I force myself to meet her gaze. "It doesn't matter. There's nothing you can do about it, anyway." I turn my back to her and open my bedroom door. "I'm going to hike out to the canyon. I want to see the bridge and take some pictures. Where's Papa Dan?"

Mom's stare burns the back of my neck, and I know she's debating with herself. Should she press the issue of Hailey or let it drop? Lucky for me, the latter option wins. Her sigh sounds like it weighs fifty pounds. "He's napping. He shouldn't walk that far, anyway."

Kicking off my sandals, I grab my sneakers and sit on the bed. "He's not sick, is he?"

"Just tired. For some reason, he spent all morning wandering around the mulberry tree."

The watch. I feel the blood drain from my face. *He was searching for where I dropped Henry's watch.* Hoping Mom doesn't notice my startled reaction, I hurry to change my shoes.

"Before I forget," she says, "we have internet service now. It's a little slow pulling it up out here in the country, though, so you have to be patient." She pauses, then adds, "If you don't want to call Hailey, maybe you could at least shoot her an email."

I could, but I won't. Why should I? I don't owe Hailey anything, not even my time.

149

I strike out toward the part of the canyon that borders our property. I'm not sure why I've waited so long to go to the bridge. Maybe because I have mixed feelings about seeing the place where Henry died. A part of me is curious, but another part doesn't want to imagine him taking the plunge, and I'm pretty sure I won't be able to wipe that image from my mind once I've been there.

I snap shots while I walk. A twisted mesquite tree. A jutting rock formation. A trio of tumbleweeds scampering across the field. After a few minutes, I rest beneath a small grove of cottonwood trees beside a boulder that's shaped like a bench. The rock formation is so unusual that I squat to get a shot of it, positioning the camera in front of my face.

Panic slams into me. I freeze.

Tate's look-alike lies stretched out along the smooth rock, a faded gray guy in a colorless world. His hands are laced behind his head, his booted feet crossed at the ankles. A violin lies across his lap. He stares beyond me with narrowed eyes, his face molded into a crooked half smile.

My pulse thunders in my ears as I stumble backward and land on my butt, my hat flying off my head, the camera strap tugging at the back of my neck as it falls. I pick up the camera, look again, and gasp. "Who are you?"

He stays as still as the rock—as if he's a part of it.

"Are you Henry?" I whisper, but of course he doesn't answer, doesn't blink. His hair remains unruffled by the gusty breeze that tousles mine.

A voice inside my head tells me to run as fast as I can

and not look back. But I'm paralyzed by the fear that, if I move, he'll reach out and grab me. I have to force myself to lift my hand to take the picture. Once it's shot, I grab my hat, put it on, and scoot backward, until I'm far enough from the rock that I feel safe to stand again. The camera bangs against my hip as I run, but I don't stop. My lungs feel like they're about to pop as I sprint across the field.

I hit a trail that weaves through another sparse grove of trees. The trail turns sharply at the far side of the grove, and ahead steel girders curve up into the sky like the arched skeletal spine of a giant centipede. The sight stops me short. Panting, I glance back, afraid I'll see the guy from the bench rock coming after me, relieved when I find that I've outrun my delusion, at least for the moment.

I turn around, lean forward at the waist, plant my hands on my thighs, and try to calm down. The bridge looms ahead of me. It's a spectacular sight. Larger than I ever imagined, tarnished and daunting and eerie . . . like Henry. Maybe the bridge absorbed Henry's essence when he fell from its side. I can't wait to capture the image on film, but when I look through the camera lens, my breath catches in my throat. He's there—the guy from the bench rock. Henry. Standing at the far end of the structure, bent over the railing, staring down into the craggy canyon below. My stomach folds in on itself when he steps up onto the railing's lowest rung.

No! Don't jump! I grip the camera so tightly my knuckles ache. But as fast as the thought flashes through my mind, another one follows. *He moved.* I zoom in, and just as I realize the guy on the bridge isn't Henry but Tate, he steps down and starts walking across the bridge toward the trail, looking down at his feet. I lower the camera and turn to go, anxious to escape before he sees me.

But only a few steps down the trail, I stop. I'm so tired of Tate's game, whatever it is. I'm ready to confront him, to come right out and ask what I did to tick him off. I swing around, and when he sees me walking toward him, he pauses a few seconds before he continues my way. *Coward,* I think, then wait until he's only a few steps away before calling, "Do you want to talk to me?"

"No, why?" He pauses. "I was just heading home."

I shrug. "I thought you might want to tell me what's bothering you."

"Nope. I'm good." Tate starts past me.

I sigh loudly, then murmur, "Jerk."

Tate stops walking, turns, and narrows his gaze on me. "I'm a jerk?"

I didn't mean for him to hear me, and at first my polite instincts insist that I apologize then slink away. But then my pride kicks in. Why should I apologize? He *has* been acting like a jerk. "No, you're an *ass!*" I shout. "And I guess you couldn't care less, right?"

"What people think of me is none of my business."

"Wow. You're a tough guy, too."

"Maybe I am. So what?"

"Well, I'm not impressed." I turn my back on him and stomp off down the trail toward the bridge.

Less than a minute goes by before a shrill whistle pierces the air. Hesitating, I glance over my shoulder. Tate starts jogging toward me. *You finally want to talk?* I think. *Fine.* I won't blow him off and leave, but I won't meet him halfway, either.

Stopping in front of me again, he jams his hands into his pockets, a sheepish look on his face. For one long, awkward moment that feels like ten, we both stare down at our shoes, silent. Then Tate clears his throat and says, "I'm sorry. Can we start over?"

My eyes lift to his.

He gestures toward the bridge. "So, what do you think? Pretty cool, huh?"

"It's amazing. I didn't expect it to be so—" I can't find the right word to describe the awesome sight of the towering structure.

"I know," he says. "I've tried a million times to write about it—you know, do it justice, but I can never explain how incredible it is."

My irritation begins to melt like butter in a microwave. How can someone who's so frustrating and rude most of the time also be so tuned in to what I'm thinking? I doubt many guys would see the beauty in a bridge, much less feel it deserved to be portrayed in a flattering way. Still, I'm not going to let down my guard. I don't completely trust this warmer side of Tate. I've experienced it once before and learned the hard way how fast he can go from hot to cold.

"You're probably better at it than you think," I say.

"Believe me, I know as well as anyone how insecure writers can be. When my mom's in the middle of whatever book she's working on, she's always convinced it's total crap and her career is ruined. Then she turns it in and her editor loves it or she gets a good review or a ton of fan letters and she struts around like she's the most talented writer on the planet. That lasts until she starts the next book, and then it's the same routine all over again." I roll my eyes. "She can be a real drama queen." Embarrassed by my nervous speech, I look down at my shoes again.

Tate laughs. "In my case, though, what I'm working on *is* crap."

I glance up and make a face. "See? You're no more secure than my mother."

Tate falls silent. He pulls his hands from his pockets and taps his fingers against his thighs. "You were right, by the way. I have been a jerk."

"An ass," I correct. "No kidding."

"I don't know what's wrong with me sometimes. What happened a second ago—I was just in a bad mood. It wasn't anything you did."

"That doesn't explain the way you've acted toward me every other day since I started school here."

He clears his throat. "I guess I haven't made things any easier on you—being in a new place, I mean. Moving so much must suck."

"Yeah, well, we move a lot, so I guess I'm used to it."

"Really?"

"No." We both laugh.

"Why *did* you move to Cedar Canyon?"

For some reason, anger jabs at me again. *"Excuse me* for upsetting you by being here."

"Is that what you think?"

"Well, you've acted like you despise me ever since you found out I wasn't just some girl passing through town. Someone you could flirt with at your uncle's café then forget about."

He lowers his head, then looks up at me slowly, moving only his eyes. "I don't despise you. It's just . . . some stuff happened, and I guess I sort of took it out on you."

"Like *that* makes sense. What stuff? What did I have to do with it?" I cross my arms.

"Nothing. It's my dad, mostly. He's been on my case about a lot of things."

"Football, you mean."

"How did you know that?"

"I heard you two arguing behind the press box the night of the Watermelon Run." When he scowls, I add, "I was at the top of the bleachers taking pictures and then you were just *there*. I couldn't help overhearing."

"It doesn't matter. Dad is fanatical about me playing college ball."

"You don't want to?"

"I don't care about football. I never have."

"Then why do you play?"

"It's a really big deal to him."

If my dad were alive, would pleasing him be so important to me that I would do something I hated just to make him happy? Maybe that's what's going on with Tate, but I get the feeling there's more to what's bothering him than just his dad and football. His mom, for starters. Probably not a good idea, though, to let him know that Mary Jane and J. B. blabbed about that, so I decide not to bring up the subject. "I read in the paper that you pretty much won the game single-handedly last night."

"I don't want to talk about football," Tate says. "I just wanted to apologize and say that I hope we can start fresh. You know . . . maybe be friends?"

I hope he can't tell how ridiculously happy that question makes me. But since he deserves to sweat a little, I make him wait for my answer. I suppose I'm feeling cantankerous, as Papa Dan used to say.

"Well?" he asks. "Any chance of that?" Tate's lighthearted tone of voice and the teasing glint in his eyes don't hide his discomfort. I recall Bethyl Ann's claim that he used to be really full of himself, and I'm pretty sure he's not used to apologizing for anything.

"That depends," I finally tell him. "Will you let me read something you wrote?"

"I don't know . . ." Tate's brows tug together. "I'll think about it."

"What's to think about?"

"It's embarrassing." He kicks a rock and it skips across the trail. Slanting me a look, he says, "I might, if you'll let

156

me see some of your photos."

"We'll see." A smile twitches my lips. "Maybe if you behave yourself and act nice for a change."

"I'll try. It'll be hard, though."

"I realize it's not in your nature."

We grin at each other, then he offers me his hand. "Truce?"

"Truce," I say, and we shake.

Tate nods toward the bridge. "You want me to give you the tour?"

"Sure." We walk along the trail side by side, and I can hardly believe how our relationship has gone from agonizing to awesome in less than an hour. If only the same thing could happen with everything else in my life.

After dinner, I go up to my bedroom and log on to the internet on my laptop computer. I want to research nightingales to see if Bethyl Ann is correct that they don't exist in North America. I think she's wrong. The bird I saw in the hedge looked exactly like the picture of the nightingale in the library book.

Before I begin a search, I think about Mom's suggestion that I email Hailey, and I can't resist checking my inbox. I have fifty-one messages—most of them spam, though five are from Hailey. And from Colin? A big, fat zero.

A few days ago, it would've stung to find out Colin didn't care enough about me to try to get in touch. Not anymore. When I think of him now, I don't feel anything at all. The truth is, Colin was never really mine, only a dream. Maybe my change of heart regarding him has a little to do with Tate.

Yeah, right. Who am I fooling? It has *everything* to do with Tate. I don't know why he's being so nice to me all of a sudden; I'm just glad he is. We didn't talk about anything earth-shattering at the bridge. He just told me a little of its history—how it was originally built in the 1920s to make it easier to get from one side of the canyon to the other. The bridge isn't used anymore, except as a hangout for teens. That must've been the case for decades, because the graffiti Mr. Quattlebaum complained about dates back to as early as the 1950s. Tate also mentioned the legend about Henry's suicide, but he didn't add any information I hadn't already heard.

I delete all the spam before opening Hailey's first message.

Tansy, I can explain what happened. I've always had a thing for Colin. But I knew you liked him so I tried—

I hit Delete without reading the rest. Though I'm over Colin, Hailey's disloyalty still hurts.

Outside my window, the bird begins to trill. I enter the word *nightingale* into the search box on the computer screen just as Mom pokes her head into the room. "What'cha doing?" she asks.

"Researching nightingales," I answer before adding the

lie, "for a science assignment."

"That sounds interesting." She smiles. "Well, I'm turning in early. Good night."

"'Night," I say, keeping my gaze on the screen as she closes the door. I click on the first link that comes up. It's a bird-watcher's site and it confirms what Bethyl Ann said. No nightingales in this part of the world.

Baffled, I close the site and open the second link. A quote written by the poet Percy Bysshe Shelley appears. I remember seeing a book of his poetry on the desk in Bethyl Ann's bedroom the day I had lunch at her house. The quote reads: "A poet is a nightingale, who sits in darkness and sings to cheer its own solitude with sweet sounds; his auditors are as men entranced by the melody of an unseen musician, who feel that they are moved and softened, yet know not whence or why."

A quiver of recognition hums through me.

"You're early tonight," I whisper to the serenading bird outside, feeling Henry's pull.

It isn't easy, but I manage to wait until midnight to make sure Mom is soundly asleep before I slip from my room. I'm anxious to go up to the turret, but I still stop by to check on Papa Dan. Mom locked his door from the outside. I twist the deadbolt Bill Dilworth installed and let myself into his room. The sound of his raspy, staggered breathing makes my chest ache. "Sleep tight," I whisper, tugging the fallen sheet up over his shoulder, realizing our roles have reversed; he used to tuck me in at night, used to murmur the same words I say to him now: "Don't let the bedbugs bite. I love you."

Stepping outside his room, I close the door but can't bring myself to engage the deadbolt. I get halfway down the hallway before I stop and go back, knowing what I have to do, whether I like it or not. Bitter tears scald my throat as the lock clicks into place beneath my fingers. "I'm sorry," I whisper.

Moments later in the turret, I look at the photos I developed earlier, now hanging on the drying rack. I linger over the one of the empty bench rock in the grove of green cottonwoods before moving on to the shot of Papa Dan in the driveway. In it, he is an old man—the grandfather I know, not a teenager. He leans against Bill Dilworth's truck, not an old-fashioned car from out of a gangster movie. Whisking my fingertip across his image, I think how unfair it is, how hard to have to stand by and watch him wither away.

My nerves stretch tight as I sit in the velvet chair by the window. I study the items on the round table: the envelope of photos from City Drug, the teardrop crystal, Henry's journal. Beneath my palm the leather is smooth in places, bumpy in others.

A poet is a nightingale . . .

What does my nightingale poet want to say to me tonight? I'm not sure I want to know. The moment I found the journal, I felt my sanity slipping away like sand through my fingers. Maybe I shouldn't read Henry's poems anymore.

I slide the top photograph from the envelope, the one of Papa Dan squinting up into the mulberry tree. Henry's pocket watch still lies on the ground at his feet. Is that what my grandfather searched for all morning?

The nightingale's song plays through my mind, so pretty it brings fresh tears to my eyes and a longing for something that I can't name.

. . . his auditors are as men entranced by the melody of an unseen musician, who feel that they are moved and softened . . .

The crystal captures the lamp's glow and winks at me. I want my grandfather back. Maybe that possibility exists, maybe not. But I'll never know unless I take the chance.

Aiming the teardrop at the picture, I turn it slightly until a prism of light stretches between the two items. The prism shimmers and surrounds me. The image in the photograph widens.

I slip through.

12

"Henry! You dropped your watch. I hope it didn't break."

Henry grabs the mulberry tree's lowest branch, pulls himself up, and climbs to the next branch, then sits on a sturdy limb near the top of the tree. "I don't care if it breaks. Keep it, Daniel. I don't want it anymore."

"I can't take your watch."

"You aren't taking it. It's my gift. That watch might be worth a lot of money someday. If you don't want to carry it, store it in one of those fancy little boxes you make."

"I never keep them," Daniel says. "I give them away."

"You really should make one for yourself," Isabel tells him.

The phantom I first saw in the tree and the boy beneath it have come alive. They move and talk like actors in a black-and-white movie. Without question, I accept the teenage boy, Daniel, will grow up to be my grandfather. I accept, too, that I inhabit someone else's body—a girl named Isabel. I'm not sure how I know her name, I just do. I know everything she knows. I feel her emotions, speak her words, think her thoughts as well as my own. And it seems right, the most natural thing in the world. It's almost as if we're both inside her body—Isabel and I. But she's the one in control; I can only follow along, listening and watching as if I'm a passenger.

Isabel wonders about the note of sarcasm in Henry's tone when he mentioned the boxes. She blames it on his strange mood today and silently forgives his condescending attitude toward their best friend. Linking her arm through Daniel's, she kisses his cheek. "I love the box you made me for Christmas. I keep my favorite trinkets inside it."

Daniel grins, then releases her arm and bends to pick up the watch. He wears a coat and a scarf, a woolen hat and heavy boots. The timepiece he holds out toward Henry is a deep, glossy gold—the only speck of color in this drab, neutral world. "But your folks gave it to you for your birthday," he protests. "It must've cost 'em a pretty penny."

"They have plenty more pennies," Henry scoffs. "I don't want anything from them. Not anymore."

Isabel's heart aches for him. She wonders how his parents can be so cruel. They leave him alone too much. Mrs. Peterson always accompanies Mr. Peterson on his business trips, and they take more vacations than anyone she knows, even during the months when Henry is in school and can't join them. Isabel's folks never leave her alone.

"I'm sure they love you," she says to him, pulling her coat more snugly around her. Her fingers are numb inside her mittens as she shades her eyes against the sun's white glare and gazes into the tree branches at Henry. "You must miss them. It has to be just awful staying out here with that moody Miss Ivy all the time. I thought she resigned?"

"After I put a bullet in my foot, you mean?" He *laughs*. "What Father wants, Father gets. He doubled the old bat's salary to bribe her back."

Daniel looks at Henry suspiciously. "You didn't really shoot yourself on purpose like everyone says."

"Didn't I?" Henry cocks a brow.

"Stop that!" Isabel scolds. "The way you talk, it's no wonder people—" She catches herself.

"Think I'm insane?" Henry says, feigning a wicked laugh. "Don't look so grim, Isabel. I don't mind being the town's Mad Hatter. In fact, I like it."

The toll of a bell diverts Isabel's attention to the farmhouse across the way—the Quattlebaums' farmhouse. No, not anymore. Not here. The farm belongs to Isabel's family; her father is the farmer I've seen through my camera lens in my own world—somehow I know that. He's out there now, shoveling snow in the yard. He props the shovel against his body to play fetch with their Labrador retriever, Kip. Isabel giggles as Kip runs toward the barn to retrieve the ball. "Daddy is in for it now," she says. "Kip will want him to play for the rest of the day." Her father pulls off his glove and blows on his fingers to warm them. He doesn't tolerate the cold. Once he's inside the house, his hands will throb as he warms them over the fire.

"What do ya want to do today?" Daniel passes Henry's watch to Isabel, and I feel the weight of it in her hand. "Remember when we spent Saturdays playin' hide-and-seek in the canyon? Now, that was fun. Too bad we're too old for games like that now."

"Says who?" Henry asks derisively. "Tell you what . . . we'll change the rules to make it more interesting." He winks at Isabel.

"Instead of one person hiding and two seeking, Isabel and I will hide together, and you'll have to look for us, Daniel."

Heat creeps from beneath Isabel's coat collar and climbs up her neck and face to warm her cheekbones. Until recently, Henry treated her and Daniel the same—as slightly amusing, slightly annoying younger siblings. He never winked at her or made flirtatious suggestions. Their shared glances didn't startle her or make her pulse stutter, as they do now. She is confused by his increasing attention, by his dark, unwavering stare and the unfamiliar feelings it stirs inside her.

The bell rings a second time. Isabel feigns annoyance, though she's really relieved. Slipping Henry's watch into her coat pocket to hold for him until he comes down from the tree, she sighs and murmurs, "I'd better go."

"So that's how your mother calls you in now? By ringing the bell?" One corner of Henry's mouth curves up. "I think I'll call you Bell from now on. It fits."

"That is a good name for you!" Daniel agrees. "You're always interruptin' and makin' noise." He dusts snow from his mittens into Isabel's face.

Shrieking a laugh, she scoops up a fistful of snow and tosses it at him, and in that small part of Isabel's mind that I now occupy, I think how wonderful it is to see my grandfather so young and strong, so healthy and happy.

"You're askin' for it now, Bell!" Daniel yells, reaching for more snow.

Henry jumps from the tree and takes Isabel's arm, casting a dark glance over his shoulder at Daniel. "Bell is my name for her, not yours."

A stunned look of apprehension flashes across Daniel's face, and I feel the pressure of Henry's fingers through Isabel's coat sleeve as her gaze darts between the two of them. "I need to go home," she murmurs, a sudden wariness humming beneath her skin.

Henry draws her a few steps farther away from Daniel and gives her arm an even harder squeeze. "It's a quarter past eight," he says quietly. "You just got here."

"I'll come back when I finish my chores."

He frowns at her father across the field. "They'll just find another excuse to keep you away from me."

Daniel begins whistling, and she looks over to see him packing snow into a ball. At first, Isabel thinks he hasn't heard her conversation with Henry, but then Daniel glances up, their eyes meet, and she realizes she was wrong. She can't tell from his expression if Daniel feels excluded, or if he's worried about her. Or both.

When Daniel returns his attention to the snowball, she lowers her voice and says to Henry, "I'll tell Mama and Daddy that Daniel is with us. They think the world of him."

"And what about you?" Henry's black eyes search hers. "What do you think of Daniel?"

"I love him, of course." Amused by his jealous scowl, Isabel nudges Henry and grins. "Silly goose, not like that. Daniel's like a brother to me."

"Promise you'll come back."

"I promise."

"After lunch, if not before." Henry holds tight to her arm until she nods her agreement.

"Ouch!" Daniel cries.

"What's wrong?" Isabel calls.

"I cut my hand."

Breaking away from Henry, she rushes to Daniel and stoops beside him in the snow. She takes the fist he cradles against his chest, asking, "How did you manage this?"

"There was a sliver of glass in the snow. It sliced right through my glove."

Isabel removes her mitten, then peels the glove off his injured hand. A small gash lines the inside space between his forefinger and thumb, black blood oozing from it. But as she probes Daniel's warm flesh, I'm shocked to see the blood turn crimson. "You should clean and disinfect this; it's deep," she tells him. "You might need a stitch or two."

Henry comes over, takes hold of Daniel's arm, and helps him stand. "Come on. We'll get Miss Ivy to do it."

Noticing Daniel's hesitance to go with him, Isabel says, "That's okay. He can come home with me. Mother will tend to it. She has the supplies in her first-aid kit."

Henry's eyes narrow; he shrugs, then drops Daniel's arm. Nodding impatiently toward her father's farm, he says, "Hurry home, then. Take care of Daniel and get your chores done, Bell." He stomps off, headed for his house.

Confused and upset, Isabel watches him go. I want her to defy Henry for acting as if he owns her. She knows she should, and a part of her wants to, but if she obeys him, they'll be together again sooner, and Isabel wants that most of all. "Let's go," she tells Daniel quietly.

Snow crunches beneath their feet and a brooding silence stretches between them as they cross the field. Midway to the house, Daniel murmurs, "Are you okay?"

"You're the one who's hurt," she points out, glancing at his injured hand. But her chest is so tight with emotion that she can't hold the words in any longer. "Who does Henry think he is? Ordering me around like that . . . implying that you should back off."

"Since you brought it up . . ." Daniel stops walking, cradling his injured hand against his stomach, pressing his loose glove to the wound with his opposite hand. "Henry's changed. . . . He seems, I don't know . . . dodgy, I guess. Like he's after somethin'."

Pausing alongside him, Isabel asks, "Why would you say that?" But deep inside, she knows exactly what he means; she's noticed the changes in Henry, too.

"You know I've always looked up to him. In some ways I wish I could be more like Henry and not give a whit what anybody thinks of me. But lately . . ." Daniel shakes his head as he glances back at the Peterson house. "I'm not sure I trust him anymore." There's an uneasy look in his eyes as he adds, "That thing with the gun . . . him shootin' himself . . ."

Isabel is torn between defending Henry and admitting she's worried about him, too. Not that she doesn't like some of the changes in him: the smooth, deep caress of his voice when he speaks her name; the way his eyes darken when he looks at her; the tender way he touches her at times. But she's also noticed his arrogance, especially toward Daniel. "He's always had an edginess about him," she says. "And I don't believe for a second that he shot himself. He's only joking."

"That's nothin' to joke about. Besides, it's more than that. I'm startin' to think everyone else might be right about him. If not for him saving my life, I'm not sure I'd keep comin' out here." Daniel looks down at his hands and lifts the glove to inspect the wound. "That and the fact that I don't want to leave you alone with him."

"Don't worry about me. I can take care of myself." Isabel hugs him, filling me with emotion. This boy wrapped tight in my arms will grow up to be my grandfather—my best friend.

While I absorb his warmth, Isabel is distracted by the hope that Daniel doesn't notice the breathless sound of her voice and guess the truth—that she longs for time alone with Henry, that lately, it's almost all she thinks about. "You know how moody Henry can get," she murmurs. "That's nothing new. But he's harmless. And as for him saving you—I don't want to see your friendship with Henry end, but if that's the only reason you spend time with him . . . You were what? Eight years old when he rescued you?"

"Nine. He jumped in and pulled me out of the river, Isabel. I couldn't swim. He risked his life."

Irritation at Henry rises up in her again. "That certainly doesn't give him the right to treat you like a bug on his shoe." She looks back at the Peterson house. "When we were little, Henry and I only had each other for company most days, being way out here so far from town. Next to you, he's my best friend. If he wants to snarl at me, fine. But I won't let him treat you like that. I'm going to say something to him."

"No, don't," Daniel says quickly. "I'll deal with whatever's bugging Henry. You just watch out for yourself. I don't like the way he looks at you."

"Tansy? Why are you up here so early? Are you okay?"

A spear of pain slices through my neck from sleeping crouched in the chair. Sitting up, I reach to rub my sore muscles and realize my fingertips are numb.

Mom calls my name again as she pounds on the door.

"I'm fine, Mom. Just a sec." I open the drawer on the round table and slip Henry's journal and the crystal inside. The photo of Papa Dan under the mulberry tree slips from my lap when I stand. My heart pounds as I bend to pick it up. In it, Henry's timepiece no longer lies on the ground at my grandfather's feet. I reach inside my pajama pants pocket and pull out the watch, trying to convince myself that I imagined seeing it in the photo before. No other explanation makes sense. Not much of anything makes sense anymore. Quickly I place the photograph and the watch in the table drawer, too.

Mom's worried face greets me when I open the door. "You scared me to death. I went to your room and saw your bed hadn't been slept in. I called and called for you."

"I was processing film. I sat down to look at some of the photos and must have fallen asleep." Hearing the chatter of birds outside, I yawn and ask, "What time is it?"

"Ten o'clock."

"In the morning?"

"What did you think?" Mom frowns. "With that dark plastic over the windows I guess you can't tell night from day."

I rub my eyes. "Wow, I really did fall asleep."

"You shouldn't be up working so late."

"You do it, Mom. I've found you asleep at your desk lots of times."

"That's different. You really scared me."

I feel bad for worrying her. "Mom . . ." Taking her hand, I say, "I'm okay. Really."

She hugs me tightly. "Come downstairs. Let's eat pancakes."

"You made pancakes?" I look at her. "I didn't smell anything burning."

Grinning, she swats at me. "I didn't make them; you're going to."

I manage to smile as I follow her out of the turret, but all I can think about is what happened last night. I don't know what to believe anymore; it seemed too real to be a dream. The wimp in me wants to pretend it never happened, to put Henry's treasures back in the cellar and never look at them again. But I'm also curious—too much so to give in to fear. Who was Isabel? It's beyond weird that I felt as if I was inside her, experiencing everything through her eyes and emotions. I don't even know what she looks like. Did she really exist in the past? Were she and Papa Dan friends? If only he could tell me. Stepping into the photograph added more questions to my list instead of giving me answers.

My knees feel like they're made of pudding as I walk with Mom to the kitchen. "How about I put strawberries and whipped cream on the pancakes the way Papa Dan likes them?" I ask her, swallowing a surge of nerves.

She wiggles her brows. "Sounds yummy."

No matter how hard I try to push it aside, last night's dream crowds my mind as I make batter and heat up the griddle; deep down, I don't really believe it was a dream, but I don't know what else to call it. Despite feeling so unsettled, I manage to put breakfast on the table. But three bites into my stack of pancakes, I notice the strawberries are dark gray. The fruit doesn't look rotten, just colorless. I'm about to ask Mom how the berries look to her when, beside me, Papa Dan reaches for the syrup bottle. I glimpse a tiny white scar on his right hand in the space between his forefinger and thumb, the same place where Daniel cut his hand. I grasp his wrist gently and ask, "What happened here?" His gaze lifts slowly to mine, and I feel as if a rain shower of needles is cascading over my skin. Barely able to breathe, I ask Mom, "Has he always had this?"

"The scar? I don't know." She sips her coffee. "I'm not sure I've ever noticed it before. Why?"

I shrug. "I was just wondering."

I study Papa Dan's tired green eyes. He looks so old, but in his face, I still glimpse the boy he once was, the one I met last night. He makes a weak noise in his throat, then pulls his wrist from my hand and pushes away from the table, his shoes shuffling against the floor as he leaves the room. I look at his plate, and notice he didn't take even one bite of his pancakes. He eats less every day. I haven't heard

172

him whistling this morning.

The truth I've refused to accept sinks slowly to the pit of my stomach and lodges there like a boulder in a pond, heavy and hard and immovable. My grandfather won't be with me forever. We might not have much more time together. I sit back, remembering that Mom took him to see a doctor in Amarillo last week. How could I have forgotten to ask about their visit? "What did the doctor say?" I ask her now, pushing the words past the lump in my throat. "About Papa Dan?"

She sets down her coffee mug. "He's lost a lot of weight since his last checkup in San Francisco. That's one reason he seems weaker."

A tear trickles down my cheek. "He's quieter, too."

"The doctor said that's not unusual for someone with his condition."

"His condition." I look down at my plate.

Mom covers my hand on the tabletop. "He's holding his own, Tansy. He's hanging in there. And the doctor said he's not in any pain."

No physical pain maybe, but he's hurting inside—I see it in his eyes. What is it about this house, this place? Memories of Henry? Of Isabel? Why would that disturb him? He was always such a happy man, so upbeat and positive and encouraging to everyone. He looked out for people. After seeing the way he was with Isabel, I realize he was always that way, even when he was young.

Stabbing a strawberry with my fork, I lift it up in front

of Mom. "Do these look funny to you?"

She shoots me a baffled frown and shrugs. "No. They look as good as they taste."

"You don't think they're a little dark?"

"They're a pretty shade of red, if you ask me. I bet you could sell a picture of these pancakes to Aunt Jemima. It would make a beautiful ad." Mom picks a strawberry from the bowl and pops it into her mouth.

My stomach protests as I stare at the piece of fruit. I lower the fork to my plate and squint at the six or seven other gray strawberries topping my pancakes.

"What's the matter? Aren't you hungry?" Mom asks.

"I've sort of lost my appetite," I tell her. Along with my mind.

Late in the afternoon, I sit in the turret with Henry's journal open in my lap. I want to find out if he really did hurt himself on purpose, and if so, why. Maybe then I would understand what's bothering Papa Dan. Do Henry's poems hold clues that will lead me to the answers? Clues about his feelings toward Papa Dan? For Isabel? Maybe. But when I read his words, they seem to be written for me rather than Isabel or my grandfather:

Listen
Be patient
Open your eyes
Don't be afraid

Don't believe lies
Reach out
I'll guide you
Open your mind
Listen

I clutch the journal to my chest, thinking how nice it would be to have someone guide me, to tell me who I can trust and who I can't. Hailey fooled me. Is Bethyl Ann fooling me, too? And am I stupid for giving Tate a second chance?

Henry's right; even if he could answer all my questions, I'm afraid of visiting his memories. And even though I feel connected to him through his words, *he* frightens me, too. When he looks at Isabel, when he touches her, it's as if he's also looking at me . . . touching me. I don't know if I have any control over her actions; if Henry tried to kiss me and I wanted to stop him, could I make Isabel say no even if she didn't want to?

I know her mind; she's also a little afraid of him. Isabel isn't used to guys treating her like a girlfriend. Especially not Henry. She's never even been kissed. But as much as the change in their relationship freaks her out, she also likes it. Henry may be dangerous, but she still wants to be with him. In that way, Isabel and I are the same. Because no matter how much visiting Henry's world scares me or how dangerous it might be, I still want to go back and be with him. Most of all, I want to be with Papa Dan. In Henry's memories, my grandfather is young and strong. He talks to me, teases me, protects me like he used to.

I close the journal and place it on the round table, confusion clouding my mind. I'm wrong; Isabel is the one my grandfather talks to and teases—it's Isabel who he worries about. She's his friend in the past, not me. I only *feel* as if I'm the one. But maybe that's enough. At least I get to hear him laugh and see the same twinkle in his eyes I remember, the one that's no longer there. If I continue to go into the photographs, maybe I'll learn something about this house and his relationship with Henry that could help me figure out what's upsetting him now, and I could stop it and give him some peace.

Though it's early in the afternoon, the plastic over the windows makes the turret room as dark as midnight. The nightingale must be confused about the time, too; I hear it singing, calling to me. Beneath the glow of the lamp, I study the photograph of the stone bench I passed on the way to the canyon yesterday, and a sense of calm falls over me. I lift the crystal and tilt it to catch the light. . . .

. . . *Once again I am Isabel, sitting beside Daniel on the hood of Mr. Peterson's new Packard on a rutted road beside a field of winter wheat. The sun shines bright, as it has since midmorning. The heat quickly melted much of the snow, leaving only small, scattered islands of slush in the dead grass between the field and the car.*

Across the way, on the bench rock beneath the grove of cottonwoods, Henry plays his violin while, beside me, Daniel plays his harmonica. They've reached a truce of some sort; Isabel is relieved about that. Henry hasn't snapped at Daniel or made any

176

snide remarks all day. She senses that it's a fragile reprieve, since a weak current of tension vibrates just beneath the surface of their cordial words.

Henry's deft hands coax a slow, sad melody from the violin cradled between his shoulder and chin. In harmony, Daniel's harmonica emits a mournful wail like the whistle of a lonesome train. When the song ends, Daniel lowers the instrument from his mouth, and Henry props the violin beside him. Reclining on the rock, legs crossed at the ankles, he clasps his hands behind his head.

"That was beautiful," Isabel tells them.

"Let's play another one before I have to go," Daniel says. "My parents'll have my hide for bein' gone all day. I'll have to do double chores tomorrow after church, and then I'll be up all night with my studies."

"Why did you have to remind me?" Isabel groans. "I have a history assignment due Monday."

Henry blows out a noisy breath and sits up. "Would you two forget about school for a change? Ditch on Monday. Come out here with me instead."

Although it's a bad idea, Isabel is glad he invited Daniel, too. She hopes Henry is past his silly jealousy, that he'll treat Daniel as he used to, like the good friend he is.

Daniel drops the harmonica into his pocket, lifts his cap, and scratches his head. "I don't know. I'm strugglin' with mathematics as it is. Besides, if my parents found out—"

"They'd have your hide?" Henry scoffs. "Fine. Bell and I will have fun without you."

Daniel tenses, and Isabel sighs, frustrated by the return of

Henry's spiteful attitude. But her annoyance scatters like smoke in the wind when Henry's attention focuses on her. His sleepy, dark gaze makes her forgive him, makes her forget they aren't alone.

"Isn't that right, Bell?" Henry asks quietly.

Something in his eyes, in the deep, smooth tone of his voice unsettles and excites me as much as it does Isabel. She wonders when her feelings for him shifted from simple friendship to something more complex while I wonder how I can suddenly be so drawn to Henry despite the rude, dismissive way he treats my grandfather.

"She's at the top of our class," Daniel says, tugging his cap back over his eyes. "She wouldn't play hooky, would you, Isabel?"

"You're right, I couldn't," she says, but the quirk of Henry's mouth assures that he doesn't believe her any more than she believes herself. If Isabel can find a way to do so without her parents finding out, she'll spend Monday with Henry. He knows that's true, and so does she.

Henry picks up his violin and begins to play a jig. The music slowly softens Daniel's rigid brow. Grinning, he jumps off the car, grabs both of Isabel's hands, and pulls her off, too. She shrieks as they twirl around in a dizzying spin that sends Daniel's cap flying off his head. I love the strength I feel in Daniel's hands, the sound of his laughter, the light I see in his pale green eyes. Surprise ripples through me. His eyes are green! They're as green as spring grass. And the hair falling across Daniel's forehead is auburn while Henry's is a honeyed shade of blond, his narrowed eyes as blue as the sky. All around us color blooms—the field becomes yellow, the rocks russet red, the earth a dark shade of brown. Only Isabel's *clothes remain gray—or are they mine?*

I think of the gray strawberries I ate this morning when I was another girl in another world, and an intriguing possibility sifts through me. If I don't go back, will Isabel's clothes change color, too? Turn red or yellow or tangerine? I have the strongest feeling that if I were to stay in Henry's world, my other life would become the drab illusion and this one my reality. I would become *Isabel, not just listen and watch from inside her. And I would finally fit in, belong somewhere completely for the very first time. Best of all, I'd have decades ahead with my grandfather. No more standing back, helpless, watching him weaken and fade away.*

As Daniel and Isabel twirl, I look across to the bench rock, dizzy and giddy. Henry's beckoning gaze wraps around me. It seems to whisper, You can feel like this forever.

Scents of perfume and chalk, sweat and stale cigarette smoke mingle in the stuffy air of my first-period class. Mom dropped me off a few minutes ago, and I noticed that every person in the school parking lot wore black, gray, and white. "Someone must have died," I said, looking back at Mom and thinking how pretty her skin looked against the emerald green of her blouse.

She frowned and asked, "What makes you think that?"

Panic knocked the air from my lungs when I realized the color in everyone's clothing had faded; everyone's except Mom's, that is. At least that's how it looked to me. Then Bethyl Ann tapped on the van window, and I could breathe again. She wore a hot pink T-shirt with the words *Shakespeare Is My Homeboy* on the front. A pale yellow barrette held back one side of her stringy brown hair.

Feeling detached from everyone around me, I zero in now on that pink shirt and yellow barrette as I cross to the front-row desk beside her. Bethyl Ann is bent over a notebook scribbling madly. "Hey," I say, slipping into my seat.

She glances up. "Sorry. No time to talk. I had an epiphany for my story a second ago." She lowers her head and starts writing again.

Everyone is extra rowdy, since Miss Petra is out in the hall. How can they act as if nothing's different? Can't they see that the world is washing out around them? My sense of detachment intensifies. Fighting back my anxiety, I unzip my backpack on the floor at my feet while glancing around the room, hoping to see someone in color besides Bethyl Ann. Sure enough, I notice a splash of red in the very back—Tate's shirt. He lifts his hand in a semi-wave. I nod and smile a little, relieved that he hasn't transformed again to his prior stuck-up self now that we're back in school.

The bell rings. Miss Petra enters the room in a bright blue blouse and instructs us to get out our books. She shuffles through her satchel and pulls out a stack of papers and a paperback novel.

I'm taking my textbook and a spiral notebook from my backpack when Shanna strolls in nonchalantly, as if she isn't late. Ignoring the scolding look Miss Petra sends her, she walks to her desk, which is directly behind me, right next to Alison and Rooster Boy Jon Jenks.

"Quiet down, people," Miss Petra says as she walks around to the front of her desk and perches at the edge of it, the paperback book in her hand. Opening the cover, she says, "We're going to begin reading *The Bell Jar* by Sylvia

Plath for a few minutes each day."

I like Miss Petra. She makes English interesting, and she's my favorite teacher here. As she begins to read aloud, I stare at the sky blue threads woven through her blouse as if they might hold me together. Fear spirals up from my stomach to my throat. I have no idea why Miss Petra, Bethyl Ann, and Tate are the only people at school that I see in color, but I'm desperate not to lose sight of any of them; I can't let them fade away, too. If I do, I'm afraid I'll also lose myself. Completely and permanently.

"Hey, Zombie Girl."

The hiss behind me is too quiet to reach Miss Petra's ears. *Rooster Boy.* Either Shanna or Alison muffles a laugh as a tiny white tidbit of paper sails past my head. When a bit of paper strikes Bethyl Ann's ear, she looks over her shoulder, squints, and flares her nostrils. Another wad lands in her hair, and she lifts her middle finger and scratches the back of her head with it, eliciting snickers from everyone behind us.

I slink lower in my chair, hardly noticing the *ping ping ping* of paper balls against my head, neck, and back. I concentrate instead on the lilting rhythm of Miss Petra's soothing voice, and soon my thoughts drift to Henry, Daniel, and Isabel. I wonder what they're doing today. Crazy, I know. Henry is dead. Daniel is home with Mom, an old man in his eighties. If Isabel ever really existed, she's either dead or really old, too. Still, I can't stop thinking about the plans Henry made for the three of us—*us*—as if

I'm one of them. That's another thing that scares me; after last night, I'm not sure where Isabel stops and I start.

I take a chance and pull my gaze away from Miss Petra's blue blouse to look out the window. Relief sweeps through me when I see the vibrant oranges and yellows of the leaves on the trees. Questions whisper through my mind: Did Daniel skip school to spend the day with Henry and Bell? Or did Henry and Bell spend that long-ago Monday together alone? To find out, I'd have to risk stepping into the photos again. The thought of doing so makes my insides flutter like the leaves drifting down from the tree branches outside.

Why am I afraid? So convinced another visit would end differently than my prior ones? Wouldn't I come back just as easily as before? I'm not sure what triggers my return. I've never needed to use the crystal to bring me home. I just vanish . . . and here I am.

A noisy gust of wind pulls my attention beyond the window to the parking lot and the billowing American and Texas flags. *"Bell and I will have fun without you. Won't we, Bell?"*

The wind falls silent as quickly as it flared, and I hear the faint singing of a single bird, its sonorous tune jarringly familiar. My skin prickles, and my head feels as if it could drift off my shoulders and float around the room. Something inside me shifts, and all my doubts clear away. Suddenly, more than anything, I want to be in Bell's world. It fits me better than this one. I'm not as brave as

Bethyl Ann. I can't stand up to these kids and pretend that I don't care how they treat me. Maybe losing myself completely would be the best thing that ever happened in my life. I draw a calming breath. I want to be Bell. I want to experience her emotions, think her thoughts instead of my own. I want to be with my grandfather when he was young and healthy.

A tumbleweed rolls across the school lawn. A fast-food wrapper follows, then another scrap of trash and a cluster of leaves. They scatter toward the street and disappear behind a parked car. I imagine the windowsill encrusted with snow, patches of white on the yard beyond the panes. In my mind, Henry's gaze caresses me, and the touch of his hand brushes away Miss Petra's voice and every other sound except the nightingale's song and the thud of my heartbeat. I want to be with Henry even more than I want to be with Daniel . . . or Tate. This afternoon when I go home, I'll tilt the crystal until the prism of light appears. I'll wait until it stretches and consumes me. Then I'll scatter, too, like the leaves and the trash, disappear from my world and reappear in Bell's.

I glance over my shoulder at my classmates, all of them black and gray and white—their skin, their hair, their clothing. Everyone here is dimming while Henry's memories become more vivid each time I visit. Isn't that a sign that I belong there?

Facing Miss Petra again, I close my eyes, think of Henry . . . his golden hair . . . his eyes on mine. . . .

"Zombie Girl."

The nightingale falls silent in an instant. My eyes fly open. More pea-size damp paper balls ping against the back of my neck, and the real world rushes over me like a heat wave.

"Tansy Piper." Flinching, I look at Miss Petra. Her book is closed. She stands now, holding a paper out toward me and smiling. "I'd like you to read your short story to the class. Why don't you come up to the podium?"

I wait for her to say, *Unless you'd rather not.* Or even, *Would you prefer I read it for you?* Not that I want my story read at all, especially in front of this group.

Miss Petra doesn't give me an out, so I push away from my desk. The podium seems a hundred miles away. Murmurs follow me as I walk toward it. Quiet laughter. Whispers. I wish I held Henry's crystal tightly in my hand so I could disintegrate into a billion tiny particles before their eyes, become a part of the atmosphere, present but unseen. When I reach Miss Petra, I take the paper from her, then step behind the podium, glad for the barrier it provides.

I glance up and my focus is instantly drawn to Tate's red shirt at the back of the room. His eyes find mine. He smiles. To calm my nerves, I try to pretend he's Henry—he's who I need right now, not Tate. But though their features are the same, I see the differences in the way they dress, the length of their hair, the way Tate holds something back when he looks at me while Henry's emotions pour out of his eyes.

185

Though Tate gives me a nod of encouragement, I'm humiliated to have to read my story in front of him. To calm myself, I dart a look at Bethyl Ann's T-shirt, a pink beach ball drifting on a pewter sea. She gives me a thumbs-up, then flashes her patriotic braces. And just like that, every embarrassment I've ever had about Bethyl Ann's friendship evaporates. She took me under her wing, as Papa Dan used to say, no questions asked.

Drawing a breath, I begin to read my story aloud. It's about a girl who sees things others can't because they don't pay attention. She feels set apart, alone in her difference. Some people ignore the girl; others completely forget she exists. Little by little, she disappears. Despite the growing shame that presses against my chest from the inside, I read with a steady voice. *Let them laugh,* I think. *I don't care about anyone here.* Soon I'll be with Henry and Daniel.

When I finish, silence cloaks the room, and for a second, I wonder if everyone tiptoed out while I read. I look up at Tate, my heart banging against my rib cage. He's not smiling anymore. He seems sad for me and, *ohmygod,* I don't want that. I don't want anyone to feel sorry for me, especially him. I'm sure Tate knows I'm the girl in the story; everyone probably does. I quickly look away from him, see Shanna sneering. Rooster Boy studying me with a curiosity he's never shown before. Straight-A Alison blinking at me, her eyes full of . . . *something.* Something I don't want from her any more than I want Tate's sympathy. Compassion maybe? Understanding? Or is it pity again?

I turn to Miss Petra, hoping she'll end my misery. She clears her throat and steps toward the podium. "What a lovely story, Tansy," she says, smiling kindly. "Excellent work."

My face burns as I hurry to my desk. I sit just as the bell rings and the room erupts with a dozen conversations. Chair legs scrape against tile, and shoes shuffle as students rush from the room.

Miss Petra walks toward me, pausing beside my desk. "I'm sorry I didn't ask you first if you'd be comfortable sharing your story," she says. "I realize now that I should have, but it was just so wonderful it didn't occur to me that you might mind."

"It's okay," I murmur, my face still burning from embarrassment.

"Keep up the good work," she says, then returns to the front of the room.

"Tansy!" Gathering my books, I turn to Bethyl Ann. She's stuffing her spiral notebook into her book bag, her eyes wide with surprise. "Ohmygosh! Why didn't you tell me you inherited your mom's writing talent?"

I focus on her pink shirt, her yellow barrette. *She's real, she's real,* I tell myself. *Don't let go of her.* I don't understand what's going on with me. One minute I get caught up in missing my grandfather, in my feelings for Henry, and nothing else seems to matter. When that happens, I'm ready to say good-bye to this world, to become Bell and be with Henry and Daniel. The next minute, I snap out of it, and the thought of disappearing into their realm panics me. The truth is, I'm not sure if my feelings for Henry are mine or Isabel's. I barely know him. I still want to spend time with Papa Dan when he was young, but I would worry so much about the grandfather I already know and love if I was no longer here for him. And I'd miss my mom.

And then there's the not-so-little problem that I would be completely insane, locked away in a madhouse somewhere, if I let myself believe that I was living in my grandfather's past as a girl named Isabel.

Shocked to realize how mentally unhinged I've become, I murmur to Bethyl Ann, "I didn't inherit Mom's talent. But thanks for saying so."

She leans close to me and whispers, "You did super. The natives were impressed."

For some reason, her nice words clog my throat with tears. Slipping my books into my backpack, I say, "Come on," and nod at the door. "I'll walk with you to your next class."

Bethyl Ann's face turns a soft shade of pink that matches her *Shakespeare Is My Homeboy* T-shirt. "Let's go hand in hand," she says, "not one before another."

"If you're expecting me to hold your hand, you can forget it."

She giggles. "Relax. It just seemed an appropriate quote. It's from—"

"Let me guess . . ." I stand and round the desk. "It's Shakespeare."

"Right. *The Comedy of Errors.*"

I sling my backpack over my shoulder and spot Tate at the back of the room, still at his desk, watching me. He stands and starts to come over. Afraid of making an even bigger fool of myself in front of him, I hurry to leave, with Bethyl Ann chattering beside me.

"Tansy," Tate calls, and we both pause and turn. Bethyl Ann goes silent as he crosses the room. "Hey, Stinky," he says to her, stopping in front of us.

I flinch, but she just lifts her chin proudly, looks him straight in the eye, and replies, "Hey, yond Tate."

Tate blinks at her and his brows tug together before he shifts his focus to me. "I liked your story," he says.

"Thanks." I feel myself blush when I look into his eyes. Since Miss Petra has left the room, I add, "I didn't realize when I was writing it that the whole class would hear it."

"Yeah, that was sort of lame of Miss Petra to put you on the spot like that."

"She apologized," I tell him. "Not many teachers would."

After a few moments of Tate and me silently staring at each other, Bethyl Ann coughs to get my attention. I'm ashamed to admit that I forgot she was waiting beside me. "Well, I'd better go," I tell Tate.

He continues to look at me with those Tate-a-licious blue eyes of his, as Bethyl Ann would say. "See you in history," he murmurs.

I face the door, and Bethyl Ann and I start out. She makes a huffing sound, arches a brow, and says quietly, "Forever, and forever, farewell, Cassius! And good riddance, if I do say so myself."

I frown at her. "What is that supposed to mean?"

Sighing heavily, she answers, "After that nauseating display of emotion, I have a feeling you wouldn't like my explanation." Bethyl Ann doesn't give me any time to pretend I don't know what she's talking about. As if it's some big secret she and I share and nobody else should hear, she leans close to me and whispers, "You want to do some more Henry research at the library after school?"

I feel Tate's gaze warm the back of my neck and think, *Henry who?*

The last bell rings. I can't leave the drab hallways of Cedar Canyon High fast enough. Pulling my hat from my backpack and my cell phone from my purse, I hurry out of the building.

I call Mom but don't get an answer. This morning, I asked her to wait an hour after school before coming to get me. She told me to pick up Papa Dan's prescription at City Drug and she would meet me there. I hope she didn't get caught up in her work and forget.

A sense of normalcy sifts into me once I'm away from the school grounds. The world outside is like a crayon box filled with dozens of colors in varying shades. Briefly, I wonder why only my life at school has lost its hue, but at the moment, I don't really care. I'm just so glad to feel calm again.

Ignoring the wind and the stares of people I pass, I snap shot after shot as I slowly make my way toward Main

Street, my mind crammed with thoughts of Tate. Ever since he stopped me from running away after English class, the prospect of leaving this world, mentally or otherwise, to live with Henry in his surreal existence seems too disturbing to consider. I can't deny that seeing my grandfather happy and whole again might make it worthwhile to say good-bye to everything here. But could I really give up my photography? And, most of all, Mom? As mad as she makes me sometimes, I couldn't be happy without her and my camera. And now that things with Tate are starting to get interesting in a very nice way, I'm not sure I could willingly leave him behind, either.

Besides, I'm not completely certain that the desire to become Isabel was ever mine to begin with. Henry probably planted it in my subconscious. For some reason, *he* wants me to merge with Isabel—that's what I'm starting to think. Could it be that without me she doesn't exist? That she never did? Maybe she's the one whose name I should be looking for in the library's archived newspapers.

The fact that I'm even wondering about such impossibilities might be what freaks me out most of all. Becoming another person? Stepping into the past? Falling for a ghost? Get a grip, Tansy. It doesn't take an MIT graduate to figure out that Tate's the one I'm falling for. That's why I made Henry resemble him, why I'm imagining Henry's steamy, hot stares. Because I wish *Tate* would look at me that way.

Still, I can't deny that whenever the nightingale sings,

it's as if Henry takes over my thoughts, as if he controls me, beckons me to him through the bird's song. I can't seem to resist his lure.

Lunacy. I obviously do need to see a shrink. I don't want to think about it.

I keep walking, pushing all my worries aside, emptying my head by concentrating on thoughts of Tate and the real-life images on the other side of the camera lens. For a while, it works. I'm caught up in the pattern of sunlight and shadow on a lawn. A squirrel nibbling a pecan. A spiderweb stretched across the broken windshield of a rusty truck.

Time passes too quickly. I make my way down a side street, headed for City Drug on the corner. As I near Main, I see someone leaning against the side of the building, a girl with her arms crossed and her head bent down. I'm almost alongside her when I realize it's Alison and that she's crying. Now that she's away from the school, I see her in color. Her shorts are turquoise blue, her sleeveless shirt yellow and white. I stop abruptly, hoping to turn and get out of there before she spots me, but it's too late. Alison looks up.

Backing up a step, I say, "I'm sorry." What I'm apologizing for is a mystery to me. Her tear-ravaged face just gets to me, that's all. As much as I don't like the girl, I also don't like seeing anyone so upset. I start to hurry past her, but then she makes a sobbing sound and I stop again. "Do you need me to get someone for you?" I ask.

Alison shakes her head. "No, it's okay. It's just—" Her

face scrunches up. "I made a C minus on my algebra test and . . ."

Her words trail away along with my compassion. I'm pretty sure she can tell by my expression that I think a C– is a pretty lame reason to have a meltdown on the street. Poor, perfect Alison, stripped of her straight-A title. Boo-hoo. She'd never survive what I've been going through.

She tilts her head defensively. "I just don't know how to tell my parents. Especially my mom," she says in a quavering voice. "Cs don't merit scholarships, you know? And algebra this year . . . I'm just not getting it."

Wow. Does every single parent in this town have some sort of perverted obsession about their kid earning a scholarship? I have no idea what to say to Alison, so I don't say anything. I just stare at her with my mouth hanging open.

"I saw you the other day at lunch," she says, swiping at her eyes with the back of her hand. "When I was in the alley with—" Her eyes dart to her feet, then up at me again. "He's not what you think."

News flash, Alison: I haven't wasted a second thinking about your boyfriend. I clench my jaw to hold back that sarcastic reply. Why does she think she knows what I think? Alison Summers just can't seem to stop judging me, for some reason.

"I don't know how I'd explain him to my parents, though," she continues, her voice barely more than a whisper. "You know . . . if they found out somehow."

So she did see me snap their picture. And now she's afraid I'll rat her out or blackmail her. "Don't worry about it," I mutter.

"But I do—"

"Alison!" a woman calls from the front of the building in a frantic, strained voice. "Alison, where are you?"

"I'm here, Mom!" Alison yells back, quickly wiping more tears from her face. "I'm coming." She shoves a strand of pale blond hair over her shoulder, takes a couple of measured breaths, then steps away from the wall. Hurrying around it to the front of City Drug, she leaves me alone on the side street.

I wait a second before walking to the front corner of the building and looking down the sidewalk. Alison and her mother stand outside the entrance to City Drug. They talk a moment before heading toward a blue Suburban parked at the curb. "Don't scare me like that again, honey," I hear her mom say. "You said you'd wait in the car."

"I was just talking to a friend," Alison answers.

A friend? I huff a humorless laugh as I walk to the pharmacy door, open it, and step inside. Bethyl Ann's reluctance to talk to me about Alison still puzzles me. So does her bizarre loyalty to a girl who rarely says more than hello to her each day.

J. B. stands behind the prescription counter at the rear of the store, using his shoulder to hold the phone to his ear while he types into a computer. Mary Jane waddles around from behind the register. "Hey, your grandfather's medicine is ready," she says. "Your mom called and said you'd be by. I'll get it." She makes her way slowly toward J. B., walking as if she has a watermelon between her knees.

"Mary Jane!" a woman calls from the cosmetic aisle. "Could you help me find—"

"Hold your horses, Rita," Mary Jane interrupts the woman. "Geez Louise, there's only one of me." She finally reaches J. B. and he hands her a sack. Mary Jane turns around and duckwalks toward me. Pushing through a low, swinging gate, she returns to the register. "You want this on your mother's account?" she asks.

"I'll pay." I pull Mom's cash from my pocket and count out the bills.

"*Whoa*," Mary Jane says. Easing onto a stool, she cradles her belly. "This kid's determined to rearrange my intestines, then kick them to kingdom come." She nods me over. "Come feel this."

"That's okay." Touching her stomach seems too personal. Like something only a friend would do.

"No, really. Come here. Have you ever felt a baby kick?" I shake my head, and she says, "Well, now's your chance."

The swinging gate squeaks as I push through. Stuffing the cash back into my pocket, I lower my backpack and camera to the floor behind the counter.

Mary Jane reaches for my hand. "Here." She presses my fingers beneath her rib cage. Her stomach is hard and tight, like a rubber ball, not mushy and soft, like I expected. "Now . . . wait just a sec," she murmurs.

I flinch when something firm pushes against my fingertips then rolls toward Mary Jane's navel, which protrudes through her shirt like a bony, clenched knuckle. "Oh . . . wow," I whisper. "That's weird. I can actually *see* it."

"Kind of reminds you of that movie *Alien*, doesn't it?" She laughs then burps. "Excuse me. Indigestion."

A grin twitches my lips. I pull back my hand. "Thanks for letting me feel it."

"Anytime."

I pick up my backpack and push through the swinging gate, then take the cash from my pocket again. As I'm handing it to her, an idea strikes me. Before I can change my mind, I unzip my backpack and remove the large manila envelope of photographs I brought with me to school today to show Bethyl Ann. Shuffling through them, I find the one of Mary Jane with her kid's class. "Here," I say, drawing my lower lip between my teeth.

"Oh!" The tension in her face melts away. "Did you take this?"

"I, uh, hope that's okay," I stammer, startled by her reaction. "You looked so . . . I don't know." *Joyful.* That's how Mom described Mary Jane's expression in the photographs with the elementary school children. It's the right word, but I'm too embarrassed to say it.

"Look at me!" Mary Jane sounds thrilled and amazed. "I actually look *happy*."

J. B. comes around the corner and joins her. "You? Happy? Now that's something I've got to see." He nods at me. "Afternoon, Tansy."

"Hi."

Mary Jane chuckles. "I look like a circus tent."

"More like a hot-air balloon." The words slip from between my lips before I can stop them. I slap a palm over my mouth and mutter, "I'm sorry. I didn't mean . . . I meant you look joyful. Like a hot-air balloon. I—"

"It's okay." Mary Jane giggles and punches J. B.'s arm since he's laughing, too. "I do look like a hot-air balloon."

"And joyful," J. B. adds. "I never thought I'd see the day." He looks up from the picture and into my eyes. "So your mother isn't the only talented gal in the family. I knew you were a photographer, I just never guessed you were a pro, as young as you are."

"Thank you." Emotion gathers in my chest like a bank of storm clouds. His compliment makes me feel proud and awkward at once. "I've been doing it a really long time. My, um, grandfather, he bought my first camera for me when I was really young."

"Could I have a copy of this?" Mary Jane asks, holding up the picture.

"Keep it. I have another that's almost identical," I tell her.

"Thanks, Tansy. I really love it." Mary Jane lays the photo down and slides off the stool. "I'd better go help Rita." She pushes through the swinging door.

J. B. nods toward the envelope I left open on the counter with a few of the other photos sticking out of it. "May I take a look?"

"Sure."

J. B. studies another shot of Mary Jane with the school kids, then moves on to the picture of Bethyl Ann and Hamlet. "Interesting," he says while looking at Rooster Boy in a rare serious moment on the sidelines of the football field after school, his bobcat head off as he waves to an old woman on the sidelines—his grandmother, according to Bethyl Ann. The last shot is of Alison at cheerleading practice, her head turned away from the other girls, her eyes uncertain and expectant, like she's watching for someone out of the camera's range. She looks as unsure of herself as I feel 99 percent of the time. I feel a sudden tug of compassion for her that catches me off guard.

"These are really good, Tansy." J. B. glances up from the shot of Alison, and I see a flicker of sadness in his eyes that stirs my curiosity even more about Bethyl Ann's loyalty toward her. "You've caught them all at their best," he adds as he gathers the photos together. "Folks around here tend to be a bit cautious when it comes to anything new. Eventually they tend to come around, though. Cedar Canyon's full of good people. They're loyal as can be once you get to know them."

I study my fingernails, hoping he won't see that my face is twisting into the repulsive crybaby face I hate so much. I get what J. B. is trying to tell me, but he doesn't understand. Being the new girl all the time isn't easy. I've moved so much that it's hard for me to let people in. And the truth is, I guess I'm not very different from everyone else in town, at least on the inside. I mean, it took me a while to accept Bethyl Ann.

I wish I could rewind my life, go back to my first day here, and give Cedar Canyon a chance. I didn't want to risk liking the town or anyone in it. I just wanted to force Mom to keep her word and move us back to San Francisco. Then, after finding out about Hailey and Colin, I was sure I'd only wind up hurt again if I tried to make friends; I'm still afraid of that. And now it seems too late to try to start over with the people here. I wouldn't know how to begin, and the very thought of it scares me, anyway.

I look up and see J. B. brush a finger along the edge of Alison's picture on top of the stack. "Have you shown this to her?" he asks.

I shake my head.

"Maybe you should. I bet she'd like it." He slips the photograph into the envelope with the others, then hands it to me. "I bet they all would—everyone you took a picture of. They'd love seeing your work."

I leave the pharmacy telling myself I should put Henry's things back in the cellar and try to straighten myself out, face what's happening to Papa Dan, and make my life here work. I wish that could be as easy as it sounds.

As I pause at the curb to wait for Mom, a breeze sweeps over me with just enough chill in it to scatter goose bumps up my arms. I close my eyes, imagine a whisper on that thin, cool wisp of air . . . *Listen . . . be patient.* . . .

The earth seems to tilt, but I know I'm only thrown off-kilter by the tug of Henry's words. Until I visit the world inside the photographs—*his* world—one more time, how can I make any decisions about my future? He's trying to tell me something. How can I give up on him?

14

"Stay with me longer, Bell. I'm not ready for you to go."

I'm with Henry again as Isabel, climbing the sloping trail that leads out of the canyon bordering his father's property. Sunshine warms the winter day. We've spent most of it outside, walking, picnicking, and sitting beneath bare-branched trees while Henry played his violin.

"I can't stay." Avoiding his gaze, Isabel remains focused on the path ahead and the scenery around us. With each step she takes, more and more colors appear to me like magic. It's as if she pushes a giant paintbrush in front of us, streaking ribbons of rust, dusty pink, and milk chocolate across the canyon wall. Throughout the day, sounds have intensified: wind-rattled tree limbs, the honks of geese flying high overhead, an occasional rustle of an animal in the brush.

"You can't stay, or you won't?" Henry asks.

"Do you realize the trouble I'll be in if Mama and Papa hear that I wasn't in school today? I shouldn't have done this."

Isabel can't stop fretting over the consequences she's bound to face for her behavior. This morning she gave her friend Louise a note to take to the teacher, saying that she was sick. She forged her mother's signature on the note, and it still stuns her to think she did something so dishonest and bold. Lately, Henry has that effect on her.

She glances across at him, and Henry's smug grin assures me he knows that, despite her worries, Isabel doesn't really regret their stolen time alone; he's aware of the power he has over her—or is it me that he's smiling at in that self-satisfied way? Me who he's happy to be maneuvering like a character in a video game?

Isabel swats his arm. "Don't look at me like that! If Miss Lee calls the house to check on me, I want to be home to catch the phone before my mother does."

"Ah," he says, teasing her with his narrowed gaze. "Aren't you the sneaky one. Pulling the wool over your sweet mother's eyes."

"Stop it. I feel bad enough as it is. But it's not only that, Henry. I'll have points deducted on my report for turning it in late. And I can't even imagine what Daniel must think of me for skipping school."

"Daniel." He spits the name. "He's the real problem, isn't he?" Angry slashes of red slice Henry's cheekbones.

Alarmed by how quickly his lighthearted mood turned to anger, Isabel peers down at the trail again. Before my eyes, with each touch of her boots gray winter grass becomes amber and brown. "Daniel a problem? What are you talking about?"

"You're always so worried about him. Poor Daniel. What about Daniel?" he mimics in a mocking tone. "I don't want him around all the time. Not anymore. He's jealous of us."

Isabel's laugh is short and baffled. "Daniel's not jealous. He's our friend. He worships you and, lately, you treat him terribly."

"Don't be naive." Scowling, Henry stops walking and sets the basket and his violin case on the trail beside him. "Daniel doesn't like it one bit that you and I are becoming closer." He grasps Isabel's arms, and I feel his fingertips press into her flesh. "I won't let him come between us, Bell. Do you understand?"

She twists free of his hold and touches his cheek. "Daniel isn't jealous. He doesn't feel about me the way—" Isabel lowers her eyes.

"Say it." Henry lifts her chin with his fingertips, forcing her to look at him—forcing me to.

"Daniel doesn't feel about me the way you and I feel about each other," she whispers, and I feel the flutter of her pulse as if it's my own as Henry's lips curve into a smile. She probes her mind for a safer topic, as unnerved by the intense way he searches her eyes as I am. "You shouldn't skip school, either," Isabel says weakly.

"Don't change the subject, Bell. What are you so afraid of?"

Everything, she thinks. She is afraid of the unfamiliar emotions strumming inside her, afraid if she gives in to them something will go wrong and she'll not only lose Henry's love, she'll ruin their friendship, too. Still, she smiles and tells him, "I'm not afraid of anything. You're the one who's avoiding questions."

Henry's grin slides off his face. He lowers his hand. "You know why I don't like to go to school. I might as well be a leper there."

"They just don't understand you."

"And you do?"

"Of course I do. Better than anyone." Isabel tilts her head, starts walking again, headed for the wagon bridge that looms ahead. She glances back at Henry, and sees him grabbing the basket and his violin case. "You're different than everyone else," she calls to him as he hurries to catch up to her. "They're used to the same old bores, day in, day out."

"You mean themselves?" They both laugh. "The fact that I'm different is why most people avoid me."

"They haven't given you a chance. Maybe if I talked to them—"

"I've lived here my entire life, Bell. They've had plenty of opportunities. The problem is, they're afraid of me."

"Henry . . ."

"They are." He shrugs. "They can rest easy. I've decided to quit school."

"No!" She pauses and grabs his arm, stopping him, too. "You can't quit now. You'll graduate soon. And what about college?"

"It doesn't matter." Pulling away, he continues on up the trail.

"But it does!" Isabel exclaims, following after him. "If the others knew you the way Daniel and I do, they'd treat you better." An idea forms in her mind—one that I wish I could make her think twice about before mentioning it to Henry. If she brings it up, she'll be setting something in motion she might not be able to stop. She takes a breath, then blurts out the words before I can stop her—if I even could; I'm still not sure I have any control over Isabel's actions. "Go with me to the Winter Dance tonight, Henry," she says. "Spend some time with everyone. I was planning to go alone, but—" She smiles up at him, thrilled with the proposal now that it's out. "Be my date. Daniel is taking Louise. It'll be fun."

"You mean Daniel didn't ask you?" When Isabel refuses to take his bait and engage in another quarrel about Daniel, he says, "Your father won't let you leave the house with me. He doesn't trust me around his little girl." Henry smirks and arches a brow. "I can't imagine why, can you?"

I feel the warmth of Isabel's blush. "Papa doesn't have to know. I'll meet you there. Daniel already said he would come out to give me a ride after he picks up Louise."

"So he's taking both of you?" Henry's smug expression turns into a scowl. "Daniel is becoming quite the Casanova."

"Louise is his date. I'm only tagging along."

"Once your folks discover you played hooky today, I doubt they'll let you go at all. Even with do-gooder Daniel."

"If I hurry home, they might not find out. I can grab the phone if Miss Lee calls to check on me. She'll believe what I say; I know she will. I've never given her any reason to doubt me before."

At the top of the trail, Isabel and Henry pause to catch their breath. Henry sets the basket and violin case at his feet then walks over and steps onto the wooden planks of the bridge. With a quick glance back at Isabel, he grasps the narrow steel railing with both hands and pushes himself up until his feet are on top of it. Crouched down and gripping the rail, he peers into the deep, craggy canyon below.

"Henry! Get down! You'll fall!" Isabel's panic is like an electrical shock. She rushes over to the bridge's arched entrance, stopping short of stepping onto the floor, afraid the touch of her foot might create a ripple that would send him tumbling over the side.

Henry turns and looks back at her, his face unconcerned. "Would you even care?" He slowly stands, lifts his arms out wide, balancing precariously.

"Why would you ask me such a terrible question?" she shrieks. "Of course I'd care. Now get down. Please!"

Henry's mask of indifference slips, and I see the anguish in his eyes. "I'm so lonely when we're apart. I miss you," he says, his voice a quiet rasp.

"I know," she whispers. "I feel the same way."

Crouching again, Henry takes hold of the railing and hops down onto the bridge's wooden planks. He crosses to her. "Do you?" he asks, reaching for her arm.

"You know I do."

I feel the truth in Isabel's words. I understand her need to be with him. Whenever I return to my own world, I almost ache to be with Henry again. Or is that only a leftover remnant of Isabel's emotions? Her yearnings? Which are hers and which are mine and where is the division?

"Your parents treat you like a little girl," Henry says, pulling her into his arms. He lifts one hand to her cheek, presses his other hand against the small of her back. I smell the starch in his shirt, feel his suspenders, as Isabel's palms skim across his shoulders. Henry's lips brush hers . . . once . . . twice. So soft, so warm, his kiss. His lips taste like the fresh mint Miss Ivy put in their picnic tea. Isabel wants the kiss to go on and on and on . . . so do I.

But then Henry's head shifts; his mouth presses harder; he pushes against her spine too tightly. Apprehension pricks my desire like a needle, and Isabel pulls her head back quickly, a startled look in her eyes.

"Come to my house tonight after the dance when your folks are asleep," he murmurs.

"Your house? But Miss Ivy—"

"She sleeps like the dead."

Isabel tries to step out of his embrace, but the pressure of Henry's grip intensifies. "I'm afraid," she whispers. "What are we doing?"

"Don't be afraid. Not with me. I love you."

"Of course you do." Tears fill her eyes. "We're friends."

"Did that kiss feel friendly, Bell?"

Isabel and I both know what he's implying and it's true. She and Henry have moved beyond friendship. There's no going back to the way things were. But as drawn as she is toward their new relationship, she mourns the loss of what they've left behind. Their love feels exciting, deliciously dangerous, but their friendship was safe and comforting, and Isabel knew what to expect.

As if Henry reads her mind, he says, "Things change, Bell." He reaches into his coat pocket and pulls out a necklace—a crystal teardrop pendant on a long gold chain. "I bought this for you." He leans back, places the chain around her neck, hooks the clasp, and says in a tender voice, "When the crystal catches the light, it shines like your eyes."

"Henry . . . it's lovely. Thank you." She strokes the cool, smooth pendant with her fingertip and I recognize the cut of the glass; I know the feel of it by heart, the power of its light. "But I don't have anything for you," she says quietly.

"You gave me the leather journal."

"That was a birthday gift. I want to give you something—"

"It doesn't matter. I'm crazy about it. I haven't written in it yet, but I will. I'm waiting until I have the perfect poem. One that will describe just how beautiful you are."

"I'm not beautiful."

"You're all the more so because you don't know it." He caresses her cheek. "You're all that matters to me, Bell. You're all I have. Without you, I'm alone. I'm nothing."

She turns her mouth into his palm, murmurs, "Please don't say that. It isn't true." As she pulls back, Isabel glimpses two thin red crisscrossed scars just above his wrist and gasps. *The rumors about Henry slap her in the face—slap me. And in that instant, my fear of Henry overrides my other feelings for him. If he's not afraid to hurt himself, would he hurt Isabel, too? Would he hurt me?*

Henry jerks his hand away and tugs his sleeve down as Isabel lifts her gaze to his. She grasps for a reason other than the obvious to explain what she saw. But though his cuff covers the physical evidence, he can't hide the truth—or the pain—in his eyes.

Henry's mouth curves up at one corner. He lifts his chin, defiant. "Will you come to the house tonight, Bell?"

"Oh, Henry . . ." She hesitates, then quietly concedes. "I will, if you'll meet me at the dance. Afterward, I'll go home then slip across to your house after Mama and Papa go to bed."

Alarm shoots through my thoughts. I want to tell her not to do it, but would she hear? She saw his wrist; she knows that he's disturbed, that his mind isn't right. She senses that his obsession with her is spiraling out of control. But Isabel's thoughts tell me that she isn't worried about herself, only Henry. She hopes if she goes to him, maybe then he'll tell her what troubles him so. Maybe then she can help him.

"All right, I'll go to that silly dance," Henry says. "But only if you'll let me take you. Have Daniel drive you over."

"Mama and Papa might see his car at your house."

"Then tell Daniel to bring you here to the bridge. I'll be waiting with Father's car."

Don't, Isabel, I whisper silently. Why won't Henry just ride in Daniel's car with the rest of you? Why is it so important to him that the two of you go alone? But if my warning gets through to her, she ignores it. Isabel presses her lips together, then looks away from Henry. "Daniel won't want to do it," she says.

"Convince him." Henry leans closer to kiss her again, but before their lips touch, he tenses and steps back, muttering, "Speak of the devil."

Isabel turns to see Daniel approaching, hands jammed into his coat pockets, his shoulders hunched, his face pale and tight. There's a strange look in his eyes. Suspicion, perhaps. Possibly disapproval. Worry, for certain.

Worry for her.

I jerk awake and know immediately I overslept. I want to stay in bed all day, my head tucked under the pillow to shut out the light. I'm so tired, I feel as if I haven't slept at all. Was it a dream? Or did I step into a memory last night? Will those questions ever be answered? I remember sitting in the turret, holding the crystal and photograph, the shimmer of light that grew and enveloped me. As before, it was all so real. So confusing.

Maybe I should roll onto my side, pull the covers over my eyes. I doubt Mom will notice if I don't get up and go to school. She's at the point in her book where she's as obsessed with the story as I am with Henry; in a way, she's not even here. She's as lost to me as Papa Dan is.

I stare up at the ceiling. Papa Dan always understood me. Mom tries, but my grandfather just seemed to know what I was feeling: my loneliness whenever we moved; how hard it is to fit into a new place. Having my grandfather with me made facing everything so much easier. Without him, I feel so lost and scared. So alone.

You're all I have. Without you, I'm alone.

The same words Henry spoke to Bell. Or did he speak them to me? Are we the same person? Was I Isabel in another life? Another time? She loves Henry, but is she wary of him in spite of her love? Or is that distrust only mine? I know one thing for sure: Whatever it is that haunts Henry's eyes is deeper than loneliness. More desperate. Doesn't Isabel see that, too? At first, I knew how to separate our feelings, our thoughts. I knew which were mine alone and which were hers. They aren't so easy to tell apart anymore. If I became Isabel and didn't come back here, could I save her from Henry's obsession? Could I save myself?

Uncertainty grips me as tightly as Henry's hands gripped Isabel when they stood on the bridge overlooking the canyon. As distrustful as I am of him, I understand his need for Bell. He was as isolated as I am out here at this house, in town, at school, in a crowd of people, most of whom didn't care to know him at all. As much as I'm starting to like Tate, I don't identify with him like I do with Henry. With each new poem of Henry's that I read, I'm more certain than ever that he knows my mind, as impossible as that sounds. Decades separate us, but he still knows me. Henry and I are the same in so many ways. We've never belonged anywhere; we've always been outsiders. Maybe we need each other, too.

I think of the red scars on his wrist and feel a twist of fear for both Henry and Bell. Maybe I could save them both.

The thought jolts me; I'm afraid of what it means. Henry's world is becoming too real to me, with color, movement, and sound. While this world, the real one . . . I scan my room. Last night, before I closed my eyes, the walls were pale blue. Now they're white.

I sit up, hug myself, and feel the muscles in my upper arms trembling. *Not here, too,* I think. Not at home, my only safe place. Other than the strawberries at breakfast day before yesterday, everything has stayed in color here. It's only at school that I see things in black-and-white.

Schizophrenia. The word escapes that hidden place in my mind where I locked it away the last time it taunted me. I try to push it back, but it's grown too strong; it glares at me, huge and hideous, refusing to be ignored anymore. Papa Dan would tell me to face it, find out what it means. He used to say that understanding a problem helps you conquer your fear of it. I want to believe that, but as much as I trust Papa Dan, I'm not so sure it's always true. There's no cure for insanity, is there? Maybe I'll go to the school library, look up the disease, see if the symptoms match what I'm experiencing. But if they do, how will that make me feel any better?

Drawing my knees to my chest beneath the covers, I whisper, "I'm okay . . . I'm okay." There must be another reason that will explain what's happening to me. One that makes sense. One that doesn't include ghosts, time warps, or anything else that doesn't exist. One that won't prove I'm going nuts. All I have to do is talk to someone. Take a chance again. I consider telling Mom, but I know I'd end up in a doctor's office in no time flat, and I'm not ready for that. Tate? Not a good idea, either. Our friendship still feels too new and fragile for me to start dumping my problems on him. I'm afraid of what he'll think, and I don't want to scare him away. That leaves Bethyl Ann. Despite her horrible social skills, she's megasmart in every other way. Plus, other than Mom, I trust her more than anyone else, and she wouldn't judge me. As much as she loves horror novels, she'd probably be psyched about the possibility that her one and only friend might be going insane.

I climb out of bed and dress, then go up to the turret, where I take the crystal and put it into my backpack. This afternoon, I'll shop for a chain so I can wear the pendant around my neck like Bell did. Somehow having it close makes me feel safer, as weird as that is.

I find Mom on the front porch with Papa Dan. He's in the swing, and she's in a patio chair, tapping away on her laptop. She says I can take the van to school this morning; she and Papa Dan aren't going anywhere today. I go back inside for the keys, then tell Mom good-bye and cross to my grandfather, where he sits in the creaking swing, whistling quietly as he stares into the distance. A chill scatters across my skin when I recognize the slow, sad tune. It's the same one he and Henry played for Bell a long time ago, the same one the nightingale sings each night outside my window. Or am I imagining that, too?

Papa Dan's round glasses magnify his eyes. I kiss his cheek and ask, "Did you sleep better last night?" He pats my arm—a good sign that he's more alert this morning. "I hope you have a good day," I tell him. "I love you, Papa Dan. Good-bye."

"'Bye," he echoes in a weak voice as I start down the steps.

In the van, I sit for a minute and watch Papa Dan through the windshield. Mom has her head down, concentrating on her work; she doesn't notice that I haven't left. My grandfather has become a shadow of the big, strong man that I once knew—a shadow of the man he was only a month ago.

My eyes burn as I finally back out of the driveway. The house towers in front of me—I study it, from the turret all the way down to the bottom porch step. Even with the fresh white paint and the new black shutters the Dilworth brothers put on, it seems to brood, as if the secrets it shelters have infected every plank of wood, each pane of glass.

The final bell rings as I pull into a parking space at Cedar Canyon High. I run to the building and open the door to a monochrome movie. I break out in a cold sweat, shivering uncontrollably. They're fading . . . everyone; am I fading, too? Now I understand why I need the crystal near me. Reality is becoming a bad dream and I feel trapped inside it; that tiny teardrop in my backpack might be my only escape. Or is it a crystal bridge into another sort of nightmare? I imagine it shimmering inside my pack and feel an overwhelming urge to take it out.

A wave of dizziness washes over me, my vision narrows, and suddenly I'm sure I'm drowning. Planting a hand against the wall, I dip my chin to my chest and try to breathe. Someone touches my shoulder, but I don't look up. "Go away," I choke out. "I'm okay." I don't want anyone to see me like this. I need to get a grip.

Keeping my head down, I manage to draw several deep breaths of air, and when I feel steadier I walk down the hallway toward my homeroom. As I approach the girls' restroom, I feel strangely pulled to go inside, to take out the crystal and feel its weight in my hand. I push on past, terrified of the irresistible need to give in to the urge.

Mrs. Tilby faces the blackboard at the front of the class. I slip in without her noticing and take my place next to Beer-for-Breakfast Shanna, across from Rooster Boy. And Tate. I can't look at him. What if he asked me something? How would I answer him? I don't trust my voice to work.

Taking another deep breath, I glance up, and find him squinting at me with a worried expression on his face. He mouths, *You okay?* I nod and dart my gaze away. I'm going to ruin everything with him. I don't even know why I care. Isn't Henry the one I want to be with now? Or is that Isabel thinking through me? Ohmygod, I can't think straight. I don't know what I want anymore. I don't even know who I am.

I'm reaching into my backpack for a book, and my fingers brush across the smooth crystal. A tingle shoots up my arm. Startled, I jerk my hand back. The glass, usually so cool, was warm—almost hot. I fumble for the book, find it, pull it out, then open the cover and stare down at the page. More than anything, I want to get out of here, go to the restroom, escape.

A few minutes later, the first-period bell rings. I gather the book and my backpack, push away from the table, and hurry toward the door, where I slam, face-first, into Tate's back. The book falls from my hand and smacks the floor between our feet.

"Whoa," Tate says with a sharp laugh, turning to face me. He backs up and searches my eyes. "You in a hurry to get somewhere?"

I stare up into his face, so like Henry's. *Look at me like he does,* I think. *Give me a reason to want to stay here, to hang onto my sanity.* But I see a hesitance in Tate's eyes that I've never seen in Henry's. And I realize at once that, for some reason, Tate is as unsure of me as I am of him, as afraid to get too close.

"I'm sorry," I say, and stoop at the same time he does to grab the book. All I can think about is the crystal, the envelope of photographs in my backpack, an empty stall in the girls' restroom three doors down. I am in a hurry, Tate. I'm in a hurry to get to Bell's world, where I can breathe again. I can almost feel Henry's fingertips digging into the flesh of my arm and see the intense blue shine of his eyes.

Should I be running away from him instead? Is he causing everything here at school to fade? Trying to frighten me away from here? Trying to draw me back to him? If so, it's working. But if I go, what else will fade when I return? If I return. What if Henry won't let me?

I look up into Tate's eyes again. They're blue, not gray. Vivid and bright. A lifeline. I don't look away.

"What's wrong?" he asks.

"Nothing," I lie, but I can't stop trembling.

He lifts my book from the floor and hands it to me. We both stand. Tate's gaze flicks away, then back to me, wary. "You seem—I don't know. Like you're mad at me or something."

"I'm just having a weird morning." Like you wouldn't believe.

"Why did you tell me to go away before class?"

"I didn't."

"You did. Out in the hall. You looked like you were freaking out."

I'm mortified to realize that he was the person who touched my shoulder. "Sorry about that. I sort of had a bad night."

Tate laughs a little. "All those creaks in the Peterson house kept you up, huh?" When I don't respond, he adds, "I heard that a lot of their old stuff is still stored out there."

"Yeah, they left some things," I answer, still trying to calm down.

He tilts his head. "You find anything interesting?"

Thinking of Henry's treasures, I shrug. "Just an old velvet chair and a table I put in my darkroom."

"You have your own darkroom?"

I nod. "In the turret."

"Sweet." He hesitates, then says, "I was wondering . . . you want to have lunch with me today?"

I do want to go to lunch with Tate, almost more than anything. Almost. I'm more anxious to talk to Bethyl Ann, to tell her what's been happening to me ever since I moved here. Now that I've made the decision to confide in her, unloading the two-ton weight I've been carrying around on my own for so long feels too urgent to postpone, like I'll get crushed if I put it off even one more day. "I have something I have to do at lunch," I say.

Tate's eyes shift past me. "Okay. No big deal." I see him shutting down, shutting me out. He calls to a guy down the hall to "wait up," then mutters to me, "See ya later," and takes off like he can't get away from me fast enough.

Stupid, Tansy. Stupid, stupid, stupid. Why didn't I say I'd like to go to lunch with him another time? Thank him for asking? Something to let him know I wasn't just brushing him off? I watch Tate weave through the people in the hallway, wishing I had the nerve to catch up to him, to explain, to walk with him to our English class. But I can't bring myself to do it. So as kids rush by me in the hall, I stand alone, wanting more than anything to duck into the restroom, close myself in a stall, and take a trip into Henry's world on the crystal's luminous beam.

15

At noon, Bethyl Ann and I sit on the stadium bleachers eating our sack lunches while Hamlet pants at our feet. He waits patiently for our crumbs to fall, his tail thumping out a spastic rhythm on the ground. I drop a few on purpose while mentally rehearsing the best way to tell Bethyl Ann that I have the hots for a guy who's been dead for more than seventy years. I don't know why I'm so antsy. She'll probably just spout off dialogue from a Shakespeare play that won't make any sense at all.

"Did you see Jade Malloy in the hall this morning before homeroom?" Bethyl Ann asks. When I shake my head, she says, "What a doofus. She had a Britney Spears moment and shaved off all her hair. Mama says she does outrageous things to get attention."

"Beth . . ." Unable to concentrate on her chatter, I fold my sack and slant her a look. "Do you believe in supernatural stuff?"

"Like what, for instance?" She pulls a toothpick from

the brown paper bag and goes to work on a chunk of apple that's stuck in her braces.

I take a sip of my soft drink, trying to appear nonchalant. "Hauntings . . . time travel . . . possession. Stuff like that."

"Ohmygosh!" Bethyl Ann lowers the toothpick. The bleachers squeak as she bounces up and down. "Your house *is* haunted. I knew it! It's Henry Peterson, isn't it?"

"*Shhh.*" I look around. "This has to be our secret, okay? You have to promise. I don't want anyone else knowing I even brought this up."

She nods enthusiastically. "Mum's the word. The natives shall remain clueless. Now tell me everything! Don't leave out one tiny iota. Do you think the house has a place memory, or do you think it's an intelligent haunting?"

Wow. She's not only a Shakespeare geek, she's a ghost geek, too. "What's the difference?" I ask.

"Don't you watch *Psychic Detectives*? Or the Syfy channel or—"

"No. I don't watch any of that."

"A place memory is like a tape playing the same thing over and over again. The ghosts are unaware of you," she explains. "But if it's an intelligent haunting, the ghosts are trying to contact you for some reason."

"I don't know. I mean, I'm not sure I even believe in ghosts."

"But you said—"

"It's confusing." Hamlet nudges my hand until I pat his cold nose. "Things have happened I can't explain."

"Like what?" She leans toward me and whispers, "I'll keep it a secret, I promise."

Focusing on Bethyl Ann's face, I take the plunge. "I see things sometimes," I say quickly. "And hear things. Things that my mom doesn't see or hear."

"Oh. My. *Gosh*." Her eyes widen more and more with each word. "What about now?" she whispers, glancing around. "I mean, do you see something right this minute?"

I shake my head. "It usually only happens when I'm looking through the camera viewfinder." I take a deep breath to steady the fluttery feeling inside me. "On the mornings I'm not at school, I hear a bell over at the Quattlebaums' farm at eight fifteen, and when I look out the window I see a man shoveling snow. A big black dog runs up to him. The same thing happens every time."

"But it's too warm for snow."

"Exactly. And the Quattlebaums don't have a dog."

"Wow." She puts the baggie of apple slices into her sack. "That's trippy."

"I know. At first, I thought I must be dreaming, but one night I woke up and—" I hesitate. *Can* I trust her? What if she tells someone in school? It wouldn't be long before the rumor spread that I'm certifiable. She might even tell her parents or Mom.

"Don't stop now!" Bethyl Ann shrieks. "What happened? You're *torturing* me." Before I can answer, her gaze darts toward the tennis courts. "Get thee to a nunnery. Look who's coming," she mumbles. "The ever-brooding Cassius himself. Or considering the gushy way you two look at each other of late, maybe I should start calling him Romeo."

"*Shhh,*" I hiss, when I see Tate approaching the bleachers.

She waves at him, and calls, "Welcome, Cassius!"

"Hey, Stinky." He pauses in front of us. "My name's Tate, by the way."

I sigh heavily. "And *hers* is *Beth.*"

Looking sheepish, Tate shoves his hands into his pockets. "I thought it was Bethyl Ann."

"Then why did you call her Stinky?"

Bethyl Ann grins. "Yes, do tell, Cassius. Why did you?"

"Habit, I guess. I'm sorry," he mumbles. "I didn't mean anything by it."

"No worries, Cassius. And neither do I. Mean anything by calling you Cassius, that is." Bethyl Ann looks smug.

Tate glances at me, then down at his shoes. He gently kicks the edge of the bleachers, and when he looks up again, our eyes meet and hold.

Bethyl Ann claps her hands together. "Well . . . that's my cue to exit stage right."

Anxiety shoots through me at the thought of her leaving me alone with Tate. I'm embarrassed by the way I acted this morning, and I feel bad about turning down his lunch invitation. If Bethyl Ann leaves, I'll feel obligated to explain myself. Besides, now that I've started telling her about Henry, I want to finish. It's a relief to talk to someone about everything that's been happening. "You don't have to go," I blurt out.

"Au contraire, Tansy Piper," she says. "A cue is a cue."

Tate's brow furrows as he watches her and Hamlet walk away. At the center of the tennis court, Bethyl Ann stops and tosses her empty plastic soda bottle for the dog to retrieve. I give her my full attention so I won't have to look at Tate.

After a dozen silent seconds, I say, "I guess it's my turn to apologize to you now. This morning . . ." I look up at him. "I'm sorry I acted so weird. You know how you said you've been going through some stuff?"

His shoulders lift. "Yeah."

"Well, so have I. I didn't mean to blow you off about lunch. I needed to talk to Bethyl Ann about something important, that's all."

"Not a big deal." Tate reaches down to the ground, picks up a pebble, rears back his arm, and tosses it over the top of the bleachers. "I came over here to ask if maybe you wanted to go do something after school. We could go get a coffee or something."

"Cedar Canyon has a Starbucks?" I tease. "I must've missed it."

He laughs. "No Starbucks, but there is a place on the highway."

"Ah. The Dairy Queen."

"Funny." Smirking at me, he continues, "You need someone to show you around. Just because this isn't San Francisco doesn't mean we don't have some cool out-of-the-way places."

"I didn't mean to make fun of Cedar Canyon."

"Sure you did." He grins. "Well? Do you want to go?"

I glance toward Bethyl Ann. Meeting Tate after school will mean missing my chance to talk to her alone today. But I'm afraid if I say no to him, he won't ask me again. "Okay," I say. "I was planning to take some photographs around town after school, and I need to shop for a necklace chain. But I guess I can do that another time." I cringe inside when I hear the uncertainty in my voice. He's going to think that I don't really want to go with him. Why couldn't I just say okay and leave it at that?

"We can still shop for one," Tate says a little cautiously, like he's afraid of saying the wrong thing and making me change my mind. "And I wouldn't mind tagging along while you take pictures."

I stare at him a minute. He looks so much like Henry! My heart spikes when I look into his eyes. Still, I'm not completely comfortable with Tate's sudden friendliness; if he has ulterior motives, I should probably find out what they are before I start liking him any more than I already do. "You'd be bored," I warn, and watch Tate's smile disintegrate.

"I wouldn't be bored, but that's okay." He shrugs. "I won't bother you." He starts off across the courts toward the parking lot.

"Hey," I shout, shielding my eyes from the sun with my hand. "Don't be so sensitive. If you want to tag along, you can."

He stops walking and glances back at me with narrowed eyes. "I'll think about it," he says.

I can't help smiling as he walks away.

Tate is waiting for me outside the building at 3:05. "I changed my mind," he says, falling into step beside me. "I *am* going to bother you." He grins, and I find it hard to exhale.

We head for the highway that runs near the edge of town. Clutching my camera like a security blanket, I snap one shot after another. I don't pay much attention to what I'm shooting; I just need to keep my hands busy and my mind off Tate. I like all this unexpected interest he's showing in me way too much. I wish it was possible that it didn't stem from some self-centered agenda on his part. I wish that—*big surprise*—the realization of how much he enjoys my company hit him like a lightning bolt from the sky. But I don't believe it. Some things are just too good to be true, and this feels like one of them.

Pausing at an intersection, I lower the camera to reload the film. "So . . . what kind of necklace are you looking for?" Tate asks.

"Just a chain for a pendant."

"A pendant? You mean like a locket?"

I'm baffled by his interest in my jewelry. I don't want to talk about the crystal. If I did, I'd confide in Bethyl Ann, not him. I don't have that much faith in him yet. "It's just a piece of old costume jewelry. Something I've had for a while," I lie.

The sky is hazy. I smell dust in the air. Hoping a dust

storm isn't going to hit before we reach the coffee shop, I quickly finish reloading the film and we walk a block in silence until we reach the highway. I gesture to the Dairy Queen on the other side. "I was right," I tease, yelling to be heard over the sound of an approaching eighteen-wheeler. "Some coffee shop. You got me here under false pretenses."

"That's not it!" he yells back. "Come on. You'll see." When the truck passes by, he takes my hand and we run across the highway.

Behind the Dairy Queen, one block down, we enter a tiny yellow house with a sign in the yard that says THE MUSE. It's a colorful, artsy place with a nice eclectic vibe— so unlike anyplace else I've been in this town. Papa Dan would've called it "hippie-dippy." I read the menu written on a chalkboard above the counter and order a soy chai. Tate orders plain old coffee. As we slide into chairs on opposite sides of a table from each other, he says smugly, "What did I tell you?"

"Okay. You win. This is a great place." I sip my chai.

Watching me, Tate says, "Tell me more about the Peterson house. I've always wanted to go inside."

"It's drafty," I say. *Lonely. Confusing. Scary.*

"And haunted," he adds without so much as a chuckle.

"You said that like you believe it."

"Not really. But anything's possible, I guess."

I study Tate, hoping that maybe I've misjudged him. Maybe he would keep an open mind if I told him about Henry.

"It's probably none of my business," Tate says, "but is everything good with you?"

"What do you mean?"

"It's just . . . your short story in English. The one Miss Petra made you read." He reaches across the table and lifts the brim of my hat, tilts his head, and squints. "And you look really tired."

I shiver. Maybe because of his nearness. Or maybe because he sees too much. I know how I look; I saw myself in the mirror this morning. Bruise-colored smudges beneath my eyes, a too pale complexion. What if I *did* tell him everything? The reasons why I'm losing sleep, why I'm so jumpy, so moody? The urge to confide in Tate is strong, but what would he think of me? He's nothing like Bethyl Ann. I can't imagine that he'd accept my story without hesitation. Even if he didn't run as fast as he could in the opposite direction to tell the entire school, how could I make someone like him understand why I'm finding it harder to leave Henry's memories? That I'm starting to believe that the world inside the photographs is where I belong? How can I admit that I'm obsessed with a brooding phantom or explain what it means to me to see Papa Dan so happy and whole again?

Lowering my gaze, I say, "I've been worried about my grandfather. He isn't well."

"What's wrong with him?"

"The doctors aren't sure, exactly. It's some kind of dementia."

"Like Alzheimer's?"

"Sort of, I guess."

"Oh, man . . . I hope he gets better."

"He will. He has to." But deep inside, I know a recovery is unlikely, and that thought hardens my throat as I lift my cup and take another sip.

Tate leans back against his chair and looks around the coffee shop. "This is nice, right? Me bringing you here? I've been behaving myself." He grins.

I scowl at him. "What are you getting at?"

"You said if I behaved myself and acted nice, you'd show me some of your pictures. I'd like to see the ones you took this afternoon."

"I said *maybe*. And *you* said you'd let me read some of your writing."

He winces. "I said I *might*." We smile at each other, neither one of us ready to commit to anything. Deftly changing the subject back to me, he says, "I've never been in a darkroom before. My mom used to take a lot of pictures, but she didn't develop them herself."

"She doesn't take pictures anymore?"

"I don't know. Maybe. She and my dad divorced and Mom moved to Austin."

I don't want to be a phony and pretend that's news to me. And no words are going to make him feel better, so I decide to just say what I think. "That sucks."

"Yeah. Just life, though, I guess." A long silence, then, "She didn't even ask if I wanted to go with her. She just . . . went."

227

The words *I'm sorry* sit on the tip of my tongue, but he's probably heard them a hundred times. That's what everyone says when something bad happens. *I'm sorry you have to move, Tansy. I'm sorry your grandfather's sick. I'm sorry you never knew your dad. I'm sorry, I'm sorry, I'm sorry.* Then they're free to forget your problems. They've said what's expected of them. But *I'm sorry* doesn't really change anything.

"If your mom had asked, would you have gone with her?" I say.

"I don't know. Maybe."

"You must really miss her."

"I'm also pissed at her."

"I would be, too. It seems like I spend half the time mad at my mom, but it would be weird not to have her around."

Tate downs his coffee and pushes the cup aside. He seems uncomfortable talking about his mother, so this time I change the subject. "I have a question," I say to him.

"Okay. Shoot."

"Why are you suddenly being Mr. Nice Guy? The truth this time. I mean, that first night I met you at the Longhorn you were a big flirt. Then when I saw you again at school, you acted like you hated my guts. Now you're buying me coffee?"

"I told you the truth at the bridge. I don't have a good excuse. Blame it on a bad mood." Tate dips his chin, and his grin shoots my heart to the ceiling. "If I tell you I'm sorry a hundred more times, will you forgive me? 'Cause I'll do it, if that's what it takes."

"That's an easy out," I say to him, voicing my earlier thoughts. I turn toward the window, trying not to laugh, ignoring the glances from kids I recognize from school sitting at other tables, studying and talking.

"I never apologize unless I mean it," he insists, then grinning, he leans in across the table and says, "I'm sorry . . . I'm sorry, I'm sorry, I'm sorry . . ."

On about the tenth *sorry* I say, "Stop!" and the laugh escapes. "Just buy me another soy chai sometime and we'll call it even. On second thought, an ice-cream soda. At City Drug."

He looks pleased with himself. "Okay. Tell your mom not to pick you up after school tomorrow. I'll bring my car, and after we visit J. B. we'll drive out to the canyon. Have you been down the trail beside the bridge yet?"

I think of the winter picnic with Henry and shake my head. "No," I say. *Not as myself. Not in this lifetime.*

While Mom taps away on her laptop in the chair across the room, Papa Dan and I sit side by side on the couch eating popcorn and watching *Pirates of the Caribbean.* It's one of my grandfather's favorites. He thinks Captain Jack is funny. I think he's funny, too, and that Johnny Depp is possibly the hottest old guy I've ever seen. When the movie reaches that scene where Captain Jack says, "Why is all the rum gone?" Papa Dan chuckles.

His laugh has always made me feel happy, inside and out. As far back as I can remember, it was my morning "hello," my "welcome home" after school, one of the last sounds I heard before I closed my eyes at night. I didn't know how much it meant to me until I started hearing less of it. I wish I had a tape recorder close by so I could capture the sound to play back years from now when I'm sad.

I watch Papa Dan and make a vow to myself not to go up to the turret tonight, not to read Henry's journal or look at any photographs or the crystal, which I put back in the turret after school. I never got around to buying a chain for it, and that's probably a good thing. My Henry fixation keeps growing like the weeds Mom pulls from the flower beds; no matter how many times I try to tug it up by the roots and toss it aside, it sprouts again.

The prospect of becoming Bell forever is both enticing and unsettling. Whenever I think about it, a strange urgency spirals up inside me. One minute I want to become a permanent part of Henry's world and be with him more than anything, and the next minute the thought of that scares me senseless and Tate is the only guy I want to be around. I'm sure I should see a doctor and have my head examined, but I'm afraid I wouldn't be able to deal with what I found out about my mental state. I need to do *something*, though, make up my mind, one way or the other.

Mom's fingers pause on the keyboard. She looks up at me and smiles.

I remind myself of my promise: I'll stay out of the turret for a while, away from Henry's things, the photographs. I'll be okay if I stop thinking about him. Everything will go back to normal, and Mom will never find out about any of it; she won't have to worry about me.

When the movie ends, we all go upstairs. I take Papa Dan to his room, tell him good night, close the door, and lock it. In my own room, I check my email and open a couple of Hailey's emails. They both start with an excuse, so I close them without reading to the end. I turn off the computer and curl up in bed, facing the window, listening to the nightingale sing. Moonlight spills through the parted curtains and washes over my face. Henry's voice whispers through my mind. . . . *Tell Daniel to bring you here to the bridge. I'll be waiting with Father's car.*

The nightingale's song is so pretty and sad . . . like poetry. . . .

I push back the sheet and get up, crossing the room to the window and shoving the curtains aside. Silver light bathes the backyard. I open the window wide. The nightingale trills louder, the melody of its song weaving through my thoughts. What if I *did* climb the stairs to the turret? If I read another poem . . . took out the photographs . . . the crystal? If I slanted it just so and lost myself in its shimmer? Would I find myself alone with Henry on another night? Would he kiss me like he did at the edge of the canyon? I've been kissed before but never like that. I'm sure no one else will ever make me feel the way he did. No one else could. Not even Tate.

A breeze flaps the curtains. I turn around and toss away the promise I made to myself. Four steps and I'm at the door, my hand on the knob.

A rattling noise outside startles me, and the nightingale abruptly stops singing. I return to the window, lean out, and look down. In a hushed voice, I call, "Papa Dan? Is that you?" Did I forget to lock his door?

A shadow creeps across the cellar and moves toward the barn. I suck in a breath when it takes the form of a person. Flinching, I grab the curtain, hide behind it, then peek out again in time to see the figure disappear behind the dilapidated building.

I try to relax, telling myself I did forget to lock Papa Dan's door. He might be down there looking for something he thinks he misplaced. The pocket watch maybe.

For at least a full minute, I stare into the darkness below, waiting for my grandfather to reappear. He doesn't, so I leave my room, intending to climb the stairs to the turret and get the watch, so I can show it to Papa Dan and coax him back inside. I'm sure that's what he spent so much time searching for beneath the mulberry tree the other day. But when I reach his bedroom door, it's closed and locked. My grandfather was not the shadow I saw outside.

I think of the sheriff's warning about prowlers, and a tremor snakes through me. Every nerve I possess screams at me to go get Mom. What if the person I saw tries to get into the house? I start for her room but pause when the nightingale's song drifts down from the turret and a sudden sense of calm settles over me. *Get the watch. Show it to Papa Dan in the morning, so he'll relax.* That's what I tell myself as I climb the stairs—any excuse to go up to the turret, to be near Henry's things. I know it's a bad idea, but I can't seem to stop myself. I go in, open the drawer, take out the journal, and read his next poem.

Return to the place where you belong;
It hasn't changed; it's waiting,
Stalled in time till you arrive
To right a senseless wrong.
Here you will find the laughter you've lost,
The missing piece of a broken heart
Chipped away without a thought
Of the terrible cost.

Come back to the one who's strong;
I haven't changed; I'm waiting,
Stalled in time till you arrive
To thaw my frozen song.

Closing the journal, I murmur, "I want to, Henry." I do. Going to Henry is like stepping onto a roller coaster. I know I'll lose control of my feelings, that I could get hurt, but there is a sort of thrill in that, and the danger tugs me against my will. I think of his eyes, and heat spreads from the top of my head down to my toes. I want to feel Henry's gaze on me again. I want my pulse to scatter and my stomach to drop. I want everything his poem promises.

Suddenly I recall Daniel's warning to Bell to watch out

for herself around Henry, and I know it's good advice for me, too. In my mind, I see the red slashes on Henry's wrist, the defiant, troubled look in his eyes when he talked about shooting himself in the foot. What if he tried to coax Isabel to do something that would be a mistake and cause her trouble? Could I control her reactions? Change her mind? I doubt it. When I'm there, she seems to control me, not the other way around.

Listen to Daniel, I tell myself.

I'm putting the journal back into the drawer when the crystal draws my gaze. An urge to touch it overwhelms me. I long to stroke the cut glass, to feel it smooth beneath my fingertips. My hand trembles above the drawer. But then I think of Papa Dan and Mom asleep one flight below while a stranger roams our property, and I turn my head so I can't see the crystal. Still feeling its pull, I curl my fingers into my palm, and take a breath.

Quickly, I glance again at the drawer, open my hand, and lift the watch, leaving the crystal behind. Exiting the room, I close the door behind me and hurry down to the first floor, double check all the doors and windows, then take the stairs up again to Mom's room. I reach to open the door, then pause. Maybe what I saw was only my imagination. A trick of the moonlight, a flicker from the past. Another delusion. I shouldn't worry Mom just yet—take the risk of exposing my shaky mental state. I'll go back to my own room first for one more look. If I see something, then I'll wake her.

Placing the watch on the nightstand beside my bed, I cross to the open window and scan the yard, the shadows around the barn. Except for the chirp of crickets, the whisper of the breeze, it's quiet outside. Even the nightingale is silent. The curtains billow. An autumn chill rides the wind, so crisp and cool that I shiver. Who did I see? Who stepped out of sight behind the barn? Could it have been Henry's ghost? Has he been watching the house? Watching *me*? And waiting?

I awake the next morning curled up on the floor beneath the window. I watched the yard most of the night, then dozed off sometime just before dawn.

Before I leave for school, I walk out to the storm cellar. One edge of the door is splintered, as if someone tugged at it with a crowbar. Someone who wants inside the cellar. Someone or *something*. Crouching, I run my hand across the damaged wood. Maybe whoever did this was afraid that using a hammer to break the padlock would make too much noise. Or maybe I stopped him when I called out to Papa Dan.

Twice now, I've seen a figure in the yard at night. It *must* be a flesh-and-blood person; a padlocked door wouldn't stop Henry, would it? Can't ghosts walk through solid objects? I'll have to ask Bethyl Ann. But if it's not Henry, then who? And what is he—or she—after? I know I shouldn't let another night pass without warning Mom. But I want to talk to Bethyl Ann first, since she's such an expert on the supernatural.

When I arrive at school, I find another black-and-white movie in progress behind the doors. Even Miss Petra has faded. Bethyl Ann has an eye doctor appointment at lunch, so we can't resume the conversation we started yesterday before Tate showed up. I take advantage of the time by going to the school library and reading about schizophrenia. Apparently no medical test exists to diagnosis it. A doctor decides a person has the condition based on the presence of certain "psychological disturbances." *Agitation. Disorganized thinking. Hallucinations that might include all the senses—seeing things, hearing voices and other noises, experiencing scents and textures and tastes.* Feeling shaken and hopeless, I read about the final symptom: *Delusions.* My heartbeat picks up. *People suffering from schizophrenia may believe that their irrational judgments and beliefs are factual . . . claims of being cheated, hassled, or that others are out to get them . . . bizarre fantasies of someone trying to send messages or control their actions by peculiar means . . .*

Fighting tears, I close the book, prop an elbow on the table, and cradle my head in my hand. No need for me to see a doctor who couldn't tell me anything I don't already know. I have every symptom in the book. Ever since we moved here, I've been agitated over the way Alison and her groupies treat me. And Tate. Even Hailey. Haven't I felt like they're "out to get me"? And Henry's memories . . . they're real to me now. The more I'm there, the more they come alive. In his world, I see and hear, taste and smell. I feel the cold and Henry's touch. More and more, I'm certain Henry is controlling my actions, that he's trying to send me a message. But it's all in my head. Warning signs that I'm sick, that I have a mental disorder. Proof lies on the pages in front of me.

I leave the library on edge, and stay that way for the rest of the day. When the last bell finally rings, I find Bethyl Ann and Tate waiting for me in the hallway outside my classroom. "You want to go to the library and do some more research?" Bethyl Ann asks. Glancing across at Tate, she lowers her voice and adds, "For our *history project*."

"I can't." I cut my gaze to Tate, then back to her. "Tate is driving me out to the canyon." Even if that wasn't the plan, I wouldn't want to go to the library with Bethyl Ann. Not now. I want to forget about Henry Peterson. Push him out of my mind. Feel normal again, at least for a few hours.

"Oh," Bethyl Ann says, shriveling like a punctured balloon.

"You can come with us," I say quickly. "We want you to, don't we, Tate?"

"Uh . . . yeah. Sure."

"I'm not stupid," Bethyl Ann says in a pinched voice. "Truth is truth to the end of reckoning. Another time, Cassius. I'm sure you'll be waiting with bated breath until then."

I pull her aside. "Come with us. I mean it."

"Far be it from me to stand in the way of lovers." She crosses her arms.

"It's not like that." I peek across at Tate and feel myself blush. He leans against the wall, his hands shoved into his jean pockets, pretending he isn't paying attention to us.

Bethyl Ann gives me an *as if* smirk. "It's okay. Mama won't let me go into the canyon without an adult, anyway."

Sometimes I forget how young she is. But I can't stand for Bethyl Ann to feel left out, so I try to make it up to her. "Tomorrow we should eat lunch at City Drug's soda fountain. I'll buy." I don't care about being seen with her anymore. Bethyl Ann has the right idea: *Natives be damned*.

"The soda fountain is always packed at lunchtime," Bethyl Ann points out, then adds more quietly, "It'd be hard for us to talk about you-know-what. Oh, and I forgot. I can't have lunch tomorrow, anyway, because Daddy's taking me. It's his birthday. We always have lunch together on his birthday. It's a tradition, or I'd try to get out of it."

"That's okay," I tell her. I'm not disappointed. I no longer want to tell her what's been going on with me. I know it's all in my head now. I don't need Bethyl Ann to confirm it. When we get together, I want to do what normal girls do. The things Hailey and I once did together. Gossip about boys and school. Look through magazines and laugh at the sleazy hoochie clothes the models wear. "Tomorrow after school, do you want to come home with me and meet my granddad?" I ask.

Her chin lifts, and her eyes brighten. "Will your mom be there?"

I nod. "She'll pick us up."

Bethyl Ann squeals. "I didn't get a chance to talk to her when we met the other morning, and I probably would've just babbled anyway. I can't even imagine visiting the home of a real-life author!"

"Please." I roll my eyes. "It's not a big deal." I glance at Tate and see that he's trying not to laugh.

"Do you think your mom will let me see her office?" Bethyl Ann asks.

"I'll show it to you myself, if you promise not to get so excited you pee your pants."

Ignoring my sarcasm, Bethyl Ann says, "I'll ask my mom and call you tonight. I'm sure she'll say yes, as long as I'm home for dinner and Daddy's birthday cake. Should I bring snacks? Mama makes the best Rice Krispies Treats in the whole wide world."

"Sure, Beth. Whatever."

Taking hold of my arm and pulling me farther from Tate, she murmurs, "We'll talk some more about you-know-who then, okay?"

"We'll see." I cast a nervous glance in Tate's direction, hoping he doesn't think that Bethyl Ann is referring to him.

A few minutes later, Tate and I pull out of the school parking lot in his old Ford Blazer. I'm trying not to think about what I read in the library book, but that's all I *can* think about. I'm so tense, I feel as if I'm standing on the railing of the bridge, like Henry did in my delusion.

Tate glances across at me. "So you and Stink—"

My glare cuts his sentence short.

"You and *Bethyl Ann* are good friends, huh?"

Feeling defensive, I snap, "Is that a problem?"

"I was just asking." He smiles.

"What?" I cross my arms, aware that I'm overreacting because of all I found out about myself today. Even though it's not Tate's fault that I'm psychologically disturbed, I can't keep from lashing out at him. It's not every day a person discovers that they belong in a mental ward. And isn't this one of my symptoms at work? Agitation?

"I didn't say anything," Tate mutters.

"Beth is the only person who's been nice to me since I've been here."

His brows lift.

"Go ahead. Say what you're thinking."

"It's nothing."

"Just say it."

He shrugs. "Some people think you're kind of hard to approach."

The statement hits me like a splash of cold water in the face. "Some people like who? Straight-A Alison Summers and Beer-for-Breakfast Shanna? Or possibly Rooster Boy?"

Laughter sputters out of him. "You pretty much summed up Alison and Shanna. Who's Rooster Boy?"

"The bad comedian who sits next to you in homeroom."

"Jon Jenks?" He laughs again. "Why'd you call him that?"

"He struts around like a rooster, but he's really just a scrawny chicken." Tate snickers and drives while I stare out the window and fume. "I guess you think it's easy moving to a new school. What was I supposed to do? Show up on the first day and introduce myself to everyone? Shake their hands?"

"I'm sorry. Don't be mad." He chokes back another laugh.

"Maybe I have been hard to get close to, but that didn't stop Beth."

Tate sobers and says, "I don't have anything against Bethyl Ann, but you've got to admit that she's weird."

"She's only thirteen. Everyone needs to give her a break. Have you ever thought how it would feel to be that age again and so smart that they stuck you in high school with a bunch of jerks who treat you like crap?"

He squints straight ahead out the window, and after a few seconds says, "I guess you're right. I'm sorry."

"You keep saying that." I think about all of Hailey's pathetic attempts to apologize in her emails and only get angrier. Apparently, Tate's no different than her or the other assholes in this town. "I don't feel like going to the canyon anymore," I tell Tate. "Just take me home."

"Tansy—" He curses quietly.

"If you don't want to drive me there, then I'll just walk. Pull over."

Tate shakes his head and exhales a noisy breath. "Relax. I'll take you home."

The next day after school, Bethyl Ann follows me up the stairs to my room, carrying the plate of Rice Krispies Treats her mother made. "I like your hair," she says out of the blue. "Does your mother cut it?"

Relieved that her chatter isn't about Henry, I look over my shoulder at her. "I wouldn't let Mom near my hair with a pair of scissors. I went to a salon in San Francisco."

"There's only one hairdresser in Cedar Canyon. Sherry Combs."

"Sherry *Combs*?"

She nods. "Scout's honor."

We pause on the landing. I glance at Bethyl Ann's stringy hair and crooked bangs. "Does Sherry Combs cut yours?" If she says yes, I'm looking for a salon in Amarillo.

Bethyl Ann shakes her head. "No, Mama does." As we start down the hallway, she adds, "I've been thinking it might be fun to have a makeover, now that I have a friend who knows about clothes and cosmetics and hair."

"You do?" I lead her into my bedroom. "Who?"

Bethyl Ann smirks. "Don't be humble. I brought some magazines we can look through for ideas."

"I'm not much of a makeup person," I say, stopping in the middle of the room to take off my backpack and toss it into the corner. "I seriously doubt that anyone at school admires the way I look, anyway. I might only get you noticed in a way you don't want."

"This is for me, not the natives."

Ever since Mom picked us up at school, Bethyl Ann has vomited words like she ate the dictionary. That's fine with me, since I haven't felt much like talking today. Avoiding

Tate has left me exhausted. I'm more than a little mortified that I got so upset and made him drive me home yesterday. It just stung to hear what people were saying about me.

I was too depressed to do anything when I got home. And tired. After dinner, I fell asleep watching television and didn't get off the couch until Mom woke me at bedtime. I barely made it up the stairs, and I was asleep again the second my head landed on the pillow. If the nightingale sang, I didn't hear it.

"What sort of look do you have in mind?" I ask Bethyl Ann, crossing the room again and closing the door, ready to take my mind off my troubles with some meaningless girl talk. I hope she doesn't ruin things by bringing up Henry.

Her eyes blink excitement at me. "Whatever you decide. I'm in your hands, oh beauty guru." She plops onto my bed with a bounce.

I quickly look her over as I take off my hat and run a hand across my short locks. "You'll have to lose the hair barrettes. In fact, you'll have to lose the hair. You want me to cut it today?"

She grins. "Would you?" When I nod, Bethyl Ann leans forward and whispers, "First I want to hear more about your visions—the ones you were telling me about the other day at lunch before Tate so rudely interrupted."

Great. I knew the reprieve couldn't last.

With an eager glance around the bedroom, she lowers her voice and asks, "Have you seen Henry? Is he here now?"

"That's not how it happens." I walk over to the dresser

to get the plate of snacks, then join her on the bed. Setting the plate in front of her, I kick off my shoes. "Do we have to talk about this right now?"

Her eyes widen as she unties the laces on her dingy sneakers. "Of *course* we do. You can't just tell me something like that and expect me to forget about it. Besides, I've been wondering about this house being haunted for a really long time."

"What made you think it might be?" I ask.

"Remember when I told you I came over here that day when Mama was visiting Mrs. Quattlebaum?" She leans closer and in just above a whisper adds, "I went down into the cellar in your backyard. Don't tell Mama. She'd be really mad at me for trespassing. I didn't stay long, though. I got a creepy feeling down there."

"You sensed something?" Bethyl Ann nods again, and I pick up a Rice Krispies Treat, nibble the corner, wondering how to explain . . . where to start. Anyone would get a creepy feeling down in that cellar. She obviously doesn't understand that what I've experienced is a lot more involved. Should I just tell her I'm delusional and leave it at that? Or should I tell her what's been happening and let her make her own decision?

"Well?" She pulls off one shoe then the other and drops them onto the floor.

Watching Bethyl Ann closely to gauge her reaction, I say, "It's like I go back into the past and I become another person who was my age a long time ago."

She stares at me with her mouth open, and just when I begin to think she's gone mute, she says, "Oh. My. Freakin'. *Gosh*. Henry Peterson is *possessing* you?"

"Not exactly. Henry's not the person I become." For the next few minutes, I tell Bethyl Ann everything while she nibbles and gasps. I begin with finding the box and end with stepping through the photographs and into my grandfather's past. I explain about the nightingale's song. How the past world is becoming more vibrant while this world is dimming. How I feel as if I'm living through Henry's girlfriend while I'm there.

"Holy schmoley." Bethyl Ann sits back against my headboard, blinking rapidly. "Does mental illness run in your family?" Her words drain the blood from my face. She must notice my reaction, because she nudges me and says, "Oh, geez. No offense. But if you want me to help you figure this out—"

"No, you're right." I try to swallow the lump that lodges in my throat like a pebble. "I'm losing it. I'm epically schizo." My voice cracks the word in two.

"Maybe," Bethyl Ann says in a matter-of-fact way, as if schizophrenia is no more serious than the common cold. "But we should rule out all the other possibilities before we lock you away." She grins.

"This isn't funny." I can't help it—my face scrunches up.

Bethyl Ann's expression changes to one of alarm, like she's afraid I'm going to spaz out. "Oh, darn." She scrambles to the edge of the bed. "I didn't know how upset you were—I'll get your mother."

"No!" I catch her arm. "I'm afraid she'll take me to some doctor who'll stuff pills down my throat until I turn into a zombie." Sniffing, I let go of her arm.

She studies my face, scoots back, and murmurs, "I understand. I didn't mean to make light of things. I just want to look at all the puzzle pieces. How else are we going to see this clearly and understand what's going on?"

Something akin to hope seeps into my heart. "By *puzzle pieces*, you mean rational explanations, right?"

She beams. "Exactly."

"In my case, there aren't any."

"Au contraire. We talked about an intelligent haunting the other day. That's one really trippy possibility."

"You're teasing me," I say, ashamed of my pouty voice. "You think I'm making this up for attention or something. Like Jade Malloy shaving her head."

"Untrue. I totally believe you."

"And I totally *don't* believe you." I press my lips together, concentrating on the wind-bent mulberry tree outside my window. The leaves are turning yellow and brown, and the driest ones rattle on the branches like hoarse voices from the past.

Bethyl Ann nudges me, and I look at her out of the corner of my eye. She plants a fist on her hip, making her bony elbow stick out like the point on a triangle. "Do I look like a close-minded naysayer to you? I *do* believe you. You might have a ghost or a demon on your hands. I've watched

Ghost Whisperer. I've seen *Psychic Detectives.*"

"So what?" I say, refusing to look at her straight on.

"So I know what I'm talking about. Things happen all the time that we can't explain logically *now* but that someone will figure out *later*. This might be one of those."

"Go on," I say cautiously, afraid to hope that she's not just trying to keep me from unraveling at her feet like a spool of thread.

"Throughout history smart-alecky know-it-alls have pooh-poohed things they didn't understand. In the scheme of things, it wasn't that long ago that the pope threatened Galileo with torture if he didn't say that he'd been wrong about the earth circling the sun." She sniffs and lifts her chin. "I am *not* a smart-alecky pooh-pooher."

Hope spreads through me like sunshine after a rainstorm. Leave it to Bethyl Ann to find a way to combine science with the supernatural and sort of make sense doing it. I'm so relieved by her attitude that I could hug her. It feels good to have the secret out, to be able to talk about it with someone who doesn't automatically think I'm whacked out.

Facing Bethyl Ann, I smile so wide my cheeks hurt. "You don't know how awful it's been, having to keep this to myself. I'm so afraid I'm going crazy. That's the most likely explanation, isn't it? I mean, the nightingale . . . I did some research and you were right. They aren't in North America."

She looks smug. "You doubted *moi*? The smartest almost-fourteen-year-old in the county?"

"Sorry about that."

"The bird might be an illusion." She sits straighter. "Of course! Henry is playing a trick on you. There's a supercool Shelley quote that says a poet—"

"Is a nightingale. I read that. It's like the bird's song pulls me to Henry. I make up my mind to stay away from his things, then the bird starts singing and I can't go up to the turret fast enough to get my hands on that crystal."

"And then you become his girlfriend," she says in an awed whisper, clapping her hands together. "That is the coolest thing I've ever heard in my life!"

"More like terrifying."

As if she doesn't hear me, Bethyl Ann exclaims, "You become *Isabel!*"

I go still. "How did you know that?"

Bethyl Ann frowns. "You told me."

"I don't remember saying her name."

"You didn't?"

"I don't think so."

Her brows wiggle. "I told you I found a bunch of articles about Henry in the library archives. I must've read something about Isabel being his girlfriend in one of them."

"It's strange that you can't find those articles now."

"I'm not a walking, talking index, you know."

She looks at me as if I'm accusing her of something. I do feel an odd sort of suspicion but of what, I'm not sure. Bethyl Ann doesn't have a devious bone in her body. Sighing, I sit back. "Sorry I'm acting so weird."

Her face crinkles into a grin. "I guess you're entitled, considering your conundrum." She bites off a chunk of her Rice Krispies Treat and, munching, says, "Let's start at the beginning. Tell me about that picture of this house your mom found."

"It was with some of Papa Dan's things."

She studies the room, from ceiling to floor. "Something really, really bad must've happened here when he was a kid for it to still bother him so much. I bet he and Henry were both in love with Isabel." Her eyes widen. "I know! Maybe Henry got jealous and beat up your grandpa!" Her hand flies up to her mouth. "Maybe Henry tried to *kill* him!"

"I don't think Daniel—my grandfather, I mean—I don't think he was in love with Isabel. They act more like sister and brother."

"Oh. Wow. You talk about them like you were there. If this is a haunting, you *were* there. You were *her*. Wow, wow, wow." Bethyl Ann sits back again and purses her lips. "As for things starting to fade here . . . Hmmm." She cocks her head. "Am I in color now?"

"You're always in color. You, Mom, Papa Dan." My eyes flick away from hers briefly as I mutter, "And Tate."

"Ah, Cassius."

I don't know why she calls Tate that, but I don't dare ask and risk launching her into a rambling explanation. "Until yesterday, I was seeing Miss Petra in color, too."

"Interesting." Her eyes narrow.

"What do you think it means?"

"You said in Henry's world you're seeing more color, and hearing more noise, right?"

"And smelling scents and feeling textures and tasting. It's as if this world becomes a little less real to me as the one inside the photographs becomes *more* real."

"That makes sense."

"No it doesn't; it's completely bizarre." The second the words exit my mouth, a realization hits me. I grab Bethyl Ann's hand. "Oh my gosh. The people I still see in color here are the people I like most. The ones I'd miss if I left."

Her face brightens. "And I'm one of them?"

"Apparently."

"I'm honored. But that doesn't explain Tate." Her eyes narrow. "Or *does* it? Well, well, well. Silly me."

Anxious to divert the conversation away from Tate, I say, "Explain why everything is only colorless at school. And why does it all return to normal after a little while?"

"That's not true about school being the only place you see in black-and-white." Sweeping an arm around the room, she adds, "You said these pale blue walls were white when you woke up the other morning. And the strawberries you ate for breakfast were gray."

Sighing, I slump back against the headboard. "If there's no consistent pattern, how are we supposed to figure this out?"

"Chin up, Tansy Piper. Maybe it's a gradual process. As you see more color in Henry's world, you might start seeing less here and for longer periods of time—at home and everywhere else. You might even stop *hearing* things here and lose your other senses, too. If your theory about the people you care about is right, then it makes sense that your house would fade more slowly than school, because your home means more to you than school."

Sarcastically, I mutter, "That makes me feel a whole lot better."

"It's only a hypothesis. It's also possible that this will end as quickly as it started."

"And maybe Hamlet's going to start quoting Shakespeare, too."

I'm about to ask Bethyl Ann if a ghost would have any reason to use a crowbar to pry open the cellar when a knock sounds at the door and Mom calls, "Can I come in?"

"Sure."

She opens the door and steps across the threshold, holding her phone in her hand. "That's not Hailey, is it?" I whisper. "I don't want to talk to her."

"No, it's for me," Mom responds. "But someone's here to see you. That cute kid who flirted with you at the Longhorn Café."

"Tate?" I swing my feet off the bed and stand.

"Is that his name?" Mom wiggles her brows. "He's got a great smile."

"*Mom*." The thought of Tate on my front porch right this second almost paralyzes me. "He's smiling? That's good news. Maybe he won't bite my head off then."

Bethyl Ann mutters, "There's daggers in men's smiles."

Shifting her attention to Mom, she explains, "That's from *Macbeth*, not *Julius Caesar*, but nevertheless quite appropriate when referring to young Cassius."

Mom stares blankly at Bethyl Ann a moment, then she slides her gaze toward me and arches a brow.

"I don't try to make sense of her anymore," I say. Nodding at the phone to postpone having to face Tate, I ask, "Who are you talking to?"

"The sheriff," Mom answers, adding, "So are you two just going to leave Tate down there waiting?"

"You go," Bethyl Ann says to me. "That'll give me a chance to snoop through all your drawers while you're gone." One corner of her mouth curves up.

I'm sure she's teasing, still I'm relieved I locked the journal in the turret, just in case I'm wrong. She may know everything about Henry now, but I still feel protective of his thoughts and words.

Mom chatters into the phone to the sheriff as I follow her downstairs, but I'm too nervous to pay any attention to her end of the conversation. When we reach the first floor, she covers the mouthpiece with her palm and yells toward the door, "Nice to meet you, Tate." Sending me a goofy smile, she heads for the kitchen.

"Hi," I say to Tate, stepping onto the porch.

"Hi." We look at each other and our eyes dart away at the same time. "I thought you might want to go to the canyon today," he mutters. "We won't talk about Bethyl Ann."

"She's here."

He hesitates before saying, "She can go with us."

"She's not allowed."

"Oh, yeah. I forgot." His jaw muscle spasms. He backs up a step, reaches into the pocket of his jeans, tugs out a tiny plastic bag, and offers it to me. "I bought this for you," he says.

My pulse skips like one of Papa Dan's old vinyl record albums. "What is it?"

"Open it."

I take the pouch and pour the contents—a silver necklace chain—into my palm. It's so beautiful and I'm so amazed that he gave it to me that I can't speak.

"It's for your pendant," Tate explains. "You, um, said you needed a chain for it, right? I just thought . . . I mean, since we didn't get around to looking for one the other day." He clears his throat. "I hope it's the right kind."

"Thanks. I love it." Even more, I love that he cares enough that he bought it for me. *Tate* bought it for *me*. Only a few days ago, I wouldn't have believed this could ever happen. Not in a million years. I finally meet his gaze, and all I can think about is the fact that Henry gave me a necklace, too, except it was gold. And after he hooked the clasp at the back of my neck, we kissed. Actually, Henry kissed *Bell*, but I felt the brush of his lips all the same. I lower my focus to Tate's mouth. Would I like kissing him as much?

He takes another backward step, inching so close to the edge of the porch that I'm afraid he'll fall off. "Well, see you at school," he says, then turns toward the yard.

"Tate?" I close my fingers around his peace offering as he faces me again. "Mrs. Pugh is picking up Bethyl Ann at five thirty. I mean, I know it's a long drive out here—"

"It's not that far. I only live about four miles down the road."

"If you want to come back—"

"Is five forty-five okay?"

"I'll be ready."

We share a quick smile before he turns and takes the steps down into the yard.

17

Bethyl Ann's bangs are choppy now, but in a good way, and her long locks are clipped to chin-length. I plucked about a million and one hairs from her unibrow, and now she has two arched ones with a nice, smooth space between them. I brushed a tiny bit of blush on her cheeks, a touch of brown mascara on her stick-straight eyelashes, and clear gloss on her lips. For her "signature *avant-garde* flare," as Bethyl Ann now calls it, we decided to put a maroon streak in her hair. Only one, on her left side in front; I didn't want to go overboard. I had a bottle of color left over from last year when I tinted my own hair.

We went out to the barn, and I dug through some boxes of my old clothes. I don't know why Mom bothered moving them, but I'm glad she did. They're a little outdated but not in Bethyl Ann's usual geeky way. We hauled a box up to my room, and I put different styles together until we found a mix that was right for her. Bethyl Ann labels it the "eclectic look" and swears it's how she'll dress from this day forward.

She takes this makeover thing way too seriously, but I'm sort of psyched about that, since she looks really great. I can't wait to see how everyone at school reacts tomorrow.

Bethyl Ann turns away from the mirror and hugs me so tightly that my lungs deflate. "Thanks," she says.

I didn't mind helping her. It pushed Henry to the back of my mind for a while. When she finally lets go and I can breathe again, I say, "No problem. It was fun. And you look hot."

"But do I look *older*?"

"Way older."

Beaming, she plops down onto my bed, and as she studies my face, her smile slowly dims. "Don't take this wrong, but you've been looking sort of wiped out the past few days. Do you feel bad?"

"No, I just haven't been sleeping that great, though."

"Because of the visions?"

"Yeah." I shrug. "That and other things."

Fluffing her new bangs, she gives me a knowing look and says, "Oh, I get it. You mean Tate. So you're going out with him later, huh?"

"Not going out, exactly."

"He likes you, I can tell. Not just for a friend. He *likes* you, likes you."

I attempt to look indifferent. "He's just going to show me around the canyon so I can take some photos."

"Oh, happy dagger! Please try to control your excitement."

"It's just that . . . I'm a little afraid of spending time with him."

"Afraid? Why?"

"Because I do like Tate and—" Blinking, I turn toward the window. "When I'm with Tate, sometimes I feel like I'm cheating on Henry." I pause and look at her again. "Now tell me you don't think I'm nuts."

"I think you're confusing yourself with Isabel. Who wouldn't? Geez, you're getting inside pictures, going back to the past, living through her." She sighs. "Such stuff as dreams are made of."

"It's weird. I like both of them." Embarrassed by the admission, I add, "And they even look alike. Almost exactly."

"Henry probably knows you like Tate, so he makes himself look similar so it will be easier to woo you and get his message through."

"Why doesn't he just tell me his message instead of tormenting me?"

"It's not that easy."

"Why not?" For some reason, her that's-just-the-way-it-is attitude exasperates me. "Is there some unwritten rule among ghosts that they have to make everything a big puzzle for us humans to solve, or what?"

"It could be a lot of reasons. Spirits try to communicate in different ways."

"Great. How are we supposed to figure any of this out then?"

She tilts her head. "Have you seen any things over and over again in your visions?"

"I don't know, why?"

"He might use symbols for clues to try to get through to you. Something he knows means something to you. One of those ghost guys on TV sees yellow roses when a female is coming through, because those were his mom's favorite flowers. That kind of association thing might be what Henry's using, too."

The ring of the bell at the Quattlebaums' farm comes to mind. The farmer and the dog showing up at 8:15 in the morning. The nightingale's song. "I guess the bird could be a symbol, but nightingales don't have any special meaning for me," I tell Bethyl Ann. "Besides, I think Henry *is* the nightingale, as weird as that sounds. I mean, he's a poet and that Shelley quote says—"

"A poet is a nightingale!" Bethyl Ann claps her hands together and grins. "You're right. Henry *is* a poet. He *is* the nightingale. He's having all kinds of fun playing off Shelley's quote to seduce you."

"I don't know about seduce." The word makes me squirm. "Summon maybe."

"Seduce, summon." Bethyl Ann waves a dismissive hand. "What's in a name?"

"You could be right. I've actually been thinking the same thing." The nightingale's song always tempts me to return to Henry's memories, and Henry's poems speak to me. "I love his poetry," I say quietly. "It's like his words were intended for me, in a way. When I read them, I hear his voice, like he's talking to me."

"That's so *romantic*," Bethyl Ann says wistfully. "It must *kill* you to be away from him." She heaves a dramatic sigh and murmurs, "Never was a tale of more woe than this of Tansy and her Henry-O." She frowns. "Or is it a 'story'? I can't remember the quote exactly."

All at once, I miss Henry so much that I can't stand it. Is he lonely without me? Does he need me? Oh, God . . . is he hurting himself? Hoping Bethyl Ann doesn't notice my sudden distress, I say, "He wrote those poems a long time ago when he was alive. They couldn't have been written with me in mind."

"How do you know he wrote them a long time ago?"

"What are you saying? That he wrote them as a ghost?"

"It's possible."

"How? I read the first one just a few minutes after we got here."

"Maybe he's a fast writer." She giggles.

I send her a chastising look, and say, "The only other thing I can think of that he might be using as a way to communicate with me is my camera. It definitely means something to me. That's how I first saw him, too. Through my viewfinder. And I go into his memories through photographs I take."

Bethyl Ann sits straighter. "Aha! Now we're getting somewhere."

"Where?" I ask, frustrated. "It still doesn't make any sense."

"Patience, grasshopper. Let's think about the crystal. How is it significant to you?"

"It's not. Anyway, I think we're off base. Maybe we should be trying to figure out what they meant to Henry or Isabel, not me. I mean, the crystal obviously meant something to them. He gave it to her as a gift."

"Yes, but for you he turned it into a transportation device. Maybe it's also some kind of key." She glances toward the door of my room. "Have you found any hidden locked passages or rooms in this place?"

"No. I don't know where they'd be."

"Duh." She crosses her eyes. "*Hidden?* Must I define the meaning?"

"Funny," I say sarcastically. "The Dilworth brothers have been over every inch of this place painting and making repairs. I think they would've said something if they had found secret rooms or passages."

"Darn," Bethyl Ann says, frowning. "What about that man and dog? What could they mean?"

I look toward the window, picturing the Quattlebaums' farm across the field. "The man is Isabel's dad, and Kip is her dog. They just seem to signify what was going on at the time of that particular memory . . . what Papa Dan, Henry, and Isabel were seeing."

Bethyl Ann purses her lips. "Was anything special about that day?"

"I don't know. It was the first time Daniel admitted to Isabel that he didn't trust Henry maybe? The first time she admitted to herself that she thought of Henry as more than a friend?" More discouraged than ever, I say, "I don't have a clue what any of this means. I'm not even sure my feelings for Henry are all coming from Isabel. I felt connected to him the minute I read his first poem, before I even knew about her."

"Can I read the poems? Maybe if I did, I'd feel a connection, too, and I'd have a better idea of what's going on."

"I don't know. . . ." I feel an embarrassing twinge of jealousy, like I don't *want* her to feel a connection to Henry.

Bethyl Ann shrugs. "That's okay. If you're not ready."

"Don't be mad."

"I'm not. Some things should remain between lovers, I guess." She falls back against the pillows. "There's nothing more dreamy than a love triangle. You and Henry. Henry and Bell. You and Tate."

For some reason, her dramatics make me laugh despite my misery. "Speaking of . . . there's another reason I feel weird about spending time with Tate. He was friendly; then he wasn't; now he's friendly again. And he blames that on a bad mood? Sometimes I think he's being nice to me for a reason."

"Duh. He's a guy. Aren't they always nice to girls for a reason? They want to—you know." Wiggling her brows, Bethyl Ann stands and starts across the room toward her book bag in the corner. "Not that I know firsthand," she adds.

"Besides that," I say.

"Maybe he just likes you." She carries her bag to the

bed and sits beside me again. "At least his taste is getting better. You're a big improvement over the prior object of his affection."

"Who?"

"Shanna."

"Oh." That's not something I wanted to hear. "Why did they break up?"

"He probably got sick of her being so mean. Shanna cheated on Tate every time he turned his back."

Recalling how horrible it felt to be betrayed by Hailey, I sympathize with Tate, even if he was stupid enough to hook up with someone like Shanna. "So I guess Alison's just like her, since they're always together."

"No, Alison's okay." Bethyl Ann's gaze shifts away as she unzips the book bag and begins stuffing her magazines inside.

Curious over her sudden silence, I say, "I saw her crying outside City Drug."

She looks up. "Alison?"

"Yep. Turns out she was upset over a stupid grade. Then her mom came out and overreacted, too—not about the grade. She freaked because she didn't see Alison."

"Don't think Alison and Shanna are the same, 'cause they're not," Bethyl Ann says defensively. "Alison can be trusted."

"Okay. I'm sorry." I scowl at her. "I don't get why you're so protective of her, but I won't say anything negative about perfect Alison again."

Bethyl Ann lowers her bag to the floor and stares down at it, plucking at the ends of her hair as if she can't believe the unfamiliar shorter strands are her own. Finally, she looks up at me and says quietly, "For the record, I'm pretty sure you can trust Cassius, too."

"How do you know?"

"I've known Tate forever. He might've been a grump when you first got here, but, alas, what fools these mortals be. Especially mortals of the male persuasion." She sighs. "The course of true love never does run smooth. Give poor Cassius a second chance."

We drag the box of clothes downstairs for Bethyl Ann to take home. Mom gasps when she sees her. "Look at you!" she squeals, then proceeds to gush over the amazing transformation of Stinky Pugh. She says Bethyl Ann looks "hip," which proves how totally out-of-touch Mom is, but I understand what she means, and I agree.

Unfortunately, when Mrs. Pugh arrives, she isn't as thrilled. Bethyl Ann's mother gapes at her, then starts to cry. Mom puts an arm around Mrs. Pugh's shoulders, and they take off toward the living room to talk. Mrs. Pugh seems better when she returns to the kitchen, but she won't look at me, and she watches Bethyl Ann like she's searching for glimpses of the daughter she remembers.

I wait until they leave before telling Mom I'm going to the canyon with Tate for a while. She keeps her back to me as she washes a head of lettuce under the kitchen faucet.

"Is there something you want to talk about first?" she asks.

"I can't think of anything."

"You look exhausted. Have you been sleeping okay?"

"I'm sleeping fine," I lie. "Quit thinking something's wrong with me all the time."

"It just seems like something's troubling you. I'm glad that you're making friends here, but is school causing you any problems?"

"It's all good, Mom. Really. Where's Papa Dan?"

"Upstairs napping." She turns off the tap and shakes water off the lettuce into the sink.

"Has he been outside during the day when I'm at school?"

"Not alone. Why?"

I open my mouth to tell her about the cellar door, about seeing someone out there a couple of times during the night. But then I think of the psychology book I read in the library, of the schizophrenia symptoms that match mine so closely . . . and I can't do it.

She sets the lettuce on a cutting board, grabs a towel, and dries her hands. "What is it?"

"Nothing. I just worry about him, that's all."

"I know, sweetie. Me, too. But right now, I'm more worried about you."

"Don't be."

She's quiet for several moments, then says, "We're having company for dinner."

"Tonight?"

"I invited Ray Don, so be back here by seven, okay?"

"*Sheriff* Ray Don?"

"That's right." Laughing, she tries to pop me with the towel, but I jump back, avoiding it just in time.

"Why is the sheriff coming to dinner? Are you *dating* him?" Mom doesn't date. She only flirts outrageously and breaks hearts. When she doesn't answer me, I say, "*Mom.*" I don't know if I can handle any more change in my life right now.

"I hear a car outside," she says. "It's probably Tate, and you'd better hurry. You only have about an hour and a half."

I stare at her.

Mom stares back. "Be careful, okay?"

I run upstairs to get my camera, and ten minutes later Tate and I are walking into the canyon by way of a trail that seems oddly familiar. As I shoot photographs, he asks questions about developing film in the darkroom. I try to explain the process, then, ignoring my guilty feelings of betraying Henry, I offer to show him sometime. I think the invitation is what he was after in the first place.

We take a cutoff onto a different trail that leads beneath the bridge. Pausing, I step back and look up. The jutting cliff beside the bridge's entrance reminds me of the place where Henry and I stood the last time I saw him, the place where he kissed me when I was Bell.

When I was Bell. Ohmygod.

I really hope Bethyl Ann knows what she's talking about when it comes to ghosts. Otherwise, I'm destined for a mental institution.

Tate stops beside me, shielding his eyes from the sun with one hand as he gazes up at the bridge. "They say Henry Peterson used to stand on the railing. Apparently, he threatened to jump more than once before he actually took the leap."

An image flashes before my eyes—Henry on the railing with his arms out, looking at Bell and asking if she'd even care if he fell. Fear and dread weave through my body, winding through muscle and bone, twisting and tangling around my lungs.

"The rumor is that he jumped because of a girl," Tate goes on.

The knots in the tangle pull tight, cutting off my air supply and making me gasp.

Tate jerks his head around to look at me. "It's just a stupid story."

"It's not stupid; it's terrible. He was a real person." Humiliated by the harsh, emotional tone of my voice, I avert my gaze and try to calm down. "Do you believe it?"

"That he jumped? I guess."

"I don't get why people are so sure of that. I mean, if he used to walk the railing, couldn't he have slipped and fallen?"

"Maybe. But from what I've heard, the dude was pretty intense. And, like I said, supposedly he'd made threats."

"Beth says he hurt himself on purpose. That once he even shot himself in the foot." I won't admit that I actually read the rumor about the shooting in the newspaper archives; I don't want Tate knowing I'm so obsessed with Henry that I've been doing research.

Tate's brows lift. "I never heard that, but I guess it fits."

We start walking again, and after a few seconds I ask, "What about the haunting part? Do you believe that, too? You said the other day that anything's possible."

"I was joking. You're the one who lives in his house. What do you believe?"

"I don't know. I've heard some things I can't explain, and sometimes I feel . . ." I look down at the trail, hesitant and self-conscious.

"A presence?" he asks, and I hear that note again in his voice, the one that makes me think he knows more about Henry than he's letting on.

My laugh is dismissive. "I'm sure it's my imagination. You know, because of all the talk. We hadn't been in town half an hour before the Quattlebaums came over to tell us all the superstitions about the house. Now every time I hear a creak or rattle, I imagine it's his ghost walking around."

Tate laughs. "Well, if you run into Henry, tell him hello for me."

Henry wouldn't like that. He'd be jealous.

I flinch. Whoa, where did that thought come from?

Uneasiness drifts down on me like a spider's web as we continue to follow the trail. When we reach a curve, I gaze over my shoulder for another look at the bridge, and pause.

Lifting my camera, I take a picture of the place where Henry last stood . . . and shudder.

When the numbers on my digital clock click over to midnight, I switch on my lamp and sit up. The nightingale sings louder tonight . . . longer. An hour ago, I stuffed cotton balls in my ears, but I can still hear the bird calling faintly, and I can't sleep. The sheet and blanket are twisted around my legs. I have too much on my mind. The rumor Tate told me about Henry committing suicide because of a girl, for one thing. Was it Isabel? Was she there when he jumped? I'm horrified that Isabel might've seen Henry fall to his death.

The sudden change in Tate still bothers me, too. The necklace chain was such an unexpected gift. Was it just a peace offering? Or something more?

I also can't quit thinking about Mom. Sheriff Ray Don stammered his way through dinner tonight. Whenever he looked at Mom, which was 98 percent of the time, I expected syrup to leak from his eye sockets. But that's not what worries me; he's nice enough. I mean, he devoted 1 percent of his attention to me and 1 percent to Papa Dan. He didn't leave my grandfather out of the conversation like a lot of people do. Because Papa Dan is so quiet, it's too easy to forget he occupies the same room.

Since I've decided to make more of an effort to befriend the natives, and because I knew it would please Mom, I gave the sheriff some photographs I shot of Cedar Canyon.

Mom *was* pleased. Maybe too pleased. I'm not sure why, but the way she acts around Sheriff Ray Don bothers me. She's her usual flirty self but nervous, too. I've never seen her act skittish around anybody. She hopes people like her, but if they don't, she takes it the way Bethyl Ann would; Mom won't apologize for who she is or feel bad about it. But tonight she couldn't quit verbally kicking herself for being a bad cook, a fact that never bothered her before. She seemed upset that her overdone roast beef was as tough as damp tree bark.

Yawning, I untangle myself from the covers and take the cotton from my ears. I'll never get used to the West Texas wind. Gusts are blowing so hard outside, I wouldn't be surprised to wake up tomorrow, walk out the door, and find myself in the next county. A tree branch scratches the side of the house. The rafters rattle and pop. But I still hear strains of the nightingale's song—they wrap around me.

My backpack sits on the floor, propped against my desk, the crystal pendant and the envelope of photographs I've started carrying with me to school inside it. Only the pocket watch and journal remain in the table drawer upstairs, and I don't need them to do what I have in mind—what I can't seem to resist doing whenever the nightingale sings.

The crystal chills my fingers as I pull it out of my pack, as if every one of Bell's winter memories are compressed inside it. The necklace chain Tate gave me lies on the nightstand. I pick it up and thread it through the tiny loop at the top of the pendant. After securing the chain around my neck, I pull out the photos, shuffle through them, pausing on one of the front entrance of Cedar Canyon High. Excitement mixes with apprehension as I study the marble columns, the arches, the tall narrow windows above. "What could you tell me?" I whisper. After what I learned from Tate today, I'm more worried than ever about Henry—about Daniel and Bell. Her most of all. Do the answers to what happened to them lie behind that row of massive double doors in the photograph? What went on inside the school building when Isabel, Henry, and Papa Dan were students?

All at once I'm cold, but even so, sweat sheens my forehead. Whatever happened, it's over; I can't change it. I can't save Henry or Bell. I can't spare my grandfather the memories that haunt him. But I still have to do this; I have to go back, if only to see Henry again. I'm really starting to like Tate, to think about him as much as I think of Henry. I don't want to feel guilty when I'm with Tate. What if he asks me to homecoming? I try to imagine that. The dress I would wear, the mum he'd buy me—such normal things I can't help smiling. Maybe I should tell Henry that I can't see him again. Maybe then he'll just tell me his message straight out and I can put an end to all this and move on with real life.

A sense that Henry hears my thoughts creeps over me. I feel the grip of his hands on my shoulders as surely as if he stands in the room. His anger that I would consider saying good-bye seems to vibrate the air.

I hold the photo in front of me, and with my other hand,

lift the crystal from where it rests against my chest. A tilt to the right and it catches the lamp's glow. I wait, hold my breath, and tilt it to the left. A bright prism of light streaks out and blinds me. . . .

. . . *I'm inside a school gymnasium packed with students wearing festive, formal clothing. Isabel's mother made the taffeta dress I wear and the material is itchy against my flesh—her flesh—Isabel's, mine.*

"Jeepers creepers, where'd you get those peepers?" Isabel sings along with the music playing on the phonograph. She stands close to the wall, tapping the toe of her keg-heeled shoe against the wooden floor and waiting for Henry to bring her a cup of punch. He's been gone too long, a quarter of an hour, at least.

With her hands clasped in front of her, she watches the dancers gyrate and spin beneath the giant, white paper snowflakes suspended from the ceiling. Spotting Daniel and Louise dancing on the far side of the room, Isabel calls out to them and waves, giggling when Daniel stumbles a little. He never could cut a rug, *she* thinks. He has no rhythm. *If I could, I would tell Isabel that will change. That he will learn to jitterbug and two-step and waltz in college. That he and my grandmother will win a contest and take home a gold trophy that Daniel will still keep on his dresser when he is an old man.*

The music changes to Glenn Miller's "In the Mood," and Isabel hums along with the song. She thinks about the picture the newspaper photographer took of her with Henry, Louise, and Daniel when they arrived. Louise had been humming off-key when the photographer approached them, and Isabel was laughing at her tone-deaf friend. She had been so excited about Henry accompanying her to the Winter Dance that it didn't occur to her until the flashbulb flared that if the Gazette prints the shot, her parents will see it and know that she was with Henry tonight.

She's wondering how she will explain that, when a few feet away, she hears someone say Henry's name. Isabel turns and sees Doris Collier, Margaret Thompson, and Betty McCoy with their heads together, whispering. She follows the direction of their gaze and her shiver scatters through me. Henry strides toward her, watching her with hooded eyes as he slices through the dancers like a blade, parting couples with each step he takes. He carries a cup in one hand, a silver flask in the other. Boldly, he lifts the flask to his mouth and drinks.

A shock wave jolts through Isabel, and her hand flies up to the bauble she wears above the neckline of her plum-colored dress—the crystal pendant Henry gave her. Alarmed by the look in his eye, she quickly searches the dance floor for Daniel and Louise, hoping they'll come to her rescue and help her calm whatever storm is brewing inside him, but she can't find them.

Henry reaches her side and hands her the cup. She smells liquor on his breath. "Let's go," he says, then lifts the flask and takes another swig.

"Put that away," she whispers, praying no chaperones have seen him. "You'll get kicked out."

"Too late," Henry slurs. He nods across the gym to where Mr. Owen, the principal, watches them with crossed arms and narrowed eyes. "He says he'll be calling my folks tomorrow." Henry laughs bitterly. "If he figures out how to reach them, maybe he'll let me in on the secret. Not that they'd give a rat's ass what I'm doing, anyway."

Before she can ask any questions, Henry grabs her wrist and starts walking. "Our coats," Isabel stammers, but he doesn't stop. It's all she can do to keep up with him as he heads for the exit. Punch sloshes from the cup she holds and onto her dress. She manages to set the cup on a table beside the door just before they step outside into the frigid night air. The door slams shut behind them. Snow crunches beneath their feet.

Halfway to the curb, Isabel hears the door open again. Music blares, then muffles. Someone yells, "Henry!"

Henry comes to an abrupt halt, and Isabel stumbles. They both turn to see Daniel rushing toward them.

"Where are you going?" Daniel asks.

Henry leers at him. "I've been asked to leave."

"I heard. You're drunk."

"Am I, now?" Staring defiantly at Daniel, he takes another long, taunting drink from the silver flask.

Tears of humiliation form a hard knot in Isabel's throat. Shivering, she whispers, "Henry, stop." She can't bear to look at Daniel. She knows what he's thinking—that they've been wrong about Henry all these years, that everyone else is right. He thinks Henry is unhinged and peculiar, that he should be locked up in a hospital somewhere. That she is almost as crazy for loving him. Why is Henry doing this to her? To himself?

Despite his behavior tonight, despite the horrifying slashes on his wrist—proof of his troubled soul—she longs to defend Henry. Defend herself. She loves him, and that fact builds her resolve to stand by him, no matter what anyone thinks, even Daniel.

Daniel calls her name and she lifts her chin, steadies herself, and meets his gaze squarely. "I told Mr. Owen I'd see you home," he says, offering her his hand. "Come inside. We'll get Louise."

"I'm not going anywhere without Henry."

Concern flickers in Daniel's eyes. "We'll take him, too. He shouldn't be driving. The roads are icy, and he can barely stand up."

"Don't talk about me as if I'm not here," Henry snaps, slipping the flask into his jacket pocket. "You're not taking me anywhere." He tightens his grip on Isabel's arm, and they start down the sidewalk again.

"Let me help you," Daniel pleads as he follows behind them. "Henry, you're fried."

"Go back to your boring new friends," Henry snarls over his shoulder.

"Think of Isabel, Henry. Even when you're sober, you drive like a madman."

We reach Henry's car, and he releases Isabel's arm to open the door.

"Let me take you home, Isabel," Daniel says. "Your folks will never forgive me if I let you go with him."

I feel her loyalty to Henry, her denial that he might hurt her, and at once it becomes my own. Our love will keep us safe and save him, make everything right again, make him all right. And then an image of the bridge creeps in to cloud my certainty and with it . . . fear. What if he takes her there now? What if tonight is the night? What if we see him—

Dread washes through me, but I don't sense Isabel's awareness of it. With everything in me, I try to make her feel it, too, try to weave my thoughts into her brain until she hears them whispering through her mind as I hear hers. Her legs are mine, so why can't I make her step away from the car, away from Henry? "I'll be okay," she tells Daniel as she moves past the door Henry holds open for her and climbs into the car.

For the first time, I realize how little control I have over the situation. I am completely at Isabel's mercy. What happens to her will happen to me until I go back to my own world—the real world. But what if I don't go back this time? What if I'm stuck here in this car alone with Henry? If I can't reach Isabel, can I reach him? Reason with him? Resist him? Stand up for myself? Even if I can, can I make Isabel do the same?

It's no use. How did I ever think I could tell Henry good-bye or anything else? Why won't he say what he wants me to know, give me his message and let me leave?

"Isabel," Daniel says, "you're asking for trouble."

She knows that Daniel isn't referring to the icy roads and Henry's inability to drive; I know it, too, and I'm afraid.

Henry closes the door, takes a breath, then swivels around and punches Daniel in the face. Isabel shrieks as blood spurts from Daniel's nose and he stumbles backward, slipping on the icy sidewalk and landing on his tailbone. Before he can get up, Henry runs around to the driver's side of the car and jumps in. He starts the engine and takes off.

"Why did you do that?" Isabel cries, grasping his arm.

"Daniel needs to mind his own business." The car swerves left to right as Henry looks down at his jacket and fumbles in the pocket for his flask. Pulling it out, he opens it using only one hand, then lifts it to his mouth and drinks.

Isabel stares out the front window at the layer of snow and ice encrusted on it. Bracing herself, she clutches the sides of the seat and yells, "You can't see! Slow down. You're driving too fast." She squeezes her eyes shut when the car hits a bump and veers off toward the side of the road. Her head snaps back as they lurch to a stop nose-down in the ditch.

Before she can catch her breath, Henry is leaning over, kissing her, pressing her back against the seat. I taste the alcohol on his breath, feel the pressure of his body, and my own emotions surge up, overpowering Isabel's. I feel trapped . . . threatened. But it's Isabel who places her hands to his chest, Isabel who tries to push him away. "Stop!" she breathes against Henry's lips. "Don't do this . . . please."

Henry pulls back, and I taste tears on Isabel's lips. "Henry," she whispers, "why are you doing this?" She lifts her hand to his face and brushes her fingers across his cheek. "What's wrong with you? What's wrong?"

Henry tenses. "What's wrong with me?" Raw pain sizzles in his glare. Scooting over, he reaches to open the glove box and pulls a metal scraper from inside. Then he throws open his door, letting in a gush of cold air. "You're no different than the others," he says in a pinched voice, climbing from the car.

Shivering and aching, Isabel watches Henry scrape snow and ice from the windshield. When he finishes, he climbs in beside her again, starts the engine, and throws the vehicle into Reverse. The tires spin in place as Henry steps on the gas—

—I startle and exhale as the world around me transforms. The photograph slips from my hand and flutters to the floor. I clutch the crystal with fingers that are as cold as my toes. My head throbs, making me wonder what jolted me back. Then I hear it . . . a noise outside, carried by the wind. The nightingale goes silent.

Remnants of the terrifying experience in Henry's world crowd my mind as I make my way to the window and look out. Tattered clouds cover the moon. Tree branches bend and sway. Shadows dance across the lawn. I move to the other window that overlooks the cellar and barn, squint, and look closer. The shadows part and, between them, I see someone bent over the cellar door.

Adrenaline shoots through me as, inhaling sharply, I turn and press my back to the wall. Why doesn't Mom ever hear the prowler outside? If she has, wouldn't she have mentioned it? Wouldn't she have gone down to investigate? Her room is at the front of the house, so maybe she's too far away to hear. Or, like the ringing bell at the Quattlebaums' farm and the nightingale's song, maybe the noise is only meant to reach my ears.

I know I should wake her and tell her someone is trying to break into the cellar. Tell her about the door's splintered edges. We could take a flashlight and check it out together. Or call Sheriff Ray Don and ask him to come.

But what if I did and we didn't find any sign of an intruder near the cellar? What if the wooden door is smooth? Intact? What if I'm the only one who sees the damage?

She and the sheriff will know I'm messed up, confused, out of my mind. Mom will ask questions, and I won't be able to look her in the eye and lie. Would she take away my camera? The photographs? Henry's crystal and the journal? They're my only links to him. My only links to Daniel. And Bell. As terrified as I am of going back to the other world, I know that I have to, if only for her. I have to find a way to help Isabel. Even as I think that, I know how crazy it sounds. Whatever is going to happen to Bell has already taken place. I can't undo it. Or can I?

I concentrate on pacing my breaths. I'm afraid to tell Mom about the prowler, and I'm afraid not to. But there's only one thing to do; I have to handle this myself, my way.

Pushing away from the wall, I hurry toward my bedroom door, open it quietly, slip down the stairs to the screened-in back porch, and let myself out. The wind moans as it rushes around me, so loud I can't hear anything else. Stubbly grass scratches the soles of my feet when I step into the yard, and goose bumps scatter up my bare legs. I crush the hem of my T-shirt together between the fingers of one fisted hand and walk toward the cellar, stopping short when I see a figure crouched over the door. One arm rears back. The shadowy figure is holding something. "Who's there?" I call in a quaking voice.

The shadow wobbles, jumps up, and runs behind the barn. I follow, but the pebbles poking my bare feet slow me down, and by the time I circle to the back, the prowler is nowhere in sight.

Panting, I stand beneath the cloaked moon, staring across the field. Wind whips the long grass, turning it into a dark sea of waves that crash in my ears, drowning out every other noise in the night. But soon the gusts subside to a breeze, and the roar calms to a *shush*ing sound. I hear the blades of the old windmill creaking, see its shadow towering in the distance like a broken lighthouse. Something tickles my toes, and just as the clouds part and a flicker of moonlight filters through, I glance down and see paper fluttering beneath my right arch. Crouching for a closer look, I raise my foot. Not paper, a *feather*. Tiny and brown like the nightingale. I try to grab it, but another sudden, hard gust blows it out of my reach, and the feather floats away into the black sky.

Gazing across the field, I wrap my arms around myself. Tomorrow night, if the prowler comes back, I'll be ready . . . whether it's Henry's ghost or a flesh-and-bone person.

18

The next day, I forget to remove Papa Dan's beret before homeroom. Mrs. Tilby is in a horrible mood. She doesn't waste time telling me to take it off; instead, she marches to my table and tugs the hat off my head. The laughter in the room dies quickly beneath her stern glare. Mrs. Tilby returns to her desk, scribbles on a pad, then brings me a detention slip.

Across the lab table, a monochrome Rooster Boy mouths, *Zombie Girl*, his lips wrapping grotesquely around each syllable, his wink exaggerated. Beside him, Tate watches me with an expression on his face that I can't read—worry, maybe, and something else. I turn away from his gaze, and as everyone heads for their next class, I hurry out into the hallway and disappear into a pewter sea of students before he can stop me.

The gloom continues through first period. I spend the entire class trying to ward off a panic attack. After finding the bird feather last night, I went back to bed, but the incidents with Henry and the prowler kept replaying through my mind until all the details became jumbled and intertwined. I didn't even doze, and I feel as if I'm sleepwalking today.

When class ends, I escape to the restroom and close myself in a stall, dizzy and sweating. The photos are inside my backpack. I have Bell's crystal around my neck, hidden beneath my shirt. I pull it free, comforted by its silky smoothness.

I'm afraid to see Henry again, but I have to make sure that Bell is safe. I'm so worried about her. Did he take her home? Did they make it back safely on the icy roads? *Did Henry hurt her . . . or himself?* After the way he acted that night, maybe I shouldn't even care what happened to him, but I do. I want to look into his eyes, tell him everything will turn out okay, even though I know that's a lie. I want to rub my thumb across the scars on his wrist and take away his pain. How can I love him and be so afraid of him, too?

The zipper sounds loud in the silent restroom as I tug open my backpack. My fingers find the photographs without searching. I do what I have to do and wait for the shimmer of light to transport me. . . .

. . . *The sun's rays weaken with twilight's approach. Henry chases Isabel up the trail. Near the top, she squeals, dodging his outstretched arms. Too late. He catches her wrist, tugs, and we tumble to the snow-dusted ground. During our playful scuffle, she manages to scoop up a handful of snow in her glove and toss it at him. Laughing and red-faced, he rolls her onto her back and pins her wrists at either side of her head.*

"Let me up! It's freezing down here!" Isabel cries.

A glint lights Henry's eyes. "Say 'uncle.'"

"I won't!"

"I guess you'll just have to freeze then."

She glares up at him, says, "Uncle," so quietly I barely hear the word.

"Louder." He tightens his grip. "Say it like you mean it."

"Uncle!" she yells. "I'm turning into an icicle!"

"Then I'll just have to melt you." He kisses her slowly until she stops struggling and kisses him back. Then he lifts his head and looks at her in a way that turns me inside out. Shifting his weight, he stands and pulls her to her feet.

Isabel frees her wrist from his grasp, and then dusts snow off her shoulders and the back of her hat. "You're a tyrant, Henry Peterson." She tries to sound miffed, but it's impossible to be angry with him—impossible for Isabel and for me. How long has it been since I last laughed as much? In this world—as Bell—maybe only yesterday. But in my other world—as Tansy—I can't remember the last time I've felt as giddy or had so much fun.

Bell has forgiven Henry for his behavior last night at the Winter Dance and for what happened afterward. Now that I'm here and understand her reasoning, I find myself forgiving him, too. The alcohol turned him into a stranger. Henry didn't scare or hurt us; the stranger did. The stranger was forceful and dangerous, not Henry. Isabel has convinced herself of this; I want to believe it, too, and so I push my doubts aside.

"Don't pout." Henry draws her closer. "Why didn't you sneak

over to the house last night after I dropped you off? You said you would. I kept my end of the bargain and went to that ridiculous dance."

Isabel drops her gaze. "I wanted to come, but—"

"Were you with someone else?"

His sudden harsh tone startles me. "Of course not!" Isabel protests. But then the memory of a face flashes through my mind, one resembling Henry's yet different enough that I know it isn't his but Tate's. I have the strangest feeling that Isabel sees it, too. "No," she repeats more softly, looking down again. "I was home in bed."

"Were you afraid?" Isabel nods, and he lifts her chin until I look into his eyes. "What happened last night . . . it won't happen again, Bell . . . I'm sorry."

"I know," she whispers.

"What did I tell you?"

"Not to be afraid of us being together."

He smiles. "Will you trust me next time?"

She nods again.

"Good, because I waited for you, and I was disappointed. Don't disappoint me again, Bell. I need you."

For just a moment, Henry's eyes look like the stranger's did last night, and his voice holds the same intensity. I'm not sure if the ripple of unease I feel is my own or Isabel's—or if we share it. But the realization that the stranger is a part of Henry brings with it a powerful, unsettling dread. Is it possible to keep that side of him at bay?

"We're together now," Isabel says quickly, desperate to smooth the ruffled edges of his anger and chase away his terrifying twin.

"It isn't enough," he tells her. "I want you with me all the time."

She steps away from him. "What are you saying?"

He catches her hands in his. "Do you want to be with me?"

"You know I do, but how?"

"We could go away."

"I can't leave Mama and Daddy. They'd never let me go."

"They don't have to know. We'll plan it so they won't miss you until it's too late."

The idea of running away with Henry frightens and thrills Isabel at once. "I don't know, Henry," she says. "Where would we go?"

"Somewhere they'll never find us. I don't want to have to sneak around to be together anymore. Do you?"

I look down at Isabel's shoes as she whispers, "No."

A recent lecture from her parents comes to mind. I'm not sure how I know what they said, since I wasn't there, but I do. They insisted that Henry is "trouble" and that she shouldn't see him. When they found out she skipped school to be alone with him, they forbade her to spend time with him outside of class. We're only here now thanks to Louise. Louise wasn't happy about it, but Isabel talked her into providing an alibi again today. I realize, though, that she's only buying time. The photo from the Winter Dance is bound to appear in the evening newspaper or, at the very latest, tomorrow's edition. When Isabel's parents see it, I won't be surprised if they send her south to live with her aunt, just as they warned her they would. Isabel is also afraid that's what they'll do.

She lifts onto her toes and kisses Henry's cheek, wondering how she would bear living so far away from him. Even though her feelings for Henry are new, she knows that if forced to choose between him and her parents, her mother and father will lose. "Mama and Daddy are suspicious," she whispers. "They watch me like a hawk."

"How did you manage to meet me today?"

"They had an appointment in Amarillo they couldn't miss. Mama called Louise's mother to arrange for me to go home with her after school. Louise went to Daniel's to study, and her mother thinks I'm with her." She glances toward the trail. "I should hurry to Daniel's house now to meet them. Will you drive me? They'll be back soon."

"Only if you promise you'll run away with me. I'll take care of you. I'll take care of everything."

A shiver of apprehension scatters through her. "But how will we live?"

"There's plenty of money in Father's safe. Enough to last until I find work."

"You can't steal from your parents, Henry. It isn't right."

Henry's jaw hardens. "They owe me a lot more than money. Maybe this will finally get their attention."

Struck by the implication of his words, Isabel says softly, "Is that what running away with me is really all about, Henry? Trying to get your parents' attention? Am I only another scar on your wrist or bullet in your foot?"

Henry's face falls and he flushes a deep shade of red. He drops her hand and looks away.

She reaches for him, but Henry turns his back to her. "I shouldn't have said that," Isabel murmurs.

"If you think that's all you are to me, then you don't know me at all."

She touches his shoulder. "I'm trying to make sense of all this, Henry. I'm trying to understand what you're going through . . . what you need."

He faces her then, and when he looks into her eyes, I'm certain it's me that he sees. "I only need you," he whispers, his blue stare penetrating and clear. "I need you to believe in me."

A shiver rattles up my spine, and in that instant there are only the two of us—Henry and me. He knows. He knows that I'm inside her. And just when I think I'll come apart if I look at him another moment, Isabel turns away from his gaze, and I can breathe again. I see the bridge in the distance, so solid and imposing and intractable. Larger than anything else around it. Bolder. Beautiful and eerie. Different and out of place. Henry is the same as the bridge. Without him, life would be empty. As empty as the canyon would be without the bridge.

"What about Daniel?" she asks quietly. "I couldn't keep such a secret from him. He'd be so hurt when he found out. And I can't imagine never seeing him again."

"I didn't say you couldn't see Daniel again. He could go with us."

Isabel looks at him. "You'd let him?"

He skims a gloved fingertip across her lower lip, and I feel the tingle all the way to my toes. "I'd do anything to have you with me, Bell. Anything. You can't tell Daniel what we have in mind, though. Not yet. Don't even hint at it."

"Why not?" Emotion wavers in her voice. "He won't tell anyone. Why are you being so mysterious? You're scaring me."

"Don't be scared. I just know Daniel. He'd try to discourage us. Let me work everything out first. Then he'll see that leaving is the right thing to do for all of us. We don't belong here."

No, I think, that isn't true. *Henry is the only one who doesn't belong here. Isabel loves Cedar Canyon, and so does Daniel. She loves her family, the school, her friends. But if her parents stand by their threat, she'll be forced to leave anyway, sent to her aunt's. She takes a moment to weigh her options—living with a woman she barely knows or running away with Henry. The choice is clear to both of us. There is no choice.*

"Okay," *she reluctantly agrees.* "I'll go."

Henry crushes her against him, and laughter bubbles out of me. "Meet me here at midnight," *he says.* "I'll tell Daniel to come, too. By then I'll have a foolproof plan, and he'll be forced to agree it's a good one."

"Tonight? You don't mean for us to leave then, do you? Not so soon . . ."

"We'll just convince Daniel. It'll be safer at midnight. There'll be no chance of anyone following us or overhearing our plans."

"I don't think Daniel will leave Cedar Canyon or his parents just so you and I can be together."

"That's his decision to make."

A prairie dog darts from a nearby stand of brush and across the trail beside us. Startled by the sudden movement, Isabel jumps, and Henry holds her tighter. She rests her head on his shoulder and I look through her eyes at the sunset. It's getting late, and Isabel knows we should leave, but Henry's skin smells of campfire smoke and soap, and his breath is scented with the hot chocolate they drank earlier.

Life with him would always be an adventure. Henry may not be

safe, but Isabel and I agree that every moment spent in his arms is
worth the risk.

"Kiss me, Bell," he murmurs.

Lifting my head from his shoulder, I raise onto my toes and press
my lips to his—

—the second-period bell shrieks, and suddenly I'm startled back into the restroom stall, breathless and disoriented, my mouth still tingling from Henry's kiss. On the other side of the stall door, feet shuffle past, moving faster and faster until, finally, the last pair of shoes disappears. Peeking out, I find the restroom empty.

I return the photograph to my backpack and leave my hiding place, torn about Henry's plans, shaken and excited at once. Were he and Bell together when he died? If only I could figure out what went wrong, maybe I could change it and they could be together forever.

We could be together.

Do I really want that? What about my own life here? Mom and Papa Dan. Bethyl Ann. Tate; I care about him, too. And he seems to care about me. But are my feelings for him as strong as my feelings for Henry? Maybe I wouldn't love Henry as much if Isabel's emotions weren't mingled with mine whenever I'm with him; I don't know.

After splashing cold water on my face at the sink, I glance into the mirror, pause, and stare. A girl I barely recognize stares back. Dry lips. Bruised crescents beneath both eyes. Three zits on my forehead—neighborly companions to the one on my chin. Hair smashed flat from the beret—

not my glossy, dark San Francisco hair. Sad, dull hair that needs washing. The mirror reflects an image of the sort of girl who'd duck and run if someone whispered "boo" and wiggled their fingers. I'm sick to think I've been walking around in public looking like this. I should've listened to Mom's concerns as well as Bethyl Ann's and Tate's when they told me how tired I look.

Confusion, anxiety, and exhaustion lace together inside me. What have I been thinking? Guys like Tate aren't interested in girls who look like social lepers. Who *are* social lepers. Why is he spending time with me after school? I've been stupid to believe he could care about me. What does he want? Is he playing some kind of prank? Acting on a dare? Is everyone laughing behind my back?

Salty tears sting my lips. I think of Tate's strange expression as he watched me in homeroom, that subtle look on his face I couldn't define, and I realize he wants something from me, but I have a feeling it isn't what I'd hoped. I can't believe I thought for one second he might ask me to homecoming. That I would go to the game wearing a mum decorated with ribbons and a glittery 10—his football number. Homecoming and the whole mum thing is such a big deal here in Podunk that everyone is already talking about the event, even though it's weeks away. I've always thought Homecoming was a corny tradition, so why do I even care if I go or not?

My throat burns, but I don't glance away from the mirror. Blinking . . . blinking . . . I look deeper into my eyes, watch a subtle shift take place, two images merging, superimposed. Sniffing again, I go still. My eyes . . . they're brown now, not green. They're larger, too, the lashes thicker. "Bell?" I whisper. Is hope or dread the emotion I feel coursing through me? I don't know the difference anymore.

A second bell sounds, the abrupt noise startling me like a thunderclap. I avert my attention from the mirror for only a second and, when I look back, my own green eyes stare back at me, red-rimmed and swollen.

The restroom smells like ammonia. I gulp in huge breaths of the pungent scent, stunned to realize that I've spent an entire forty-five-minute class period in here. At the sound of laughter on the other side of the door, I grab my backpack and dart into a stall again, unwilling to let anyone see me like this. I sit on the toilet tank, my feet on the lid.

A gust of noise blows into the restroom, voices I don't recognize bitching about a homework assignment. A stall door slams. Water rushes from a tap. Another gust. A toilet flushes. More voices mix in with the others. One with a husky, haughty edge that's familiar, probably from all the cigarettes she smokes while drinking her morning beer.

"*God. What* is his problem?" Shanna groans.

The assignment bitchers leave, their voices trailing behind them and into the swell of hallway noise. The door thuds shut. A book bag hits the floor, followed by a sharp sandpaper sound, then the smell of menthol and sulfur. I scoot quietly backward until I'm pressed against the wall.

"You're going to get caught again and sent to detention."

This voice has a soft lilt, full of care and concern. Straight-A Alison.

"Big freaking deal," Shanna says. "You won't snitch on me, will you?"

"Have I ever?"

"You want one?"

"Not here."

"You are *so* middle school sometimes. You worry too much. As if half the school staff doesn't sneak smokes in the teachers' lounge." More water in the sink. "He *quit* the *team*. I heard Coach Dryer is furious. Tate won't even tell him why."

Tate quit football? I think of the times we've been together after school. Even yesterday when he came over to the house, it never occurred to me that he must be missing practice.

"I feel bad for him." Alison sighs. "Maybe he's still messed up over his mom."

"He was always *pissed* at her. You know that."

"Who isn't pissed at their mother sometimes? Most mothers don't *leave*."

"Now that you mention it, he did quit calling me about the time she left."

Cigarette smoke filters through the crack between the stall door and the divider. I hold my breath and try not to cough as I peek out.

Alison and Shanna lean against the sinks. A smoldering cigarette lies next to the faucet. Shanna picks it up. "I am so *into* him, but he doesn't even care anymore. God, how could I be so stupid? I broke up with Derek for him. This summer Tate couldn't stay away from me, but ever since school started, I haven't heard one word from him."

"*Shhh.*" Alison jerks her head toward the door. "Someone might come in."

"I don't care. Everybody knows Tate dumped me. They all think he's acting weird, too." She takes a drag off the cigarette. "I mean, he's hanging out with that creepy California chick." A stream of smoke pours from her mouth. "At first I thought the guys put him up to it. You know, as a dare or something. But nobody is laughing. Which can only mean one thing."

Alison scowls. "What?"

"What do you think?" Shanna huffs, her face screwing into a smirk. "She probably puts out like a Pez dispenser."

I press my fingertips to my temples, humiliation rising up to choke me.

"That girl is a mute freak like her grandfather," Shanna goes on. "The only time I've heard her speak is when she read that report in English. Did you *hear* it? Whack jobs like her grow up to be serial killers."

"I think you just didn't get it," Alison says.

Shanna props a hand on one hip. "Oh, right. I guess it had some deep *philosophical* meaning that I'm too stupid to understand."

"I just don't want to judge her. I don't really know her, and neither do you."

"What more do we need to know?" Shanna asks. "I mean, she's tight with Stinky. For that reason alone, why would Tate give her the time of day unless they're doing it?"

Stepping away from the sink, Alison says, "Come on. I feel bad for Tansy. Can you imagine how hard it would be to move to a new place during high school?"

"You feel bad for everyone."

More voices gust in from the hallway as the door opens, and Shanna puts out her cigarette in the sink. Alison says hi to someone I can't see who says hi back to her. She and Shanna pick up their book bags and leave.

I scoot off the tank and sit on the toilet lid. The person who interrupted Shanna and Alison starts peeing in the stall beside mine. Pressing my forehead against my upraised knees, I wrap my arms around my shins. At least I was wrong about Tate trying to win a bet or play a joke on me. That is, if Shanna knows what she's talking about. But now I'm more confused than ever.

Creepy California chick. Serial killer. Mute freak. Whack job.

There's no stopping the sobs that burst from my throat. I should just leave. I could go away right this minute to a colorful place full of laughter, eyes that look at me as if I'm important, fears that thrill as well as paralyze. But something tells me if I did, I'd find myself standing on the bridge overlooking the canyon at midnight. And this time I wouldn't return; Henry wouldn't let me. He'd be waiting to take Bell away.

I think of Mom. Of Papa Dan at home, frail and silent. Would he miss me? Mom would. Losing me would destroy her. It wouldn't matter if I disappeared physically or just zoned out mentally. Her life would never be the same. How can I even consider causing my mother that sort of pain? I try to swallow the sounds of my weeping, but the tears strangle me and I only cry louder.

"I will speak daggers to her," Bethyl Ann's scratchy little voice says from the next stall. "Just say the word, Tansy. I'm not afraid of Shanna."

Her kindness and loyalty pull more sobs up from a place deep inside me.

"You want me to stay?"

"No, go on," I manage to choke out. "I'm okay."

Her toilet flushes. Her stall door opens. Her shoes—mine from last year—appear beneath my door and pause. "If you need me—"

"I know. Thanks."

Her footsteps move away from the stalls. Water splashes in the sink as she washes her hands. The faucet shuts off, and seconds later, the restroom door opens then closes as the third-period bell rings.

I remain on the toilet until I'm drained of tears and my body stops shaking.

Somehow, I managed to avoid Tate all day, but he was waiting for me outside the building after I served my detention time in the office and left to go home. He asked me what was wrong, why I'd been dodging him, and all I could think to say was that I didn't feel well. Which isn't entirely untrue; in fact, it's an understatement. He wanted to come over, but I told him I was going to study for an economics test then go to bed early. I don't think he believed me.

Tonight at dinner, Mom tried to make conversation, but I knew if I said a word I'd burst into tears, so I stuffed spaghetti into my mouth and kept my eyes on the plate. I felt her watching me, though. I felt her worry seeping into my pores, the same worry I heard in her voice, even though she was trying to sound cheerful. I see it now, too, in her tense expression when I glance across the living room and catch her watching me instead of the television. I've been staring at the program for the past hour while sitting next to Papa Dan, but I couldn't tell you what's on. I keep thinking about what Shanna said and how Alison jumped to my defense. And about that feather I found last night. The one that I stepped on while chasing the prowler who vanished into thin air. Will the prowler show up again tonight? If so, will it be a person or Henry's ghost? Will I finally see a face that will click a puzzle piece into place and give me some answers?

I mull over the things that Bethyl Ann brought up about Henry having a message for me, about ghosts using symbols and connections to get through. The only sure connection I have to this house and to Henry is Papa Dan. He's my grandfather, and if there's any truth to my visions, he and Henry were once friends. And enemies. Until we moved here, nightingales had no significant meaning to me. Neither did crystals or pocket watches or poetry journals.

Rosewood boxes.

I sit straighter and study Papa Dan, remembering again the beautiful boxes he used to make. *Of course.* Why didn't I think of it before? Maybe Henry's message is for my grandfather, not me. Maybe I'm just the vessel. Could Henry be reaching out to me through what I find most meaningful—my photography—so that he can give me a message for Papa Dan? This house, the nightingale, the rosewood box, and Henry's treasures . . . they must've all meant something to my grandfather once. They're a part of the memories that connect him to Henry. I recall the voice I heard in my grandfather's room our first night here. Was that Henry? Did he realize then that he would never get through to Papa Dan alone because of his illness, and so he chose me to help him?

"I've got some homework to do," I say abruptly, and push to my feet. I'm anxious and excited to get on with the night, to find out if the prowler is Henry or someone else and, I hope, move one step closer to the answers that will make sense of what's been happening to me. I glance at Mom. "G'night."

She sits forward. "Good night, sweetie. Get some sleep after you study. You look completely exhausted."

"So you've said a bajillion and one times."

"And you've told me a bajillion and *two* times that you're fine, but I'm not sure I believe you."

I don't want her to start bugging me again about keeping a diary or, worse, asking me questions, so I turn my attention to Papa Dan. He's snoring softly, his mouth open slightly, his chin on his chest. "You want me to take him up?" I ask Mom.

"Would you?"

"Sure." I lay my hand on his shoulder and murmur, "Papa Dan? Wake up." He stirs and blinks groggily at me. "Let's go to bed," I say. He stands, and I lead him out of the living room and up the stairs.

A few minutes later, with my grandfather settled in his room, I tell him good night and close his door. My thoughts return to Alison, and I climb up to the turret and gather all the photos I've taken of her. There are more in my backpack, and when I go down again to my bedroom, I take those out, too. One by one, I tear them up and toss them into the wastebasket, saving only the one of her at cheerleading practice. The one where she looks like she's watching for someone, hoping, expectant, her perfect mask off for once. I wonder if it was her boyfriend she was waiting to see, but it doesn't matter. It's none of my business. And I don't need proof anymore that she's not as perfect as everyone thinks. I'm sure she knows that; I don't need to remind her. I don't need to remind myself anymore, either. But for some reason, I can't bring myself to destroy this particular picture. I really like that image of her.

I return the picture to my backpack, then stare blankly at the study sheet for Monday's economics test. Soon the television quiets downstairs, and I hear Mom make her way to her room. I wait an hour, then sneak into her office to find her camera. Then I return to my room and dress in jeans and a T-shirt, sneakers, and a black zippered hoodie. Tonight, instead of my 35 millimeter, I'll use Mom's digital, since the flash isn't as bright. It's less likely to startle whoever or *whatever* is sneaking around outside the house. Plus, I won't have to spend any time developing photos in the darkroom. I'll be able to see the digital images in seconds.

I slip downstairs to the kitchen and out the door. At the cellar, I use the combination Mom told me to open the lock, then I lay the padlock on the ground to make it look as if someone forgot to put it back on. If the prowler shows up, I'll wait until he or she or *it* goes down, then I'll return. They won't get away without coming past me. Of course, if it's Henry, I suppose he could transform into the nightingale and fly out of my reach.

Making my way to the mulberry tree, I climb up. The moon is bright tonight. From high up in the branches, I have a great view of the backyard, the barn, and the cellar. Settling back on a sturdy limb, I pull Mom's camera from my sweatshirt pocket and wait.

The wind gusts, making the tree sway. Hanging on, I try to gauge the passage of time. Fifteen minutes. Twenty. The knobby tree limb jabs my butt. Lowering the camera to my lap, I try to concentrate on something safe to distract my mind—conjugating Spanish verbs, working math problems—but nothing works.

A stain of darkness, deeper than before, spreads over the cellar door. I look up and watch a train of clouds chug slowly across the moon. My eyelids feel heavy, my consciousness drifts, and a memory floats through my mind. Summer in San Francisco when Papa Dan was still himself . . . the two of us setting our alarms for dawn . . . climbing onto the roof . . . a glow on the horizon . . . colors blending . . . pink and purple . . . gold . . .

A creaking noise jerks my mind back to the present. I sit upright and grab the tree limb tighter with one hand and Mom's camera with the other. Below, I see someone lifting the cellar door, their back to me. My heart is frantic as I raise the camera, aim, zoom in. I can't tell who it is. *Click. Click. Click.*

The prowler turns on a light, aims it into the cellar, starts down the steps, and disappears. The door closes.

Leaning back against the tree trunk, I gulp in air to steady my nerves. Pushing a button on the camera, I bring the first photo into view on the LCD screen. The image is blurred, so I click to the next one, my heart thumping hard and steady. This one is clear but small. I use the zoom to enlarge it, see someone in jeans, an orange jacket with writing on back that I can't make out. *Definitely not a ghost.*

Shrinking the image again, I click to the next one and enlarge it as much as I can. Squinting, I lean closer and stare at the LCD screen, tensing when I recognize the number 10 beneath a name that I still can't read. It doesn't matter; I don't need a name. I know which Cedar Canyon High football player wears the number 10.

Tate.

19

Anger, betrayal, and humiliation build to a crescendo inside me. Dropping the camera into the pocket of my hoodie, I scramble down the tree. Tate has been hanging around me because he wants something. Something he thinks is in the cellar. Henry's things? The journal, crystal, and pocket watch are all that were down there when we moved in.

Did Henry use the crystal and his journal to communicate with Tate, too? That would explain why Tate was so angry and rude to me after I moved here. Mom and I padlocked the cellar door. He couldn't get to Henry's things anymore. But why didn't he just tell me he'd left them down there? That they were his? Why did he have to use me? Pretend he liked me? Sneak around?

My feet hit the ground, and I take off across the yard. What would I have done if Tate had told me the treasures were his and he wanted to get them out of the cellar? I would've known he was lying. I wouldn't have handed them over, no questions asked. I already felt a connection to Henry. His poems speak to *me* . . . were *meant* for me. Not Tate or anyone else. Whatever Henry's message is, I'm the only one who might be able to get it through to Papa Dan. But if Tate had been honest with me, maybe I would've confided in him about Henry and we could've figured this all out together.

When I reach the cellar, I see a large hammer lying on the ground beside it. Bending over, I grab the door handle and tug.

"Who's there?" Tate yells up at me, and a bright light shines in my face. The aromas of mildew and earth surround me. A pause, then, "Tansy?" The light beam shifts away from my face. "What are you doing here?" he asks.

White spots dot my vision—the result of the bright light in my eyes. Squinting, I ask, "What am *I* doing here? What are *you* doing? You're the trespasser, not me." I start down the steps, not even trying to hide my anger.

"You unlocked the door, didn't you?" he says. "You were *expecting me*. How did you know I'd come tonight?"

"I'm not as stupid as you think I am, and you're not as sneaky as you think you are." Midway down, I stop. The fact that he had an ulterior motive for spending time with me is all I can think about, and my emotions lodge in my throat. I have to choke out my next words. "What do you want, Tate?"

"I don't want anything, and I don't think you're stupid."

"That's why you started being nice to me, isn't it? You thought if you weren't able to break in here, you could convince me to *let* you in."

"That's not true."

"See? You *do* think I'm stupid. Well, you're too late. I found the box my first day here. It was under the last stair, exactly where you left it." The steps creak as I take another one down. "It's still there, but I took the journal and the watch into the house. The crystal, too." My vision finally adjusts to the muted glow of the light, so I can see his face. His eyes don't lie; I'm right. "That's what I thought," I say. "You wanted the things in the box, and you were mad because we padlocked the cellar door."

Tate's gaze shifts away.

"Why do you want them?" When he doesn't answer, I say, "You could've just asked me for them."

Crickets chirp outside. The rustling leaves on the mulberry tree seem to say, *Hush . . . listen . . . be patient.*

Tate stares at me a long time, then says, "Before you moved in, I hung out here a lot. The box . . . I do want it back. But that's not why I've been nice to you."

"You hung out here? Why?"

His hesitation hangs between us like a wire stretched tight. "Never mind. You can keep the box and the stuff in it. I don't care anymore." He starts up the stairs, but before he reaches the step where I stand, the door above us drops with a *bang* and a cloud of debris swirls down. We both start coughing as a rattle sounds overhead, and Tate rushes up the remaining steps. Slamming his palms against the door, he shouts, "It's locked!"

"Are you sure?" I hurry to help him.

Tate goes still and asks, "Hear that?"

Whistling. The quiet tune moves away from the cellar door. "Papa Dan!" I yell, and bang the door with my fists.

"Your grandfather?"

"I guess I forgot to lock his bedroom door. Sometimes he wakes up and wanders around."

The whistling drifts farther away. We both bang and yell and rattle the door. "If we can hear *him*, he has to hear *us*," Tate says.

"He might not be wearing his hearing aids. He's basically deaf without them." I don't mention that even if my grandfather hears us, it doesn't mean he'd know what to do.

"Great." Tate lowers his fists at the same time I do. "Let's keep trying. Sooner or later, your mom's bound to hear us."

"It's the middle of the night! She might not hear us for hours. Did you bring your cell phone?"

He shakes his head. "It's at home charging."

I move down to the center step and sit. Tate bangs on the door a couple more times before giving up. Then he sits two steps above me. I notice for the first time that the light he's carrying is shaped like a lantern instead of a flashlight. He sets it beside him. The beam seems weaker than before. "I'm not sure how long this light's gonna last," he says. "It's a solar lantern; I haven't charged it in a while." Our eyes meet, and a shiver ripples through me. I look down at my shoes. We're stuck here until Mom discovers I'm not in my room. If I weren't so upset, this might be funny. Or even exciting. I'm trapped with Tate Hudson and his moody blue eyes in a musty, dark cellar worthy of an appearance in a Millicent Moon novel.

Minutes pass that seem like hours. We don't talk. We don't look at each other. Words I want to say but can't crowd my mind, making my head hurt. Then the light dies, and blackness drops down on us like a lid on a box. I hear Tate's breathing, hear the thump of my heartbeat.

"You never said why you used to hang out here," I say, just to break the silence. "You have a thing for breaking and entering or what?"

"Funny," he says, mimicking my cynical tone. "I bought the lantern so I could read and do homework." He pauses, then continues, "And I came here to get away from my dad. I always thought it was bad having him on my back about football, but him not talking to me is worse."

I don't know if Tate's trying to play on my sympathies or if he's just changing the subject to postpone having to explain what he's doing in my cellar. But, either way, it's working. I flash back to that night at the Watermelon Run and the insensitive things his dad said to him. "He doesn't talk to you?" I ask cautiously.

"He doesn't talk period. Not much. Not since Mom left."

I tug the hood over my head. "If you treat him like you treat me, then I don't really blame him."

"I already apologized for the way I acted when you first came to town."

"Sure, you did. So if your attempts to break in here failed, you could ask me to show you the haunted Peterson cellar."

"That's not true. I apologized because I was sorry. And because I like you."

I want to believe him, but I'm afraid to let down my guard. Since arguing with him isn't getting me anywhere, I change the subject. "I heard you quit the team."

"Yeah."

"I bet your dad's not happy about that." He makes a huffing sound, and I ask, "What about your mom? Is she upset about it, too?"

"I haven't told her. But she'll be fine with it. Mom knows playing football isn't what I want to do." Tate's quiet for a long time, then he says, "It's probably stupid, but I want to focus on my writing. There's a student contest I want to enter. If I win, I'll get some college scholarship money. My mom encouraged me, but Dad thinks it's a waste of time. He says there's no future in it for me."

"Well, you can tell *him* my mom makes her living as a writer."

"I know."

"That's why we moved here, to answer your question."

"My question?"

"The other day at the bridge? You asked why we moved here."

"Oh, yeah. And you got mad at me again."

"Me? You're the one who can't make up his mind—" I sigh. "Forget it."

After a long, tense silence, Tate asks, "So what does

your mom's writing have to do with Cedar Canyon?"

"She thinks she has to live where her book is set. The one she's working on now takes place in a town like this."

"No offense, but that's weird," he says with a laugh.

"I know. If she stays in one place too long, she turns into a walking nerve ending. There's more to it than her books, but I won't go into how messed up my family is."

"Whose isn't?"

The wind buzzes through the cracks in the cellar door. "If you want me to ask her to give you some writing advice, I will," I tell Tate.

"That's not why I've been nice to you, either, if that's what you're thinking."

"It's okay. It's not a big deal."

"I never even thought about getting her advice until you said it just now."

I'm not sure I believe him, but I decide to give Tate the benefit of the doubt.

"Man, it's chilly in here," he mutters.

"I know. I've never lived anywhere else where it can be so warm during the day and then so cool at night. Until I moved here, I thought Texas was always hot."

"Yeah, well, the Panhandle's not like the rest of the state." His feet tap out a stuttered beat on the step below. "You mind if I come down there?"

"I don't care." The stair above me creaks, and I scoot over. Tate eases in beside me and, instantly, I'm warmer.

The silence between us stretches until Tate says, "Before

you moved in, sometimes when I came out here I'd break into the house and look around."

"So it was you the Quattlebaums saw?"

"They saw me?"

"Sheriff Dilworth told us they'd reported spotting a prowler over here. He said there'd been a break-in."

"I didn't take anything from the house," Tate says defensively. "I was only looking around."

"I guess I ruined all that. You coming here, I mean."

He shifts beside me. "It's no big deal."

"So when did you find the box?"

"I found the crystal first. It was buried in the creek bed beneath the bridge. I know it sounds stupid, but I felt like it led me to the cellar. That's when I found the box with the pocket watch and the journal inside. It freaked me out because the watch was stopped at 12:22. Supposedly Henry killed himself sometime after midnight."

12:22. What would Tate say if I told him I keep resetting the watch, but whenever I open it again, it's always stopped at that time?

"I guess you read his poems?" I ask.

After a long silence, Tate says, "Yeah, I read them."

"They're beautiful. He seems so . . . I don't know. Troubled, I guess." When he doesn't respond, I say, "If it's okay, I'd like to keep Henry's journal. And the crystal . . . it's the reason I wanted the necklace chain. So I could wear it." I reach up to where the pendant rests beneath my jacket. "But if you want it back, I understand. The watch, too."

"You can keep everything."

"Really? You sure went to a lot of trouble to try and get to that box before I did."

"I just couldn't quit thinking about Henry Peterson killing himself. And his stuff . . . it was like—" Tate exhales a noisy breath.

"What?" *Say it,* I think. *Tell me I'm not the only one who feels Henry's pull.*

"Nothing." Tate laughs a little. "I don't know. It's just a stupid ghost legend."

I dig my fingertips into my arms. I want to tell someone besides Bethyl Ann what's been going on—to tell *him*. "I'm not so sure," I say slowly. "That it's stupid, I mean."

"What are you talking about?"

The wind seems to claw at the door above us. "Henry Peterson contacted me," I blurt out before I can change my mind.

"You're saying he's been in *touch* with you?" Tate asks, disbelief in his voice.

I take a deep breath and tell him everything, starting with the night I woke up at 12:22, when I heard a voice in Papa Dan's room, and ending with the last time I stepped through the shimmering crystal beam and into Isabel's memories. "Henry wants me to meet him at the cliff at midnight. He wants me to run away with him."

"You mean Bell," Tate says with a hesitant tone. "He wants Bell to meet him, right?"

"Don't you understand? When I step through the crystal

beam into a photo, I *am* Bell. And the next time I go, I have a feeling I won't come back."

"You won't come back *here?*"

The confusion in Tate's voice makes me think I was wrong about him sensing Henry's presence, too. I'm afraid I made a mistake by telling him so much. "I know I sound crazy," I tell him. "But what's even crazier is that I feel like I don't have a choice. I *have* to go. I *need* to do what Henry tells me to do. And, in a way, I *want* to." Although I know Tate can't see me in the dark, I turn my face away from him before murmuring, "I guess you're probably thinking I'm crazy now, like everyone else does."

"Who said you're crazy?"

I think of Shanna and say, "Nobody important."

"Well, I don't think that." He tugs at the cuff of my sleeve, his fingers brushing my wrist and making me shiver. "You're freaking me out, though," he says softly.

"I thought that since you found all Henry's things like I did, maybe you'd sensed him, too," I murmur. "I mean, you said that the crystal led you to the cellar and the box."

"I may have felt something, but nothing even close to what you're telling me. It was just my imagination going wild because of all the stories about this place."

"So . . . what's happening to me?" My voice falters.

"Your imagination's going wild, too. You just have a stronger one than I do. That's what scares *me*, since I'm the one who wants to write fiction." He laughs a little at his joke, but he sounds more nervous than amused. "Look, you've been through a lot. Moving . . . your granddad being sick . . . dealing with all the jerks at school. Anybody would want to escape." He's quiet for a few seconds, then asks, "Could you be dreaming? It sounds like a lot of the times this has happened have been at night when you're about to go to sleep or early in the morning right after you wake up."

"One of the times I heard the bell ringing over at the Quattlebaums', I was outside walking with Papa Dan. And the times I looked through the camera viewfinder . . ." I exhale a frustrated breath. "I would've had to have been sleepwalking. That's kind of a stretch to believe, don't you think?"

"And what you're telling me isn't?"

I prop my elbows on my knees and drop my face into my open hands. "I know."

Tate's arm wraps around my shoulders. "Promise me you won't go back into the canyon without me," he says. "And that you'll stay away from the bridge."

"Okay. I promise." I lean against him.

"You should put the things we found back in the box and get it all out of your room and the darkroom so you won't be tempted to look at any of it."

I'm reluctant to do what he asks, which scares me, too— the fact that I'm afraid to be without Henry's treasures. "Where would I put them?" I ask.

"I could keep them." My back stiffens, and he quickly adds, "Don't think that's what I've been after all along, because it's not. We can put them back under the stair if you want. I'll nail it down so the box won't be easy for you to get to. Just in case."

It's humiliating to admit that I'm so obsessed with Henry that Tate has to lock up his possessions just to keep me away from them. Swallowing my pride, I whisper, "Okay."

"If you feel like you have to have them for some reason, tell me and we'll take them out together. Promise?"

"If *you* promise not to tell the whole school about this."

"I won't tell them anything. Deal?"

"Deal."

"I think we should seal it."

I give a jittery laugh. "With a handshake?"

"I was thinking more like a kiss."

Tate's fingers touch my cheek and slide around to the back of my neck. His mouth finds mine, and I taste spearmint. Wrapping my arms around him, I skim my fingers across the 10 on the back of his jacket. He pulls me closer, and I sink into him.

I was wrong; Henry isn't the only guy who can make me dizzy and limp-kneed. Clinging to Tate, I ignore the chill of the crystal against my chest and kiss him back.

"Tansy!"

Mom's frantic voice weaves into my dream. I see her running from room to room inside the house, wild-eyed and pale as she throws open doors. When she reaches the turret, she steps inside and sees photos scattered across the floor. Bending, she picks one up and gasps. I'm inside the picture, beneath the mulberry tree, standing in the snow next to Henry and Papa Dan when he was young.

"Tansy!"

I stir and open my eyes. Thin spears of light slice the darkness above. Someone has their arms around me. After a few seconds, I realize that it's Tate and that we're in the cellar. I sit up, hear Mom call my name again, and understand that her voice is not part of the dream.

In a groggy voice, Tate says, "What?"

"It's my mom." Pushing to my feet, I make my way to the top of the stairs and bang on the door. "Mom! Over here!"

In seconds, Tate is beside me and pounding, too. "In the cellar!" he yells.

"Mom! We're locked in the cellar!"

"Tansy! What in the world are you—" She sounds louder now, closer. I hear scuffling, then a rattle, a squeak, and a groan. The door lifts and daylight pours in, along with a good amount of dust.

I squint up into Mom's surprised face. "Hi."

"Are you okay?"

"Yes," I say, coughing and brushing dirt from my hair. She takes my hand and pulls me out.

Tate climbs up behind me, carrying the dead flashlight. "Hello, Mrs. Piper." He looks down at his shoes.

Mom stares at the two of us, frowning. "Tate, right?"

He nods. "Sorry if we scared you."

Mom's eyes are suspicious. "What were you doing in the cellar?"

"It's a long story," I murmur.

"I love long stories. Why don't I make some breakfast while you clean up and Tate calls his parents? Then you can both tell me what happened."

Tate brushes off his jeans, then bends down to snatch the hammer off the ground. "I think I'll just head home. Thanks for the breakfast offer, though." He looks at me. "See ya later, Tansy. I'll call you. Maybe this afternoon I can come back and fix that stair." His eyes say what he doesn't—that he'll nail it shut with Henry's things inside.

"The stair?" Mom glances down into the cellar, then at the hammer Tate holds. "The bottom one is loose," I tell her, feeling defensive, though I'm not sure why since I haven't done anything wrong. "Tate offered to repair it so no one gets hurt."

Half an hour later, I'm showered, dressed, and eating scrambled eggs with Mom and Papa Dan at the kitchen table. "I heard a noise outside last night," I explain. "When I looked out the window, I saw someone and I thought it might be Papa Dan, so I went after him. I guess I forgot to lock his door. I'm sorry."

Papa Dan blinks across at me when I say his name.

"The cellar door was open when I got there," I continue. "I expected to find Papa Dan inside, but it was Tate. I went down to see why he was there and then the door closed and we were locked in. I think Papa Dan didn't see either one of us go down there. He had to be the one who locked it." Aware that I'm jabbering, I look into my grandfather's eyes. "Did you lock the cellar last night, Papa Dan? You can tell me. I won't be mad at you."

Papa Dan smiles at me and keeps eating his eggs.

"This all sounds a little strange, Tansy," Mom says.

Ignoring her, I lean closer to Papa Dan and say, "You know we don't like you wandering around outside at night. It's dangerous."

"Why would the cellar door have been unlocked in the first place?" Mom asks.

"I was down there taking pictures recently. I must not have secured the padlock and that's how Tate got in." The eggs weigh heavy in my stomach. So do the lies. I hate being dishonest, especially with Mom.

"And Tate wanted to get into the cellar in the middle of the night because . . . ?" Her eyes narrow.

"He used to go down there before we moved in. It was sort of his place to get away." I shift my attention to my plate and force another bite of eggs down.

"Tansy . . . look at me." I meet her gaze. "I'm glad you're making friends here. And I don't mind if you have a boyfriend."

"He's not—"

"But," she interrupts, "I want to know if you've been meeting Tate down there."

Heat infuses my cheeks. "No, Mom!"

She studies me with pursed lips until the distrust slowly melts from her eyes. "Okay." She sighs. "But next time you hear a noise outside at night, wake me up. What if it hadn't been Tate or Papa Dan? What if it had been that prowler the Quattlebaums saw?"

"I know. I'm sorry. I won't do it again."

My cell phone rings in the next room. I jump up to get it, silently thanking the caller for saving me from any more of this humiliating conversation. Bethyl Ann is on the other end of the line when I pick up.

"I'm keeping Mama company at the library," she says, sounding excited. "I decided to continue looking for articles about Henry or your grandfather, and I found something."

"You did?"

"It's a picture I saw once before. A long time ago. That's why I probably remembered Isabel's name the other day."

"It's a picture of Bell?"

"I guess it's her. She's with Henry and your grandpa and another girl at a high school dance. Underneath the photo it says . . ." Bethyl Ann clears her throat. *"Left. Isabel Martin, escorted by Henry Peterson. Right. Louise Irving, escorted by Daniel Piper."*

The picture the newspaper photographer took of Henry and Bell at the Winter Dance! Gripping the receiver so tightly it shakes, I shut my eyes, and suddenly it's Henry's hand I'm holding instead of the phone. I smell the liquor on his breath; hear the music playing in the school gym on that long ago night; hear Louise humming beside me.

316

"It's a funny picture, actually," Bethyl Ann goes on. "Isabel looks like the cameraman caught her off guard. Her mouth is open, and she's raising her hand like she's trying to stop him from taking the shot."

Of course, I think. *She didn't want him to take it. If the paper printed it, her parents would see her with Henry.*

"And you should see their clothes," says Bethyl Ann. "The girls are all dressed up in these really old-fashioned dresses, and the guys—"

"What does he look like?" I interrupt, my heart ticking like Henry's pocket watch.

"Your grandfather?"

"No, Henry. Does he look like Tate?"

"Tate Hudson? Why would Henry Peterson look like—"

"Does he?"

"I can't really tell. The picture is blurry where his face is. But you can see the others. Your grandfather was such a cutie patootie. I'm not saying he isn't now, but you know what I mean. *Hot* cute." She giggles. "Gosh, now that I think about it, that's really an embarrassing thing for me to be saying about your—"

"Bethyl Ann." I lift my gaze to the ceiling. "Are you going to be there awhile?"

"Yep."

"I'll ask Mom to let me take the car and come over there."

"Good. You'll want to see this." She lowers her voice. "So you really think Isabel Martin is *your* Bell?"

"I guess I'll find out when I see the picture."

"But you don't know what she looks like," Bethyl Ann says.

"It's weird, but I'm just sure I'll know if it's her or not."

"Why didn't you say her name was Martin? Bethyl Ann asks. "Isabel Martin died not too long ago."

"Did you know her?"

"No, I just remember reading her obituary in the paper. She moved away a long time before I was born. Before my parents were born, even."

Only Bethyl Ann would remember the details of a stranger's obituary. Something Mom said recently about Papa Dan crosses my mind. Something about a girl he grew up with sending him a letter. "Beth . . . how long ago did Isabel Martin die?"

"I don't know. A year maybe?"

Could Isabel be Papa Dan's friend? The one whose lawyer sent the letter that made him want to come back to Cedar Canyon? "What about the other girl in the photo?" I ask Bethyl Ann. "Do you know her?"

"Louise Irving? I'm not sure. She looks like my old Sunday school teacher Mrs. O'Malley, only without the gray hair and reading glasses. I think her first name is Louise, too, but I would have to ask Mama. Mrs. O'Malley is nice. She used to live down the block and she made me cookies when I was little. They had these little chocolate drops in—"

"Wait. Mrs. O'Malley is still alive?"

"She's in a nursing home in Amarillo. You know Mary Jane at the pharmacy? That's her granddaughter."

"Ask your mom if Mrs. O'Malley's name was Irving before she got married, okay? I'll be there as soon as I can."

20

The image of Henry and Isabel, Daniel and Louise in the old newspaper photo imprints on my brain like a tattoo. The Winter Dance scene seems familiar, as if I were there when it was taken. Henry's face is as blurry as Bethyl Ann said, as if he turned his head the second the camera snapped. I recognize his suit as the one he wore that night at the school when he drank too much. As I touch his image, the same mixed feelings of love and apprehension that Isabel felt that night sweep through me, and I long to feel his hand in mine and look into his troubled eyes, to try to make him happy.

Louise Irving looks exactly as I remember her. And Papa Dan is the same as he is when I step through the crystal's beam and into the memories. He is Daniel—Isabel's best friend and protector. His grin makes me smile, but at the same time, I ache inside. He grew up to be more than my grandfather; he was also *my* friend and protector. I miss him—the young man he was and the old man he became—

the man he was before he got sick.

Isabel Martin, though, is the person in the photo who captures my interest and holds it. It's the first time I've seen her face, yet I *know* that the pretty girl with pale hair, wide eyes, and a long, straight nose is Bell. Though the photograph is black-and-white, I know the taffeta dress she wears is the color of wild plums. I also know that the sleeves make her arms itch and that the skirt swishes when she walks. She wears the crystal pendant. Henry's crystal. The one he gave to her . . . to *me*.

In the photograph, Papa Dan and Louise smile into the camera, but Isabel looks startled and alarmed. Though I can't see Henry's face, I know Bell felt the heat of his gaze at that moment. I've been inside her skin, behind her eyes. Even if Tate comes up with a hundred more rationalizations, I'm not sure he'll ever change my mind about that.

"Is that them?" Bethyl Ann asks quietly, and when I say yes, she whispers, "Wow." Louder, she says, "Mom told me Louise Irving is Mrs. O'Malley."

I look up. "She did? I have to find a way to go see her."

Her eyes widen. "Hey! Mom and I are going to the mall in Amarillo this afternoon. You should go with us. We could visit Mrs. O'Malley at the nursing home."

"You think your mom would take us?"

"Sure, she will. And we can make Mrs. O'Malley some cookies." Grinning, she adds, "Let's go ask."

When Bethyl Ann tells her mother our idea, Mrs. Pugh beams at us like we're a couple of saints. She gets off at noon, so Bethyl Ann and I rush over to the Pughs' house to make chocolate peanut butter drop cookies, and I call Mom to fill her in on the plan.

Bethyl Ann already has all of the baking ingredients on the counter by the time I finish talking to Mom. "I can go," I tell her.

She opens a cabinet and takes out a big metal bowl and an electric mixer. "I hope Mrs. O'Malley can answer some of your questions about Henry."

"Me, too."

I lean against the counter and watch as she flips through a cookbook. "Bethyl Ann . . . I never did thank you for being there for me the other day at school when I was so upset in the restroom."

She looks up from the cookbook, and her brows tug together. "I'm just sorry Shanna was such a meanie to you."

"Why *is* she so mean?"

"Mama says it's just her nature. Some people are flowers, and some are thorns."

I smile as she returns her attention to the cookbook. "What about Alison Summers? I know you don't think she's a thorn, but why would she hang out with someone like Shanna if that's true?"

Bethyl Ann lays the open cookbook down on the counter. "Alison's not mean." She takes the lid off a canister. "She and Shanna have just been BFs forever, that's all. And—" Catching herself, she blinks and looks down at the measuring cup she holds in one hand.

"And what?"

"I don't want to gossip about Alison."

"Hey, I told you all my secrets."

"It's not my secret. It's not a secret at all. I just feel bad for her."

"Because?" When she doesn't answer, I say, "She defended me to Shanna before you came into the restroom. And she didn't even know I was there. It surprised me."

"It shouldn't have."

"Why? What's going on with her?" When she doesn't answer, I say, "When I saw Alison crying the other day, what do you think she was really so upset about? Surely she wasn't really that bummed over making a C minus. And why did Mrs. Summers freak when she didn't see Alison the second she stepped out of the store?"

After a few moments of silence, Bethyl Ann finally says, "Mama told me Mrs. Summers can't get over her grief. And that Alison still feels guilty."

"About what?"

"Okay, I'll tell you." Bethyl Ann blows her bangs off her forehead and puts down the measuring cup. "Alison had an older sister named Amelia."

"Had?"

She nods. "Last year, they were in a car accident and Amelia was killed. Alison was driving."

"Oh no," I murmur.

"She only had her learner's permit and wasn't supposed to drive without an adult in the car, but I guess she talked

Amelia into letting her. The wreck wasn't Alison's fault, though. Another car ran the light at the intersection on the highway."

"That's terrible," I say. "Mrs. Summers must be afraid of something bad happening to Alison, too."

"I know. Everyone adored Amelia. She did everything right. She had just found out she was getting a scholarship for a full ride at UT after she graduated. She never got into any trouble, either. And she was always nice to everybody, even me."

"She sounds just like her sister." *Except for the being nice to Bethyl Ann part,* I think. *Ignoring someone and standing by while others abuse them is not my idea of 'being nice.'* "Everybody adores Alison, too."

Bethyl Ann blinks at me, fidgety all of a sudden. She measures out a cup of flour. "This is the part I'm not supposed to talk about. It was told to Mama in confidence."

"You can trust me," I say quietly.

She pours the cup of flour into the bowl then turns. "Mama found Alison crying in the library one Saturday, just before closing time," she says quietly. "She told Mama that she and Amelia were arguing when they had the wreck, and she keeps wondering if she might've hit the brake earlier if she hadn't been distracted. Then she said that she should've been the one who died."

"Why would she say that?"

"She said because Amelia was so good."

"And Alison isn't?"

"Alison has changed since the wreck. She didn't always try to be so perfect. She was a lot more like all the other natives at school."

"Like Shanna, you mean?"

"Sort of. You know, boy crazy, average grades, drinking and smoking sometimes. She even got caught a few times sneaking out her window at night to meet her boyfriend."

Thinking of the guy in the alley, I ask, "Who is he?"

"Some older guy. She doesn't see him anymore."

I decide to refrain from telling Bethyl Ann that's not exactly true.

"But now she feels like she should try to be like Amelia, I guess."

"Replace her, you mean. For her parents."

She nods. "She probably thinks they wish if one kid had to die, it would've been her instead of her sister. I don't think that's true, though. Her mom's not like that."

Alison's misery over a C– on a test makes sense to me now. "I don't know what to say. All this time, I thought she was just a phonier version of Shanna."

"*Shanna.*" Bethyl Ann makes a face. "I wish Alison would bid her a long farewell. But they've been close since first grade, and Shanna only got mean in the last couple of years. Besides, she hardly left Alison's side for weeks after the accident, so I guess Alison overlooks a lot of Shanna's bad behavior because of that." She turns away again, measures another cup of flour. "Don't feel bad about what you thought. It's hard to know about a person. Who you can trust and who you can't."

She's right. I think of Hailey and Colin. And also about the fact that, only last night when I caught Tate in the cellar, I thought he couldn't be trusted, but now I've told him all my secrets.

"This is a wonderful idea and a very nice gesture, girls," Mrs. Pugh says, glancing back at me through the rearview mirror. "I've been a neglectful friend to Louise these past months. I really should visit her more often."

As Bethyl Ann and her mother chatter to each other up front, I tap out an impatient beat against the floor with the toe of my shoe and watch farmland and cattle pass by outside my window. Mrs. Pugh drives her rattling old station wagon ten miles an hour under the speed limit. It's going to be a long forty miles.

"Bethyl Ann didn't tell me your grandfather grew up in Cedar Canyon," Mrs. Pugh says to me after a while. "How did he know Louise?"

"I think they dated once or twice in high school."

"I'm sure she'll be pleased as punch to have you update her on everything that's happened to Mr. Piper since he moved away. Louise loves to talk. Her body is worn out, poor thing, but her mind is still as sharp as a tack."

Mrs. Pugh wants to visit Louise before we go to the mall, so once we hit the Amarillo city limits, we head straight for the nursing home. The place smells like a hospital, and old people are everywhere—in the lobby, in wheelchairs along

326

the hallway, in the rooms we pass by. A few of them glance up, smile, and greet us. Others remain hunched over, looking down at their laps like they don't even notice our presence. Some people stare at televisions through glazed eyes. Nobody laughs or talks much.

Watching them, my chest feels tight. I'm glad Papa Dan doesn't live in a place like this, surrounded by people yet all alone. I'm glad he has Mom and me, and we have him.

Mrs. O'Malley's door is open. She sits in a chair beside her bed. The television volume is too low to hear the program, but she doesn't watch it, anyway. She's gazing out a window overlooking the barren courtyard below. Mrs. Pugh knocks, and the old woman turns startled eyes our way. They brighten with recognition when she sees Bethyl Ann's mom. Then Mrs. O'Malley smiles, and goose bumps scatter up my arms. I can see the girl from the newspaper photo within the old woman. Isabel's friend Louise.

"Well, look who's here!" She pushes herself upright in the chair. "Come in this room! How lovely to see you, Georgia."

"Don't get up," Mrs. Pugh says as we enter. She rounds the foot of the bed and faces Mrs. O'Malley, reaching her hands out for the older woman to grasp. "Louise, you're a sight for sore eyes. How are you?"

"I can't complain. It's so good of you to come." She turns to peer at Bethyl Ann and me. "And who do we have here?"

"It's me, Mrs. O'Malley. Bethyl Ann Pugh." Bethyl Ann lifts the tin she carries. "My friend and I made cookies for you. Chocolate peanut butter drops, just like you used to make for me."

"Come over here and let me see you, honey. You're so grown up, I didn't even recognize you." When Bethyl Ann goes around to stand beside her mother, the old woman adds, "My land, you look like a model in a magazine."

"Tansy gave me a makeover." Bethyl Ann glances across at me, and her mother frowns, her mouth puckering up like a prune.

"What fun!" Mrs. O'Malley exclaims with a wheezy chuckle. "Thank you for the cookies, girls. I know I'll enjoy them." Her eyes shift to mine. "You're Tansy?"

"Yes, ma'am. Tansy Piper."

She studies me more closely. "I once knew some folks named Piper. Way back when I was a girl."

"My grandfather grew up in Cedar Canyon. His name is Daniel Piper."

She claps her frail hands. "Daniel Piper. Yes! He was a good friend. I haven't heard from him in years."

"He lives with my mom and me. We just moved to Cedar Canyon recently."

"Daniel is in Cedar Canyon?" Her voice quiets on the last word and she peers past us, as if she's looking at something only she can see. "How is he?"

"He's—" My throat closes and tears fill my eyes. "He doesn't talk much anymore. I'm not sure what he remembers."

"I'm so sorry to hear that, Tansy. Your grandfather and I

had some wonderful times together when we were growing up. Going to parties . . . hiking in the canyon." She chuckles again. "He could be quite a show-off sometimes. Daniel could identify a bird just by its call. He tried to teach me, but I could never catch on."

I think of the nightingale and wonder if Henry remembers that about Papa Dan, too. "He used to tell me stories about the two of you growing up here," I say, feeling guilty over the lie. "He talked about someone named Henry, too." I pause, then add, "And a girl called Bell."

Mrs. O'Malley's eyes soften. "He must have meant Isabel Martin. She and I were close as girls. Really, she was my best friend." Smiling, she shakes her head. "But I couldn't compete with Daniel and that Peterson boy. They were thick as thieves, those three. I never understood what she and your grandfather saw in Henry. He was a peculiar young man."

Placing the cookie tin on Mrs. O'Malley's nightstand, Bethyl Ann sits at the edge of the bed and asks, "Did he really do a swan dive off the bridge into the canyon and kill himself?"

"*Bethyl Ann,*" Mrs. Pugh scolds. "There's no need to be so blunt."

"Well, everyone says he jumped." Bethyl Ann crosses her arms and in a pouting voice adds, "It's not a national secret."

"Even though the authorities called it a suicide," Mrs. O'Malley says, "his folks insisted he was pushed. But there was no proof of that."

"*Pushed?*" My stomach plummets.

Shifting her attention back to me, Mrs. O'Malley says, "Your grandfather found him. Did you know that?"

"No," I say quietly, exchanging a glance with Bethyl Ann.

"It was the next morning," the old woman continues. "A day or two after the Winter Dance, as I recall. Daniel told the authorities he was supposed to meet Henry at sunup to hike into the canyon. They often hiked together. That's when the Petersons started pointing fingers."

"At my grandfather?"

"Yes. But I took care of that. I was at Daniel's house when Henry called and made plans for the hike." She sounds as if she's still angry that anyone would suspect my grandfather might be involved in anything so terrible. "What a sad, sad day that was. Poor Daniel. He was beside himself with grief. And Isabel . . ." She sighs. "Lord, that Peterson boy was obsessed with her. And her with him. Some of the things she'd tell me . . . I worried about her. He was manipulative and wild, and he had a terrific temper. He wanted Isabel to run away with him. She confided in me and promised she wouldn't go, but I had a feeling he'd change her mind. After Henry's death, I wondered if she had refused him and he couldn't bear it, but Isabel wouldn't talk about any of that. Not with anyone, even me."

"So you agree with the authorities that he jumped?" I ask.

330

"I wouldn't speculate, though I'm certain your grandfather had nothing to do with it. That sort of violence wasn't in Daniel's nature. I'm sure I don't have to tell you that. No one in town was surprised when they called Henry Peterson's death a suicide."

"Why?" I ask, though I'm sure I already know the answer.

"Rumors had circulated about his mental instability for years. Henry had threatened to kill himself before. Or hinted that he might." She shakes her head and *tsks*. "He did the craziest things. More than once, I saw him walking the railing on the bridge. Isabel worried about him, but she also defended him. For a while, your grandfather did, too. Henry pulled Daniel out of the river when they were small boys. Back then, there was actually water in it. Daniel felt indebted to him."

Mrs. O'Malley looks down at her folded hands. "After Henry's death, Isabel was never quite the same. She left town after graduation and never came back. Went south to live with an aunt, I believe."

The quiet stretches on too long, as if the story had cast a haze of gloom over the room. "Let's move on to more cheerful topics," Mrs. Pugh says, breaking the uncomfortable silence. "I should fill you in on all the Cedar Canyon news, Louise. Let's see . . . now where should I start? Did you hear that the Hinkles' pet pig, Tilly, is nursing a stray kitten that Vivian Hinkle found hiding in a pot of mums?"

I call Mom from Bethyl Ann's house. "We're back."

"I'll come get you. Then we need to buy groceries."

"Would you bring my backpack? It's in my room. I need to give Alison Summers something that's in it. On the way home, could we stop by her house?"

"Sure. After we finish at the store, we'll go by." Mom sounds curious, but she doesn't question me.

I've been thinking over J. B.'s suggestion that I show Alison the photo of her at cheerleading practice. After what Bethyl Ann told me today about the car wreck and Amelia's death, I think maybe I should *give* Alison the photo. It may sound as crazy as everything else I've been thinking, but I'm no longer so sure she was looking for her boyfriend that day. Maybe it was her sister. Maybe Alison sensed Amelia's presence. Or maybe she was remembering happier times when Amelia watched her cheering from the sidelines. I guess I could wait until tomorrow and give Alison the photograph at school, but Shanna is always glued to her side, and I don't really want an audience. I'm sure Alison wouldn't, either.

On the way to Alison's house, I consider telling Mom what Mrs. O'Malley said about the rumor involving Papa Dan, but for some reason I can't make myself bring it up. My grandfather would never do anything so terrible, but still the story disturbs me.

We pull to the curb in front of the pretty brick house on Caprock Street. Clutching my backpack, I step outside and make my way up the walk to the front door. A horse whinnies nearby. I take deep breaths, tell myself I'm doing the right thing, and ring the bell.

The door opens, and there she stands. Alison isn't wearing makeup, only a big blob of what looks like zit cream right between her brows. "Oh. Hi," she says, her expression a mix of curiosity and surprise.

"Hi. I, um, brought you something." I unzip my backpack. "The other day in the school restroom between second and third period? I was in one of the stalls when you and Shanna were talking about Tate Hudson and me and—"

"Oh . . ." She lifts a hand to cover her mouth, and her eyes widen. Then her face scrunches up as if she's going to cry. "I'm *sorry*. I didn't mean—"

"No, it's okay. I know she's your friend, so I won't mention what I think of Shanna, but I heard what you said and—" I pull out the photograph. "I want you to have this." Handing it to her, I add, "Photography is my hobby and—"

I stop talking when she looks at the photo and goes still.

"I hope you don't mind that I took it," I say.

Her face reddens, and I'm afraid that I made a mistake, that she's going to be upset with me. "That other time—when I was in the alley with . . ." She looks down. "I saw you. You had your camera then, too. Did you—"

"I shouldn't have taken your picture with him. I'm sorry."

Panic flashes in Alison's eyes as she glances over her shoulder.

333

"Don't worry." I lift a hand toward her. "I got rid of them. I tore them up and threw them away. I'm going to destroy the negatives, too."

Her breath rushes out. "Thanks. My parents . . . if they knew, they'd kill me. They're just—"

"I won't say anything. I promise." I glance back at the car. "Well, Mom's waiting. I'd better go." Swiveling around, I start down the walk.

"Tansy?" When I look back at her, Alison lifts the photo and says, "Thanks for this. It's really good. We should do something sometime. You know, go to a movie or something."

I hesitate a second, then say, "Okay."

"Bethyl Ann can come, too, if she wants."

"That'd be fun."

"Did you have anything to do with her makeover?"

I nod. "It was her idea, though."

Alison smiles. "She looks great."

"You should tell her. Beth would love the compliment." I smile back, then turn around and head for the car.

The nightingale kept me up most of the night, so I sleep in on Sunday morning. Tate comes over after lunch, and I know without asking why he's here. While he talks to Mom and Papa Dan, I run upstairs and tuck the journal and pocket watch into my camera bag. But then the nightingale begins to sing again, and my hand pauses above the bag's zipper. Bell's crystal pendant feels as cold as ice below my throat, and I feel Henry's pull. Trembling, I take out the journal, open it to the place I left marked with a paper clip—his next poem . . .

A wicked wind's blowing
Bitter and cold
Telling me that it's over
That your love has grown old
Whispering lies
I know can't be right
The wicked wind blowing
Through my mind tonight

It takes every ounce of my willpower to make myself close the journal, to put it back in the case and secure the zipper, to pull the strap of the camera bag over my shoulder and walk into the hallway. But at the staircase, I hear a gust of wind whistle through the eaves of the house and Henry's words play through my mind . . . *whispering lies I know can't be right* . . .

I start up toward the turret instead of going downstairs. But then I hear Tate's laughter in the living room, and just like that, the spell is broken. "Sorry, Henry," I whisper, glancing toward my bedroom, where the nightingale's call seems more faint than before. Turning, I hurry to join Mom and Tate.

"You mind if we go out for a while?" I ask Mom. "I promised Tate I'd give him a photography lesson in exchange for him repairing the cellar step."

"My tools are in the car," he explains to her.

"Okay," Mom says, looking from me to Tate and back again, a flicker of suspicion in her eyes.

Tate and I head out the front door to his Blazer. "I tried calling you a couple of times yesterday," he says.

"I went to Amarillo with Bethyl Ann. I had my phone off part of the time because we were visiting someone." He takes a hammer, nails, and a flashlight from the front seat while I tell him what I learned from Mrs. O'Malley about the Petersons' accusations toward Papa Dan.

"Sounds like Henry's folks were just looking for someone to blame," Tate says as we take off across the yard.

"That's what I believe, too. I mean, what parent wants to think their kid committed suicide? It must've been a terrible time for them, even if they weren't the world's greatest mother and father."

I open the padlock and, this time, carry it with me into the cellar. Tate snaps the flashlight on. Taking a deep breath, I remove the crystal necklace and hand it to him. Then I take Henry's things out of the camera bag and put them into the rosewood box.

When I pass the box to Tate, he searches my face and asks, "You okay?"

I nod, even though I'm really so nervous that I can't speak.

Smiling, he pushes my hat brim back and gives me a peck on the lips. "You still haven't shown me any of your photos or your darkroom," he says, as if to take my mind off what I'm giving up.

"And you still haven't let me read any of your writing," I point out, grateful for the distraction.

Tate's grin widens. Stooping, he places the box under the stair and nails the plank over it, and I'm sad and relieved at the same time, if that makes sense. I'll miss being with Henry . . . seeing Daniel; I'll miss experiencing Bell's life through her eyes. But the thought of going back there frightens me too much, especially since no matter what rational explanations Tate comes up with, I'm sure after seeing the newspaper photo that I haven't imagined or dreamed anything that's happened. Henry's ghost is real. And I have visited his past life.

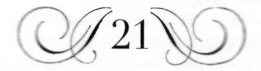

21

Mom goes to her office after dinner to finish writing a scene. I make sure Papa Dan is settled and content in front of the television; then I climb the stairs to his bedroom. Guilt prods me for snooping in my grandfather's personal things, but I don't know what else to do. I need answers about his past, and he can't give them to me.

I think of the picture album he took away from me when I was little. What didn't he want me to see? Was he afraid I would ask questions he didn't want to answer? Did those particular photos bring back memories he wanted to forget? After what Mrs. O'Malley said, that makes sense. Being falsely accused of pushing someone off a bridge would be horrible, especially if that person was one of your best friends. If I'd gone through something like that, I'd want to wipe it from my mind, too.

The fact that Henry's parents believed he was pushed from the bridge makes me feel sick inside. *Pushed. Killed.* Is that why Henry's spirit can't move on? Maybe he didn't jump, and he wants the truth known. Maybe the message he wants me to give to Papa Dan includes the name of his killer.

In my grandfather's closet, I locate a box filled with his photo albums and some scrapbooks my grandmother made. The forbidden album's cover is blue canvas, like brand-new denim jeans. I take it out, start to open it, then stop myself. Tucking the album under my arm, I go downstairs, pausing inside the living room doorway. "Papa Dan?" I say.

His eyes brighten when they settle on my face.

Crossing the room, I sit on the sofa beside him and place the album in my lap. I reach for his hand, bring it to rest atop the canvas, and cover his long, bony fingers with mine. "I've always wanted to see these, but if you still don't want me to, I'll put it back," I tell him.

He lowers his gaze to our hands, to the book beneath them, then returns his attention to my face. I search the pale green eyes peering at me from behind his thick round glasses and wonder if I only imagine the flicker of understanding I see in them.

"I want to hear about when you lived in Cedar Canyon. Back when you were my age. No matter what happened, I'll understand."

Tears sting my eyes and flood my body with dread. *He could not have pushed Henry. Papa Dan would never hurt anyone. Not then, not now. Unless . . . What if he had to hurt Henry to protect someone else?*

Papa Dan stares at the album, and something about

339

the sound of his exhale makes me think the sigh has been trapped inside his chest for years . . . decades. Beneath my palm, his fingers move. I open the album cover.

The photographs make me smile. Papa Dan as a boy with his parents. Papa Dan at a picnic at the town park. A birthday party with Papa Dan and four other kids, all about age six, around a kitchen table with a cake in the center; they wear pointed hats and chocolate-icing smiles.

I turn the page to more pictures taken somewhere in the canyon. A line of boys, eleven years old, maybe twelve, wade through a muddy creek, splashing one another. A second turn of the page and my grandfather's image grows older. Now he is a teenager, standing alongside his parents and another couple. Isabel Martin poses between the man and woman, who must be her parents, based on the resemblance. The six of them stand in front of a farmhouse. I think I recognize the background as a field midway between our house and town.

When I turn another page, Papa Dan lifts his hand and touches it. All the photographs display this house and the grounds surrounding it. Many seem familiar, like the frozen black-and-white scenes I've seen through my camera's viewfinder. In several, Papa Dan poses with Isabel and a young man that I know at once is Henry, though his face doesn't look at all like Tate's. He looks nothing like the Henry I've talked to and walked with. Only the sharp glint in his eyes is the same, the taunting expression. I know him . . . and I don't.

Doubts I'd pushed aside rush back to crowd my mind. Could the Henry I met be a product of both the truth and my own creation? In my mind, did I make him resemble Tate because I wished so badly for Tate to like me?

With a sinking sensation, I look across at my grandfather. All my life I've found comfort in his eyes, strength in his face. But now a tear trickles down the paper-thin skin of his cheek. "Papa Dan," I whisper, and follow his gaze to the news clip he touches, the one from the *Cedar Canyon Gazette* back in the forties. He and Louise Irving, Henry and Isabel Martin at the Winter Dance. The paper is glued to a sheet of stationery that lies loose on the album page. Staring at the teardrop crystal Isabel wears, I lift the sheet and turn it over. On the back, four names are scrawled in faint black ink beneath the yellowed glue. Daniel, Louise, Henry, *Bell.*

My heart beats too fast as Tate's explanations play through my mind. Years ago, when I was little and I found this album, before Papa Dan caught me and took it away, did I see this photograph? Did I see the crystal pendant around the girl's neck, then flip over the picture and read the names on back? Did it all stay locked away in my subconscious? I could have glimpsed the photos of the house then, too. When we moved here, seeing it for real might have released the memories trapped in my mind. I was lonely, confused, afraid of starting over, of trusting again. Did my mind play tricks on me because of that? When I looked through the viewfinder and everything seemed familiar, did I remember these photographs and flash back to them?

I guess finding Henry's treasures *could* have set off my imagination. Maybe the Quattlebaums said Henry died sometime after midnight, or I heard it somewhere else and just forgot. Maybe, in my sleep, I am setting the pocket watch back to 12:22. Maybe I wove the stories I've been told about Henry into these photographs, created a place and time where I wouldn't be lonely or afraid anymore, where I belonged. A place where I could talk and laugh forever with the one friend I've always known I could rely on. My best friend. My grandfather.

That makes more sense than visiting a ghost's memories.

"Tansy?" At the sound of Mom's voice, I look up. "Didn't you hear the phone ringing?" she asks.

"No, did it?"

"Yes, it's Tate." She moves closer to the sofa, hands me the phone, and looks down at the album. "I don't think I've ever seen these before."

"I don't know if I have, either." My voice trembles, and I catch the perplexed look Mom sends my way before I stand and head for the kitchen, the phone in my hand.

"Hey," Tate says. "Sorry to call you on your home phone, but you didn't answer your cell. What are you doing?" When I tell him, he says, "See? You saw the photos before and read that girl's nickname and your mind invented the rest. I told you there was a good explanation."

"You sound like I should be relieved to know I'm crazy."

342

"Not crazy, *dreaming*. That's better than being manipulated by a ghost, isn't it?" When I don't respond, he adds, "You still think that's what's happening, don't you?"

I lean against the kitchen table. "No, you're right." Forcing a laugh, I continue, "They were some really vivid dreams, though."

"Sounds like it." I hear relief in his laughter. "You care if I come over?"

"I have a lot of homework. Maybe tomorrow after school?"

"Okay." A long pause, then, "You're not going to do something stupid like go out to the canyon, are you?"

"Are you kidding? I'd be afraid to go out there by myself after dark."

"You sure?"

"Positive." That's not a lie. I *will* be afraid. I look out the window. "Would you tell me something?"

"What?" Tate asks.

"You hinted that you felt a weird pull from the crystal when you found it. Like it drew you to the cellar." I pause, then ask him, "What do you think that was?"

"I don't know." His voice sounds sheepish. "At the time, I guess I thought that it would be cool if there *was* a ghost and he was trying to get a message through to me about his death or something." He laughs. "Which is so stupid that I can't believe I just admitted it."

"You thought it would be *cool* if that was possible? Or you actually kind of felt like that's what *was* happening?"

"Maybe I felt it, but only for a minute. It was my *imagination*. And it's your imagination, too. Quit thinking about this, Tansy, okay?"

"I was just asking."

He's quiet for a few moments, and I have a feeling he doesn't believe me. "I guess I'll see you at school tomorrow," he finally says.

Guilt gnaws at me when we hang up. I don't like breaking a promise, but later tonight I have to take the rosewood box from beneath the cellar stair for Henry's sake and Papa Dan's. I'm more sure than ever that Henry has something to say that my grandfather needs to hear—and that neither of them will find peace until that happens.

Maybe that's just a delusion on my part, and maybe it isn't, but I have to find out once and for all—and that means taking out Bell's pendant again. If Tate's right and I'm dreaming, the crystal conjures the dreams. If he's wrong, I step through the shimmer of light into the memories of a ghost.

Either way, I have to see Henry one more time. For him and my grandfather. For Isabel and myself.

I think of that tear streaking down Papa Dan's cheek and feel an urgency to know what happened with my grandfather, Bell, and Henry. I believe that truth is what Henry has been trying to lead me to all along.

Curled up on the velvet chair in the turret, I open Henry's journal to the last page and read.

If only . . .
A different time, a brighter moon,
A wiser word, a longer hesitation,
A calmer voice, a tighter grip,
Another plea, a quicker realization.
Your regrets won't—

Something bumps softly on the other side of the door and brings my head up. I lay the journal aside and glance at the pocket watch. I reset the timepiece after bringing it up here. 11:45. I'm wasting precious minutes.

I take the necklace from the table, put it on, and secure the clasp at the back of my neck. The photograph of the bridge lies across my lap. I lift it with one hand, lift the teardrop pendant away from my chest with my other hand, and position it over the photo until it captures the lamplight. A bright shaft of light spears toward the picture. Another bump sounds. A squeak. I glance up as the door opens and see Papa Dan peering in at me from the hallway. His startled eyes meet mine as the prism's light stretches up from the photograph, expands, and surrounds me. . . .

. . . A cloud-dappled moon as round as a china plate sits high on a sky of thick black velvet. Bundled up in his coat and hat, Henry stands on the bridge, his back to me, staring into the dark hole of the canyon below. Calling his name, I hurry through the snow toward him, and he turns, relief and happiness smoothing the worry from his face.

"Bell . . . you're here!" He crosses to the entrance of the bridge to

meet me, hugs me quickly, then steps back and takes both my hands in his. "I parked Father's DeSoto on the road at the trailhead. If we hurry, we can make it across the state line before anyone realizes you're not in bed asleep." Still holding one of my hands, he starts to step off the bridge.

I pull back, shivering against the bitter cold wind. "But you said we weren't leaving tonight. That we would talk to Daniel about our plans."

"There's no time. If we don't go now, we might never get a chance. Your parents—"

"Where's Daniel?" I glance to the opposite side of the bridge. "He's meeting us here, isn't he?"

"Not unless you told him to."

An animal scratches in the dead brush nearby. Wind whistles a warning across the open mouth of the canyon. "But you said—"

"I was going to tell him, but I knew Daniel would never go along with this. He would have gone straight to your parents. Did you say something to him?"

"No. Why?"

"He was asking a lot of questions today . . . acting suspicious." A fine white mist floats from Henry's mouth as his breath meets the chilled winter air. "To throw him off, I said I'd meet him here to go hiking in the morning."

"I can't just leave without saying good-bye to Daniel and Louise. They're my best friends."

"And I'm not?" His brows pucker.

I touch his wind-chapped cheek. "Things are different between us now."

Henry smiles. "We need to hurry. The town's supposed to get

socked in by heavy snowfall in the next couple of hours. We'll have to outrun the storm." He starts off again.

Holding tight to his hand, I step off the bridge behind him, follow a few steps, then stop.

Pausing, too, Henry faces me and asks with exasperation, "What is it now?"

"If I'd known we were leaving tonight, I would've packed my bags. What will I do without my clothes?"

"I'll buy you more clothes."

"I would've left my parents a letter. I can't just disappear. They'll be worried sick about me. And it wouldn't be right if they heard about us leaving secondhand from—"

"You told someone?"

"Only Louise," I murmur.

Henry drops my hand and curses.

"I'm sorry. I needed to talk to someone about all this before I could decide. Don't worry. . . ." I pull on his sleeve and peer up at him. "She doesn't know we're leaving tonight. I let her believe she'd convinced me not to go."

"Why did you tell Louise, when I asked you not to say anything?" he snaps.

I look down at my boots. "I was afraid . . . unsure." In a whisper, I add, "I still am."

"Don't you know what will happen when your folks see that photograph the reporter took at the dance? They'll send you south to live with your aunt."

"If I tell them how we feel about each other, they'll have to understand!"

"How do you feel, Bell? I'm not sure anymore." He turns away and steps closer to the precipice of the cliff that drops to the creek bed below.

"I love you," I say quietly. "But I want to finish school. I want—"

"I can't stay in this town another day, Bell; it's smothering me." He shakes his head and faces me again. "But I can't be without you, either."

Henry grabs my upper arms, and his fingers press hard enough to bruise my skin through my coat. "Let go! I can't do this. . . . I can't."

"You heard her, Henry. Let Isabel go." Daniel emerges from the shadows, his stride long and hurried, his eyes narrow and tense.

"This is none of your business, Daniel!" Henry shouts as he inches backward, dragging me with him toward the jutting lip of the canyon beside the bridge's entrance.

The anger evaporates from Daniel's eyes when they shift to mine. "Louise told me you were meetin' him tonight. She was afraid he'd pressure you to go with him."

"Louise should mind her own business, too," Henry says.

Daniel glares at him. "You're a bad liar, Henry. I figured the hike was just to throw me off."

A sudden gust of wind blows my skirt around my shins as I look from Daniel to Henry. "Try to understand," I plead. "I don't want to sneak away like we've done something wrong. Henry, please . . . let me go."

The desperation in his eyes stabs a blade of fear into my chest. "I won't let go of you, Bell. Not ever."

"Listen to me, Henry," Daniel says, the soothing tone of his voice in contradiction to the look of alarm on his face.

Henry takes another backward step that brings us nearer to the edge of the cliff. *"Leave!"* he growls at Daniel.

"Watch out!" Daniel thrusts a hand toward us.

Panic rises up in me as I glance into the dark crater behind Henry and struggle to pry myself free of his grasp.

Daniel lowers his voice, says calmly, *"Henry, look behind you . . . you're too close to the edge. Let's talk on the bridge."* When Henry doesn't budge, Daniel risks another cautious step toward us.

"Stay back," Henry warns, his grip tightening on my arm. *"I told you this is none of your business, Daniel. Go home."*

Daniel's eyes dart to mine. *"It's okay, Isabel. I won't leave without you."* Paralyzed, I lower my gaze to his outstretched hand. *"Grab my fingers,"* he says.

I will my free arm to lift, and before Henry can stop me, I reach out to Daniel in one quick motion. He jerks me toward him, causing Henry to lose hold of my arm.

"Run!" Daniel yells.

But I only back away out of reach, unwilling to leave the two of them alone, afraid of what they might do to each other.

Daniel jabs a finger toward Henry. *"I don't know what's gotten into you. If you want to leave town, go ahead. But stay away from Isabel. You heard what she said. She doesn't want to go with you."*

"You're jealous." Rage contorts Henry's features. *"You can't stand it that she loves me instead of you."*

"Stop it!" I yell. *"Don't argue. Please, I can't stand it!"*

"Isabel is my friend," Daniel says, ignoring me. *"I won't let you force her to do somethin' she doesn't wanna do."*

Henry starts around him, headed my way. *"I'll do whatever I* damn well please, Piper. Just try and stop me."

Daniel snags Henry's shoulder as he walks past, jerking him around. The punch he throws connects with Henry's nose and knocks him to his knees. Shaking off the blow, Henry stands, staggers, then dives into Daniel. Arms swinging, they move closer to the edge of the cliff.

"Stop it!" I scream, rushing over. "Stop!"

They keep shoving each other, punching and grunting and grabbing, cursing each time a blow lands. I watch every movement, and when they finally separate, I wedge myself between them. "Don't do this!" I yell, looking from one red face to the other.

Panting and watching each other, they both back up a step—Daniel away from the cliff, Henry toward it.

Daniel grabs my hand. "Let's go, Bell."

Fear, love, and confusion tangle inside me when I look into Henry's eyes. But now the fear is for him, not myself. I can't go with him. But if Mama and Papa send me away, what will become of Henry? Who will he turn to without me here?

I link my fingers with Daniel's, my heart aching at the look on Henry's face. "Go home," I plead with him. "You aren't thinking straight."

Squinting at me, he drags his glove across his eyes as I turn to leave. But before I can take a step, Henry utters, "Bell." Anguish as ragged as the canyon wall fills his voice. "Don't leave me alone. Please. I don't want to go away without you."

I look back at him, and my heart shatters into a million splintered pieces. "Stay then . . . stay here in Cedar Canyon with me." I lean toward him, reach out with my free hand, grasp

Henry's fingers, connecting myself to him on one side and to Daniel on the other.

"Please come with me, Bell," Henry coaxes, squeezing my fingers. "It's what you want. What we both want. You know it is."

Daniel must sense my uncertainty. He drops my hand, says, "It's your decision, Isabel. But this is your life we're talkin' about."

I search Henry's face for several long moments, then shake my head and sigh. "I'm sorry." I taste tears on my lips. "Go home, Henry. We'll talk about this tomorrow."

"I won't be here tomorrow," he says, and his eyes turn to ice. He hauls me against him, twisting my wrist.

"You're hurting me," I gasp. The mouth of the canyon yawns only inches behind Henry, the black hole so deep that even in the moonlight I can't see the bottom of it. Beside us, the bridge looms, a dark giant arching into the sky. It beckons to me, offering safety. "Please," I say quietly, trying to steady my voice. "Let go of me . . . Henry . . . we'll fall. Let's step onto the bridge."

"Let her go." Daniel's voice quivers like a plucked string on Henry's violin.

Henry laughs, and in that instant, I know that the stranger inside him has taken over. Panicked, I push against his chest with my free hand, and when he doesn't budge, I slap him hard across the face.

Henry flinches, and his startled eyes grow wider. He releases me with one hand, but at the same time his other hand swings up, and I think he intends to grab me again. On instinct, I shove his chest, and he stumbles backward against a rock the size of my dog.

Henry's mouth opens. Panic flares in his eyes. Arms flailing, he gasps as his legs fly out from under him. His right hand grasps at the crystal pendant that rests against my coat, and the chain around my neck snaps. I clutch at his coat sleeve and feel the scratch of wool against my skin as the fabric slips through my fingers.

"No!" I shriek as Daniel lunges forward, grabbing for Henry's foot. But it's too late. Henry topples backward into the canyon's gaping, dark mouth.

"Henry!" Daniel and I both scream at once. Dropping to my hands and knees in the snow, I crawl to the edge and peer deep into the black chasm.

An alarm shrieks in my head, growing louder and louder until it drowns out my own rising screams. I press my hands to my ears, dizzy and sweating, my mind unraveling, twisting, curling, tangling like a dropped roll of film. Before me, the canyon's mouth seems to open wider. I squeeze my eyes shut and wait for it to swallow me, too.

Daniel's voice breaks through the shattering noise in my head. "Isabel!" he yells. "Turn around. Take my hand!"

The screeching resumes, fills my brain, the pressure building until I'm sure my head will explode. I press my palms harder against my temples.

"Isabel . . ." My name again, spoken quietly now, a calm, steady note at the center of a storm. "Move away from the edge. Look at me. Take my hand."

I open my eyes, but I can't move, can't stop staring at the place where Henry stood only moments ago.

"Tansy . . ."

Tansy?

I blink. Blink again. Not Bell. Tansy . . .

"Move away from the edge."

My lungs burn from exhaustion. I taste salt on my lips; I hear myself sobbing. With shaky arms, I somehow manage to push onto my knees, manage to turn and glance up.

Tate reaches out to me.

"Tate?" I cry. I take his hand, and he pulls me into his arms. "Did you see him? Henry fell! We have to help him!"

Tate strokes my hair. "You were sleepwalking. Dreaming. Henry isn't here."

"He was, though. He *was.*" I lift my head from his shoulder and look into his eyes. "Henry didn't jump off the bridge; he fell off the side of the cliff. And no one pushed him. Not on purpose. It was an accident. I saw the whole thing. Maybe that's why his ghost reached out to me through the journal. He wanted everyone to know the truth."

"There isn't a ghost, Tansy."

"But—"

"There isn't a ghost. There never was." Tate holds my gaze. "*I* wrote those poems."

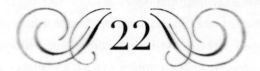

22

"You?" I step back. "You couldn't have."

"I should have told you before, but I was embarrassed." Tate looks down at his feet and exhales noisily before meeting my gaze again. "That's why I wanted in the cellar. So I could get the journal back before anyone found it."

"No . . . I don't believe you." Hurrying to the edge of the cliff, I look down, desperate to find Henry, but all I see is darkness. I search around my feet for the rock that threw Henry off balance, but it isn't there.

"Tansy," Tate says, "let's go. I'll explain everything once you're home."

His Blazer sits roadside at the trailhead, not Mr. Peterson's shiny DeSoto. Climbing in on the passenger side, I shut the door, lean my head against the window, and close my eyes, shaking all over.

"I can't believe you walked all the way out here alone in the dark," Tate says quietly.

"I don't remember walking." I remember sitting in the

darkroom, the photograph, the crystal. My grandfather's face before I stepped through. *Papa Dan!* What did he see?

"How did you know I'd be out here?" I ask Tate.

"I didn't. After we talked on the phone, I had a feeling something was up with you. I couldn't sleep, so I called your cell and tried texting you. When you didn't answer, I almost called the house, but I didn't want to wake up your mom. So I drove out to your house to see if the box was still in the cellar. I wanted to make sure you hadn't taken it out and done something crazy."

"What were you planning to do? Try to break the lock again?"

"I don't even know. I just got in the car and took off."

I cock my head to study him. "But you came to the canyon. . . . Why?"

"When I pulled into your driveway, I saw your grand-father in my headlights. He was walking in this direction."

"Papa Dan was walking out here?" I grip the edge of the seat with both hands.

"He seemed pretty upset. He had one of your pictures of the bridge. I took him back to the house, and your mom ran into the yard when I pulled up and said you were missing. I told her I thought I knew where you were, and that I'd find you and bring you back."

I cross my arms, my muscles tense and trembling. Papa Dan must've been in bad shape, or Mom would've come with Tate to look for me. "Hurry," I tell him. "I bet she's going nuts right now."

Tate nods, keeping his focus on the road.

"I don't understand about the journal," I say.

"Neither do I." He sends me a quick, self-conscious glance, then adds, "You know I told you I used to come out to the house and read?" When I nod, he continues, "Sometimes I'd try to write, too, but after my mom left, it was like all my words dried up." He pauses for a breath, then says, "Then I found the journal. The pages were empty; it was just an old book with nothing in it. And the crystal . . . when I took it out of the box . . ." Tate's fingers clench and unclench on the steering wheel. His gaze darts my way again. "It was weird. . . . I'd go there straight from school. I didn't even think twice about it. It was like I was *supposed* to write in the journal, like I was meant to fill those empty pages. The words started flowing out of me and I couldn't write fast enough. And the poems . . . I couldn't believe what I was reading, that I'd written them. I didn't want Dad to find them, so I left the journal in the cellar."

"In the box with the other things," I murmur.

"Yeah. After that, every time I went back there, I'd take out the crystal and the journal and the same thing would happen. The poems . . . I mean, the handwriting is mine, but the words and the thoughts . . . I don't know. I relate to a few of the poems, but some of them I don't even understand. It's almost like they didn't come from me, like they were—"

"Henry's," I finish when he hesitates. "Like he was writing them through you."

Tate frowns. "But that's impossible."

"But you thought it, too, didn't you? That's what you meant when you told me you felt as if Henry's ghost was trying to tell you something."

"I told you I don't believe in ghosts."

"Then how do you explain what happened?"

A long silence, then, "I can't."

The house comes into view, the windows aglow with light. Just as Tate pulls to a stop in our driveway, Mom and Papa Dan step onto the porch in their pajamas and robes, holding hands.

"Should I come in with you?" Tate asks.

"She'll want to talk to both of us. I guess it's time I told her everything." I sigh, nervous about confessing to Mom, but also relieved to finally have it all out in the open.

Tate reaches across the seat and covers my hand with his, as if to let me know that we're in this together.

I open the door.

An hour later, I tell Tate good-bye while Mom goes upstairs to check on Papa Dan; he went to bed right after Tate and I came home. I guess he only needed to know I was safe before he could calm down enough to sleep.

When Tate's Blazer disappears into the shadows on the road, I go back inside the house and lock the door. I return to the kitchen, where, moments ago, Tate, Mom, and I had sat around the table talking. After Tate brought me home, even though Mom was pressing me to sit down and explain, I immediately ran up to the turret. I placed Henry's treasures into the rosewood box and brought it downstairs. Mom needed to see it all in order to understand. The crystal and the watch; the journal, too. Tate's poems. Now everything remains on the table where we left it, even the journal. Tate surprised me by leaving it here.

I pick it up, and when Mom enters the room again, say, "I guess Tate forgot this."

"You can give it to him at school tomorrow." She pulls out a chair and sits down beside me.

I look into her eyes. "How's Papa Dan?"

"Resting, but still not asleep."

That's not what I meant by my question, and she knows it. He's been less agitated and restless the past couple of days, but physically he's weaker, more fragile, less quick to move.

"How about you?" Mom's brows draw together. "Are you okay?"

"I think so." I open the journal. "I still can't believe Tate wrote these poems. Now that I think about it, some of them could be about his mom leaving, though. You should read them."

"I'll ask Tate if it's okay first." She smiles. "We writers are sensitive about sharing our work."

"You think he's right, don't you? You think that I've been dreaming, too."

Mom hesitates, then says, "That makes the most sense."

"What about the things I saw through my camera? I was wide awake then, Mom."

"I don't know, sweetie." She clasps her hands together on the table.

"Other than hearing that scream the first night we were here," I say, "have you had any more weird experiences or seen anything strange?"

"I've been spooked once or twice, but that goes along with my job." Another smile teases her lips.

I take a deep breath and, before I can change my mind, say, "I still think Henry used my photography to get through to me. And he used Tate's writing to get through to him. Maybe he was trying to reach you, too."

She tucks a strand of my hair behind my ear. "I said dreaming makes the most sense, and it does. But I'm open to other possibilities, Tansy."

"Like maybe I'm losing my mind?" I stare down at the table, and the knot of tears inside my chest begins to loosen. "That's what you think, isn't it?"

"No." She nudges me gently with her elbow until I look at her. "I know you're stronger than that. I've been worried about you, though. You've been through so much. Maybe . . ." She looks into my eyes and shrugs. "Some things that happen in this world can't be explained. If you believe Henry Peterson's ghost reached out to you and Tate, I won't argue." Mom starts to say something else, then, changing her mind, looks away.

"But?" I prompt.

Tears fill her eyes. "I can't help thinking that I caused this."

"You? How?"

"By moving you so much. You don't have roots . . . a place to call home or steady friendships. The stress of this move on top of Papa Dan's illness—maybe you were so lonely you—" Breaking off, Mom averts her gaze.

"What? Made up an invisible friend?" I ask, humiliated.

Her face scrunches up, like it always does when she's trying not to cry. "You've paid the price for my silly selfishness. You don't know how much I wish I could go back and change that. But I can't." A tear trickles down her cheek. "I'm sorry."

I reach up and wipe the tear away. "You're making your really gross crybaby face, Mom. I've told you a bajillion times it's not a good look on you." She laughs a little, and I say, "None of this is your fault. And don't worry—I don't need to see a shrink. Not anymore. I was getting pretty close, though."

Laughing, I squeeze her hand. I reach again for the journal, flip to the last page, and read the poem I started earlier tonight but never finished. My heart beats harder with each word on the page, and I know without a doubt that Henry wrote this poem, if not the others. Through Tate, yes, but the message is from him . . . and I know who he meant to reach. Papa Dan already knew that Henry didn't jump off the bridge. Henry had something more that he needed to say to my grandfather.

Handing the journal to Mom, I say, "Just read this one.

Tate won't mind. Maybe then you'll understand why I believe what I do."

Mom hesitates before taking the journal and lowering her gaze to the page. After a minute, she looks up at me with stunned eyes. "Oh, Tansy . . . do you think . . . ?"

I lift the journal from her hands, and without another word, we both stand and leave the room, headed for the stairway.

Lamplight glows beneath Papa Dan's bedroom door. Pausing next to it, I say, "I'm going to tell him good night."

"He'll like that." Mom touches my arm. "If you want me to sleep in your room with you tonight, I will. Or you can sleep in mine."

I used to do that as a little girl when I was scared or sad or upset. But I'm not any of those things now. Not anymore. Still, it would be nice to have her close by, to reach out in the darkness and feel her beside me. Like me, my mom's not perfect, but she's mine. "If I get lonely, I'll let you know," I tell her.

She gestures at my grandfather's door. "He was really worried about you tonight. He loves you so much."

"I know."

Mom kisses my cheek, then heads for her room, leaving me in the hallway. I tuck the journal beneath my arm and knock on Papa Dan's door. After a few seconds, I open it and poke my head into his room.

He sits at the edge of his bed, a sheet of beige stationery across his lap. The mattress springs squeak as I settle beside him. "I'm sorry I scared you tonight."

His eyes meet mine, and I realize that though I may never totally convince Mom or Tate about Henry, my grandfather knows the truth. He saw me step through the shimmer of light from the crystal beam. He spoke to Henry on those nights when I heard his voice and another's—Henry's—in this very room.

I glance down at the stationery in his lap, and chills chase up my spine. The name Isabel is scrawled in neat script at the bottom. "May I read it?" I ask him, and he lifts his hand off the page.

Dear Daniel,

I hope this letter finds you well. I've thought of you often through the years. You've remained one of my most cherished friends, despite the miles that have separated us and the long silence between us. You are a true friend in every sense of the word.

To protect me, you honored my wish, though I realize you were never comfortable with that decision. I want you to know that I regret placing you in such an awkward position. I was a foolish, terrified girl in the beginning and, later, a cowardly woman who couldn't bear the thought of a scandal.

You were right; we should not have kept such a terrible secret. It was wrong of me to ask you to. Wrong and unfair. Not only to you but also to Henry and his family. Doing so harmed all of you. Our secret even harmed me.

I spent what should have been the best years of my life worrying that someone would find my crystal pendant in the creek bed below the cliff, and that the necklace would tie me to Henry's death.

I wish I'd been as brave as you—as willing to tell the truth and face any consequences. What happened was an accident, and surely that would've been proved in the end. Years back, when I saw you at your mother's funeral, your eyes revealed the suffering you've endured for allowing everyone to believe Henry committed suicide. If your guilty feelings extend further than that, you're wrong. You bear no fault in his death, either.

I thank you every day for stopping me from running away with Henry that night. But I was the one afraid to speak the truth. I'm the one who chose to ruin Henry's reputation, not you. I'm ashamed to admit that I have remained a coward to the end, as I've waited until I'm an old woman at death's door before writing this letter. Should you decide to expose the truth, you have my blessing. I hope you will forgive me for not giving it sooner.

I wish you and your family good health and happiness.
Your friend always,
Isabel

I lower the letter to my lap and look into my grandfather's tired eyes. "She's right," I whisper, reaching for his hand. "It wasn't your fault. Or Isabel's, either. Henry didn't blame you two. I know he didn't." I open the journal to the last entry. "Henry wrote this poem for you, Papa Dan. Listen, I'll read it to you."

If only . . .
A different time, a brighter moon,
A wiser word,
A longer hesitation,
A calmer voice, a tighter grip,
Another plea,
A quicker realization.

Your regrets
Won't alter fate, or turn the tide. . . .
If blame's to cast,
Then blame my dedication
To blind desires, obsessive love,
Lust for control,
Selfish manipulation.

"Henry blamed himself, not you or Bell," I say. "He couldn't rest until you knew." I hug my grandfather, and I feel his thin, worn body relax. "He wanted you to be at peace, too, Papa Dan. You and Isabel. You've blamed yourself for too long. What happened wasn't your fault. You have to move on and forgive yourself."

Papa Dan sits back and looks at me. In his face I read what he can't say: I have to move on, too. I smile at my grandfather. A lip-quivering, eye-watering, full-blown crybaby smile.

I'm pretty sure that, somewhere inside his mind, Papa Dan understands that I got his message. Just like he got Henry's.

The nightingale sings outside my window, but not the mournful tune I've come to know. Tonight its song is happy and calm. Peaceful.

I dream of Henry. He sits on the bench rock beneath the willows, playing on his violin the same happy tune that the bird sings while my grandfather and I twirl to the music.

Winter is over. The earth and sky are rich with the colors of spring. Papa Dan is no longer young but an old man whose green eyes twinkle behind his glasses. "Hang on, Tansy!" he shouts. "Don't be afraid."

We hold hands and spin, faster . . . faster . . . until he becomes a streaking blur of pink and purple, gold, and pearly white light. "Wait!" I cry. "Slow down!"

"Don't worry, Tansy girl. I won't let go."

"I can't see you!"

"I'm here . . . all around you. Do you feel me?"

The colors blend; the light brightens. "Yes! I feel you." He wraps the warm wind around me like a cocoon, and I'm filled with a sense of peaceful security.

"I'll always be here," Papa Dan says. "I'll never let you go."

Something as soft as a feather brushes my cheek.

"Tansy." I hear my grandfather's voice, filled with love and happiness. His husky chuckle drifts on the air.

"Tansy?"

Light floods the room and startles me awake. I squint, blink, and sit up. Mom kneels at my bedside. She pushes hair from my forehead with her fingertips. Her brown eyes are glossy, her face pale and sad. The house is quiet and still. Too still. "Mom?" I whisper.

"Oh, sweetie . . ." She closes her eyes, as if she can't bear to see my face when she speaks the words she needs to say.

But she doesn't have to tell me. *Papa Dan.* I know.

We wrap our arms around each other, rock back and forth.

Outside my window, the tree sways. The wind rattles the panes against the frame. The nightingale warbles, and for the first time, another bird answers his call. Dawn stains the horizon with streaks of pink and purple, gold, and pearly white light.

I'm here, Tansy girl. All around you.

The colors blend, the light brightens. *I see you.*

And do you feel me?

A sense of calm surrounds me, just like the crystal's luminous light once did.

Stroking Mom's hair, I watch the sun rise over her shoulder, remembering another dawn, one I witnessed with my grandfather on the roof of our house in San Francisco.

"Yes, Papa Dan," I whisper. "I feel you . . . I do."

Months Later

Mom takes the last two candy canes from the box, then hands one to me and the other to Bethyl Ann. I hang mine near the top of the Christmas tree, beside a cracked snowman I made in third grade out of Play-Doh. "Why do you keep this?" I ask Mom.

"Because I love it," Mom answers, placing ornament containers into the clear plastic tub where she stores them.

Bethyl Ann finds a bare spot near the bottom of the tree and hangs her candy cane over the branch. "Oh, that one's so cute!" she exclaims, pointing to an old ornament—Santa in cowboy boots and a ten-gallon hat.

"Papa Dan gave that to me in third grade," I say. "The Christmas before we moved to Austin."

"As I recall," Mom adds, "he said it was to help you get ready to be a bona fide rootin' tootin' Texan."

No matter what new state we moved to, he would always say something like that. *Just think, Tansy girl, you're going to be a bona fide Georgia peach . . . a bona fide Okie from Muskogee. . . .*" But in each place, we only stayed long enough for me to feel like a bona fide outsider. Except here. Thanks to Bethyl Ann, Tate, and Alison.

Bethyl Ann steps back and surveys the tree. "Isn't it super?" She claps her hands together and begins singing an off-key version of "O Christmas Tree." I join in, and so does Mom. We don't make it through the first verse before a car horn honks outside. "Darn and double darn," Bethyl Ann mutters. "That's my ride. I'll see you tomorrow at school." In the driveway, Mrs. Pugh's ancient station wagon backfires.

"School," I groan. "Don't remind me."

"Only one more week until winter break," Mom says in an upbeat voice. "You can hang in there that long."

"Actually, I'm not looking forward to the break." Bethyl Ann sticks out her lower lip. "Romy is spending the holidays in Orlando with his grandparents."

Romy Bernard, a freshman, moved here midsemester from Tulsa. By the end of his first week, he had joined band (he plays the tuba), started a chess club (he, Bethyl Ann, the principal, and the school janitor are the only members), and stole my best friend's heart. Romy is teaching Bethyl Ann how to play tuba, too, and she plans to join band in the fall, although I can't imagine that Cedar Canyon High needs more than one tuba on the field during halftime at the football games.

"How will I ever get through two weeks without seeing

him?" Bethyl Ann presses a hand over her heart. "O Romy, Romy, wherefore art thou, Romy?"

Mom laughs, and I roll my eyes.

At the door, Bethyl Ann turns to wave. "Good night, good night! Parting is such sweet sorrow. In case you didn't know, that's from—"

"We *know*, Bethyl Ann." I raise my brows.

"You're no fun," she teases, closing the door. Mom's phone rings in the kitchen. She goes to answer it while I gather the decoration tubs and haul them to the storage closet. When I'm finished, I join her in the kitchen as she's hanging up the phone.

"Who was that?"

"Ray Don. He said he read Tate's article in the newspaper this morning. Apparently, people in town are already buzzing about it. Henry Peterson's suicide has been a legend around here for a long time."

I waited until last month before talking to Mom about sharing what Isabel said in her letter to my grandfather. After a lot of thought, I decided Papa Dan would have wanted the truth told. I believe that's what he intended to do before he got sick. Mom agreed. But first we contacted our landlords—Henry's descendants—and Isabel's family. Instead of being upset like I'd predicted, they were all amazed by her letter. Even the Petersons. Everyone agreed that the truth should be told, so Tate wrote the article, and I provided photographs I took of the bridge, our house, and Henry's treasures.

Tate asked Mom to help him write the article, but once he started, he didn't need her. The words flowed onto the page and, this time, they were definitely his, not Henry's.

"Is Ray Don coming for dinner?" I ask.

"Not tonight."

"Why not?" The sheriff has joined us for dinner every Sunday night for the past couple of months. The truth is, I have sort of become used to him hanging around.

"I told him I wanted it to be just us tonight." Mom cocks her head, her eyes on mine. "I want to talk to you."

"Ooo-kay." Anxiety flutters in my chest.

"I finished *The Screaming Meemies* last night," she says.

"That was fast."

"I told you I'd hurry." She pulls out a chair and sinks into it.

I search her eyes for the signs that are always there when she finishes a book. Restlessness. Sadness. For the first time ever, I don't see any of that.

"We had a deal," Mom says. "I plan to keep up my end of it, since you've kept up yours. I've seen you making a real effort to fit in here since Papa Dan died. If you want to stay, we will; you can graduate here. But if you're not happy, I'll move wherever you say."

"Really?"

She nods, and a sudden rush of happiness almost knocks me over. Before I know it, I'm beside her chair and we're hugging each other.

I imagine leaving Cedar Canyon, moving to a city

again. Restaurants and movie theaters. Museums and rock concerts. I liked Seattle when we lived there. And Nashville. I wouldn't mind going back to one of those places and starting over again. No more Shanna or Rooster Boy to taunt me. I see the two of them in color now, by the way, as well as the rest of the kids and teachers at school. I hear them clearly. Honestly, sometimes I wish Shanna and Rooster Boy *would* fade away, though. Poof. No more misery.

I sit in the chair beside Mom, trying to picture going back to San Francisco, but I can't see myself there anymore. In too many ways to count, I'm not the same person I was when we lived there. Would I have anything in common with Hailey anymore? I'm not mad at her now for stealing Colin. He doesn't compare to Tate, so I ended up being the winner in the end. I even emailed and told her so. But the truth is, it still bothers me that she was so disloyal, and I don't see us ever being close friends again. Even so, I finally read all her emails. I had to hear her apology and put what happened behind me.

I think about Tate and Bethyl Ann. Even Alison. In spite of her pom-poms and the totally lame pep rallies she loves so much, we've become friends. Saying good-bye to the three of them would be just as hard, if not harder, than leaving San Francisco was for me.

"Well?" Mom says. "Where are we going next? Someplace new, or somewhere we've already been?"

"What about your next book? Don't you need to live

where it's going to be set?"

"A deal is a deal. Besides, I haven't decided where it's set. It depends on what *you* decide." She leans closer to me. "Wherever it is, it might be nice to plant a few seeds there . . . see if they take root." She pats my shoulder. "You don't have to decide just now."

I watch her closely. "You and the sheriff—"

"Don't let our relationship affect your decision one way or the other. We're not that serious." My mother actually blushes.

Before I go to bed, I sit in the darkroom on the velvet chair, the rosewood box in my lap. I lift the lid, take out Henry's pocket watch, and open it. *Ten o'clock*. It's kept the correct time since the night I watched Henry fall from the cliff, the same night that Papa Dan died.

I touch the pendant, think of putting it on one last time, then decide against it. In my heart, I know that when Henry was stumbling and he grabbed the necklace from Bell's neck, the crystal captured their memories and trapped them inside.

Holding my breath, I slant the crystal over a photograph, the one of Papa Dan standing in our yard looking up into the branches of the tree. A part of me wishes the prism of light would shimmer, stretch, and wrap around me so I can step through and talk to my grandfather again. But, though the light catches, it doesn't spread; I knew it wouldn't, and I finally accept that's how it should be.

I'm relieved instead of disappointed. Henry's spirit holds the memories now. Both he and Papa Dan have finally found peace. And so have I. I wonder if they both know how much they helped me.

I've made my decision about where I want to live. I'll tell Mom in the morning, but right now I have something else I need to do. I turn to the side table and pick up a pen and the pretty blue notebook full of blank pages Mom bought for me at the Food Fair our first night here.

Dear Diary,

I've learned what can happen when I keep my thoughts, fears, and hopes bottled up inside, so I've decided to take Mom's advice and start spilling my guts to you. Maybe that'll keep me from going peanutty and make her stop bugging me.

I've been through a lot lately, but I'm starting to feel okay now. Here's the thing: No matter where I go, sad things will happen to me, hard things. People I love will die, and sometimes I'll have to tell friends good-bye. I'll meet people who won't like me, and I'll know loneliness. I don't like it, but that's the way it is.

But, unlike Henry, I won't hide away at this old house or anywhere else, living in a secluded world of my own making, not anymore. I won't ever lose myself again. If I've learned anything from this whole weird experience, it's that if I take the time to look beneath the surface . . . of people, of myself, of life . . . I'll find wonder. I'll find strength. And more love and acceptance than I ever imagined.

Which brings me to Tate Hudson. Wow. Sometimes the
real world shimmers, even without the crystal.
Sanely yours,
Tansy Piper

Closing the notebook, I set it aside. I start to place the crystal in the rosewood box, then pause, wondering if Henry and Bell would care if I kept it. I touch the silver chain around my neck, the one Tate bought me. It's beautiful, even without a pendant—though he promised to soon buy me one of my own. I'll let him pick it out . . . well, maybe I'll give him a hint or two about what I'd like.

I put Bell's crystal next to Henry's pocket watch and close the lid on the box. Tomorrow morning before school I'll drop by the library to give Mrs. Pugh the rosewood box so she can display Henry's treasures in the local history section. Then I'll go to school and start making my own local history—as a bona fide Cedar Canyon Bobcat.

book. While researching this novel, I called upon my friend and fellow booklover Renae Haiduk to let me spend a day in her science classroom at Panhandle High School in Panhandle, Texas. Many thanks to Renae and her fun, friendly, and extremely well-behaved students for allowing me a glimpse into their daily lives. And thanks to the entire Panhandle High School staff, as well, for welcoming me into their school and classrooms. My research of life in a small Texas town also took me to the quaint community of Canadian, Texas, where many gracious residents eagerly showed me the ins and outs of the businesses, restaurants, and historical sights around town. Thank you, Canadian! A heaping helping of gratitude to my closest friend from my own teen years, Donna Stamp, for telling me about the Watermelon Run and inspiring the Cedar Canyon version of that small-town tradition. Thanks also to my teen mentee, Summer Baker, for helping me keep my teenage lingo current and for teaching me the difference between nerds and geeks; Bethyl Ann thanks you, too! I'm not sure I could ever write a book and remain sane without the input and encouragement of my fabulous critique group: Linda Castillo, Anita Howard, Marcy McKay, and April Redmon. Thanks and much love to you, ladies. You rock! I am also fortunate to have a wonderful family that keeps me from spending too much time inside my own head. Gratitude and love to Jeff, Ryan, and Jason for making me laugh and keeping me solidly planted in the real world . . . most of the time. The best coffee baristas in the Texas

Panhandle work at Roasters on Soncy; thanks, guys and gals, for your delicious java, your welcoming smiles, and for often having my "usual" poured and waiting when I walk through the door ready to write. Finally, although chances are good that they will never read this acknowledgment, I'd like to thank Mychael Danna, composer of the *Girl Interrupted* soundtrack, Alan Silvestri, composer of the *Identity* soundtrack, and the various composers of *The Mothman Prophecies* soundtrack for their beautiful, eerie music—it set the mood and immersed me in Tansy's world!